Sister Saint, Sister Sinner

Peg Herring

Sister Saint, Sister Sinner

Editor: T. Zenzcak
Copy Editor: R. Hodges

ISBN: 978-1-944502-34-8

Chapter One

Nettie-December 25

Under a black, starless sky, the Michigan State Police detective followed GPS directions, fishtailing along the snow-packed gravel road until she came to a driveway populated with two squad cars, lights flashing; an ambulance, its grill facing the road and back doors open; and a pickup truck with an irregular strip of rust along the rocker panel. At a low, flat-roofed building she exited the car, taking small steps so as not to slip on the narrow, icy path. Though it wasn't snowing, she'd lived her whole life in Michigan, and the smell of the air said snow was imminent. In an hour, maybe less, flakes would fall, innocent and beautiful as individual entities, but mighty and perilous in accumulation.

An un-roofed, un-bannistered platform made from used two-by-fours served as a no-frills porch, and on it a uniformed sheriff's deputy paced back and forth, boots stomping and posture hunched as he struggled vainly to stay warm. He'd called the state police to the scene, as was customary in murder cases. The detective had seen him before but didn't know his name. "Merry Christmas," she said, her wry tone acknowledging the aggravations of working on a holiday.

"Same to you, Detective Belizek. I ain't seen no wise men, but your wiseass buddy Tyler is inside."

The deputy opened the battered wooden door, and Belizek entered a long, narrow room that had probably once been a barracks. She imagined exhausted migrant workers asleep in rows of bunks at either side, photos of their family members taped to the iron frames or thumb-tacked to the wall above them.

The detective's nose twitched at the strong smell of cigarette smoke. A blue haze hung in the air, coating the unshaded bulbs overhead and blurring their glow. On either side of the door, sheets of particle board formed a rough entryway, blocking wind and cold. At the far end, unpainted drywall partitions carved out two rooms, one on either side of a narrow hallway.

In the room on the right, crime techs bent over a body sprawled across a rumpled bed. When the door closed, Belizek's team leader turned from watching them and invited her forward with a tilt of his head.

"What have we got?"

"Three shots, up close. Guy died quick." Tyler stepped aside, and she entered a room that would have been depressing even without the presence of a corpse: second-hand furniture, crooked, broken blinds, and not a touch of adornment, unless you counted dust. It smelled like violent death, but under that was a masculine scent, juniper, she thought. On the floor was a rifle, beside it a plastic ID marker. No doubt it had already been photographed from several angles. "Name's Caleb Green. No record as an adult. Some misdemeanors as a teen."

"He lived here?"

"On and off, I guess." Tyler gestured behind them. "The place is hers."

Turning, Belizek saw that the entry wall had blocked her view of a woman who sat slouched at a '70s-era dinette table. Tall, with wiry gray hair, a long face, and eyes that drooped like a Basset hound's, she wore jogging pants and a t-shirt spattered with blood. With robotic movements, she raised a cigarette to her mouth every few seconds, drew smoke deep into her lungs, and then rested her hand on the table again. Before her lay a phone and a box of tissues. She seemed unaware of the detectives' presence.

Belizek spoke softly to her partner. "What happened?"

His answer was a shrug. "That's Janet Waller, who's lived here since 2004. She called 9-1-1, said there'd been a shooting, gave the address. Since then, we've got nothing from her."

"You think they had a fight?"

"Hard to say." He shifted his feet. "She's probably in shock, so I thought maybe another woman might get more out of her."

Belizek suppressed a grimace. Uncomfortable interviews were often dumped on her with the excuse that as a female, she was somehow better equipped to deal with traumatized people.

Approaching the woman, Belizek touched her softly on the arm. "Ms. Waller, is it okay if I ask you a few questions?"

She blinked slowly, as if waking from sleep. Her mouth moved, but in the end she merely nodded. The techs had begun packing up their equipment, and Tyler approached. "Um, they're finished, so—"

Belizek turned to the woman. "Is there a place we can speak privately?"

Taking a final drag, Waller crushed the butt in the half-full ashtray. Without a glance at the corpse or the team dealing with it, she led the way to the empty bedroom.

As plainly furnished as the rest of the place, this room was much cleaner than the one where the dead man lay. The bed was loosely made, sheets, blankets, and a quilt laid across the mattress but not tucked in. A small shelf on one side held a book, an ashtray, a pen, and a lamp with a fake cowhide shade that Belizek guessed hadn't been Waller's choice. The most interesting part was a shelf unit stuffed with books. They were stored upright, sideways, and even in the two-inch gap between the feet and the floor. Belizek stepped closer to see what someone who lived in a shack read for entertainment.

The answer was apparently everything: Malcolm Gladwell, Richard Castle, a new theory of brain function, an old Georgette Heyer novel, and a history of the Peloponnesian Wars. Waller's appearance didn't suggest such eclectic tastes. *I guess we don't always look like what we are.*

Waller paused when she realized there were no chairs in the room. After a moment she moved to a corner and leaned a shoulder against a battered wooden armoire. Gesturing at the bed she said in a gravelly voice, "Have a seat."

Belizek obeyed, ignoring the box spring's squeaks of protest. Bracing herself with one hand, she felt the softness of the handmade quilt, thin from many washings, under her palm. A relic of happier times? "Ms. Waller—"

"Nettie."

"Nettie. This is your home?"

A deep line between her brows grew deeper. "Home, sweet. Like they say."

"Do you own or rent?"

Reaching into her pants pocket, she took out a pack and lighter and extracted a new smoke. The lighter produced only scratching sounds the first few times she tried it, but finally a flame appeared.

After she'd sucked in the first lungful, Waller replied, "Family property. We've owned it since the 1800s."

"The dead man, Caleb Green. He was staying here?"

The brow reacted again. "Yeah."

"Can you tell me what happened tonight?"

Nettie's gaze met hers. "I shot him."

The abruptness of the admission shocked her, but Belizek recovered quickly. "I need to know *why* you shot him."

The detective tried to wait out the silence that followed. In training, they were taught to let the witness, suspect, whoever, tell the story in their own way. *Silence bothers people*, the instructor had claimed. *Because they can't stop themselves from filling it, they reveal things they don't intend to.*

In this case, the silence went on and on, and it felt cruel to play amateur psychologist. "Who was Caleb Green?" the detective asked gently, "Why was he here in your house?"

The woman drew on her hand-rolled cigarette, and the acrid smell of cheap tobacco again stung Belizek's nose. Stowing the lighter in her pocket with an impatient movement, Nettie Waller said, "He was my son."

DDD News Station 22, Detroit – December 26, 2023

> Authorities report a shooting death last night near the town of Berlin in St. Clair County. Caleb Green was living with his mother, Janet Waller, and had gone to bed. While he slept, Ms. Waller used a hunting rifle to shoot her son three times in the chest. Ms. Waller subsequently called 9-1-1 and reported the incident. Michigan State Police are investigating, but sources say Waller admits her son never attacked or even threatened her.

Metro Detroit News–December 30, 2023

> Janet Waller of Berlin was charged today in the death of her son, Caleb Green. The case is notable because Ms. Waller is the sister of Ruth Mandell, whose husband is running for President. It's also unusual because the accused refuses to explain why she killed her only child. A source reports that even Waller's attorney, Andrew

McMahon, can't get his client to explain the crime. Waller's admission that she was never threatened by Green resulted in a charge of murder in the second degree.

Chapter Two

Ruth-January 5

As Butch and Ruth Mandell left their limousine at the small airport that served Vienna Park, Pennsylvania, Butch slid a protective arm around his wife's waist. A herd of reporters waited, their eyes as cold as the January wind. An attractive blond shouldered her way to the front and stuck a microphone in Ruth's face. "Mrs. Mandell, do you have a comment on the murder charges levied against Janet Waller?"

"I do not." Ruth spoke firmly, though her expression remained pleasant. Butch's reassuring hand pressed at her back, and she leaned into it, feeling his strength and support.

With his free hand, Butch made an authoritative gesture, and the reporter backed off a step. Another, more aggressive one took her place. "Are you denying that Ms. Waller—"

"We're not denying anything." Butch took the lead, his manner amiable but firm. "We're simply keeping our traps shut so we don't confuse all you nice people."

Yet another reporter shouted, "Mrs. Mandell, do you believe your sister's crime will impact your husband's Presidential campaign?"

Ruth put a hand on Butch's arm, signaling willingness to speak for herself. "I'm confident the American people won't reject a decent man simply because an in-law he's never even met made a horrible mistake."

"Then you don't believe the charge against your sister should be murder?"

"I refuse to speculate." Her chin rose an inch as she finished, "Nettie is my sister, and I love her. That's all I have to say."

At that point, serious-looking men in suits inserted themselves between the couple and the reporters, escorting Candidate Mandell and his wife into the terminal. Both the cold and the reporters' questions were shut out as the automatic doors hummed to a close. Once they'd passed through security, Butch spoke in his wife's ear. "You did good, Ruthie. Shut 'em down like you were flipping a switch."

"I did *well,* Butch. The President must use the English language correctly." His face fell slightly, and she added, "But if you hadn't been holding me up, I'd probably have burst into tears."

Wyandotte Gazette—Butch Mandell Visits Detroit
Presidential candidate Hiram "Butch" Mandell and his wife Ruth arrived this morning at Metro Airport. The representative from Pennsylvania, currently in his second term in Congress, stopped briefly to speak to the crowd that braved the frigid Michigan wind.

Personable, almost folksy at times, Mandell has a captivating smile and an informal manner. "Our major political parties have failed," he told an exuberant audience. "After every election, half of the voters of this nation believe that their concerns will be ignored for the next four years, and they're probably right. First the Republicans get their way. Then the Democrats get a turn. Neither party seems able to solve a single problem.

"Americans are tired of blame getting passed back and forth, and Ruth and I see that in the support we've garnered since I threw my hat into the ring. Our Unity Project will seek consensus on the issues that divide us. My election to the office of President will show everyone in Washington, D.C that voters want—no, demand—that they support what works instead of clinging to their old, partisan platforms."

When pressed to say where he stands on issues like corporate money in politics or gerrymandered districts, Mandell contended that what one person believes doesn't matter. "Working together is what will save our nation," he insisted. "When we study problems with unity as our goal, we can put everyone's best ideas into action." In closing, Mandell raised a hand as if taking an oath. "And folks, that's not a campaign promise. It's my word to the American people."

Chapter Three

Kim-May 14

Kim Dailey pulled into her usual parking space, shut off the engine, and sat listening to the tick of some metal part cooling down. Outside the car, trash skittered across the parking lot, driven by a May wind that was both warm and strong. A take-out cup rolled and bounced toward a fence, making a hollow sound each time it hit the pavement. Kim watched it bump along as she took a few seconds to prepare herself for eight hours with people. It wasn't that she hated her job. In fact, burying herself in clients' problems and following someone else's agenda helped to push her own concerns aside. Mostly.

Still, Kim had noticed lately that her coworkers seemed like cyborgs, devoid of personal conversation. Everyone avoided topics they thought would upset her, like divorce, crackpot politicians, and sisters who murder their children.

It had started nine months ago, when her husband announced he was leaving public relations, leaving Detroit, and leaving Kim. "We married too young," Edmund told her in the self-pitying tone he'd adopted. "I got sucked into a work-for-a-paycheck rut, and now my whole life is a big old trap."

Kim admitted their relationship was stale, maybe even spoiled. They'd begun with shared goals and good sex, but a decade and a half later they disagreed on everything, from long-range goals to short-term actions. Should they buy a house or pay off their student debt? Could they afford to fly to Cabo at Christmas? Were fertility treatments the next step? Arguments led to sniping and then to screaming matches. Edmund called her a drone. Kim asked herself how Edmund's puckish manner had become so irritating. How had his jokes about chucking it all to go live on an island turned into tiresome attempts to escape responsibility? More and more, Ed had surfed travel sites and moaned that he'd missed his chance to see the world. Under every complaint was the hint that having a wife prevented him from living as he pleased.

In September of 2022, at forty-two years of age, with no relevant experience and no discussion with Kim, Edmund Dailey had accepted a job with a crew studying climate change in the

Antarctic. He intended to leave soon, he informed her, since October was the start of the season. There was no place on the crew for Kim.

Would she have gone if he'd asked her to? Probably not, but that didn't make the loneliness any easier to bear. Might they have stayed together if they'd had a child? Now, seven months later, Kim had no answers to her questions.

As her personal drama played out, Kim's sisters' lives changed drastically as well. Ruth's husband, a trucking business owner turned Congressman, had decided to run for President. While Butch Mandell's candidacy began as a joke in many circles, his support had grown quickly, and he was now a serious third-party contender. At work, Kim left the room when politics came up. Her coworkers soon learned they'd get nothing from her: no family gossip, no insider incidents, no intimate revelations of the candidate's character. Kim never expressed an opinion on Butch's platform—or anyone else's, for that matter.

Then came Christmas, and the news that her oldest sister, Nettie, had murdered her only son. Nettie contacted neither Kim nor Ruth after her arrest; they'd both heard it on the news. Kim had immediately made the two-hour trip from Detroit to Berlin, but her reward was a message written on the back of a list of jailhouse rules: *I did it. Go home and forget me.*

How does a person forget any of this? Kim asked herself. *Where's the pill that makes that happen?*

With a sniff and a sigh, she opened the car door, pulled her bag from the back, and headed inside, staggering a little against the stiff breeze. Danielle and Paula, two of the firm's personal assistants, stood waiting for the elevator. They didn't see her coming, since Paula was talking excitedly. "He's taking me out for dinner at Gianni's tonight." She held her left hand out in a comical mimic of an old Beyoncé music video. "I think he's gonna put a ring on it."

Noticing Kim, Danielle raised her brows in warning, and Paula abruptly changed course. "—And by noon today, Ms. Evans wants me to find hotel rooms for ten people who don't speak a word of English."

They murmured greetings, and for a while everyone watched the light above the doors count its way down to them. When she couldn't stand the silence anymore, Kim asked, "Anything new on the Mueller account?" The chime sounded, the doors opened, and the women rode upward as Kim's coworkers took up the state of Mueller's Home Furnishings with enthusiasm born of relief.

A few minutes after Kim reached her desk, Paula approached. "Mr. Calver wants you to bring him what you've got on the Horace account so far."

"Be right there." Her cell phone rang as she sorted papers into a folder. Checking the ID, she took the call. "Ruth?"

"Kimmie, can you come out and play?"

"Where are you?"

"Downtown. Butch is speaking to the UAW and touring a car plant. Can we do lunch?"

Kim almost said no, but conscience jabbed like a sharp stick in the ribs. Though she loved her sister, as a candidate for First Lady of the United States, Ruth attracted publicity. Looking down at her brown skirt and tan blouse, Kim tried to remember if she'd even bothered to put on makeup that morning. And when had she last had her hair trimmed? She imagined the photos in tomorrow's news, the classy, gorgeous Ruth Mandell and her dowdy, recently dumped sister. Excuses piled up in her head, but in the end, family loyalty won. "Let's meet at noon at Dana's on Woodward."

"Sorry I'm late," Kim said as she set her purse on an empty chair beside Ruth. The restaurant bustled with lunch trade, and the pleasantly greasy smell of onion rings teased her senses. "Once I hit the office, things always seem to spiral out of control."

"You work too hard," Ruth had risen from her chair, and the two embraced. Her sister was a doll, tiny, beautiful, and perfect. Beside her, Kim felt like Fiona in Ogress mode.

She'd come incognito, which lessened Kim's fear of looming publicity a little. A turban-type hat hid Ruth's dark hair, and she wore glasses with square, black frames, and bright red lipstick that was completely out of character for her. "Is that how you escape all the hoopla?"

"I'm getting really good at it." Mischief lit her eyes. "The security people have nervous breakdowns every time, but sometimes I need to be by myself."

"What a complicated life you lead, Mrs. Candidate." Kim had been surprised when Butch ran for the Pennsylvania General Assembly, but his natural charm and reputation for compromise had led to success. Now he was trying to move to the national level, which was a huge jump. While Kim wondered if Butch understood what being President would entail, Ruth seemed to take it all in stride, as she did everything else.

The waiter came to rattle off the day's specials. They ordered drinks, and Kim said, "I'm glad you called. It's been ages since we really talked."

They'd last met at Nettie's hearing in March, but there'd been little chance to reminisce. At the courthouse, members of the press swarmed around them like trout after midges. Ruth took charge, ordering, "Don't even make eye contact, Kimmie. Just keep walking." Even in taxis they'd said little, since Ruth warned that cabbies might be paid to report their conversation to members of the press.

As they sat in the stuffy courtroom where their sister waived trial and admitted to murder, Ruth showed no emotion. Kim almost broke as the detective described the scene on the night of Caleb's death, but Ruth took her hand and squeezed it. "Don't," she murmured, and Kim pulled herself together, grateful for her sister's strength and experience.

Nettie pled guilty to second-degree murder. Her attorney, Andrew McMahon, had achieved the lesser charge by insisting there was more to the story than had been told and arguing that Janet "Nettie" Waller was no danger to society. The prosecution agreed, so it was left to the judge to determine if the defendant's guilty plea was "knowing and intelligent." Kim recalled his questions to Nettie with the clarity that momentous events impress on the memory.

> Judge: In the matter of the State vs. Waller, how do you plead?
>
> Defendant: Guilty, Your Honor.
>
> Judge: Counsel, have you reached a settlement?
>
> D.A.: Yes, Your Honor. The people suggest a sentence of five to ten years.

Judge: Ms. Waller, do you know that by pleading guilty you lose the right to a jury trial?

Defendant: Yes, Your Honor.

Judge: Did anyone force you to accept this settlement?

Defendant: No.

Judge: Are you pleading guilty because you in fact killed Caleb Green without legal provocation?

Defendant: Yes.

Judge: Janet Waller, you are hereby sentenced to no less than five and no more than ten years in the Huron Valley Women's Correctional Facility.

Kim and Ruth had left the courtroom together, stopping only to hug Nettie briefly under the watchful eye of a deputy who'd see her transported to prison.

As they stepped into the gray March afternoon, reporters swarmed again, and this time Ruth spoke to them. "Our sister has not had an easy life." She put an arm around Kim's shoulders. "Cases like hers put society on trial."

"You're saying society is responsible for your sister's crime?" someone asked.

"Of course not. Nettie did what she did. But her destruction began a long time ago, in a nation that allows young people to throw themselves away, as it were. It's my belief that if our social structure were stronger, people like Nettie would be saved from their own destructive tendencies."

An extended metallic clang brought Kim back to the present. Someone had dropped a metal tray that rolled in a circle for several seconds before clattering to a stop. Across the table, Ruth hardly noticed, since she was busy studying the menu. She squinted to see it, and Kim smiled to herself. Okay with wearing fake glasses to hide her identity, Ruth was too vain to wear the reading glasses she obviously needed. When she set the menu aside Kim asked, "How goes the campaign?"

"Very well. I think voters are ready for a candidate who offers real change."

"'If not now, when?' right?"

Ruth smiled. "You'll be pleased to hear that your second-eldest sister came up with that slogan." Ruth often mentioned the difference in their ages, but Kim suspected if she asked their waiter, he wouldn't be able to say who was older. Ruth had inherited the best of both parents, while Kim had gray hair at her temples, their dad's small eyes, Mom's tendency to carry weight in her hips and thighs, and a sense of never quite having her act together.

"The slogan is brilliant." Kim took a sip of water, swallowing her question as to why Butch wanted to be President. The country was bitterly divided. Who'd want to tackle a job that hopeless?

As Ruth talked, Kim's mind wandered to the past, when she'd grown up in her sisters' shadow. Eight years younger than Ruth and ten years younger than Nettie, she'd been seven when Nettie ran away, shocking their little town and breaking their parents' hearts. She'd been eleven when Ruth married Butch Mandell, who seemed like a prince from a fairy tale. She'd been a junior bridesmaid, hair securely moussed in place and a dress that resembled a birthday cake. She'd even been allowed one glass of champagne at the reception, and she could still recall the delightful feeling of bubbles in her nose.

Her sisters had been like distant stars, moving into and through the adult world while she perfected the art of ice-skating backwards. Impressions came in vignettes: Ruth bargaining with Kim to keep her trip to Detroit to see Bon Jovi a secret from their parents. Nettie mailing her a bracelet decorated with real turquoise for her sixteenth birthday. Once she'd run away, Nettie never came home and seldom called, but from time to time, Kim got small gifts, often books. They were second or third hand, but with each came a short message. *Hey, Squirt, Think you'll like Vonnegut's stuff. Hope you're behaving and getting tons of kills in volleyball. All good here. Love, Nettie.*

But that wasn't true. Whispered conferences between Mom and Dad revealed worry for their eldest child. While Ruth delivered one beautiful, healthy baby after another and ran the Sunday school at her church, Nettie drank too much, took illicit drugs, and lived with a succession of men who treated her badly.

"Why?" Mom would ask. Lying on the floor above and listening through the heat register, Kim heard defeat in her voice. "What did we do wrong, Stan?"

"I don't know, Hon." He often repeated it. "I don't know."

Once again, the present interrupted her memories as Ruth prompted, "Kim?" The waiter stood ready to take their orders.

"Oh, sorry. I'll have the quesadillas."

"Sour cream?"

Before she could reply Ruth sang, "Lots of extra calories." Ruth couldn't see Kim's rear, which was three sizes bigger than hers, but Kim figured she was thinking about it.

"Um, just salsa," she said, trying to quell the regret in her voice. The waiter left, and she asked, "Heard from Nettie?"

Ruth's mouth turned down. "I called the prison and asked if she'd see me while I'm in Michigan. She said no."

"She won't let me visit either."

After a sniff that said the topic was exhausted, Ruth asked, "How is work?"

"You know, same-old-same-old."

Setting her elbows on the table, Ruth toyed with her water glass. "Do you like your job, Kimmie?"

Kim felt her neck tense. The nickname always made her feel like she wasn't quite grown up. Should she say something?

She didn't. "Office politics can be a pain, but it's fun working with clients, coming up with ideas, that sort of thing."

Ruth's pale pink nails clicked on the stem of her glass. "I wondered if you might consider a change."

"A change?"

"While Butch had no intention of running for national office, people love his ideas."

"Some people," Kim corrected.

Her lips pinched briefly then turned up in a smile. "Many people. We find ourselves in need of help."

"You want me to work on Butch's campaign?" Kim began sorting through her mind for polite ways to refuse. She couldn't very well tell her sister outright that she thought her husband wasn't Presidential material.

"I need what's called a 'body woman.' You'd handle media contacts and schedule my engagements."

"But I have zero experience in the political arena."

Ruth gave that a floppy wave. "I'm not a politician. I'm your sister, and I need what you do now, every day, for strangers."

Kim was shaking her head before Ruth finished. "I'm happy where I am." That wasn't completely true, but she was comfortable at Calver PR. Modest demands. No surprises.

"It's your decision, of course, but I wonder if you aren't so tied to your routine that you can't imagine anything else." Reaching across the table, she put her hand on Kim's. "I need a helper I can trust, and family is the best way to go."

"I'm sorry, but no. Thank you."

"All right. I wanted to ask you first, before I start looking elsewhere." Ruth smiled at the waiter, who had arrived with their food. "Doesn't lunch look yummy?"

Chapter Four

Nettie-June 18

A guard unlocked the cell and ordered, "Waller, come with me."

"Why?"

Unfriendly eyes focused on her like twin pistols. "Because I told you to." When Nettie obeyed without further questions, the woman's manner softened a little. "Some doctor wants to examine your head."

Her newest roommate, a taciturn woman with lizard-like eyes, made a chuffing laugh. "That won't be easy. She don't talk much."

Nettie almost refused to go, but cooperation with authority made life inside tolerable. The law had done what it had done, and she was content with it. Rising from her lumpy mattress, she stepped to the cell door and stopped, waiting for the guard to tell her what to do next. If they wanted her to see a psychiatrist, she would, but she'd stonewall him, as she'd stonewalled everyone else. *Why?* she'd been asked repeatedly. *Why face a murder charge when telling us what happened could make all the difference?* She hadn't answered, and she wouldn't, no matter how many doctors they sent.

Inside the prison, it was difficult to determine the weather. When exercise time came, Nettie often felt a rush of pleasure when she stepped into bright sunlight, as if Nature had provided it especially for her. She'd raise her face to the warmth, closing her eyes and feeling her muscles going soft.

Today was rainy. As they passed a window, she saw heavy drops of water clinging to the glass. Even so, the outside called to her. She resisted the urge to reach out and touch the pane.

The new doctor was female, and a gingery smell clung to her. Long brown hair had been pulled into a messy bun, and tortoiseshell glasses sat halfway down her nose. The look seemed like an attempt to downplay her attractiveness. *Do the boy psychiatrists assume you're a ditz because you're pretty?* Though her attitude softened slightly, Nettie didn't let it show. Admiring a woman for staking out a place in the world of men was one thing. Letting her inside the head of the murderous Janet Waller was another.

"Janet, I'm Doctor Susan Foeller."

"Call me Nettie." When the doctor looked perplexed, she explained, "It's an old Scottish nickname for Janet."

"Nettie." She made a note on her legal pad. "I'm a psychiatrist. Did they tell you that?"

"Yeah."

"I study aberrant behavior, specifically crimes that are out of character." Her gaze met Nettie's, honest and candid. "I'm interested in how and why people with no violence in their past suddenly commit serious crimes."

"I suppose you're writing a book."

"Possibly." Foeller's tone was even. "Your case intrigues me."

She felt the need for a cigarette, but there was no smoking in the visitors' area. "What do you want?"

Foeller glanced around the cheerless room: the beige walls, plastic furniture, and gray metal doors. "Are you being treated well?"

"Well enough. It's a prison, after all."

Foeller smiled. "I'm here with an offer." Taking a few sheets of paper from a folder she said, "I have permission from the state of Michigan to move you to my private, secure facility outside Richmond, Virginia, where you will serve out your time under much better conditions."

"Virginia?" Nettie's nostrils narrowed. "Who's behind this?"

The doctor's tone remained warm. "Your sister thinks you'd benefit from a less oppressive atmosphere. When she heard about our facility, she called to ask if there might be a room for you there."

Nettie shook her head. "You can tell Ruth the Blessed I'll stay where I am."

Foeller's smile wavered. "Don't you think you deserve—"

Nettie rose. "I'm sorry you came all the way from Richmond for nothing." Leaving the woman with her mouth open, she went to the door and rapped sharply with her knuckles, signaling the guard to return her to her cell.

Locked in again, Nettie lay on her bunk, staring at a water stain on the ceiling she didn't really see. Her roommate asked idly what the visit had been about, but she said it was nothing. The woman said more, but Nettie didn't respond. Instead, she listened to her mind as it replayed her father's voice, the only time she'd ever known him to cry.

In times of trouble, it had been Mom who came to deal with whatever mess Nettie had made. Dad stayed home with the cows, because that's what farmers do. She never saw him again once she left Berlin, but sometimes when no one else was home, she'd call. They'd talk about everyday things, the price of hay and the change of seasons. Often there were long silences while they both smoked and said nothing. Once, after she heard the scrape of his lighter, the first draw on the cigarette, and the exhalation of breath, he said, "Nettie, you deserve a new chance at life. Let your mother and me help you."

She'd taken a drag on her own cig before answering, "Dad, you don't know what I deserve."

"I wish—" That was when she'd heard the sob and knew she'd broken her father's heart. He hadn't said what he wished for, but she knew. He wished she'd never been born. Three daughters: one too many. Though Nettie was the eldest, Stan and Linda Kovalesky's successes had come later. Ruth was beautiful and good at everything. Kim was athletic and honest. Only she disappointed everyone, choosing to live in a drug-induced haze.

What was wrong with her?

Her parents had never given up. They tried to understand her. If for a time Nettie thought she could resume a useful life, they'd been willing, even eager, to bail her out, pay for rehab, and set her up in a new place. Mom often stayed with her for a week or two, encouraging her sobriety and taking her shopping for curtains or dishes. Though her memory was fuzzy, Nettie knew of at least three times they'd provided everything she needed to start over.

None of it had worked. Only Caleb had given her the will to change.

Chapter Five

Kim-June 20

The message that brought Kim to the front office was terse and noticeably cool. Hurrying down the corridor, she wondered what she'd done wrong. Her accounts were all up to date. She hadn't been late for work lately, though in the first few weeks after Ed left, she'd found it hard to care about clocks and calendars. As she passed from the brightly lit hallway into Mr. Calver's office (and he was still Mr. Calver, after all these years), she blinked. As usual, the blinds were drawn, and a single gooseneck lamp provided illumination. The room smelled like black licorice. Together, those things created an old-fashioned mood, and Kim often imagined an eyeshade and sleeve garters stored in the top left drawer of the old man's desk.

She received no greeting, nor was she asked to be seated. "Ms. Dailey," her employer said in a formal tone, "we've made some unsettling discoveries."

Use of the plural pronoun signaled that Calver was distancing himself from an unpleasant message. "Discoveries?"

"The financial information on a number of your accounts has been falsified."

It felt like a hammer had struck her chest. "Falsified? Mr. Calver—"

"Before you say anything, let me show you what we found."

He laid several sheets of paper on the desk before her, snapping them into place in a rigid line. A few seconds' study of highlighted areas showed that for several years, amounts charged to their biggest clients were higher than what had been entered in company records. In each case, Calver Public Relations had received only eighty percent of what clients paid.

In happier times, Ed had said they made a great team, since Kim was good with clients and he was good with recordkeeping.

"This has to be a mistake."

"It's no mistake." His tone was like a door slamming in her face. "Money was diverted. Stolen."

Should she explain how little she'd had to do with that end of things? Which was worse, being a co-conspirator or a clueless dupe? And why would Calver care? Her ex was in Antarctica, while she stood there in person, her upper lip moist with sweat she didn't dare wipe away.

"Mr. Calver, I didn't know anything about this, I swear."

"I'd like to believe you, Ms. Dailey, but legally, you are as responsible as Edmund." Folding his hands, he presented his ultimatum. "If you return the money and resign immediately, I won't have you charged with embezzlement."

When she could trust her voice, Kim asked, "How much does it amount to?"

"Almost a hundred thousand dollars."

A wave of nausea swept over her, and Kim steadied herself against Calver's desk. "I don't have that kind of money."

"I'm willing to give you three months. If you can't make recompense at that time, we will involve the authorities." He spoke as if it were a magnanimous gesture, but Kim thought of the years she'd spent at the firm, working long hours with no appreciation from this man, only a demand for more hours, more dedication."

Questions boiled into Kim's mind. Why had Edmund cheated the firm? They'd had no dire financial needs, at least until he left her with all the bills and half the income. Had Ed wanted to punish Calver for being such a hard nose? If so, it wasn't fair that he'd included Kim in his plan. And why did he need a hundred thousand dollars in Antarctica?

Then the truth struck: Ed wasn't at the South Pole. He was probably halfway between, on a beach with a younger, prettier, trimmer companion at his side.

Dragging her mind back to the immediate problem, Kim made a decision. "I'll find a way to pay back the money," she told her almost-former boss. "I'll—I will." Then she bolted from his office and the building.

She managed to make it to the car before dissolving into tears. Half blind, she started the engine and drove away, unwilling to let her coworkers see her sobbing uncontrollably. Pulling into the first available alley, she parked next to a garbage bin and cried until her noisy gulps turned to heaving sighs and finally to sniffles. By that time, the smell of rotting vegetables, cooked by the sun, wafted through the vents, turning her stomach. When she finally calmed, blew her nose and cleared her throat, Kim tried a few words aloud. Judging herself able to speak coherently, she called her attorney.

"Calver has every right to terminate you," Abigail said once Kim told her story. "He could bring the police in at any time."

"Is the deal he offered legal? I mean, if I pay him back, is it all good?"

"Embezzlement's a crime, but if your boss doesn't report it, you'd probably be okay." Abigail's voice changed. "How could you not know Ed was such a louse, Kim? Cheating the company and leaving you holding the bag? That's low."

"I thought I knew him. How could I have been so wrong?"

Her attorney sniffed lightly. "I hope you see now that none of this was your fault."

"I'll see that your bill gets paid, no matter what. You've been great through all this."

"The firm requires me to bill by the hour," Abigail said, "but I'll keep the fees as low as I can."

They ended the call, and Kim added Abigail's bill to her mental list of horrors. She needed a hundred thousand dollars to stay out of prison. She had living expenses. She had to find a new line of work. And she had to decide whether to leave Michigan or stay and face the certainty that word would get out about why she'd left Calver PR.

That led to a second round of tears, interrupted by a guy in an almost-white apron who came out the restaurant's back door and tilted his head as if to ask what she was doing back there. Waving to indicate she was okay, Kim wiped her eyes, started the engine, and backed out of the alley. The time for tears was over. Time to go home and figure out what to do.

"Mandell residence. This is Mrs. Deeds."

"It's Kim Dailey. I need to speak to my sister, but she isn't answering her cell. Can you find her for me, please?"

"Hello, Ms. Dailey. Please hold while I find out where she's gone this time."

Kim pictured the housekeeper carrying the phone through Ruth's lovely home with its high ceilings, large rooms, tasteful colors, and perfect décor. The help, Mrs. Deeds and two or three men who worked outside, were all long-time employees, as dignified as the house itself. On her infrequent visits to Pennsylvania, Kim had been pleased to note that Ruth treated them well. While she could be snobbish at times, Ruth herself was not a snob.

Listening to the faint sound of the housekeeper's footsteps, Kim guessed Ruth was in her garden, where she often went to escape when things got hectic. A week earlier, she'd claimed she needed help dealing with a constant stream of calls for favors, appearances, and donations that. *Please, God, don't let her already have filled the position.*

"Kim?"

"Ruth." A knot had formed in her throat, and the word was almost a croak.

"Sweetie, have you reconsidered coming to help me?"

Biting her lip until it hurt, Kim regained control. "Um, yes."

"That's wonderful. How soon can you get here?"

"Right away, but there are things you need to know, and things I need from you."

The explanation came in fits and starts, with lots of "I didn't know—" and "I would never—" qualifiers. Finally, Ruth interrupted, "Kim, tell me what you need to get out of this mess."

Swallowing once, she said, "A hundred thousand dollars. Maybe one-twenty. I know it's a lot to ask, but I'll pay it back."

Ruth hesitated, and Kim waited for the letdown. It was too much. They'd have to draw up some sort of contract. She'd see what Butch had to say. Digging her fingernails into her palms, Kim told herself that whatever excuse Ruth offered, she'd accept it gracefully. None of her problems were Ruth's fault, and—

Instead, her sister said, "How do you want me to send the money?"

Chapter Six

Ruth-May 30

"Mrs. Mandell, we have a situation." Gavin Croft, the gifted lawyer hired as legal advisor to Butch's campaign, had approached silently, not a whisper of shoe leather on the tiles. He paused in the doorway, and shadows from the hallway gave his complexion an unhealthy look. Though Croft was becoming an integral part of Butch's team, Ruth had never warmed to the man. She found him obsequious with a tendency toward dishonesty, but it was a point of pride for her that no one in Butch's inner circle could say whom Mrs. Mandell admired and whom she merely tolerated. "Come in, Mr. Croft."

Croft obeyed, but he stopped some distance away, as if unworthy to enter her aura. "You're looking pale," Ruth said. "We're not working you too hard, are we?"

"Oh, no, ma'am. I enjoy being a small part of such a worthwhile endeavor."

"Well, don't forget to take care of yourself. Get some sun, but not too much, mind you." She turned to business. "Now, what's the problem?"

"A reporter I know called to say he's been contacted by a man who claims he was your…friend in college." Looking down at his phone, Croft read, "Robert VanCamp?"

"Bobby. Sure, I remember him."

"His story is that you and he were engaged." Croft cleared his throat. "He says you dumped him the minute you met a man with money."

Ruth's laugh seemed to take him by surprise. "Oh, for heaven's sake. That's ridiculous."

Croft clasped his hands at his belt buckle, reminding her of a worried mortician. "VanCamp asked if the magazine might pay him to provide details. Now, this reporter turned him down, but it's likely he'll keep trying until he finds someone looking for dirt to toss on the campaign."

Croft's value, despite Ruth's personal feelings, was as a counter to Butch's idealism. In the cut-throat world of modern politics, pragmatists were a necessity. To his credit, Croft seemed to seek no attention for himself. He relished working in the background, ferreting out facts and solving little glitches.

"If I know you, Mr. Croft, you've already researched this old boyfriend of mine."

A slightly protruding eyetooth showed in his half-smile. "A little."

"Tell me what you found out."

"Robert VanCamp dreamed of making the U of M football team, but that didn't happen. He failed out after two semesters and returned to Flint, where he went to work at his uncle's auto shop. He's still employed there as a bump-and-paint man."

"Family?"

"Two wives. A girl with one and two boys with the other. Divorced from both."

"Finances?"

"Paycheck to paycheck. He's had some legal trouble, but Uncle VanCamp always bails his nephew out, believing this time he's finally seen the light."

Ruth made rhythmic taps with her fingernails on the arm of her chair. "Let's fly Bobby here for a visit. Can you arrange that?"

Croft's head twitched to one side. "You want to bring him to Pennsylvania?"

"Book a room at the Caroline Hotel under your name. I'll meet him there for dinner Saturday night."

When Croft was gone, Ruth went upstairs, where Butch was struggling to button his dress shirt. "I swear, every time a church group invites me to a potluck dinner, I gain three pounds. Lately I'm puffed up like a Christmas goose."

She crossed the room to help him with the task. "The White House has a gym. Once you're elected, we'll both get back into shape."

Sliding the top button into place, she patted the cloth flat. Butch took her hand and held it. "Are we sure we want to tackle the mess this country is in?"

"We can do it, Sweetheart. Together we can do anything."

While Butch's chances of being elected had at first been razor thin, Democrats and Republicans alike had spent any goodwill they still had with bitter wrangling among themselves and vicious attacks on each other. Voters wanted an end to the nastiness.

Butch's character was unassailable. Employees and even competitors admitted he did his best to give everyone a fair shake. And there was a romantic element to Butch Mandell's story. While he could have had his pick of women from eminent Pennsylvania families, he'd chosen a girl from a small farm in rural Michigan. Their behavior toward each other signaled that the love they'd found so long ago was still strong today.

Ignoring Butch's soft grunts as he bent to put on his wingtips, Ruth traveled in her memory back to the night they met.

At the University of Michigan in the beautiful, cool September of 1995, her assigned roommate had been Molly Corbett, a ditzy girl from Pennsylvania. Hopelessly disorganized, Molly lost important items daily and invariably went ballistic about it. Without Mom, Daddy, and the housekeeper to smooth her way, Molly transferred her dependence to Ruth, who patiently located her other earring, her misplaced I.D. card, or her assignment sheet for English 101 (inexplicably stuck behind the toilet paper roller in the bathroom). Once, busy listening to her new Green Day CD, Molly missed a midterm exam. Predictably, she'd panicked, but Ruth suggested she call the prof and beg forgiveness. The man agreed to let her take the test in his office the next day. Things always seemed to work out for Molly.

Ruth loved the glimpses her roomie provided into a life she'd only imagined. On the farm, wearing Nettie's hand-me-down jeans and shirts from Target, Ruth had pored over magazine photos of beautiful people whose clothes were created for them alone. Molly brought with her an upscale wardrobe that pushed the limits of their dorm space, and she encouraged Ruth to wear whatever she chose. Her roomie was spoiled and erratic, but for Ruth, walking across campus smelling of Obsession and wearing Prada or Versace made up for it.

Molly's stories of home fascinated Ruth. Her parents were movers and shakers back in Pennsylvania, and Molly mentioned casually people Ruth had seen on the evening news. "Uncle Bud" was a state senator. The governor had attended their Fourth of July picnic. A judge sent Molly chocolates on her birthday with a note: *Don't stop till you get that law degree!*

Anyone who was paying attention knew Molly would never enter U of M's law school. Her plan was to "party hearty" for a year or two then get married, though her criteria for a mate was fuzzy. One month, she was enthralled with a poetic grad assistant from the English department. The next it was with a guy who planned to be a professional bowler. The question of whether they were or weren't suitable husband material was never a consideration, but her enthusiasm always waned after a time. When that happened, Ruth was called upon to lie if the former lover phoned or stopped by. Molly was out. Molly was in the shower. Molly had a cold and had taken some Nyquil so she could sleep.

Molly's parents came to visit on Homecoming weekend. Mrs. Corbett was exactly what Ruth had imagined, a woman who radiated class. She wondered how she'd raised a daughter as…well, loose as Molly. Mr. Corbett, who clearly adored "Molly Doodles," smelled of pipe tobacco and wore a double-breasted suit which, though expensive, was wrong for his stocky build.

The Corbetts took the girls to a restaurant where the clientele was elderly, well-dressed, and mostly silent. Intimidated by the formal atmosphere, Ruth watched Mrs. Corbett and copied what she ordered and how she ate. Later, back at the dorm, Molly showed "Daddy" her portfolio from Art 101, leaving Mrs. Corbett and Ruth in the common room. "I believe you're a good influence on our daughter," Donna Corbett said in a low voice.

If "good influence" meant she'd hidden the worst of Molly's excesses, cleaned up her vomit, and took care of her after weekends spent at parties, Ruth decided she was. "We do okay together. I like hearing about all the places Molly's been."

Mrs. Corbett watched her daughter half-dance across her bedroom, pulling her father to a wall of posters. Taking a small carrying case from her purse, she popped it open, selected a tiny white pill, set it at the back of her tongue, and swallowed it dry. "If she makes it through the semester, you might come for a visit at Christmas." In her words Ruth heard a promise: *Protect Molly from herself, and we'll reward you with a glimpse into our lifestyle.*

"That would be great."

Molly overheard and took it a step further. "Maybe Ruth could go to the Snow Ball with me. Can you get her in, Daddy?"

Corbett harrumphed once, examined Ruth as if noticing her for the first time, and said he'd see what he could do. Molly hugged him. "My best Daddy."

"The Snow Ball is like this stupid mating ritual," Molly said when her parents were gone. "Guys check out the girls while parents check out their pedigrees and bank accounts. If your balance is in the black, if your ancestors didn't blow up any banks, and if the two of you can stand each other, Ma and Pa start preparing the prenup."

"Is it really that bad?"

"Worse." Molly added, "But everyone goes anyway."

"What would I do there?"

Molly put on a comically snobbish air. "Dahling, you'd be my personal hand grenade at the Night of the Living Unwed. I will drop you among all the mean girls I grew up with and watch them hide jealous snarls behind their wrist corsages." Ruth frowned, but Molly slapped her arm playfully. "Don't worry. No one can force *you* to marry some dork in a tux." She waved like a fairy godmother. "Dazzle the boys with your raven hair and perky boobs. Give the girls a scare. Afterwards we'll get pissy drunk and make fun of the whole bunch of them."

"Sounds great, Mol." Ruth's sarcastic tone hid her eagerness. All her life she'd wanted to stand among the glitterati and learn how it felt to be one of them. Now she'd get her chance, if she made sure Molly showed up for final exams and didn't bomb too badly.

The Grand Ballroom at the Swift Hotel was the most magnificent sight Ruth had ever seen. Decorated with snow white bouquets trailing pastel ribbons, it smelled like an indoor garden. Overhead were chandeliers as big as limousines, and the music was produced by real musicians, long-haired, serious types in slightly tatty evening wear.

Ruth wiped her damp palms one last time and tucked the tissue into her bodice. Everything she wore (except her underpants) was borrowed from Molly. Every bit of allure the girls possessed had been maximized, and Ruth knew she looked good, pale skin, lustrous hair with a bit of natural curl, and a figure that Bobby, her sort-of boyfriend, called “dynamite.”

Ruth pushed Bobby to the back of her mind. She’d fibbed, telling him she was going home for Christmas. Instead, she was here, feeling like Cinderella, right down to her puffy sleeves, sweetheart neckline, and tulle skirt.

Molly paused in the wide doorway of the ballroom, so Ruth did the same. A blushing adolescent boy checked their invitations and nodded. Two more boys approached, each extending an elbow. Ruth copied Molly, curling a hand around her escort’s arm. The boys ushered them inside, bowed awkwardly, and backed away. As the crowd assessed them, the girls surveyed the room, already awhirl with dancers. “You’re the prettiest one here,” Molly said in a low tone. “And that Ice Queen smile you put on when you’re terrified practically dares men to run up and throw themselves at your feet.”

Ruth wasn’t feeling calm at all. People who were obviously at home here moved through the crowd, stopping to kiss each other on the cheek—well, almost on the cheek. They chatted amiably, indicating long acquaintance. What was she doing here? She wasn’t rich. She had no powerful relatives. Miserably, she imagined the rest of the evening. One or two of the men might ask her to dance, but once word spread that she was Molly’s farmer-girl roommate, the bachelors present would turn back to girls from their set, girls of their kind.

A mellow bass voice spoke beside her, and she got a whiff of expensive masculine scent. “I don’t think I’ve seen you before.”

Turning, Ruth faced a young man with a strong build and a dazzling smile. Molly’s open-mouthed expression revealed that even she was impressed. Swallowing unobtrusively, Ruth looked into the man’s warm, deep-brown eyes and hoped her underarm deodorant was as good as the ads claimed. “I’m Ruth.”

“Butch Mandell,” her future husband replied. “It’s nice to see a new face among the flowers. Would you like to dance?”

Chapter Seven

Nettie-June 10

A metallic clunk brought Nettie out of a deep sleep. She started, and the pain of movement made her moan aloud. Her shoulder felt like someone had used a tire iron on it, and her cheek throbbed with each beat of her heart. Opening her eyes, she squinted at a bright, rectangular fluorescent light overhead. Glancing to one side, she saw an IV stand, a heart monitor, and an oxygen tank. As her brain caught up, she remembered. Prison. She'd been heading downstairs for lunch when a hand gripped her hair, pulling her backward and off balance. A second later, a push had sent her stumbling down the remaining steps, where she collided with the wall. Vaguely, she recalled what followed, a jumble of voices and sharp commands. Before she blacked out, a voice spoke in her ear. "I'm gonna make your life hell, and there's nothing you can do about it."

Why? She couldn't think of anything she'd done to upset anyone. She stayed to herself, kept her eyes down, and said little. She was too old to be of interest to sexual predators, too quiet to have disturbed anyone's sleep or awakened their prejudices. Who had gone out of the way to hurt her?

The shoulder was badly bruised but not broken. Her split cheek had required stitches, and the reactions of others hinted that with that and two black eyes, she wasn't pretty.

Not that she'd been a looker before. Years of dissolution had written themselves on Nettie's face, and she knew she looked more like sixty-nine than forty-nine.

Returning to gen-pop was stressful, though Nettie did her best to hide her fear. Calling herself a coward, she double-timed down passageways, kept her distance from others, and remained in her cell whenever possible. Looking down at the floor, she listened intently to the voices around her, trying to identify the one that had made the threat. Could it have been a guard? The prisoner everyone called Crazy Joan? An inmate who appeared friendly but wasn't?

Nettie had been with men who hit her, but when the abuse got too bad or came too often, she'd left. Not one of them had ever cared enough to track her down. Now there was no escape, and every second spent outside her cell was imbued with terror. Gently she touched the stitches that climbed the side of her face. Sixteen of them. Would the next attack come on the stairs? At the showers? In the exercise yard? Would she be beaten? Stabbed? Would she suffer broken bones, internal bleeding, permanent brain damage?

When Doctor Foeller wrote to offer a place in her private clinic a second time, Nettie accepted.

Chapter Eight

Kim-June 28

Kim found it maddening that she had no way to contact her ex-husband. Texts went undelivered, and her emails bounced. She composed and practiced speeches in her mind, sometimes polemics but also pleas for him to explain why he'd done it. Apparently, she'd meant so little to Ed that he hadn't minded leaving her to face his crimes. In the end, there was nothing she could do except count herself lucky that Ruth had the means and the inclination to get her out of Edmund's mess.

Before she left Michigan, Kim packed her car with boxes and headed north to close and winterize the farm, which had sat empty since Nettie's imprisonment. She called Dack Porter, a friend of her father's, who agreed to meet her there and do what was needed to protect the water lines from freezing when winter came. While he did that, Kim would deal with the contents of Nettie's house. Usable things she'd donate to the local women's shelter. Dack said she could toss anything not worth donating into the back of his pickup, and he'd take it to the landfill.

Parking her car in the driveway, Kim stopped to take in what still seemed like home. Dappled sunlight filtered through deep green leaves, making dark and light speckles along the driveway. Light mixed with darkness. Happiness blended with sorrow. Life, but also death. All in this one, beautiful place.

Dack pulled into the driveway only minutes behind her, and they entered the bunkhouse together. While he took his tools and went to the back of the building, where there were four toilet stalls and a shower tree, Kim took inventory of what she needed to get done. Released on bond during the trial period, Nettie had removed the food to discourage mice and other wild creatures from moving in. When Kim offered to help, Nettie had said she'd call if she needed her. She hadn't called.

Nettie's personality was everywhere: nothing superfluous, no knick-knacks or figurines. It smelled of dust and was littered with the carcasses of flies who'd beaten themselves to death against the windows. There were blinds, plain and cheap, but no curtains. Pans and lids hung from nails driven into the wall above the stove. Kim's footsteps echoed on the wooden floors, and the bangs and squeaks

Dack made as he worked on the plumbing were magnified by emptiness.

Caleb's room was a mess, and Kim felt bile rise in her throat. It was exactly as the police must have seen it, minus only her nephew's corpse. Nettie had simply closed the door on the scene of her crime, unable to face it again.

Forcing her nausea back, Kim dragged the blood-soaked mattress outside and wrestled it into Dack's truck. Though she could imagine the comments it would cause, she had no other way to be rid of it. As she stuffed Caleb's possessions into cardboard boxes she'd brought along, she came to a Crown Royal bag that contained several keychains, some with metal fobs, others made of wood or leather. Dumping them into the last box, she stacked it with the others atop the mattress. Then, gritting her teeth, she found a bucket, bleach, a scrub brush, and rubber gloves, drew water before Dack drained the kitchen pipes, and washed the stains from the floor and walls.

It was harder to decide what to do with Nettie's things. Kim hated the idea of her sister leaving prison someday and finding she owned nothing, but Ruth had already decided they should sell the place. In the end she kept only the lamp with the fake cowhide shade that she'd bought for Nettie's birthday one year. She'd meant it as a joke, but Nettie had called to say she loved it. The least she could do was keep that one light-hearted piece. Everything else Kim either donated or tossed, promising herself that when the time came, she'd see that Nettie got new everything to go along with her new life.

Finally, the work was done, the door locked, and the windows shuttered. Kim hugged Dack, who smelled sweetish from the antifreeze and sweaty from the work. She offered to pay for his help, but he refused in his usual gruff manner. "Your dad was my friend. A few hours' work ain't gonna kill me."

As his old pickup roared away, Kim stood looking at the property where she'd grown up. The house was gone; fire had taken care of that. The barn was rented to a local farmer for hay storage. The other outbuildings were empty for the most part. What was left here for her?

Memories, her mind whispered, *which are both everything and nothing.*

Chapter Nine

Ruth-Same Day

Entering the restaurant, Ruth squinted through the dim lighting and picked out three different men who sat at a table alone. At first, her gaze went past Bobby VanCamp, but a second look at a man eyeing the drink in his hand as if it were a lover told her she'd found him. Bobby hadn't aged well, and from what Croft said, alcohol was a major factor. As she got closer, Ruth saw that the veins on his nose stood out, making it seem to glow. Bright-blue eyes, once his best feature, were now rheumy and puffy. Despite that, Ruth raised her arms, signaling she wanted a hug. "Bobby, it's so good to see you."

Rising, he embraced her, and Ruth felt the bump of his gut against her before the rest of him arrived. Standing back, he looked her up and down. "You look even better now than you did at eighteen, Ruth."

"You wouldn't believe the amount of upkeep that takes these days." When it became obvious her companion wasn't going to, the waiter pulled out a chair for her. Thanking him, Ruth asked for white wine. As he left to do her bidding, she leaned across the table. "I hear you've been telling tales about me, Bobby."

His lips pinched together. "You and me were doing fine, and all of a sudden you're engaged to some guy from La-di-dah Land."

She gave him a direct look. "Did I ever once say I'd marry you?"

"No, but you didn't mind hanging with me until Butch Mandell showed up."

"We had fun, didn't we?"

"And now you can afford to eat in this kind of place every day." He waved at the room, the gesture loose and uncontrolled. "You can send your old boyfriend a plane ticket and stash him in a fancy hotel. You used to be a nobody from Podunkville, and now you're probably headed for the White House."

"Your outrage over our breakup comes late in the game, Bobby. It happened almost thirty years ago."

In an obvious attempt at righteous anger, he blustered, "You didn't even have the nerve to tell me to my face. That snarky roommate of yours had a million excuses, and then you were gone."

Leaning back in her chair she said, "We're face to face now."

Gliding forward, the waiter set Ruth's wine before her as if it were a gift. "Would you care to see menus?"

"Not now, thanks. My friend will order later, and you can add his meal to the room charges."

Nodding, the waiter left. Ruth took a sip of wine before asking, "What is it you want, Bobby?"

"I want you to admit you treated me like dirt." His words were followed by a mucous-y sniff of fake outrage.

With effort, Ruth managed to keep from rolling her eyes. She'd apparently become Bobby's excuse for every mistake he'd ever made. *He* wasn't a failure. The girl who'd broken his heart all those years ago was to blame.

"Mrs. Majors."

They looked up to see a large, square man standing between them, his face like a slab of slate. "Bobby," Ruth said, "this is Agent Josh Bennigan of the U.S. Secret Service." Bobby's eyes widened. "His job is to protect me from threats."

Bobby's gaze moved from her to Bennigan several times, like a comedian in a skit. Ignoring his discomfort, Ruth asked, "Will you join us?"

Without answering, Bennigan sat, waving away the waiter who hurried over to see to his drink requirements. Setting his elbows on the table, he knitted his fingers and said evenly, "Mr. VanCamp, I'll be blunt. Your presence here amounts to extortion."

Bobby reached across the table toward Ruth, and she noticed grease buried deep under his nails. "I didn't—"

At a curt gesture from the Secret Service man, Bobby stopped talking. "You've been trying to make money on this story of yours, but I know every shady thing you've ever done, from illegal poker games to cheating on child support." Through his teeth, he finished, "I can make it so your kids never speak to you again. I can get you fired. I could even send you to jail."

"Listen, you got this wrong." Bobby stabbed a finger at Ruth. "I came here because she wanted to see me." Turning his eyes to hers, he challenged, "Did I ask for anything? I never asked for anything."

Ruth turned to Bennigan. "I appreciate your help, Agent Bennigan, but I think Bobby and I can work this out."

Immediately he stood and pushed his chair back into place. "Happy to be of assistance, ma'am."

As he left, Ruth said, "Bobby. I didn't mean for you to be embarrassed, but you see how protective our people are."

"He made me sound like a criminal," he said resentfully. "It's not a crime to talk about the past."

"It is if your intentions are dishonest. Now, I'd hate to see you in legal trouble because your memories of what *did* happen got confused with what you *wanted* to happen." She rose. "Enjoy the weekend, my treat. I don't expect to hear from you again." As she left, Ruth heard Bobby rattle the ice in his Beam and Coke, signaling the waiter to bring him another.

Later, with Ruth and Gavin Croft, Bennigan expressed his conviction that VanCamp would not be a problem in the future. "The guy's no genius, but he's smart enough to know when to back off."

"An iron fist and a velvet glove," Croft congratulated them. "Very effective." When the agent returned to his duties, Croft remained behind to bring up a new concern. "Mr. Mandell is slated to give an important speech on the environment on Tuesday, ma'am, but he hasn't begun work on it yet. I was hoping you might encourage him to set aside some time for that."

"Better yet," Ruth replied, "let's you and I draft the speech."

Croft watched her closely as he said, "If you think that's acceptable."

"We can do it. Between us, we know his views well enough."

Hours later, Ruth's back ached from bending over Croft's shoulder as he typed, but the speech was in reasonable shape. She'd found him surprisingly easy to work with. He grasped her ideas quickly and followed her lead, adding only an occasional murmur of approval. Their one disagreement came when Ruth suggested an example to demonstrate the possibilities. "We should suggest using welfare recipients to sort recycled goods. Work for them; help for the environment."

Croft shook his head, though his tone was gentle. "Mr. Mandell wants nothing put forward as 'This is how we'll accomplish that.' The suggestion becomes the issue and not the idea of consensus."

"But even the mentally handicapped can be taught to toss cans into separate bins."

"Your idea is worthwhile," Croft allowed, "but your husband's refusal to give specifics gives us the advantage. Since those things will be decided at some point in the future, his current opponents have nothing to argue against."

Ruth tapped a finger on her lips. "But eventually, someone will have to make these decisions. Debating what's best in any particular instance could go on forever."

"Yes." Croft eyed her speculatively. "I'm sure you and he will discuss that after the election. I will of course be willing to help in any way I can."

Was he suggesting Ruth could become a real part of the administration, not simply a decorative addition to the Presidency? Did Croft hope she'd help him steer Butch onto certain pathways? Ruth wasn't sure how she felt about that.

Croft didn't seem to require a response. Pressing the "print" key, he moved to the copier, where sheets of paper began whirring into a tray. "I'll get this to our candidate, so he can begin learning his lines."

Chapter Ten

Nettie-July 1

The first thing Nettie liked about Martha's Place was the light. The prison in Michigan had seemed designed to shut out natural light entirely, but the renovated Virginia mansion was awash with it. The original windows were high and wide, and rather than changing that, they'd replaced the glass with panes of polycarbonate. Her escort Nettie boasted they were impervious to smashing and even bullets. Though it was meant as a warning, she was pleased to find that everywhere she went, she could look out and see the fat summer sun.

Her cell was bland, as a prison cell should be. About ten feet square, it had in one corner a sink, stool, and shower combination that granted a modicum of privacy by means of a single four-by-eight frosted-glass panel. It was a luxury to bathe and use the toilet without witnesses for the first time in months. The entry door was metal framed and solid, with a slot guards could look through when they felt it was necessary. "We don't use them unless you give us reason to," the guard informed her. "Doc wants the clients (Nettie was no longer an *inmate*) to be responsible for their own behavior."

Prisoners controlled their cell's lights, as well as the heating and cooling, within a range of fifteen degrees. Meals and group recreation came at set times, but the rest of the day they chose their own schedules. Nettie was given several options for therapy sessions, depending on the doctor's availability.

Punishment for serious rule infractions was simple: you went back to the prison you'd come from. After a day at Martha's Place, Nettie saw what a powerful incentive that was for good behavior. In her dreams, she still heard the grind and clank of gates closing on their mechanical tracks at Huron Valley. She'd usually been either too hot or too cold, with no recourse but to lie on her bunk and try to think happy thoughts. And the food! While meals at Martha's Place were simple, they were banquets compared to those served at the prison in Michigan. For a woman who had for two decades grown her own food and cooked it to suit herself, the canned, reused, and reheated gunk had been torture.

While Nettie wasn't the type to ask questions, she listened to those around her and pieced bits together. Martha's Place was an experiment in private prisons, funded in the 1970s by a wealthy Virginian whose daughter had committed suicide after being sent to a state penitentiary for selling drugs. Though its success rate was exceptional, Martha's Place had encountered financial problems in the last few years, and the building had begun showing signs of age. Software that wasn't essential was replaced with hardware, like the shiny metal padlock that replaced the keypad on the malfunctioning freezer door. Outdoor monitors malfunctioned when conditions were extremely humid. Water pressure was low at peak usage times, signaling the need for an upgrade that was unlikely to happen.

Though other inmates griped about puny showers and decrepit plumbing, none of it bothered Nettie. On the farm that first winter, she and Caleb had gone a month without running water. It hadn't occurred to her that the bunkhouse wasn't designed for year-around living, so the pipes froze somewhere underground. With no money to pay a plumber, they'd hauled milk cans filled with water from Dack Porter's place. She could still recall the weight of those cans, wet and cold against her thighs, and the thumps they made as she set them into the back of the pickup. Caleb had always hurried ahead and took up the hose, so it was he who filled the cans while Dack and Nettie did the lifting and carrying. When they finished, he would thank Dack politely for his kindness, but once, on the way home he'd asked, "Did you forget what winter's like here, Mother, or were you too stupid to care if we had water?"

Being an early riser, Nettie chose mornings for her sessions with the doctor. Cell door locks were on a timer, so at five minutes before her appointment, she heard a muted click. For fifteen seconds, the knob would turn in her hand. She stepped into the hall where Haller, one of the guards, sat at a desk. "Seeing the doc," she said, and Haller nodded. Downstairs another guard, whose name she didn't yet know, saw her approach and consulted a list. Rising, she knocked once on a door, slid her ID badge across a magnetic pad, and stood aside to let Nettie enter.

Dr. Foeller's office was painted pastel colors, one wall blue, one yellow, one green, and the last peach, with Impressionist prints hung in stationary frames on the two side walls. A vase by the door held hydrangeas, and she smelled their jasmine-like scent as she passed. The vase was bolted to the table, assuring that a hysterical prisoner couldn't launch it at Foeller. The desktop contained no loose objects: no scissors, stapler, or pens that might become missiles. The doctor was no fool, and though more attractive than most, Martha's Place was still a prison.

"Are you settling in?" Dr. Foeller asked, and Nettie swallowed a smart remark. *What choice do I have?*

"Yes, thank you," she replied. "I'm enjoying the quiet."

"We have only two dozen residents," Foeller said. "You probably met most of them at dinner last night."

She had, at least in the sense that she'd seen them. Though a few nodded to acknowledge the new "client," no one had sought her company. Gossip had no doubt preceded the unnatural mother who'd murdered her son in his bed.

Since Foeller's study focused on sudden, violent crimes committed by apparently sane people, Nettie had been curious to see the other inmates. When none of them seemed visibly disturbed, she guessed Foeller rejected openly volatile types. One advantage private prisons had over state-run institutions was that they got to choose who occupied their cells.

Foeller watched Nettie as if trying to read her thoughts. "Do you have any questions for me before I start digging into your brain?" Nettie suppressed a flash of liking for the woman. She was direct, which Nettie preferred, and she wasn't condescending. Nettie had had enough of that from so-called professionals.

"Why does my story interest you?" she asked. "Family members kill family members every day."

"What interests me," Foeller replied, "is your unwillingness to say why you did it. Most killers want to explain themselves." She made a little throat-clearing noise. "I'm hoping that in time, you'll trust me enough to tell me about it."

Nettie fingered a cigarette she'd stashed in her pocket. The rules said they could smoke outside, at least twenty feet from an entrance, or in cells equipped with smoke eaters. Not in the office. Though the need prickled in her lungs, head, and mouth, having her next cig in hand helped a little. "There's no excuse for what I did," she told Foeller, "so there's no sense in me trying to defend it."

If the doctor was disappointed, she didn't show it. "Parenting is hard. I have a daughter who's eleven, and we're already butting heads."

When she got no response to that, Foeller changed the subject. "Our rules for visitors were in the agreement you signed, but I want to be sure you understand. You get one visitor a month, subject to my approval."

"I don't want to see anyone."

"If and when a request is made, we'll talk, and you can decide." Taking a pen from a drawer, she tapped a sheet of paper before her. "You're required to participate in three ways: sessions with me at least twice a week, physical activity daily, and some sort of ongoing work or study. We can arrange computer classes in almost any subject, and we have a few instructors who come in for hands-on teaching such as metal work or fine arts. Do you have any idea what you might enjoy doing?"

Nettie glanced out the window. "Is there a greenhouse?"

"No." Foeller must have sensed her disappointment, for she added, "That doesn't mean we can't get one."

"I bet Ruth the Blessèd would pay for it." Nettie heard the odd tone in her own voice but hoped the doctor didn't know her well enough yet to identify it as envy. She was jealous of Ruth, but not for the reason others might think. Nettie didn't long for Ruth's wealth or looks or social status. What she coveted was her sister's single-minded view of life. Ruth never doubted herself. Nettie doubted everything.

"Why do you call her Ruth the Blessèd?"

"Aside from once when she stepped on a nail in our barn, Ruth has never had a bad day in her life."

"Do you think she doesn't deserve what she's got?"

Nettie snorted a laugh. "We all deserve what we get, Doctor."

"Can you admit the possibility that you might deserve better than you've had?"

"Sure." Nettie grinned. "I deserve a greenhouse." After a pause she added, "If there's anyone interested, I could share what I know about growing things."

"That's good of you."

There was a pause, and Nettie asked, "Do the sessions start now?"

"If you're ready."

She shrugged. How different could it be from rehab? "Now is fine."

"Is there a Mr. Waller somewhere?"

"I guess so, but I don't even remember what he looked like." Nettie chuckled. "He meant to save me from myself, but he soon realized that wasn't happening."

"What he wanted for you wasn't what you wanted?"

"Yeah. That."

Foeller folded her hands on the desktop. "My ex-husband had definite ideas of what a perfect wife should be. I couldn't fit into the mold."

Nettie recognized a second attempt to create commonality between them, not doctor and patient but two women discussing their lives. When she didn't respond, Foeller seemed undeterred. "How did you start using drugs?"

Every counsellor posed that question, and Nettie found it tiresome. They assumed booze and drugs had ruined her life, not the personal weaknesses that had made her want those things. Still, it was easier than explaining the murder of her son.

"I was at a party. I was fifteen, maybe sixteen, and somebody offered me a taste. The result was amazing. For the first time I could remember, I didn't feel responsible for anything. Not for myself, not for anyone else. I was free to not care. I could laugh at the crap I usually carried around like a sack of rocks." Rubbing at her arms, she added, "On that bubble of euphoria, you simply exist. Nothing you do or don't do matters."

"Drugs relieved pressures you felt to be or act a certain way."

Many therapists saw that as an "aha" moment, when they'd unraveled everything. Perhaps because she'd warmed to Foeller a little, she said softly, "It doesn't matter how it started."

Foeller got it. "The question is what made it continue."

Nettie nodded, crediting her for understanding that a diagnosis isn't the same as a cure. "Self-abusers are judged from a list of supposed causes. We're weak. We're selfish. We're troubled by the past or the present or the future." Nettie met Foeller's gaze. "The beauty of addiction is that nothing on that list matters. All the dissecting of why and judging of how doesn't reach where you live."

During times she was sober and willing to poke at her scars, Nettie had asked herself how her life went so wrong. While not as beautiful as Ruth, she'd been okay, with lots of auburn hair and a good figure. She got the female lead in *Bye Bye Birdie,* and Trent Sutfin, who was born to play Birdie, had approved. "Not only is she the prettiest cast member other than me," he'd told his buddies as he rested a proprietary elbow on her shoulder, "but Nettie can act too." The sex they began having a few weeks later wasn't bad, and Trent was admirably discreet about it. Another reason to love him.

The show's success caused Trent to conclude they belonged in the movies. "We're wasting our time in this burg," he told Nettie. "In California they want good-looking, talented people like you and me."

"What about school?" she'd asked. "You're done in June, but I have a year left."

"Where does it say you need a diploma to be the next Kim Basinger?"

His arguments had been hard to resist. In the first place, Nettie loved acting more than anything she'd ever done. Standing on the stage, with everyone watching and waiting to hear her speak or sing, was a huge rush, and it was hard to imagine how calculus or world history could improve on that. Second, she found herself more and more at odds with her mother, who said Trent was "more than a little in love with himself."

"It's confidence," Nettie had argued. "It's what makes a good actor."

Her mother had pursed her lips, signaling disagreement. After that, every time Mom hinted Trent wasn't her soulmate, Nettie became more convinced he was.

"I met this guy, and we ended up running away together," she told Foeller.

"It didn't work out?"

"No."

"That's when you went from occasional partying to seriously abusing alcohol and drugs."

"You've heard dozens of versions of the story. Mine's not much different."

"I understand that you made attempts to recover and start over."

Ruth had provided background. No surprise there. "I did, but in the end, it was always easier to let the local dealer sell me relief from caring about...everything." Her jaw tightened. "No matter what the price was, I paid it."

"And your family? Did you think they were better off not knowing where you were and how you were doing?"

Nettie's laugh was harsh, and the sound of it hung between them until she said, "Damn right they were better off." Touching the cigarette again, she added softly, "I'd write occasionally: *Got a good job. Taking it one day at a time*." Looking down at the floor she said softly, "Sometimes a lie is all you can give the people you love."

Chapter Eleven

Kim-July 3

Kim had always hated moving, but it wasn't so bad this time. While the mild weather held, she gave away her beloved houseplants, reduced her wardrobe to the few things Ruth might approve of, and sold the furniture she and Edmund had accumulated. He still hadn't answered her messages, but she was done with him anyway. Not only had he dumped her after sixteen years, but he'd also made her an unwitting accomplice to embezzlement. Kim was furious at herself for believing his tall tale about doing "work that matters to the world."

It had all been a lie. Antarctica? Really? The perfect excuse not to be reachable when his crimes were discovered.

What would she have done without Ruth? What people said about family was true. When everything in life is a pile of rubble, you turn to parents, siblings, even cousins, and suddenly there's hope for a better future.

The job Ruth offered paid well. The rest of it, the scary-large amount of money that appeared in her bank account, the airline ticket that arrived by email, and the two burly men who showed up at her door with orders to move whatever she wanted to Vienna Park and take the rest to storage, all that was Ruth making life easier for her. She was thoughtful like that: little presents for no reason. Little kindnesses at holidays. And a card every week for months after their parents died in a fire. *Thinking of you. Hoping you have a good day today.*

One bitterly cold night in February of 2003, an ancient furnace, a hundred-year-old house, and a second-floor bedroom had combined to kill Stan and Linda Kovalesky. Kim, a freshman at college, had discovered within a day that the house insurance had lapsed, the farmland had been sold off in parcels, and the remaining property was mired in tax debt.

"Bailing Nettie out of one scrape after another," Ruth said as they sat in the local library, sharing a clunky computer and trying to piece together the information needed to settle the estate. Though Ruth seldom spoke harshly of Nettie, they were shocked to learn how far her parents had gone to try to save their oldest daughter. Despite a lifetime of hard work, they'd died owning only ten acres of land. Stan's life insurance policy would cover two cremations, a modest memorial service, and about half of the property taxes owed.

Revealing a surprising talent for forensic accounting, Ruth dug out information, bit by bit. Her expression grave, she showed Kim receipts for times their mother had gone to wherever Nettie was and repaired the damage she'd done. To protect her from the scope of Nettie's problems, they'd told Kim Mom was visiting her sister in Ohio. There were payments to rehab clinics—three different ones—along with fees for lawyers, restitutions in small claims courts, and other amounts connected to arrests for drugs, drinking, and even one for prostitution, though the charge had later been dropped. Personal checks had scrawled notations like "back rent" or "damage repair" on the memo lines.

When they finally contacted Nettie, two days after the fire, she agreed to come home for the first time in over a decade. Ruth paid for a plane ticket to Detroit, and Kim offered to pick her up and bring her home to Berlin. Nettie couldn't come until Saturday, she said, a day too late to attend the service. "It doesn't matter," Ruth said when the call ended. "It's been a long time since Nettie did anything for anyone but herself."

Kim and Ruth stood side by side through the service, Ruth with her arm around Kim's waist. It was touching to have their parents' friends approach with what they meant as words of comfort. The sisters agreed that Stan and Linda were in a better place, and that God doesn't send anything we can't handle. However clumsy the words, they were well-meant. "It's probably best Nettie isn't here," Ruth commented. "These dear hearts would have no idea what to say to her."

The next day, Kim drove to Metro Airport to meet Nettie. The woman who emerged from the jetway looked much older than twenty-nine. Her skin was dull and blotchy; her hair had streaks of gray at the temples. Though Nettie picked Kim out of the crowd immediately, she stopped, apparently unsure of her welcome. When Kim opened her arms, Nettie hurried forward and embraced her. Grief flowed between them, a circuit of silent understanding.

Stepping back, Nettie asked, "Where's Ruth?"

"Trying to untangle things. All the records burned, so she's figuring it out from online files."

"Ms. Get-It-Done. Do you mind if I smoke in your car?"

She did, but Nettie had already taken out her cigarettes and lighter. "Ruth got us rooms at the not-so-glorious Berlin Inn," Kim said. "I offered to drive back and forth to save her some money, but she thinks we need to be together." Her next statement was partly a question. "We didn't know how long you'd be staying."

"Just tonight," Nettie replied. "I have to be back in Tucson tomorrow by six."

"Oh."

Nettie was mostly silent as they drove northward. Gloomy clouds hung overhead, like visual symbols of their grief. After a few minutes Kim stopped trying to make conversation, which was just as well, since the roads were slick with ice. When they stopped for Ruth in Berlin, Nettie got out of the car to greet her. After a hug that seemed too long for Nettie's comfort, they got into Kim's car and continued to the farm. Nettie was somewhat more talkative with Ruth present, and Kim felt, as she often had as a kid, that the experiences her sisters had shared as children made them close in a way she couldn't be. Still, she noted that Ruth's specific questions brought only vague answers. Nettie's current job paid the bills. Her apartment was kind of a dump but in a decent neighborhood. Life was okay.

Ruth had taken care of the pressing tasks pertaining to their parents' estate. "Stuff will come up later, but we'll deal with it." With that out of the way, they commented on the weather and the unchanging nature of Berlin, Michigan. No one spoke of the deaths at the farm and what they would face once they got there. By tacit consent, Kim and Ruth had waited for Nettie before visiting the scene of their best memories, now clouded by tragedy.

Kim pulled into the driveway and turned off the engine. They sat silent for some time, each with her own thoughts, as the temperature inside the car dropped. On their left was the old bunkhouse. Beyond it were barns, sheds, and other outbuildings. The row of apple trees lining the driveway, four each of Duchess, Jonathan, and Wolf River varieties, stood starkly black against the sky, their trunks wrapped to keep the deer and rabbits from eating the bark. Everything looked as it had when Kim was last there, except that their two-story farmhouse was now reduced to charred rafters and unidentifiable clumps of metal. The remains had collapsed into the unfinished basement, which Kim had been a little afraid of as a child. Snow coated the open crater, so the scene was starkly black and white, as if the colors of their childhood had been sucked away.

With a strangled sob, Nettie suddenly pushed her way out of the car and took a few steps forward, walking as if her feet were shackled. She collapsed in the driveway, heedless of the snow that soaked her pant legs. Hurrying to her side, Kim crouched and put an arm around her. "It's okay," she said as Nettie sobbed. "The fire chief said that the smoke killed them. They never knew what was happening."

"But I *owe* them," Nettie said, her voice fierce. "Now I can never pay them back."

"They didn't care about that." Ruth had exited the car, and she helped Nettie to her feet. "All they wanted was for you to get your life together."

"I know." Nettie wiped her nose on the back of her glove. "I know that."

They walked the property together, crying or laughing as memories bubbled up. At first Nettie said little, wiping her eyes and smoking one cigarette after another. But as stories came up about irritable cows, aggressive roosters, and beloved cats, she opened up, adding anecdotes of her own. They traded information about who had Mom's pie crust recipe and which friend Dad would want to have his tools. Kim offered to take the urns to the sextant for burial when spring warmed the ground. Last, they approached the pit that had been their home and stood staring into it. At the spot where the living room had been, Kim's boot turned up a small item that had somehow escaped destruction.

"Look, one of Mom's Hummels." Bending, she took the figurine, an old man and a floppy-eared dog, from the mud. "How in the world did it survive?"

"You should keep it," Ruth said.

"To be honest," Kim confessed, "I always thought these things were ugly."

"But it will remind you of Mom."

Setting the figurine on a charred beam, Kim turned away. "It's not like I'm going to forget her." That brought more tears.

"None of us will forget them," Ruth said. "They did the best they could for us."

With that as benediction, they turned their backs on the wreck that had been their home and returned to Kim's car, their noses tipped with red from sorrow and cold. In the silence before Kim shifted into drive, Nettie made a request. "If you don't have plans for this place, I'd like to move here with my son."

"Your son?" Kim and Ruth said in chorus.

"I had him at nineteen." Her tone was matter of fact. "Until recently, he lived with his grandmother."

"Where is he now?" Ruth asked.

"With friends in Tucson." Lighting another cigarette, she rolled the window down a few inches to let the smoke escape. "Caleb needs a stable home, and I think I can give him that here."

"How will you earn a living?" Ruth asked.

"I'll wait tables while he's in school." She gestured at the patch of land left to them. "And we'll grow vegetables to sell. It will be good for him."

Kim stated the obvious problem. "There's no house anymore."

Nettie pointed at the bunkhouse. "There's that."

Kim frowned, picturing the inside: a wood stove, antiquated plumbing, and a few pieces of discarded furniture. "We'll fix it up," Nettie said. "We'll be fine."

Ruth's voice sounded prim as she said, "There are back taxes owed."

"Given the circumstances, I think the county will let me pay in installments."

"It sounds like you've thought this through." Ruth seemed relieved. She'd probably been reluctant to propose selling the place, though neither she nor Kim would ever return to Berlin. Kim could have used the money to pay for college, but she reminded herself that a three-way split wouldn't provide that much. And it didn't matter. Nettie needed a place to raise her son. She claimed she was clean and sober, and that seemed true, though she smoked way too much. If this was her chance to build a new life, she should have it.

When Kim offered to come back and help with the move, Nettie's response was brusque. "Don't feel like you need to run up here all the time. The last thing Caleb and I need is you fussing over us." Stung, Kim backed off, struggling to reconcile her differing perceptions of Nettie: the loving sister she recalled from childhood, the irresponsible addict who'd almost bankrupted her parents, and now the prickly woman who didn't seem to want her around.

Experts said addiction was a disease, but if so, shouldn't rehab have broken the hold drugs had on Nettie? Once she came out of her drug-fog, shouldn't she have realized she never wanted to go back? Even if Nettie hadn't stayed clean for her own sake, shouldn't she have wanted to for her parents? It was hard to understand addicts, Kim decided. You never knew what to expect from them.

"I can't believe our sister never bothered to mention to either of us that she had a child." Nettie's plane had departed, and Kim waited with Ruth until it was time for her flight east.

"It was certainly a surprise," Kim agreed. "I wonder what he's like."

"She'll be lucky if he isn't brain damaged from all the drugs and booze she consumed." Possibly ashamed of her comment, Ruth added, "She seems to care about him, so that's good."

"If he's caused her to clean up her act, that's even better."

"It is." Ruth hesitated as if trying to decide whether to speak. "I tried to help Nettie once," she confided. "Some man had put her in the hospital, so I flew out to help. Once they'd stitched up her forehead and put her arm in a cast, she had nowhere to go, so the hospital wouldn't release her."

"Horrible."

"It was." Catching a glimpse of her reflection in the glass, Ruth smoothed her hair. "I took her home with me and got her into a rehab clinic. I bought her new everything: jeans, shirts, underwear, jammies, and toiletries. She thanked me a hundred times, said I'd changed her life. Five days later, she signed herself out of the clinic and disappeared." Resentment colored Ruth's tone as she added, "They called to ask what they should do with her things, since she left everything but the clothes she had on." She laid a hand lightly on Kim's arm. "I'm telling you this so you understand that Nettie doesn't want a relationship with you or with me. She'll take help when she needs it, but don't expect more than that."

Kim found the selfishness of Nettie's choices overwhelming. Time and time again, she'd betrayed those who loved her, taking their money and tossing aside their concern. The sister who'd sent little gifts and funny notes as Kim grew up wasn't the victim of Fate she'd imagined. Along with drugs, Nettie used people.

"Want a lemon water?" Ruth asked. "I'm going to get one." Kim shook her head.

While she was gone, Kim tried to summon the nerve to ask for a loan to pay for school. Ruth and Butch were wealthy, but they seemed to assume Kim's scholarship covered everything. In fact, it was less than half her tuition, so she had to make up the rest with loans and a job at a local pizza place. They could have made things a lot easier, but Kim was shy about begging for help. She wasn't like Nettie, taking from everyone, and Butch and Ruth had five children to raise. They didn't need one more dependent.

Though she hated to acknowledge it, Kim also feared that if Ruth paid her bills, she'd stick her nose into Kim's life to help her make the "right" decisions. She'd always been like that, and Dad had often teased her with the nickname "Miss Management." In the end, Kim decided that when the bills came in, she'd grit her teeth and take out more loans.

The decision seemed like a wise one when Kim got home and found the Hummel figurine, wrapped in a tissue and stuffed into a corner of her suitcase.

Despite Ruth's advice and Nettie's reticence, Kim tried to stay in touch once Nettie moved to the farm. She offered items of furniture she could spare. Nettie said she had enough. She said she'd help with renovating the bunkhouse. Nettie said she was perfectly able to pound a few nails and apply a coat of paint. Kim didn't know whether to be hurt or angry. She'd boldly asked for what she wanted, and now that she had it, Nettie seemed determined to shut Kim out of her life.

Still, they were sisters. Kim called once a month, and Nettie seemed okay with that. If Kim asked about Caleb, the answers were terse. He was in school. He'd outgrown his clothes again. Only once did she admit regret for the years she and her son had been separated. "I was a mess," Nettie said. "And the perfect little person I'd produced scared the hell out of me."

"I've heard that happens." *Not that I'd give up a child.* "You said his grandmother raised him."

"I promised myself it would only be for a few weeks, but…" She didn't finish, but Kim guessed she'd returned to alcohol and drugs. "Ten years she had him," Nettie said. "I have a lot to make up for."

Nettie knew she'd screwed up. That was good; the first step toward making things right was admitting you'd done wrong. While Kim hoped for more conversations like that, most of the time Nettie claimed Caleb was okay and changed the subject. Kim sensed he was a difficult child, possibly unhappy with a mother he hadn't known in his first decade of life.

While phone calls were enough family contact for Nettie, they weren't enough for Kim. One summer Saturday, when the sparkling sunshine drew her out of her apartment and made her miss trees and the smell of clover, Kim decided to drive north and surprise Nettie. She and Caleb had been on the farm for five years. Kim had been busy with school, and then with her job and her marriage. Still, it was silly to live only two hours away and never see her sister.

The blank space where home had once sat was still a shock, though the site had been bulldozed flat. The old bunkhouse looked much the same as the last time she'd seen it. In the open space beyond it was a greenhouse, almost empty of plants but well stocked with shovels, hoes, rakes, pots, trowels, and a wheelbarrow. The other addition was flowerbeds along the front and sides, a profusion of lilies in orange, red, and yellow. A chalkboard leaned against the mailbox post offered sweet corn, tomatoes, beans, radishes and floral bouquets. Kim knew that in addition to working at a diner, Nettie supplied local restaurants with fresh vegetables, starting with asparagus in spring, and expanding the list through the growing season. Later, she'd have potatoes for a local factory to turn into chips and fries.

Nettie's expression when she opened the door was disquieting. She clearly wasn't happy that Kim had appeared unannounced. When she stepped inside, Kim saw that at least part of the reason was embarrassment. Everything in the place was second-hand and worn out. Battered, mismatched saucepans hung on the wall over the stove. A faded couch and a lumpy recliner were covered with blankets, probably to hide tears. The TV set was old and square. The tea Nettie made for her came in a mug that said *Berlin High School.* Nettie's said *Miami, Florida.*

"I haven't got any sweets," Nettie apologized. "Caleb eats everything in sight."

"Where is he? I'd like to meet him."

Nettie seemed to struggle with whether to tell the truth. "He got into a little trouble," she finally said. "He has to do community service on the weekends."

"Oh."

"The judge ordered him to attend school, so that's good." Nettie looked away as she said it.

"I'm sorry, Nettie."

She combed her wiry hair back with spread fingers. "The school counsellor thinks he'll settle down in a year or so." That sounded like hope, not experience.

"Well, if you ever want to talk about it, I'm ready to listen." *That was dumb,* Kim chided herself. Why would the parent of a misbehaving adolescent ask a childless woman for advice? Pushing her teacup aside, she said, "Take me to your garden. I haven't eaten a carrot with dirt on it for years."

Kim was glad she'd asked, because Nettie became a different person in her garden. Happiness tinged her voice as she told Kim each plant's name, touching them lightly as if blessing them. Or perhaps it was Nettie who received the blessing.

In the months that followed, Nettie seemed to regret revealing her son's bad behavior, and when asked would breezily assert he was doing fine. Kim felt uncomfortable going to the farm a second time without being asked, and no invitation was offered. She tried suggesting they meet halfway between for lunch and some girl time, but Nettie claimed busy-ness. A crop was coming in. A package was due she had to sign for. Vacationing neighbors had asked her to go over and feed their dogs.

A phone call here and there was going to have to do.

The phone buzzed, bringing Kim back to Detroit, her condo, and 2024. After rejecting a really, *really* final opportunity to extend her car's warranty, she went back to packing for the move to Pennsylvania. Soon she'd be on the staff of a Presidential candidate. Ruth claimed the job was perfect for her, arranging events and seeing to details she was too busy to handle. "You'll be great," Ruth claimed. "You know me, so you'll know what I'm willing to do or not do."

Though she didn't say so, Kim didn't feel she knew Ruth much better than she knew Nettie, though the reasons were different. When Ruth married Butch, she'd thrown herself into becoming the perfect wife, mother, and citizen. The few times she'd visited, Kim had marveled at her sister's command of a dozen things at once: her husband's business, the children's schedules, her committee work, and the maintenance of a stunning home surrounded by amazing gardens. Active in church, and civic groups, Ruth had seemingly boundless energy and an almost magical way of getting those around her to do as she asked. Though she never demanded people do things her way, Ruth usually got positive responses when she argued for something in her logical, practical way. Once she made her case, refusal, even hesitation, seemed petty.

Kim would move in with the Mandell family in Vienna Woods. "No sense in signing a lease somewhere and then moving again in January," Ruth had said. "If you don't mind what used to be servants' quarters, you'll be perfectly comfortable and even have a little privacy."

Kim liked the idea of having a place where she could be on her own, since Ruth's house was a bit like a carnival most days. In addition to Butch's staff and a constant stream of visitors, there were children everywhere, since each of Ruth's five tended to be accompanied by a friend or six.

The two oldest were for the most part gone now. Ben was at college, and Grace had married the summer before. She recalled that when the invitation came, Edmund had objected to going, claiming there'd be too many "fakes and fops" there. He'd been so nasty that she tried to beg off, but Ruth had almost cried. "Kimmie, please come. I need at least one member of my own family to celebrate my daughter's wedding with me."

"Nettie isn't coming?"

She'd made a sound of disgust. "Nettie insists she can't leave Michigan right now."

"Why?"

"Her son had moved out for a while, but apparently he's back. He won't come with her, and I think she's afraid to leave him at the farm unsupervised."

"Why do you think that is?"

"Who knows? I don't have the energy for Nettie's dramatics right now."

While they didn't know much about Caleb as an adult, it was clear from his frequent coming and going from home that he had problems. "It must be hard on her, having a kid who can't get his act together."

"What did she expect?" Ruth asked. "I can't imagine how wild Ben would be if I weren't around to get after him when he needs it."

After the wedding, Ed had referred to Ruth's only son as "Brat Boy Ben," but Kim had insisted that all kids go through phases, and he'd be fine with time and a little maturity.

Unsure why she felt the need to defend Nettie, Kim said, "She did what she could to make up for not being there."

"I suppose." Ruth's tone warmed. "You know I love our goofy sister, Kimmie, but I'll never understand her. And I'm sure we'll love the boy, if we ever get to meet him."

Chapter Twelve

Ruth-July 14

Dinner with the family was Ruth's favorite time. She loved her family more than anything, and having them all together at her extra-long table with two crystal chandeliers lighting the meal was the best feeling ever. Though they complained it was corny, they did the "family thing" the first Sunday of every month: church as a group, then dinner. Butch sat at the head of the long table, with Ruth at the opposite end. Between them were the five kids, each entitled to bring one other person. Grace, the oldest, came with her husband these days, and Will brought a succession of lovely young women Butch struggled to differentiate from each other. The three still at home invited mostly friends from school, and it pleased Ruth to see the wonder on the guests' faces. Most modern teens had no concept of family time. They ate meals in front of the TV, with one parent present at best. It was good for her kids' friends to see a group so dedicated to each other, a family in the best sense.

Dinners followed a pattern. At first Ben did most of the talking, his handsome face lit with humor as he recounted his latest adventures. His natural gift for mimicry added to the entertainment. His tone would go high to parody a girl in his class who believed she'd been born a mermaid and then drop low as he recounted the professor's answers to her vapid arguments.

The girls listened to Ben's stories eagerly and responded enthusiastically. When it was their turn, they spoke of school, friends, and crushes, with names omitted in the latter case. Ruth noticed that they looked to Butch, hoping to make him chuckle or comment. He was their lodestar, their hero. Daddy.

After the meal, Ruth went to the library, where, seated at her desk, she invited each child in, one at a time, and spoke with them about their lives and goals. She'd done it for years, and the children loved having their mother's attention focused wholly on them for a time. After the wedding, she had invited Grace's husband to join the "Mom Chats," but he demurred. Ruth let it go. Once he recognized her value as an objective adult with more life experience than he, the boy would come around.

Her children's concerns were varied, some large, some small. As the campaign progressed, Maddy, her youngest, had become worried about life in the White House. A friend had told her a Secret Service agent would be at her side 24/7. "Will they even watch me sleep?" she asked. When Ruth assured the girl they'd have privacy in the Presidential residence, Maddy perked up. "It might be cool, I guess. Maybe I could help you decorate for Christmas."

"Great idea," Ruth said. "We'll plan it, just the two of us."

Ben came last, and Ruth sensed reluctance when he took a seat and folded his arms on his chest. *He thinks he's too old for these sessions*, Ruth mused. *If we only knew how naive we are at twenty-three.* Ben's answers to her questions came haltingly at first, but as old habits settled in, his hidden concerns came out. "How did you know you wanted to marry Dad, Mom?"

Ruth chuckled. "The first time we met, I thought, *This is the guy you've been looking for.*"

"Did he feel the same way?"

"He claims he knew before I ever said a word, though that's not very flattering to my intelligence." Guessing where the question had come from, Ruth asked, "Have you met a special girl, Ben?"

Chapter Thirteen

Nettie-July 15

Hearing a knock, Nettie called, "Come in." The electronic lock buzzed, and Dr. Foeller stood in the doorway. "Want to take a stroll with me? It's not as blazing hot today as it's been for the last week."

Getting her cigarette wallet, Nettie followed the doctor outside. The sun felt good on her back after the artificial chill of A/C, a cool she'd never been fond of. They followed a gravel pathway, for a time enjoying silence broken only by birdsongs and the splash of a nearby fountain. While Nettie tried to be distant with Susan Foeller, it was difficult. The doctor never talked down to her or treated her like a lab specimen. Neither did she presume friendship where there could be none. Still, Nettie often reminded herself that she was first and foremost a subject for study. Articles in scholarly journals on a well-known filicide were Foeller's goal for their association.

When Foeller began seeking Nettie out for more than "psych seshes," as the residents called them, Nettie gave herself no credit. They both loved to read, and they had spirited discussions of writers from Connelly to Conrad, from Hannah to Hardy. They wrestled with questions of crime, but so far it had remained objective. When it came close to personal, Nettie deftly side-stepped her own actions and returned to those of Harry Bosch or Tess of the D'Urbervilles.

Today Foeller explained her theory that critical periods in a young person's life turned their path one way or another. "They end up either Smeagol or Gollum," she said half-facetiously. When she went on to suggest that lack of parental support at a particular moment of need was a factor, Nettie disagreed, and she used her own case to make the argument. "During my 'critical period,' my dad was taking time out from his chores to drive me to drama practice by 6:00 a.m. four mornings a week. Mom got Kim ready and off to school, and then she worked for hours on my costumes for the shows. The director said she was amazing."

"They didn't realize you were unhappy?"

"*I* didn't realize I was unhappy," Nettie replied. "None of us could have predicted I'd trade my future for a mirage."

"You don't think your parents could have turned you from your destructive path?"

"I doubt it. Anything they said at that time was like static in my ears." She chuckled, but there was no humor in it. "My downfall came from hubris. I was sure that if everyone just got out of my way, I'd be amazing."

"Tell me how you decided to leave home."

"This guy I was seeing, Trent, was a pretty good actor—good for Berlin High School, and at sixteen, that was all I could see. Everyone said I was good too, and Trent and I talked about it a lot. What were we doing, hanging around this rinky-dink high school? How would we start our careers in acting when we were stuck in a microscopic dot on the map of Michigan?"

"Young people often feel the need to get out and try their wings."

"The more we talked about it, the more exciting it seemed. We'd take action, go after our destiny. If one of us said, "We need to wait," the other would say, "For what?" Trent wanted to be in front of a camera, and I believed he had what it took to make it. While I wasn't sure I was movie-star material, I figured I could get toothpaste commercials and bit parts. There are tons of those jobs, right?" Her smile showed understanding of how naïve she'd been.

"Did your parents know how much you wanted a career in acting?"

Nettie shook her head. "I was their first kid. I don't think they realized how strong a teenager's desires can be." She rubbed at her forehead, encouraging memory. "I read this article about it once. They call it dissonance reduction."

"Wanting to believe something so much that you ignore facts and evidence."

"That's what we did." Nettie took a long drag on her cigarette. "My parents encouraged my acting, but they didn't get how much it meant to me."

"And Trent's family?"

"His mom was killed in a car accident when he was four." She paused at a bench and removed some dirt from inside her shoe. "That spring, a couple of weeks after our big show, Trent's dad had a massive heart attack and died. Suddenly all the talking we'd done about making a grab for success became real. Trent got ten thousand dollars from his dad's life insurance. We figured that would fund our trip to Hollywood and keep us going until we got work."

"In entertainment."

Nettie's brows quirked with humor. "We agreed we'd both get waiter jobs temporarily, until we networked and met the right people." She sighed. "I know how stupid it sounds, but we thought that talent and drive would be enough."

"What happened?"

"We made it as far as Tucson, Arizona, and then Trent's Mazda broke down." She smiled, years of separation from the event allowing a humorous slant. "Actually, it didn't just break down. It completely gave up the ghost, which brought on our first argument. Trent said buying another car would eat up too much of our money. I didn't see that we had a choice."

The doctor's brow arched. "He had a different plan in mind."

"Not at first. For two days we had the same argument over and over. I wanted to call home, but he said we couldn't admit we'd started for Hollywood and got stuck halfway. 'Our friends will laugh, and your parents will whine that I ruined your life.' I said he didn't know Mom and Dad well enough to judge them like that. I realize now that Trent was stressed and grieving and scared, but soon we were hardly speaking to each other." She stopped to breathe in the scent of a bright-white flower on a moonflower vine. "That's pretty uncomfortable when you're sharing a motel room the size of a chess board."

Foeller waited quietly until Nettie went on. "About nine o'clock one night, Trent said he was going out for a while. I worried when he didn't come back, but eventually I fell asleep. The next morning, he came in walking on air. He'd seen a notice that this club was holding Amateur Night, so he went there and sang a number. The crowd loved it, and afterward, a promoter approached him." Nettie met Foeller's eye. "She said Trent had a great future in music."

"She."

"I didn't get it at first. I was happy for him and hoped it meant good things for us. A day later, I realized there wasn't any *us* as far as Trent was concerned."

"He left you."

"I woke up to an empty room, a hundred-dollar bill, and a note." She recited from memory. "*Nettie, it's not working out for us. Sheila's taking me to Cali, where she'll introduce me to people who can get my career on the right path. Here's money for a bus ticket home.*"

"Did his career happen?"

Nettie shook her head. "Trent is probably working at the Beverly Hills Radio Shack, if there is such a thing." She took a final drag on her cigarette and snuffed out the butt. "Life sucks, and then you die."

"No. When you were too young to know better, a guy convinced you he loved you and then dumped you."

She shook her head. "I convinced myself. Those 'You made me love you' song lyrics are lies. We do it to ourselves."

"You recognize now that you never loved Trent."

"Probably not, but I chose him. Why?" Stopping, Nettie turned toward a small duck pond. "To make Dad angry? To defy my oh-so-proper mother? To shock my teachers, make them frown and shake their heads?" She heaved a sigh. "I don't know. All these years later, I still don't."

"You wanted a different life than the one you had. That isn't unusual."

"But I ruined everything I was or might have become." Nettie knocked cigarette ash onto the ground and then swept it away with a scrape of her shoe. "I was so successful at wrecking myself that first time that I spent ten years tangled up with booze, pills, and unsuitable men. Poor choices, every one."

Chapter Fourteen

Kim-Previous December

Kim met Caleb Green ten days before his death. Since the last photo she'd seen of her nephew was from the Berlin Middle School Directory, she didn't recognize the man at her door. He was handsome, with close-cropped hair, warm brown eyes, and a grin that implied secrets. Snowflakes clung to his shoulders, melting quickly into damp spots on his brown corduroy jacket. Slung over his shoulder was a cloth sack that bulged with hard edges and soft curves. "Kim, hi," he said. "I'm your nephew Caleb."

She hesitated briefly. Living alone had made her cautious, and these days she answered the door with the chain on and kept one foot set firmly against the bottom. This man's smile was like her mother's, and his nose was pure Kovalesky. Unhooking the chain, she stepped back. "Please, come in."

As he stepped past her, Caleb's upright posture and the set of his shoulders reminded Kim of her father. He paused at the living room doorway, as if taking stock. His glance took in everything, from the Ikea tables to the neat row of houseplants sharing the only window.

"How is your mom?" Kim asked.

"Fine. I tell her all the time to call you, but you know she's not much for chatting."

That wasn't exactly true. Over the last year, Nettie had called Kim at odd times and talked for perhaps half an hour. Kim was always pleased with the contact, though she was never sure why her sister reached out. Nettie never made a request, expressed a concern, or sought advice. She talked mostly about the past, their childhood on the farm. When Kim suggested they meet, she always said no, without excuse or explanation. Kim told herself it was nice that Nettie wanted to talk, whatever her reason.

Though Nettie said little about her son, Kim had detected a pattern. He'd move out, going to work in Lansing or Port Huron or Lapeer. In a few months he'd be home again. Nettie never said what happened to the jobs that had sounded so promising.

Caleb was now twenty-nine years old. It felt odd to finally put a face to the man, to see how the boy she'd never met had turned out. He went to the couch, waited for Kim to sit in the chair where she'd left her tablet, and then made himself comfortable. "Nice place."

"It's basic." As she said it, Kim felt faintly guilty, recalling the converted barracks he shared with his mother.

Draping his arms along the back of the couch, Caleb turned his gaze on Kim. "Mom's always telling me how great you are." His voice held a challenge as he added, "I decided it was time to see Aunt Kim for myself."

"I've always wanted to meet you, but—" She couldn't say, *but your mother wouldn't allow it*. Instead, she said, "—it never worked out." *What abnormal sisters we are, a one-time circle that became a scattering of broken arcs.*

"Yeah." Caleb stared at her until Kim looked away, unsettled, and she sensed he enjoyed her discomfort. After a moment he asked, "So what does this place run a month?"

She chuckled, treating it as a joke. "Most of what I've got right now. You probably heard that my husband left me."

He blinked once, as if filing the information away. "Do you have anything to drink? Scotch, maybe?"

"Oh." Kim glanced around the room as if she had bottles of alcohol stashed everywhere. "I think there's some Jägermeister in the freezer." She smiled. "Edmund got it as a gift, but neither of us cared for it much."

"That'll work."

As she rose and went to get a glass, Kim felt faintly disquieted. While Caleb wasn't the surly, discontented type she'd imagined, something odd lay behind his casual manner and wide smile. In a weak, moment, Nettie had once confessed that her son blamed her for abandoning him. "And he's right," she'd added. "I deserve it."

"You provide what he needs now," Kim had soothed. "Love and a good home."

In a voice uncharacteristically shaky, Nettie had replied, "I hope it's enough."

Despite years of separation, Caleb was family. He'd come seeking a connection. Kim wanted him to know she cared, even if she was late showing up. She smiled warmly as she handed him the drink.

It was gone faster than she'd have believed possible. "Not bad." Setting the empty glass on the end table, Caleb looked around again. "I thought you were some big business executive."

She chuckled. "I'm employed, which is pretty good in this economy. Most firms have cut advertising and public relations budgets to the bone."

Caleb leaned forward, elbows on his knees. Though his expression was earnest, Kim suspected he intended to lie through his perfect white teeth. "I'm moving to Detroit, and I thought you could help me get started."

"I'd love to," she replied, "but I don't know anyone in transmission repair." It was a job Nettie had finagled when Caleb returned to Berlin for perhaps the fourth time. "If he likes it," she'd told Kim hopefully, "it could turn him around."

"I got out of that," Caleb said dismissively. "Too much lifting." Tilting his head, he said, "Maybe they need a guy like me where you work."

Kim straightened the magazines on the end table while she chose the right response. "They require at least two years of college." She wasn't sure Caleb had even finished high school.

"You've got no say in the hiring?"

"None. I'm sorry."

Something shifted behind his eyes. "I could use a loan. I'm gonna need first and last to get a place down here." In an easy tone that suggested it wasn't important he added, "I'll pay you back once I get work."

"I'll be honest, Caleb. Since Edmund left, I'm barely getting by. I'll give you what I have in cash, but that's all I can do." Rising, she went to her purse, aware that he watched her every move. She took all the bills from her wallet and folded them in half. Rather than setting her purse back on the stand near the door, she slid it into a drawer.

Caleb rose, stuck the bills in his jeans pocket, and went to the refrigerator. "I'll take the Jägermeister, since you don't like it." Unzipping the bag, he shoved the bottle inside.

Kim reminded herself that he was family. "Is there a phone number where I can reach you if I hear of a job you might apply for?"

He shrugged. "I move around a lot, but I'll call if I need anything." Then he was gone. No farewell, no apparent regret at the parting.

An hour later, Kim noticed that a baseball Ed had left behind, signed by Tigers' pitcher Justin Verlander after a no-hitter in 2007, was missing from its place on her bookshelf.

She told neither Ruth nor Nettie about Caleb's visit. Nettie would have been mortified to know what her son had done, and even more ashamed to have "Ruth the Blessèd" know about it. The other reason was one Kim didn't fully admit, even to herself. For once, she was the sister with a family secret. For once, she wasn't too young to understand.

Chapter Fifteen

Ruth-July 15

Ruth spent Monday morning in her yard, wearing a large-brimmed hat to keep the burning July sun off her neck. She encouraged her peonies with low-nitrogen fertilizer and discouraged bugs from crawling on them with soapy water. From a distance, the gardener tossed resentful glances sideways, jealous of her invasion into what he considered his territory.

Ruth ignored him, reveling in the feel of heavy gloves on her hands and sweat on her skin. The neat beds that surrounded the house were the only places she could relax these days and think about nothing, and the flowers were hers, planted and, until the Presidential campaign stole all her free time, tended by her. She loved the solitude and noted drolly that when a person kneels to pull weeds, others tend to leave them alone lest they be enlisted to help. Not one day lily asked her to justify her opinion on welfare. Not one dianthus questioned her husband's position on foreign aid. With the election only four months away, she'd needed a bit of time to herself before leaping back into the fire.

Lately, Butch had talked of quitting the race. As his chances for success grew, his doubts ballooned. It was all his team could do some days to keep him from announcing he was returning to his old, less stressful life.

The first time a cadre of supporters came to ask Butch to run for the Presidency as an independent, he'd said no. Ruth was much more excited at the prospect than he, and she urged Butch to reconsider. "If you don't win, so what? The deck is stacked against independents, so there's no shame in it. But if you do, think what we could do for the country."

In the end he'd agreed to test the waters. With Ruth's help, he chose a team to run the campaign, mostly old friends but with a few newcomers included for their specialized knowledge or political savvy. When speaking privately with team members, Ruth was honest about Butch's strengths and weaknesses. She suggested they allow him to focus on things he was good at, such as delivering speeches, sparring with the media, and meeting voters. Since he disliked meetings and deskwork, she advised that they minimize his involvement in strategy and planning sessions.

They'd hit a few bumps in the road, the biggest being Nettie's unexplained murder of her son. When the story hit the news, Morris Blake, Butch's oldest friend and current campaign manager, had suggested they claim that after years of separation, Ruth hardly knew her sister. Gavin Croft argued for some medical excuse, perhaps an undiagnosed brain tumor. Ruth had taken a middle path, expressing love for her sister but not in any way excusing her crime. That had turned out to be the right choice, and respect for Ruth's opinions among members of the team rose steeply.

Dr. Foeller reported that Nettie was settling in well at Martha's Place. A friendly judge had sealed the records in Michigan, so the press couldn't learn where Nettie was and pester her for the details of her story. It was win/win: Foeller had her murderer to study, and Nettie would make no headlines that embarrassed Candidate, and with luck, President Mandell.

It had also been Ruth's idea to bring Kim into the campaign. It was a way of saying to the voters, *Yes, there's a killer in my family, but look—This one is a productive citizen, and she supports Butch Mandell for President.*

What they accomplished in the last year hadn't been easy. At times Ruth felt like one of those entertainers with a table of spinning plates, moving constantly to keep them from dropping and breaking to bits. That had been another reason to bring Kim into things. She'd already scheduled a TV interview for Ruth that afternoon, which, she suddenly realized, she should be getting ready for. Reluctantly she rose, brushed the dirt from her knees, and surrendered her flowers to the man who was paid to see to them.

An hour later, she came downstairs to find Kim helping the interviewer and her crew set up. Ruth whispered, "Do I look all right?"

"You look gorgeous," Kim replied. "As always."

She'd chosen an ivory suit with green accents—the colors they'd chosen for the campaign. "Butch refused to use red, white, and blue," she told Kim as she fussed with the neckline of her top. "Too often, our national symbols are used to pander for votes. It's tacky and trite."

Kim quoted one of Butch's catchphrases to prove she'd been paying attention. "'When I'm in office, I will fly our flag proudly. Until then, I refuse to wave it, hug it, or otherwise use it for my personal agenda."

Ruth took a deep breath and let it out. "Now, I have to go charm this reporter's socks off…though she probably isn't wearing any."

She wasn't. Hallie Donaho was all of twenty-five, with blond hair that hung in uneven, twisted strands along her face. Her crew had already set up equipment to brighten the light in the interior room, and Ms. Donaho sat in the chair she'd chosen while a man tested various angles and added or subtracted lamps. He did the same for Ruth, after which he put a lapel mic on each woman and tested its levels and placement.

Though Kim had suggested the light was better on the patio, Ruth chose the library, believing it better reflected what she and Butch stood for. Family pictures hung on every wall, her favorite on a shelf behind her, where it would be visible during the interview. Ruth and Butch stood in the center, Ruth turned toward him with one hand resting lightly on his chest. Ben stood next to his father, a younger version with the same smile and direct gaze. The four girls were arranged on either side, all dark-haired and lovely. They represented what a family should be: intelligent, attractive, caring, each loving and loyal to the others and the ideals they'd been raised to value.

Finally, all was well, and the recording began. It started with soft-pitch questions about what it was like to be a politician's wife in modern America. Ruth had predicted those and memorized responses that couldn't be turned against her or Butch. After the warm-up Donaho asked, "What should we know about your sister, Janet Waller, recently convicted of second-degree murder?"

She'd prepared for that one too. "My sister has faced a lot of pain, most of it due to poor decisions she made in the past."

"At her trial, you said if we had a stronger social structure, she might not have become so lost. Can you expand on that?"

Ruth raised a hand as if she were a referee stopping play. "I'll explain, but I want to make it clear I won't be speaking for my husband. I am not, nor will I ever be, President of the United States, so my answer is simply an opinion." Returning her hands to her lap, she went on. "A strong society has firm rules that its members agree with. They understand the consequences for breaking those rules. If those rules weaken, young people often lose their way, because they act on fleeting urges rather than the universal truths that should govern behavior. The mistakes they make can ruin their lives, and they might never achieve the success they could have had."

Donaho had done her homework. "But you come from a traditional home, where you were taught strong values by loving parents. You attended church, and your community was close-knit and supportive. How did that background fail Janet?"

"It didn't," Ruth replied calmly. "We three sisters had the idyllic childhood I wish every kid could have. But as soon as Nettie stepped out of that environment, she fell into a world where nothing she'd been taught mattered. Rules are ignored. People are used and thrown away. Values are bent to fit the purposes of the wicked."

Donaho's eyes narrowed. "Are you suggesting that we need a more Christian society—maybe even a Christian government?"

"No." Ruth spoke firmly, and then she put a hand on her chest. "While I'm a believer myself, I agree with the Founding Fathers that government should not be based on religion. What I would like to see is strong codes of conduct that would help our young people navigate the difficult years."

"Where would these codes come from?"

"We could start with the family." Ruth shifted slightly in her chair. "Youth is a dangerous time. The brain is still forming, so our decision-making skills aren't fully developed. Urges run high, and patience tends to be lacking. The undeveloped conscience needs guidance, but in the last few decades, we somehow bought into the idea that kids should their make own decisions, and therefore their own mistakes."

"You'd like young people on a tighter leash. Like with curfews and chaperones?"

"Do you have children?"

A proud smile lit the woman's face. "A four-year-old boy."

"When the ice cream truck comes by, do you let him go out to meet it alone?"

"Well, no."

"Why not?"

"Because he doesn't understand traffic or money or nutrition."

"He knows about ice cream, and he knows he wants it." Ruth raised a hand, turning her palm up. "Does a fifteen-year-old understand the pitfalls of sex and illegal drugs?"

Donaho smirked a little. "I believe those things can be taught."

"But can't you teach your toddler about calories and traffic signals?"

"He wouldn't understand."

Ruth's hand turned, and she pointed a finger at Donaho. "I submit that a teenager doesn't understand the dangers of alcohol, sex, and drugs, except in the most abstract, 'It can't happen to me' sense. Like your toddler, their choices tend to be based on what they want, not on what's best for them. Parents should be their guides, but Mom and Dad are either at work or exhausted from work. Tablets and television serve as nannies, and we all know what kids find there. On even the mildest TV shows, experimenting with drugs and alcohol is presented as a 'natural' part of growing up."

"Not everyone accepts that."

"Too many do." Ruth smiled to take the sting out of her words, but she went on. "Society's least helpful examples are glorified by the press and emulated by those who have no core values. Headlines scream out the news when some 'influencer' visits a nightclub without putting on underwear. Politicians caught in extramarital affairs, in lies, or in a host of other unsavory activities simply lower their heads and wait for a new scandal to arise so that voters forget what they've done. Good people turn their heads, afraid of being called old-fashioned if they speak out." Folding her hands, Ruth asked, "What happened to the agreement we once had that our kids should be protected from the worst the world offers?"

"There are programs designed to encourage teens to make good choices."

"But their message is always blurry. 'Don't have sex, but if you do, use protection.' 'Don't use drugs, but if you do, call this helpline.' 'Don't drink alcohol, but if you do, ask a sober friend to drive you home.' What's wrong with saying with complete clarity, 'Don't do it'?"

"Isn't it naïve to think kids won't experiment with societal taboos?"

"That's why there must be education before a choice arises and consequences afterward," Ruth replied. "Some societies send clear messages on birth control to their citizens from a young age. Everyone agrees it's irresponsible to have unprotected sex if both parties aren't ready to raise a child."

Donaho nodded. "And in those countries, the incidence of unplanned pregnancy is much lower than ours."

"We know that mothers who raise children alone are more likely to suffer poverty. Their kids have higher rates of arrest and substance abuse. The minute we say, 'If you're an unwed mother, we'll support you financially,' we doom those women and their children to lives of unhappiness."

"Are you proposing that we leave pregnant teens to fend for themselves?"

"Not at all. I propose hands-on parenting where our sons and our daughters are informed, monitored, and made responsible for their choices."

"If your husband becomes President, how would he go about cultivating that sort of responsibility?"

Ruth raised a chiding hand. "Didn't I say a minute ago that I wasn't speaking for Butch? As First Lady, I would adopt strong families as my cause, but as my husband has said many times, actions taken under his leadership won't be the result of one person's opinion. It will be through consensus, with all voices heard and considered." Ruth summoned the playful smile she'd practiced before a mirror. "We've spent far too long tossing grenades across the rivers that divide us. We need to build bridges that let us meet halfway."

Chapter Sixteen

Kim-September 3

Before Kim could believe it, she'd been with Ruth for two months. In that time, Butch's star rose sharply, though both major parties did their best to dim its shine. Polls showed that a growing number of people believed the only way to truly change the country's direction was to make a drastic shift. Other independents had agendas that didn't appeal to most voters. Butch Mandell proposed problem-solving through cooperation. He promised to fill his Cabinet with competent people from both parties and outside the mainstream. When questioned about what his policies would be, Butch always said the same thing. "Nothing is written in stone. When I'm President, we'll sit down together and hash things out."

Busy juggling her sister's hectic schedule, Kim had little time to reflect on all that. Ruth's day began at six and often ran until midnight. As Kim presented questions about whether she would speak at this dinner or that march, there were periodic interruptions from her daughters. Could Maddy take a day trip with schoolmates? Should Mary Louise tell her teacher about a kid she'd seen cheating on a test? Ruth was always welcoming, turning from whatever she'd been doing to listen and respond to her children's concerns. While she waited, Kim often studied the family portraits that peppered the walls. Over time it struck her that in each one, Ruth was holding onto someone. Usually it was Butch, but if he wasn't in the picture, Ruth had a hand on the arm or shoulder of one of her kids.

Seeing that reminded Kim of a winter day when the three of them had gone outside to build a snowman. The sun turned the snowbanks too bright to look at directly, so they all squinted at the camera Mom had brought out to snap their picture with "Iceman Ike." Fifteen-year-old Nettie stood behind Kim, who was five, and Kim leaned against her, her grin revealing a missing tooth. Beside them, Ruth held Kim's arm with both hands, her black gloves stark against the tan sleeve.

Clearly, touch was important to Ruth. Kim reflected that most of the time, neither she nor Nettie initiated hugs or made physical contact. Was that part of why Edmund had left her? *Connections,* Kim thought. *Ruth is good at making them. Me? Not so much.*

As they worked their way through Kim's list each day, she realized that Ruth had been correct. They functioned well together. Ruth took Kim's word in areas where her past job had given her expertise. Kim understood that Ruth's every word in public sent messages, both overt and subliminal, about what sort of First Lady she would be. Most mornings they worked together for an hour, and then Kim went off to put their plans into practice. Like the others on staff, she worked hard for Ruth. No one wanted to disappoint "R.P.M.," as they'd begun referring to Ruth Patricia Mandell.

Kim liked most of the people she worked with, and Ruth sometimes suggested this man or that as someone Kim might date. She always said no, unready to trust in her ability to judge what was a decent man.

Kim learned that Nettie was in Richmond by accident. Since Ruth was in a meeting, she took a call from a Doctor Susan Foeller, who wondered if Mrs. Mandell might consider a visit. "I'm the other sister," Kim told Foeller. "Are you saying Nettie isn't in Michigan anymore?"

"We're a private facility on the north side of Richmond," Foeller replied. "It's only two hours by train."

"I doubt Ruth can manage a visit at this point, but I'll come if Nettie allows it."

"I'll encourage her to consider it," Foeller said. "I believe family support would be helpful to her at this point."

"Did you know they'd moved her?" Kim asked Ruth later.

"I wasn't sure if I should tell you." Ruth straightened Kim's jacket so the hem hung evenly. "She refused to see us before. Do you think Miss Stubborn will change her mind now?"

"She might if I show up on her doorstep," Kim replied. "You're always saying I should take time off. Is there a day this week that you can do without me?"

"Of course, Kimmie." Ruth squeezed her arm. "I only hope she doesn't disappoint you again."

At Martha's Place, Kim dismissed her Uber and approached a formidable metal gate set in a twelve-foot surrounding wall. A guard took her driver's license through a narrow slot and studied it carefully. Once he was satisfied as to her identity, he made a phone call. Then he pressed a button, causing the gate to slide sideways a few feet. "Please come in, Ms. Dailey. Peters will take you up in the golf cart."

"Up" meant a slight incline, at the top of which sat a graceful mansion with antebellum columns that brought images of Scarlett O'Hara tripping down the wide steps, pantaloons showing under her raised hoop skirt, while Mammy called from above about the rules of propriety. Instead, it was Susan Foeller who met Kim, a tall, pretty woman whose manner seemed more Melanie Hamilton than Scarlett. "It's so nice to meet you." She opened the door by passing a card that hung on a lanyard around her neck over a sensor. As they entered the cool interior, she added, "Nettie speaks of you quite often."

The foyer was beautiful, with a wide staircase as its set piece. Heavy draperies framed tall windows, and carved cornices and crown molding recalled craftsmen of the past. Martha's Place resembled no prison Kim had ever seen, though admittedly her experience was limited to cop shows and detective movies. A second, closer, look revealed what the lovely façade concealed: electronic locks, fixed window glass, and steel doors. Noting her interest, Foeller said, "We're very secure, make no mistake. In fact, Mary here is going to have to frisk you."

"No problem." As the woman ran a scanning wand over her body then patted her down, Kim asked, "Does Nettie know I'm coming?"

"She does." Foeller hesitated but apparently decided to be truthful. "I didn't tell her until this morning, so it was too late for her to refuse. I said it would be rude to make you waste the day on a fruitless trip."

"That isn't very encouraging."

"She's ashamed, Ms. Dailey. She claims it would be better if you forgot her."

"I disagree."

"So do I." She smiled, revealing a slight gap in her front teeth. "I don't intend to have Martha's Place become a tomb where Nettie can bury herself."

Foeller led the way up the stairs, through windows on either side Kim saw a wide expanse of lawn separated with walkways and dotted with stone benches and statuary. Stopping at a door, Foeller knocked once and then waved her ID badge over the scanner. "Nettie, your sister's here." She stepped back, allowing Kim to enter, and then closed the door behind her. An odd sensation traveled down her spine at the knowledge that she couldn't leave this room until someone came and let her out. How did that feel, day after day?

Her discomfort was deepened at a sudden dread of facing her sister, a woman guilty of many wrongs, but none more serious than the one that had brought her here. She took a breath. "Hello, Nettie."

"Kim."

At her trial, Nettie had seemed almost comatose, eyes dead, expression flat. Ruth had fussed that she should have been consulted on Nettie's appearance. "Her clothes are awful, and her hair looks like a nest of steel wool." Kim guessed Nettie had refused to cooperate with any suggestions her lawyer had made about her appearance. Today, she looked better. She wore plain gray sweatpants and a t-shirt. Her wiry hair was cut short, and the reduction of the curls she'd never been able to conquer lifted a little of the weight from her features. Her eyes had regained some of the liveliness they'd once had. Meeting her gaze, Kim saw fear and perhaps hope. For what? Understanding? Kim could not understand what might lead a person to kill, especially someone she cared for. Forgiveness? She wasn't sure that was hers to give. What could she offer?

Love. Opening her arms, Kim took a step forward. "Hey, Big Sis."

As Nettie stepped into the hug, relief made her voice shake. "Hey, Little Sis."

Nettie didn't extend the embrace, and, knowing tears would embarrass her, Kim swallowed and said, "We're not that far apart now, so I wanted to see how you're doing." The words sounded stilted, but she had to start somewhere.

"You're not in Michigan anymore?" Taking a seat on the bed, Nettie indicated the single straight chair for Kim.

"I'm in Pennsylvania. With Ruth." Briefly, she explained what had happened over the last few months.

"Your ex-husband was cheating your boss?"

"Yes."

"And you had no idea."

Kim glanced out the window. "I know. I'm an idiot."

"That isn't what I was thinking at all." Nettie set her hands in her lap, but her fingers fluttered like sea anemones.

She wants a cigarette, Kim thought. *What else can we talk about?* Her chair was next to a bookshelf, and she scanned a few titles. "You've got *The Once and Future King*. You sent me that when I was in middle school, and I loved it."

"The library guy lets me keep it up here. He says nobody else wants it, but I read bits and pieces all the time."

Touching another spine, she said, "*The Portable Mark Twain.* I remember you sent *Huckleberry Finn* for my birthday once."

"Have you read his *Letters from the Earth*?

"No."

"You're probably not cynical enough for it yet." Nettie grinned. "Give yourself a few more years."

"I'll ask if I can bring you books next time." That would occupy Nettie's long hours alone and also provide future discussion topics.

"I'd like that."

That ended that thread, and Kim licked her lips, unsure what topic to try next. Nettie rose abruptly and moved to what Kim had taken for an air conditioner. She turned it on, and a whooshing noise began. "Smoke eater," she explained, taking cigarettes and a lighter from her pocket. After lighting up, she said, "Tell me about your job with Ruth."

Kim did, describing the weirdness of modern political operations with humorous side comments. As she spoke, Nettie smiled a few times, which pleased her. When she was done, she checked her phone for the time. Dr. Foeller had suggested keeping her initial visit short. "I have to go, but it's been good to see you." Rising, she asked, "Are you okay here, Nettie?"

"Better than okay." She gestured at her surroundings. "This is way more than I deserve."

"Nettie—" Kim began, but her sister raised a hand.

"Don't bullshit me with how I'm really a good person at heart." Nettie rubbed her free hand on her pantleg, as if trying to remove a stain. "I deserve to be in a place a lot worse than this."

Kim sniffed. "If I promise no pity parties, will you let me come to see you once a month?"

Nettie's mouth twisted to one side. "Susan says I need outside contacts."

"Can Ruth come too?"

"No." It came out too quickly, and she went on, "You can visit without a lot of hoopla, but she can't. And every time my name comes up in the news, it hurts Butch's chances for election."

Kim couldn't argue with that. "All right. I'll schedule a trip as near to the first of each month as I can make it. We'll be stumping on and off, so I can't be specific."

"If you can't get away, don't sweat it." Humor lit Nettie's eyes. "Whenever you get here, I'll be available."

When the guard escorted Kim downstairs, Susan Foeller was waiting. "How was the visit?"

"She seems…at peace."

"Could we talk for a few minutes?"

"Sure." At Foeller's inviting gesture, Kim followed her into her office and sat opposite the desk. The A/C was on high, but the blinds were open. Foeller apparently liked the sunshine but not the heat.

"Has Nettie ever spoken to you about the night she killed her son?"

"No. I felt sorry for her lawyer, because he had nothing to offer in her defense."

"I read up on the case, and the press described Caleb as 'shiftless,' and 'shady.' Do you think Nettie felt threatened?"

"He was asleep, Doctor Foeller. Nettie admits he never hurt her or even threatened to." Kim fiddled with her purse strap. "I can't imagine what he did or said to make her…I mean, he was a little odd, but—"

"You met Caleb?" Her tone revealed surprise. "Mrs. Mandell said that no one in the family knew him. In fact, she wondered for a time if the boy was imaginary, an excuse for Nettie to claim the family farm for herself."

"He came to my apartment shortly before he died."

"What was your impression?"

"He was nice enough, but it felt…fake."

"What did he say or do that you found odd?"

She decided not to mention the stolen baseball. "He wanted me to get him a job at my firm, but the only position he was qualified for was janitor."

"You didn't get any sense of threat from him?"

Kim shook her head, but it was more a refusal to answer than a denial.

"I think Nettie needs to tell someone, maybe not the world, but someone who cares about her, why she killed her son. Once we know that, we can perhaps help her forgive herself."

Kim gave the doctor a rueful smile. "Is it that easy?"

"No," Foeller replied with a tinge of sadness. "But it would be a start."

Foeller's phone rang, and she pressed a button to stop it. "I should go," Kim said. "My ride is probably waiting at the gate."

"I'd like to give you my private cell number." Foeller wrote it on the back of one of her business cards. "If you ever find out something you think will help me understand Nettie, feel free to call and talk with me about it."

On the ride home, Kim stared out the train window, taking in nothing that was out there. Instead, the face of Nettie's lawyer came to mind. Andrew McMahon had shown a sincere desire to help, and he'd been frustrated by his client's silence. "Nobody thinks Nettie's crazy or evil or whatever," he'd told Ruth and Kim. "If she'd tell what happened, I might get the charge reduced to manslaughter." He'd raised his hands, revealing his frustration. "She says it doesn't matter."

Kim looked at the card Dr. Foeller had given her. If Nettie ever told Kim the truth, would she pass it on to the psychiatrist? The doctor was better equipped to help a person deal with trauma, but Nettie would consider it a betrayal. Kim slid the card into a seldom-used pocket of her purse. It was hard to know what was right when a family member went wrong.

Chapter Seventeen

Nettie-Same Day

Kim's departure seemed to suck the light out of Nettie's tiny cell. For a while she sat by the window, smoking. Her room faced the side yard, so she couldn't watch her sister go, and that was probably a good thing. About twenty minutes later, when she'd finally picked up her current book and begun reading, a knock sounded at her door. Protocol at Martha's Place was that visitors, even staff, knocked, though it was unclear to Nettie what would happen if she ignored whoever stood outside her cell. Nettie called permission to enter. There was a click, and Dr. Foeller appeared. "How was the visit?"

"She's a good kid, that Kim."

Foeller chuckled. "She's my age, Nettie. Not exactly a kid."

"I know, but I keep seeing her at six years old, the summer I taught her to swim instead of dog paddling." Nettie smiled. "Back then, she always wanted me to put her hair in pigtails, to keep it out of her way when she went out to build a tree fort or catch frogs at the pond."

Foeller smiled, no doubt pleased that Kim's visit had spurred good memories. "Would you like to go outside for a while?"

Though she suspected Foeller had pumped her sister for information she would now use to batter Nettie's defenses, it was better than remaining in the cell that still smelled faintly of Kim's strawberry shampoo. "Sure."

Passing through a succession of gateways, they exited the building. The day was stifling, and Nettie fought the urge to use her shirt to dry the damp space between her breasts. In such times, her mother's voice still sounded inside her head, reminding her what nice girls did and did not do in public.

Instead, she lit a cigarette, stopping briefly to steady the lighter. Foeller stopped too. "Kim seems to care a great deal about you."

Nettie sniffed. "Kim is one of those people who takes on debts she doesn't owe. Know what I mean?"

"I think so, yes."

"She'll come here and try to brighten my days, and she'll never get that she doesn't owe me that."

"Is that what it's about? What someone owes someone else?"

"I don't know," Nettie heard the roughness in her own voice. "I just know I don't want her to feel obligated to me."

Foeller left that alone, asking instead, "Did Kim ever meet your son?"

She pocketed the lighter. "Caleb mentioned that he'd dropped in to see her."

"Did he say why?"

Nettie frowned. "He wasn't much for explaining himself."

"But he wanted you to know he'd finally met his aunt after all these years."

A long pause. "Yes."

"Do you think you were a good mother, Nettie?"

Her eyes filled with tears, but she blinked them away. "I tried to be." After a long drag her voice steadied, and she said, "I thought I could save my son, and I thought maybe at the same time, he'd save me."

"He changed you," Foeller said. "Before Caleb came to live with you, there was often trouble with the law. Afterward, no arrests, no complaints from neighbors about loud music or noisy fights with your boyfriend. You tried to make a good life for him."

She blew smoke into the air. "You know what they say. Be careful what you wish for."

"Caleb was different than you expected?"

"You could say that." Nettie bent to crush her cigarette butt on the sidewalk and then carried the remains to a receptacle farther along the path. "He wasn't what I expected, but he was exactly what I deserved."

Chapter Eighteen

Ruth-September 4

"This Congresswoman, Rebecca Soames Bentley, is outrageous." Ruth waved a newspaper still damp from the morning's rain in front of her husband's nose. "There isn't a word of truth in anything she said about you."

Taking the paper from her, Butch scanned the article, and then set it aside and wiped his fingers on his napkin. "It's her opinion, Ruthie. We don't have to agree with her."

Picking up the paper, Ruth read from the article that had enraged her. "*While Butch Mandell is admittedly charming and honest, he lacks the focus a modern President needs. Mandell has a reputation for delegating with only the lightest efforts at oversight.*" She looked up, including Butch's two breakfast companions in her question. "How should we respond to this?"

Butch made a dismissive gesture with the hand that wasn't holding a fork. "Delegating isn't a bad thing. No one is an expert at everything, despite a few Presidents who believed they were."

"You can't say that," Ruth objected. "Voters want to imagine their President in control of every little detail. Tomorrow there'll be a cartoon in the *Times* of you sitting on a velvet cushion while little functionaries rush around waiting on you."

"Let them have their fun," Morris Blake counseled. "Most voters picture Butch here rolling up his sleeves, wading into the Washington mess, and fixing it."

Gavin Croft made a throat-clearing noise. "I could draft a response that will answer the Congresswoman's assertions. We'll assure the American public that President Mandell will personally perform the work of his office, but he will consult experts for information and advice before making his decisions, as all wise leaders do." Croft raised his hands. "What more could voters ask?"

Butch pointed an approving finger. "Get to work on it, Gavin. I'll need time to practice saying the words before the reporters start calling in."

Butch and Morris Blake went off to a meeting, leaving Croft scribbling notes next to his half-finished eggs. Observing his bent head, Ruth noted that he'd taken her comment on his paleness to heart but hadn't followed her advice to get more sun. Instead, he'd bought some concoction that turned his skin an odd shade of orange. At the back, where he couldn't easily see, pale streaks cut through his "tan." She thought about telling him to be more careful when he applied the stuff, but she didn't like disrupting his concentration. She'd mention it later.

As she rose to leave, Croft paused his writing and said, "It must be frustrating to have lies and half-truths told about you and your husband when you're trying so hard to do good for this country."

She paused, gratified that someone, even Croft, understood her anger at the unfairness of it. "I suppose the Bentley woman is paving the way for her own run for President four years from now."

"I believe that's the case."

"It would be nice if loudmouths like her could be silenced."

Ruth was ashamed to admit it, even to herself, but she was pleased to read later that week that Congresswoman Soames Bentley had been accused of funneling government money into her daughter's construction firm. Though her spokesperson insisted that was not the case and investigation would prove her innocent, it looked like her hopes for rising to higher office were ruined.

Chapter Nineteen

Kim-October 10

On the way home from her visit, the bright blue sky above the train reminded Kim of the man who'd served as Nettie's lawyer. Andrew McMahon had eyes that exact color, she recalled. He'd seemed to truly care about Nettie's case. While he couldn't share privileged information, she wondered if McMahon knew anything about Caleb Green that might suggest a motive for Nettie's crime.

In her phone's contact list, she found the number of his law office and, before she could second-guess herself, made the call. Listening to the ring, she waited for a secretary to answer or a recording to ask her to leave a message. Could she leave a message if she didn't even know—?

"Drew McMahon. Is this really Kim Dailey?"

"It is." His face came to mind, boyish and bony, with reddish-brown curls that fell over his forehead no matter how many times he pushed them back. He favored blue ties, she recalled, and took notes on a yellow legal pad, lefty, with a back-slant that stained the heel of his hand with ink. "How are you?"

"Crazy busy, but I've promised myself I'm going to take time off soon."

"I believe you said the same thing the first day we met. Did you do it then?"

"Well, no." Hearing a high-pitched squeak, she guessed he'd turned his chair away from his desk and the work he'd been doing. "I promise myself a vacation about three times a day, but then a new case comes along." After a change-the-topic throat-clearing noise, he said, "I understand you're well on the way to being right-hand assistant to the First Lady of the United States. Congratulations."

"To be honest, I'm a little nervous about the whole idea." For a second, she was tempted to confide that she doubted her brother-in-law's grasp of Presidential responsibility. She suppressed the urge, knowing that even the slightest criticism of Butch might be all over the headlines tomorrow morning.

"If this isn't a good time to talk, Mr. McMahon, I can call back later."

"Call me Drew, and we're good. I have an appointment in ten minutes, but the client is a loud talker who's addicted to her phone. We'll both hear her coming."

Suddenly Kim was unsure if she should proceed. Did she really want to get into Nettie's past now, with Butch's campaign and the unspoken but expected loyalty to Ruth that her job required? Still, McMahon had done his best to help Nettie, and he'd been discreet. Reporters must have tried to get him to tell what he learned about the Kovalesky sisters, but he hadn't. "Mr. McMahon—um, Drew, I've been to see Nettie. She still won't say why she killed Caleb."

"Huh. Even now, after she's been tried and sentenced."

"Right."

She heard him let out a long breath. "I can't tell you how many times I reminded her that I was bound by confidentiality and couldn't pass on anything she said. Every time, she'd give me that Mona Lisa smile and say she didn't need to talk about it."

"She won't even talk about Caleb with her psychiatrist, who's taken quite an interest in her."

"This is a staff doctor at Huron Valley?"

"No. Nettie was moved to a private prison in Virginia."

There was a pause as he digested the information. "How did that come about?"

"I kind of assumed you had something to do with it."

"No. I wanted to file an appeal, but she said no, so we were pretty much done."

"Can you summarize what you're allowed to tell me about the case? I was there, but it was…emotional for me."

After a moment to collect his thoughts, McMahon said, "Nettie called the police immediately after she shot Caleb. She made no attempt to hide what she'd done but wouldn't explain it either. I was appointed as counsel by the court. Your sister Ruth offered to get her a different attorney, a better one in her mind, I suppose, but Nettie stuck with me. As a client she was difficult. All she'd say was she'd done it because she had to."

"She said the same to Ruth and me."

"The county sheriff knew Caleb a little from petty crimes he'd committed as a juvenile. He really wanted to help Nettie, but neither of us knew how."

"I knew Caleb had legal problems, but I never heard the specifics."

"Two trespassing complaints, I think, and one petty theft." Hearing clicks, Kim guessed McMahon had opened a file on his computer to refresh his memory. "Caleb was sent for counselling in tenth grade after an incident in the lunchroom. The school social worker visited the home and reported that things seemed stable. Mom worked first shift, so she was there when he got home from school—not that he always attended. The place wasn't ritzy, but it was neat and there was adequate food. Caleb's clothes were clean, and he had games that were age appropriate. Nettie gave him half the profits from their vegetable stand. The only negative in her notes was a shelf of slasher movies in Caleb's room." He chuckled. "What teenage boy doesn't love slasher movies?"

"Home was okay then."

"The notes said Nettie admitted her son was moody and defiant at times, but my mom would have said the same thing about me at that age."

"I know Caleb came and went from home as an adult. Any idea why?"

"He couldn't hold onto a job. I spoke to his last employer, who said Caleb talked a good game at the interview but was pretty much useless once he got hired." His tone changed. "Sorry. I know he was your nephew."

"I appreciate your honesty."

"I think the DA's office suspected Nettie had a reason for what she did. I had no trouble getting them to agree to the second-degree charge."

"Did the police know that Caleb spent his early years with his grandmother?"

"Yes, but she's dead."

"Did you find any information on his time with her?"

"No. Since Nettie freely admitted to the crime, there didn't seem to be any point in looking back twenty years to find out if Caleb was a bratty kid before he became an irresponsible adult."

Kim's hands had grown sweaty, and she wiped one then the other on her sweater. "Do you think it might be worthwhile to look into what sort of person Caleb was? Nettie won't tell me anything, but I wonder, you know?"

"I guess you could talk to people who knew him and ask if he was a violent drunk or whatever."

"I owe my time to Ruth right now, and I don't know of anyone else who might help."

"If you were thinking of me, I've got cases all the way into next year. I can give you the name of a decent private detective."

Kim's momentary enthusiasm dissipated like a wisp of cloud. "No, but thanks. It's a crazy idea. I'm in the middle of a Presidential campaign, and Nettie doesn't even come up for parole until 2026. There's lots of time to decide whether to pursue it or not."

"I really wish I could help." McMahon sounded like he meant it.

"It was good to talk about it with you," Kim said. "Thanks for listening."

Chapter Twenty

Ruth-October 10

"Great weather for ducks." Draping his damp overcoat over the banister, Butch set his suitcase at the foot of the stairs. Rain had started early and continued all day, slowing his return home from a five-day stump tour of the Southwest. Ruth had stayed behind this time, catching up on what had been neglected at home.

While he sounded tired as he told her about the trip, Butch was also pleased at the reception he'd received. A live audience always brought out his best, and crowds all along his route had been wildly enthusiastic.

After years of sniping on both sides, the public was ready for a more positive outlook. The media, always mindful of its profit margins, shifted from initial disdain for the Unity Project to more favorable reporting. Analysts began offering articles and segments that examined what might happen "If we do as Butch proposes." For the Mandell campaign, it happened at exactly the right moment.

With the handsome, personable Butch and his well-spoken, attractive wife in the spotlight, reporters had begun suggesting a new "Camelot Couple" might soon move into the White House. While she wasn't a prideful person, Ruth felt she was an asset to Butch's campaign, despite a few objections to her more "extreme" opinions. She held firm to her belief that family had to come first. "Every child should have a parent in the home," she contended. "It would benefit kids and society as well. Robotics and technology eliminate jobs every day, but if one parent in each family left the work force, competition for workers would result in higher salaries. Families wouldn't need that second income." She always ended with a return to Butch's platform, adding, "My opinions are mine alone. The direction of our country under Butch Mandell will be decided by people working together, not by the President's wife."

"How are your sister's visits to your other sister going?" Butch had slumped into a chair and was untying his shoes. He seldom called her siblings by name, and Ruth wondered if he even realized it.

"It's been so busy that we haven't spoken privately for a while. The doctor did call to ask if we'd fund a greenhouse at Martha's Place. I said yes."

Butch grunted what might have been assent and went upstairs, leaving his shoes beside the chair. After setting them in the closet, Ruth went down the hallway to Kim's apartment. It was good, she thought as she went, that they had a home large enough to hold the growing number of helpers necessary to run a successful (fingers crossed!) Presidential campaign. Gavin Croft and two others who were single lived with them, at least when they weren't with Butch on the campaign trail. Now Kim was there too. Ruth loved having her little sister as part of their inner circle.

Kim came to the door carrying a sponge that smelled of bleach. "The housekeeper would be happy to do your cleaning," Ruth said.

"I don't mind it. Come in." Ruth followed her inside, noting small touches Kim had added to make the place her own: a philodendron that looked lonely on its stand in the corner, the guitar no one had ever heard her play, prints of lesser-known Renaissance artists, and books. She'd mentioned downsizing her collection when she moved, but it had apparently grown back.

Ruth chose a book at random. "*Letters from the Earth*?"

"Nettie recommended it." Kim quoted, "'You have heretofore found out, by my teachings, that man is a fool; you are now aware that woman is a damned fool.'"

Ruth set the book back in place. "If you ask me, Mark Twain was an irritating old grump who rambled too much. You should be going out with some handsome young lawyer, Kimmie, not reading dusty, dead authors."

"I'm in no hurry to start dating again."

With a shrug she dismissed the topic. "We haven't had a chance to talk about how Nettie is doing."

"She seems content at Martha's Place."

"That's good, because she'll be there for a long time."

Kim winced, and her gaze drifted to a window, as if she could see Nettie all those miles away, locked in and alone. "How does a person kill, Ruth? Especially family?"

"I have no idea."

"Nettie isn't the type of person to kill without a good reason."

Ruth made an impatient popping sound with her lips. "Neither of us knows her well enough to say what she would or wouldn't do, Kimmie. You never did, and I haven't been close to her for years."

"But we know what kind of person she is at heart." Kim shook her head. "That can't change, can it?"

"You probably don't want to know the answer to that." Ruth straightened a photo of their parents that sat on a low table. "Someone said you spoke to her lawyer recently, McMasters or whatever."

"McMahon." Kim seemed irritated. "Who said that?"

Ruth shrugged. "I don't know. You know how they all flock around me and chatter." She took up another book and examined the cover. "What did you and he have to talk about?"

"Nothing, really. I just thought he should know Nettie's not in Michigan anymore."

"I don't see why he'd care. She made no secret of having no use for him." Putting the book back in place with a crisp thump, she said, "I'll see you in the morning. We need to look at catering bids for next month's event."

Chapter Twenty-One

Nettie-November 6

Dr. Foeller came to Nettie's cell early on the morning after the election. "Did you see that your brother-in-law was declared the winner in the Presidential race? In a few months, your sister will be First Lady of the United States."

Nettie had pulled her chair over to the window, where the first rays of sun could warm her face. She put a bit of paper in her book to mark the place and set it on the sill. "He won, even with me dragging him down."

"I don't think you hurt their campaign. They had momentum, like the whole country woke up and said, 'This is who we want in the White House.'"

"I know the press tried to make what I did an issue."

A shrug conceded the point. "The warden from Michigan called me once to see if I wanted requests to interview you forwarded here, but I said no."

Nettie looked up at her. "The press doesn't know where I am?"

"Very few people do. I figured you'd prefer it that way."

She nodded. "I do. Out of sight, out of mind."

"Kim texted to say she's coming here today, since she's not sure what her schedule will be like for a while."

Nettie enjoyed her sister's visits, though she sensed that Kim was still uncertain how she felt about her. Their conversations focused mostly on books, exchanging favorite titles and expressing opinions on authors. When their discussions revealed differences in the way they viewed the world, Nettie often wondered how a person like Kim, almost forty years into life, still believed that people are basically good.

When Kim arrived, Dr. Foeller and Nettie met her at the gate in the golf cart. After offering her congratulations on the election, Foeller suggested Kim and Nettie walk the grounds and enjoy the mild autumn day. When they agreed, she let them out on the pathway and drove off. Their feet plowed fallen leaves as they walked, making rustling sounds that were somehow comforting.

"I still can't believe Butch won," Kim said. "I mean, we all worked really hard to make it happen. On our last trip, we hit fifteen states in twelve days." She shook her head. "I swear, that man could live on applause. Near the end I was exhausted, but he'd still be out there, shaking hands and patting babies on the butt. Ruth too. Never once did she admit being tired."

When Kim finally ran out of campaign stories, Nettie said, "Tell me what you remember about the time after I left."

Her smile faded, but she answered honestly. "Mom and Dad whispered a lot at night when they thought I was asleep. Sometimes they cried." She turned to meet her sister's gaze. "You really hurt them." It hurt to hear it spoken aloud, and Nettie's chin dropped almost to her chest. "We had such wonderful parents. Why did you go all goofy?"

"A series of unfortunate incidents." Fishing out a cigarette, she lit up. "You know I left home with Trent Sutfin."

"Yeah. Great decision."

"One of many not-great decisions," she conceded. "To be fair, when Trent left me in Tucson, he thought I'd go home." She sat down on a stone bench, and its cold surface pulled at her thighs. Kim stood a few feet away, as if reluctant to associate with the girl from those days. "I knew Mom and Dad would forgive me, but I also knew our little stunt was the talk of the town. I couldn't face going back to sitting in algebra class and sleeping in my bedroom at the end of the hall."

A small light of humor showed in Kim's eyes. "You'd have had to fight for it. Ruth took it over as soon as you were gone."

"She always wanted the room with the big closet." Nettie went back to her story. "After Trent left, the night clerk at the motel, Virgil Green, was nice. He let me move into this tiny room under the stairs that they only charged half price for. After he talked to a woman he knew at a diner, she hired me to work the early shift. The place was close enough to the motel that I could walk there and back. Virgil came in most mornings, after he got off work, and we'd talk." She ran a hand through her hair. "He was nobody's Einstein, but he was good-looking, and he liked me. At the time, I was feeling pretty unlikable."

"You two started dating."

She nodded. "I ended up moving in with him. There was no way I could keep paying twenty bucks a night on what I was making, so it seemed like a good idea."

"I'm guessing he wasn't as nice as he seemed."

"Virgil was pretty mellow when he was high, but he was downright cruel when he wasn't. While I wasn't new to the practice of chemically changing my mood, he was a serious user. It wasn't long until I was as heavily dependent as he was."

Kim skipped ahead. "You say his name was Virgil Green. Does that mean…?"

"Yes. Virgil got me pregnant." An angry gesture erased those words, and she rephrased. "It was my fault. My prescription ran out and I told myself I'd be careful, count the days and all that." She hooked her bottom lip under her top teeth briefly before continuing. "You can guess how well that worked."

"Was Virgil upset?"

"Oddly, no. He got all manly about having a knocked-up girlfriend." She made a puff of derision. "Big accomplishment."

"Was it a…healthy pregnancy?"

Nettie smiled, acknowledging her tactful wording of the question. "Do you mean did I straighten up? Yes. I quit the booze and drugs the minute I knew. I ate right and even got those vitamins for pregnant women. I wanted that baby to be healthy, because I planned to give him up for adoption."

Kim's gaze dropped to the pathway, and Nettie realized for the first time how much her sister had wanted children. *How unfair is life?* she thought. *It sends babies to the ungrateful and withholds them from those who ache to be mothers.*

"How did Virgil react to the idea of giving up the baby?"

"I never told him." Nettie wrapped her arms around herself. "But one day he found a flyer from an agency that helped girls adopt out their babies. Virgil got really mad and…"

"He hit you."

"It wasn't the first time, but this one was bad." Nettie made her voice emotionless. "I fell against a shelf edge and cut my head open. When Virgil called the EMTs, he told them I fell down the stairs."

"I bet they didn't believe that."

"I agreed that's what had happened." At Kim's incredulous look she said, "I had a broken shoulder, a bunch of contusions, and twenty stitches in my scalp. The first words out of the doctor's mouth were that I'd be off work for at least two weeks. I had nobody but Virgil to support me until I got well."

"You could have called Mom and Dad."

She shook her head. "They'd have found out about the drugs, the booze, and the baby. Everything changed when Virgil's mother showed up." Nettie's smile was rueful. "Her name was Florence, and she'd remind you of women we knew back home: rural vibe, plain clothes, hair pulled back as if she wasn't about to let it interfere with whatever she had to get done. She seemed pretty smart, and she said Virgil and I should get married before the baby came."

"Marry a guy who beat the crap out of you?"

Nettie smiled. "I know. But when she got me alone, Florence explained that once Virgil's name was on the birth certificate, he had to support the kid, even if we didn't stay married." Nettie picked a bit of tobacco off her tongue. "I know I wasn't thinking straight, because I let her talk me into it."

"What about your plan to give the baby up?"

Nettie let her eyelids go almost closed. "Florence said as soon as I held that child, I'd want to keep it. She convinced me that Virgil would settle down once he had a kid, like his father had."

"Did she know Virgil was the one who hurt you?"

Nettie cleared her throat. "She admitted he could be difficult, but if things didn't work out, she said I could move in with her and she'd help me raise the baby."

"That sounded good to you?"

"It was better than calling Mom and Dad and admitting what a mess I'd made of my life." Nettie stood, crushed her cigarette out, and immediately lit another. "Virgil and I got married at the county courthouse. After the ceremony, Florence hugged us both, bought us lunch, and then went home."

"Did things with Virgil go better after that?"

"Two days after our wedding, Virgil got killed in a bar fight." Nettie huffed a laugh. "Classy, huh? My man was big and tough when it came to smacking me around, but a hick from Oklahoma put him down with one punch."

"Which left you in a bad place."

"It did. I went into labor a few hours after the police notified me. A woman from the apartment building drove me to the hospital. I had my little boy, but there I was, absolutely lost less than a year after the last time I'd been absolutely lost. Then, lo and behold, along came Florence again. She drove me back to the apartment, showed me how to take care of Caleb, and went to work on his future. She filed lawsuits against the guy who'd hit Virgil, the bar where it happened, and anyone else she could think of who might be bullied into giving us money."

"Did it work?"

Nettie smiled. "I wasn't in on the results, but I think it did. Florence was sharp—too sharp for me."

"What do you mean?"

"Her efforts were entirely focused on getting her hands on my baby." Nettie stared across the lawn, where winter had started its slow creep across the grass, sapping its color and inhibiting its growth. "Florence sat me down on our saggy couch and informed me that I was a mess, emotionally, financially, and every way possible. Since the rent was paid for the month, she suggested I take some time to recover from the birth and clear up whatever business I had in Tucson. She offered to take the baby home with her and care for him until I was ready to be his mom." Nettie sighed. "She looked me in the eye and promised he'd be fine. 'After all,' she said, 'he's the only grandson I'll ever have.'"

"It doesn't sound unreasonable."

"No." Nettie rubbed her forehead. "She gave me some papers to sign. I hardly looked at them, just did what she said." Her tone hardened. "It was stupid. *I* was stupid."

"She took custody of the baby."

"Yes." Her eyes stung with tears as she added, "Florence was a conniving bitch, but she was right about two things. First, I loved Caleb from the second they laid him in my arms."

"That's good."

"But she was right about me being a mess too. I told myself that in a month I'd be ready to be a mom."

Kim frowned. "That isn't what happened."

"Florence and my baby disappeared. The address and phone number she'd given me were fake. The lawyer who drew up the papers wouldn't give me the time of day. Florence's last name wasn't Green. I had no way to find her, no money to look for her, and I'd made her my son's legal guardian." Her voice quavered as she added, "I deserved to lose Caleb, but still, it was hard."

"What did you do?"

"The rent was due. I had no car, no groceries, no job, and no friends." Nettie blew smoke over her shoulder. "I got a dead-end job in a bar, drank too much, and took drugs when I could get them. I lived with a string of men who knew they could treat me however they wanted." Self-loathing colored her voice as she finished, "After a few months, I got low enough to call home and beg Mom and Dad for a bailout. That first time was hard, but it got easier as time went on."

Kim pulled a dying leaf from a tree they passed and traced its veins with a finger. "They always said next time they wouldn't give you money, but they did."

"Experts talk about tough love," Nettie said, "but if your child is sitting in a jail cell, you do what it takes to save her."

"How did you find Caleb again?"

"Florence died in 2003. In her papers they found his birth certificate, so this woman showed up at my door asking what they should do with my ten-year-old son. Once I got past the shock, I said, 'Send him here.'" Nettie rubbed her nose. "I stopped drinking and gave up drugs, even aspirin. I fixed up my apartment the best I could in the few days I had. It was a studio, but I got a cot and bought one of those panels you set up to wall off a corner. I wanted Caleb to feel he had a space of his own, you know?" Her posture straightened as she recalled, "A friend at the bar cut my hair short, so I'd look more Hip Mom and less Worn-out Hag. I found a new job. The pay wasn't as good, but I'd be home when he got out of school every day." Taking a last drag on the cigarette, she stubbed it out on the underside of the bench. "I thought it would be better if my son could say his mom worked at the local grocery and not at Chubby's Bar."

"And was it?"

The smile faded. "The word *better* never really applied."

"Caleb took a dislike to you?"

"I didn't see it at first. He'd been taught to say 'Yes, ma'am,' and 'No, ma'am,' and smile right into your eyes. But under that polite shell, Caleb wasn't able to connect." She sniffed. "Maybe to anybody, but certainly not to me."

"What made him that way?"

Nettie turned to face her. "I did. It was my fault."

"Is that why you wouldn't defend yourself after he…was killed?"

"You mean after I shot him." Kim looked away, and Nettie asked, "You don't harbor any hope that I didn't do it, do you?"

"I understand that you did it, but I think you're protecting him, and that's why you're stuck in this place."

"I wasn't there to protect him when he was little," Nettie said in a tone that allowed no discussion. "It's the least I can do for him now."

Chapter Twenty-Two

Kim-Same Day

Kim became used to finding Dr. Foeller waiting when her visits with Nettie ended. "I can take you to the gate in the golf cart," she offered once Nettie had been escorted inside.

"I don't mind walking if you don't," Kim said, and Foeller stepped into place beside her.

"They're saying your brother-in-law received 54% of the popular vote, which is amazing."

Kim chuckled. "I can't believe two girls from Berlin, Michigan, are going to be living at the White House."

"You grew up on a farm, right?"

"I could drive a tractor long before I ever drove a car."

"And there's a bit of an age gap between you and your sisters."

"Mom used to say I was more like a toy to them than a sibling. Nettie was like a buddy, and Ruth was like a second mom."

"Everyone got along, then?"

"Ruth claims Nettie took any suggestion for improvement as criticism, but I suppose that's just sister stuff."

"It's good that you're getting to know Nettie now."

"Both of them," Kim corrected. When Foeller's brows lifted, she explained, "We didn't see much of Ruth once she married."

"You and your parents didn't visit?"

Kim shook her head. "Cows require attention every day, so it's hard for a farmer to get away. Ruth did fly me out for a visit the summer after I graduated high school." Chuckling, she added, "That was quite an experience for a girl straight off the farm. I got little lessons in deportment, so I didn't come off too much like Country Mouse in the Big City."

"You've all led very different lives."

"Yes. Nettie's has been too sad for too long. I hope you can help her find even a spark of joy in her life."

"She's beginning to open up to me, but I doubt she'll ever trust me as much as she trusts you."

"Family is different," Kim said. "I think it's born in us."

After a moment Foeller said, "She's never even hinted to you why Caleb had to die?"

"No." While that was true, Kim resented the assumption she'd share Nettie's secret if she had.

Foeller bit her lip. "With me, the topic of her son is still off limits."

"How did you get interested in Nettie in the first place? I know Ruth's paying for all this, and I can't imagine Nettie is happy about letting her do that."

Foeller kicked a pebble off the path. "There was an…incident at the prison in Michigan. Nettie was injured."

"Someone attacked her?"

"She's never admitted it, but I believe that was the case."

"And Ruth asked you to get her out of there?"

"Actually, Mrs. Mandell had contacted me shortly after Nettie was sentenced. She flew me to Michigan to offer her a place here, but Nettie refused." Foeller folded her hands. "After the attack, Mrs. Mandell suggested I ask again, and Nettie had indeed changed her mind."

"I see."

"She's been very generous to Nettie."

"To me, too," Kim admitted. "Where else would I have done as well?" *Especially with a charge of embezzlement hanging over my head.*

"Then you're both lucky to have Ruth Mandell for a sister," Foeller said. "Though I've only seen her on TV, she seems like an amazing woman."

"She is," Kim agreed. "I wish I had half her energy—and even a quarter of her confidence."

Chapter Twenty-Three

Ruth-January 20

Butch's inauguration as President was the proudest day of Ruth's life. Even the weather cooperated, with pale yellow sunshine that warmed the air enough to make the day pleasant. Not only did Ruth get to stand with him as Butch took the oath, but most of the speech he gave was her creation. Butch was no wordsmith, so it was her phrases, spoken in his earnest way, that would be quoted over and over by reporters. "Stitching us together" was one. In some mouths it would have sounded corny, but Butch made unifying the nation seem as simple as mending the seam in a pair of pants. Not that most of his listeners knew the first thing about mending.

Butch went on, putting the nation's future into terms of daily household tasks. Americans needed to "mow the weeds," to get a better look at their neighbors. They'd "mend their porches" to assure future safety.

What did it mean? Nothing, really, but the average citizen could interpret the words as they saw fit. If mowing weeds meant getting rid of outsiders, that satisfied one element. If to some it meant clearing impediments between peoples and cultures, that was fine too.

After the swearing-in ceremony, Butch and Ruth retreated, exhausted but exhilarated, to their temporary quarters to rest before the evening festivities began. Ruth had barely entered her bedroom and kicked off her heels when she heard a knock on her door.

Gavin Croft looked positively manic, which meant that his usual corpse-like expression was disturbed by a twitch. "He needs you."

Butch had gone to lie down for a few minutes. It had been a long day already, but they would attend balls until the wee hours. He'd looked a little gray, she recalled. Now, Croft's face was almost the same color. "What's wrong?"

Instead of answering, he gestured urgently for her to follow. Ruth obeyed, her heart feeling as though he'd taken a harsh grip on it to pull her along.

Butch lay on the bed, his face slack. Seeing Ruth, he raised one hand, but the other lay lifeless beside him. Leaning over him, she ordered, "Butch! Smile for me." The lopsided result confirmed her fears. "It's a stroke."

"I was afraid of that." Croft's hands worked as if he were kneading bread.

"When did this start?"

"Five minutes, maybe. He collapsed. I got him to the bed and came to get you."

"And no one else knows?"

"He's supposed to be resting."

"Where's Morris Blake?"

"Downstairs," Croft replied. "I thought you'd want the situation kept quiet until you have time to decide what will be done."

While Ruth trusted Blake more than Croft, the fewer who knew what was happening, the better. "All right." Taking the pad and pen from the desk, she located a contact in her phone and began writing. "Pick one person on the Secret Service detail you can trust to keep his mouth shut. Have him help you put Butch in a car. Take him to the Montague Private Hospital. Here's the address." She handed him the note. "The head doctor there, Eric Chalmers, was at school with Butch. I'll call and have him meet you there, and he'll see that the President gets the best care with absolute anonymity."

Croft processed the information, and Ruth sensed that he approved. "You're going to keep this a secret?"

"Chalmers is a long-time supporter. He'll admit Butch as a John Doe." She took a second to think. "On the way there, bandage his face and make up a story for why he has no ID. Maybe he was mugged." Seeing doubt in his eyes, she added firmly, "Until we know how bad this is, the President is officially fine."

"But—"

She held up a hand. "If a stroke victim is treated quickly, doctors can often reverse the damage. If they can't, we'll deal with it. Now choose a helper and get going."

Croft nodded as his thoughts caught up to hers. "What are you going to do?"

"Put on my ball gown and think up an excuse for my husband's absence." She quirked a brow. "A twenty-four-hour virus, maybe?"

Croft shook his head. "They'll want to send a doctor in."

"I'll think of something. Now go."

Josh Bennigan was the agent Croft chose to be his co-conspirator. Grasping the situation quickly, Bennigan called for a car, circumventing the usual protocols and procedures. Even better, he was strong enough physically to simply lift Butch into a laundry cart. Covering the cart with a sheet, he wheeled it out the back door while Croft gathered the staff and gave an over-long explanation of a family emergency he had to attend to. When he judged Bennigan had had enough time, Croft joined him, leaving Ruth to cover her husband's absence.

In the end, Ruth chose facial disfigurement, an embarrassing but not debilitating excuse. "Our newest President took a spill in the shower," she announced once Croft messaged that Butch was under Dr. Chalmers' care. "It's not serious, but he's got a lovely black eye, and he refuses to face the public."

There was talk, of course. The President was going to miss his inaugural parties because of a minor accident? Questions and speculation grew, with all sorts of silly possibilities offered.

Ruth laughed them off, insisting it wasn't out of character for her husband. "Once he got stung by a bee, right between the eyes, and he wouldn't leave the house until the swelling went down." Her cheerful resignation to her husband's eccentricities was convincing, and some found it endearing that a man of Butch's charm and power was embarrassed to be seen with a shiner.

Ruth had to take one more person into her confidence, and she chose Kim. After telling her what had happened, she said, "I'm sorry to ask you to give up going to the balls, but I need you to guard the door to Butch's room. While you're keeping people out, pray that he recovers and can start work tomorrow morning."

Kim was aghast. "You can't lie about this, Ruth. What if the President is dying?"

Ruth raised a hand. "I have every expectation that he will be able to fully resume his duties in a few days."

"A few days? Do you realize what he's got on his schedule?"

"Butch is new to the job, so there are no expectations for how he'll conduct business. If he chooses to work from the residence for a while, who's going to object?"

Kim pulled at a lock of hair, as if already punishing herself for her role in the deception. "I think it would be better to be honest."

Reaching out, Ruth took her hand and guided it back to her side. "We can't afford honesty right now, Kimmie. Even if Butch is fully recovered tomorrow, the press and the public might decide he's not fit to govern."

"And he might *be* unfit, Ruth. The Vice President should step in until we know—"

"Stockwell?" Ruth interrupted. "He might look like a wise elder statesman, but honestly, he's as dumb as your left shoe."

"But that's how the Constitution says it has to be done."

"Kim." Indicating she should sit, Ruth stood over her. "Who do you think knows better what Butch's intentions for his presidency are, me or some has-been senator chosen because he could deliver a bunch of electoral college votes?"

"Well—"

"I'm sure—I'm positive—this spell is temporary. We don't need to go through the rigmarole of transferring power and then getting it back in what? A week?"

"It seems dishonest to me."

Ruth licked her lips. "Do you think I'm dishonest, Kim?"

"Of course not."

"Then I'm going to ask you to trust me. If Butch's condition requires it, I'll tell everyone what happened, I promise. But for tonight, I'm going to smile and make jokes about how nobody believes they can slip in the shower and mess up their face until it happens to them."

When he located Ruth at her third inaugural party, Croft led her to a quiet spot to report news that was neither as good as she'd hoped nor as bad as she'd feared. "He'll live, but he's paralyzed on his left side. The doctor thinks he'll recover in a week or two, but right now, his appearance does not inspire confidence."

"That's bad. We really needed to begin from the strong position the election provided."

"Agreed." Croft's eyes hinted there was more he might say if he dared.

"But there's no way we can pretend that Butch isn't seriously ill, is there?"

An involuntary nod indicated Croft had been waiting for the question. "On the way here, I remembered that comedian who did Butch Mandell impressions. Butch once joked that he might hire the man to impersonate him at events he didn't want to attend. I don't recall his name…"

Ruth's spirits lifted. "Nathan Tanner."

Early on, Tanner's stunning resemblance to the Presidential hopeful had netted him multiple appearances on television. He'd disappeared after a few months, and rumor said his penchant for strong drink had ruined a good thing. Another comedian, less like Butch in appearance but able to show up on time and sober, had taken his place, aping Butch's direct gaze and folksy manner.

"See where he is now, will you?"

While he consulted his phone, Ruth paced. Was it possible they could pull this off?

"Mr. Tanner is currently doing a stand-up routine on a cruise ship in Alaska," Croft reported.

"How soon do you think you could get him here?"

He put a hand on her arm, and Ruth forced herself not to pull away. "Leave it to me, ma'am. I'll have him here by lunchtime."

It was later than that, but Croft informed her at breakfast that Tanner was on his way. "He jumped at the chance." Croft's nose lifted. "Of course, I didn't tell him everything, but I offered more money than he made in the last decade."

"Good. I'll keep making excuses for Butch. You get Tanner ready."

"How long do you think we might be able to manage the charade?" There was the slightest emphasis on *we*, and Ruth sensed she and Croft were now inexorably linked.

"We'll need a few days. Maybe a week."

"But this is the new President's training period, with briefings on subjects he needs to understand."

"The good side of that is he'll be expected to do a lot of listening." She cupped her chin with a hand. "Still, when he recovers, Butch can't very well ask to hear it all again. "Could we record everything somehow, maybe secretly?"

Croft shook his head, but he had a suggestion. "What if the President brings his wife to the briefings? Relatives have sat in on policy meetings in the past. Presented correctly, your presence could be seen as an asset."

"Not by the press, I'd bet, nor most of Congress either."

"Perhaps not, but the American public has often approved of First Couples who work as a cohesive unit."

"Like Franklin and Eleanor, or Bill and Hillary."

Croft rubbed his hands together. "We could easily have you vetted right away."

"And I'd go in with Tanner and learn what Butch needs to know."

"You'll cover for any mistakes he makes, too." Croft met her gaze, and Ruth realized they had formed a partnership of sorts. "I'll do what I can to help, and Bennigan and your sister will assist as well." Croft paused before adding, "Most of the responsibility will fall on your shoulders. Are you ready for that?"

Ruth chewed at her bottom lip, imagining what seemed to be impossible yet had to be done. "Let's do it. If we fail, we fail."

He made a sardonic bow. "If we fail, I will become the scapegoat. The President can do without one of his many advisors, but the First Lady can never be suspected of misconduct."

Ruth frowned. "If the substitution were discovered, what would I do?"

"Play dumb," he replied firmly. "Insist you didn't realize your husband had been replaced by an imposter." He touched her shoulder briefly, and this time Ruth managed a smile. She needed Croft, and she admitted, he'd been exactly what she and Butch needed in their first Presidential crisis.

"Call me as soon as Tanner gets in," she ordered. "Keep him off the booze, and let's hope when he crawls out of the bottle, he's got a little acting talent left."

Chapter Twenty-Four

Nettie-February 1

Nettie didn't watch much TV. World and national events held little interest for her, and she grew impatient with talking heads, self-righteous preachers, and over-dressed celebrities who spoke of saving this, changing that, or banning whatever their focus was this month. Still, she stopped as she passed through the common area and saw a close-up of Ruth's face on the screen. It was a morning talk show, and before a bright pink background, three hosts hung on her sister's every word. At almost fifty, Ruth looked beautiful. Her dark hair fell in soft waves around her face. Her clothes were fashionable but classy. She was also convincing, largely due to the certainty with which she spoke. Pride, Nettie reflected, is a useful trait. Who could be a surgeon, a quarterback, or a bomb disposal expert without the confidence to say, "I can do this"?

Not that the hosts were willing to allow Ruth her opinions. Their false eyelashes batted faster each time she spoke, filing away phrases they could chew on the minute she stopped for breath. *Like the Furies*, Nettie thought, *waiting to take the hero down*.

"The number of abortions has steadily decreased since *Roe v Wade,*" Ruth said, "yet forces on both sides keep the controversy boiling." Raising a palm on either side, she cited the opposing arguments. 'It's murder.' 'It's a woman's choice.'" Counting on her fingers, she explained, "These days, the procedure isn't necessary in most cases. We have safe birth control, so women can avoid unwanted pregnancies. We have better diagnostics, so doctors can prevent some birth defects and identify others early on. Sometimes they can even fix them in the womb."

"What about a woman's right to control her body?"

Ruth's expression remained pleasant, but the curve of her brows hinted that the question was naive. "I'm not in favor of limiting anyone's rights. We need to provide birth control, teach women to use it, and stress that no one should get pregnant unless she can provide a stable home for a child."

The inevitable questions followed. "What if birth control fails?" "What if a woman is raped?" "Would you allow abortions that are medically indicated?"

Ruth stopped the barrage with a wave of her hand. "First, we have to stop looking at the most extreme circumstances. Pro-lifers would have us believe that tons of careless women use abortion to correct the mistakes of their sexual orgies." She chuckled lightly. "Now, I've never considered any medical procedure to be fun, so I can't imagine it, but that's the argument." There were nods around the table, acknowledging the truth of that.

"Pro-choice forces," Ruth went on, "would have us believe that molested twelve-years account for huge numbers of abortions, but that's not true either. Only by looking at what's really happening can we decide the best way to proceed."

Again, there were nods of agreement, and Nettie thought, *Go, Ruth!* Under her cool eye, the topic had become less emotional, with the hope that even if differences couldn't be completely erased, serious mediation might balance deep-held beliefs with individual rights.

"President Mandell has gathered medical professionals, social workers, women's rights advocates, and educators and asked them to determine what can be done to reduce the frequency of abortions in this country. The number will never be zero, but if we attack the problem logically, it can be much lower." Flashing her beautiful smile, Ruth said, "If we stop fighting about who's right, we'll find a way forward."

Nettie went on to the greenhouse, smiling to herself as she shrugged on her jacket. Her sister was a First Lady to be reckoned with, classy and committed to a cause, as all the great ones were. Her smile twisted a little when she recalled that Ruth tended to see everything—and everyone—as her cause.

Chapter Twenty-Five

Kim-Same Day

Kim was sure she didn't sleep the whole week the actor took Butch's place. She must have, but it felt like she stared at the ceiling of her never-quite-dark-enough bedroom all night, every night, worrying about what could go wrong. What if Tanner made a comment that caused an international incident? What if Ruth's ruse was discovered? What would happen to the new First Lady? And what if the actor blabbed to the press? Or turned to extortion? What if Butch was angry when he learned what they'd done? And if the worst happened, how would they explain that the President of the United States had died in a private hospital under someone else's name?

Over and over, Kim told herself the answers were out of her hands, so there was no sense dwelling on them. Still, it was hard to watch Tanner play President Mandell. He did an admirable job, copying Butch's movements, his way of tilting his head slightly before he spoke, and his familiar gesture of removing his glasses when he had a point to make. A few reporters complained they heard nothing of substance in the first days of the Mandell Presidency, despite Butch's promise of swift changes. One editorial asked, "When do the new ideas show up?"

The administration gave daily press briefings, led by Glenda Delacroix, Esquire, an earnest young woman Ruth chose because of her ability to think on her feet. The "President" attended twice in the first four days, joking with the press corps and fielding their questions with requests for patience. "I'm getting my Cabinet together, and once we're all briefed and ready, we'll hit the ground running." With a chuckle that sounded exactly like Butch's, Tanner added, "There's more to this job than people realize, as I'm sure every new President discovers."

The President's team knew his intended Cabinet nominees and staff appointments, so all they had to do was release the names. Many were obscure, often not of either major party, and analysts scrambled to learn about them. Anticipation rose as Butch's administration took shape. At every opportunity, citizens were reminded that President Mandell would consider all viewpoints and look for new ways to move forward. The team went to work getting the nominees vetted and approved. The administration's backbone would be ready for the return of President Mandell. The real one.

Gavin Croft was named Chief of Staff. Though not well known in Washington circles, Croft had already been dubbed "the President's second brain" by those familiar with the inner workings of Butch's circle. For Ruth, Croft's presence was critical. He guided the impostor, signaling what he should do with subtle gestures and speaking for him whenever possible. Ruth and Croft discussed what they learned about the inner workings of the government, knowing they'd need to help Butch keep up in the days ahead, when he had to appear to know things he did not.

Croft admitted to Ruth that he wasn't thrilled with some of Butch's Cabinet choices, but overtures had already been made. Daniel Stone's name was submitted as head of Homeland Security. Calvin Keene, a scholarly type with hair that reminded Ruth of Lord Byron, was Butch's choice for Senior Policy Advisor. His old friend Morris Blake was nominated for the post of Attorney General.

Kim hovered at the edges of business, hearing her sister and Croft deciding their choices for the remaining posts. When Croft argued for Connor Keogh as Solicitor General, his reason made Kim uneasy. "The man is a bulldog," Croft said. "He'll keep the courts on our side and punish those who give us trouble."

Kim spoke privately to Nathan Tanner only once. The actor confessed without shame that he was terrified every time he had to "put on the purple mantle" and be President Mandell. "I've always been good at impressions," he confided, "but I'm not Presidential material, not by a long shot."

"You won't have to pretend much longer," Kim assured him. "I hear Butch is recovering nicely."

He sighed dramatically. "First job I've ever had I'll be thrilled to give up."

"You've done the country a service. With so much turmoil in the last few years, it would have been hard to ask the American people to deal with a Commander in Chief who was gravely ill."

"To be honest, this was exactly what I needed to happen." Tanner's lips formed a curve of regret. "You probably know I have a drinking problem. Doing this has given me the confidence to do without booze."

"That's good to hear."

"This snarl in the President's path will work itself out, and he'll be himself again." Tanner tugged at Butch's necktie. "I'll be myself again too, but I hope I can be a better Nate Tanner than before."

Things did work out. Despite Kim's imagined disaster scenarios, Tanner left the White House one evening at dusk for a formal dinner. At the venue, he went into the men's room with Josh Bennigan as escort. Butch was waiting there, and the two men exchanged clothes. Though Butch was slow-moving and a little overwhelmed, his natural charm covered the weaknesses. Putting on the wig and glasses Butch had worn coming in, Tanner left the building by a side door to be whisked away to an airport and a flight to Alaska.

When Kim saw the real President Mandell the next day, she tried to gauge how damaged he was. His voice was slightly weak, but since he was no longer stumping, he had little need to project. As Tanner had done, he wore makeup around his left eye to simulate a healing bruise. His limp was explained by the supposed fall in the shower. "When I hit my face, I also whacked my ankle on the lip," he told reporters in a joking tone. "Now I walk like my grandpa used to on days his arthritis acted up."

That was it for the physical after-effects, but Ruth admitted to some mental glitches. "He's very emotional," she confided, "and his memory isn't great."

"But he's seeing the doctor?"

"Dr. Chalmers was here this morning. He's pleased with Butch's progress."

Gavin Croft seemed to think their secret drew them closer, but Kim felt just the opposite. Though he was hailed as a political genius among Butch's staff, Croft's prim manner and greased-back hair repelled her. She disliked the way the lawyer slunk around the White House, appearing without warning, observing everything and everyone, and filing information away for later use. He brought on the same feeling tent caterpillars had in her childhood, when they seemed to wait in the trees overhead for the right moment to drop into her hair.

Croft's buddy Josh Bennigan was almost as creepy to be around, though he was no caterpillar. Bennigan brought to mind a terra cotta warrior statue she'd seen in a museum. He stood apart from others whenever possible, silent and stiff, and Kim couldn't escape the notion that he was capable of pulling out a sword and strike off a head without a second's hesitation.

Oddly, Croft and Ruth had bonded during the crisis. Ruth treated the Chief of Staff as a trusted friend, and while Butch dozed at his desk, the two discussed what should be done next. When they were alone, Kim hinted that she found Croft's underhanded methods objectionable, but Ruth made a dismissive gesture. "He's objective, Kimmie. While people like you wonder what *should* be done, Croft sees what *can* be done, and he does it."

Overall, Kim was pleased to be part of an administration attacking America's problems head on. Ruth was everything a First Lady should be, dignified but warm, proper but not prudish. Already she was being compared to the best of her predecessors. It was said she had Jackie Kennedy's style, Barbara Bush's likability, Hillary Clinton's energy. Kim was proud of her sister.

But she had concerns. Never fond of planning and strategizing, Butch was even less interested after his stroke. "Write it up," he'd tell Croft with a careless wave, whether that meant preparing a speech, drafting an executive order, or building a budget. "I'll say the words." Almost inevitably, staff turned to Mrs. Mandell for guidance; in fact, the President often encouraged them to do so. Fearful of stirring up the old criticism that Butch delegated too much and too often, Ruth initiated a stern code of conduct. No one was to speak to the press unofficially, not even to mention what Butch had for lunch. Breaking the code was cause for dismissal. *We must be above reproach,* the email outlining the rule read. *Only by our good example can Americans learn to trust the government again.*

A cadre headed by Ruth met every morning before the President awoke to hammer out the day's announcements and actions. When it was time to speak on a given topic, Butch learned his "lines," with Ruth as his coach and Croft a stand-in for reporters, Congress members, or experts on a given topic. Croft never went easy on his boss, but Butch took it as a game, turning challenging questions into jokes and providing glib responses. Butch came alive when cameras focused on him, and Kim couldn't help imagining him as a parrot, with beautiful plumage, clever phrases, and almost complete indifference to what he said.

Over the months of the campaign, Kim had become fond of the Vice President-Elect, Carroll Stockwell. A long-time senator who'd left his party in disgust a few years earlier, Stockwell had accepted Butch's (possibly Ruth's) invitation to join the Unity Project in hopes of healing the nation's divisions. After their morning work sessions, Ruth often sent Kim to meet with Stockwell, and the two of them worked out which events he would handle as the President-elect's representative. It became their habit to have brunch together in a corner of his office, where Stockwell kept a coffeepot and a microwave oven. He always had a selection of excellent pastries sent up from the White House kitchen each morning, and Kim found them irresistible, though she often bemoaned the calorie count.

Stockwell treated her more like a daughter than a co-worker, and since his tall frame and foggy voice reminded her of her father, she didn't mind. Insisting she had nothing to worry about in the weight department, he plied her with cream-filled buns while she informed him on matters Presidential. Over cups of specialty coffee, he also chided her for not dating. "You need to find a good man, Kim," he would admonish. "You can't keep mooning over that bum who went to Australia or wherever." She always agreed and then changed the subject. While she didn't mourn the loss of "the bum," she wasn't ready to play the dating game again. Eligible bachelors abounded in the White House, but she suspected most of them saw her mainly as a conduit to the President.

Butch's old friend Morris Blake pursued her too, though he was no bachelor. Smart, attractive, and persistent, Kim had the distinct impression that every time he looked at her, Blake was imagining her naked.

It was relaxing to spend time with Carroll Stockwell, who had no ulterior motive for being her friend. While Stockwell was laid back, Kim disagreed with Ruth's description of him as "dumb." Surprisingly unambitious for a politician, he'd sensed from the first that the President's real sidekick was and always would be his wife. Vice-President Stockwell, known as "Cary," seemed content to make whatever appearances were asked of him and otherwise remain in the background. He was, Ruth opined at one point, perfect for the job of VP.

On the first of February, Kim was surprised to find a voicemail from Drew McMahon on her phone. *Kim, it has occurred to me that suing for damages because a neighbor's tree drops acorns in a client's yard isn't what I imagined when I half-killed myself to get through law school. I could use some time away, and I was wondering what exactly you had in mind for me to do to help Nettie.*

She hesitated before contacting him. Did she still want to know Nettie's reason for murdering Caleb? Yes, she decided. Calling Drew, she navigated through the pleasantries and then said, "I want to know about Caleb's life before he came to live with his mother." She wriggled her shoulders to loosen the tension that crept up the back of her neck. "I'll pay your base hourly rate and any expenses you incur." After a beat she said, "I'm not sure what we'll learn, but I wish I'd done more for her at the time it happened."

"Then we'll do what we can now," McMahon said. "I'll be in touch."

Tracking down Caleb Green's grandmother was more difficult than McMahon expected. Without Nettie's help, it was like tossing pebbles at a puddle in the dark, but he kept at it while he wrapped up a few old cases. In mid-February, a pebble hit its mark, and he called Kim. "I've got the grandmother's name and address. If you're okay with it, I'd like to go to Arizona and talk to whoever I can find that knew her."

"You're a one-man office," Kim protested. "You'd have to close up shop."

"Hey, it's February in Michigan. If it's warmer there, it'll be worth the trip."

Two days later Drew crawled out of his rental car and stretched his cramped legs. It was a long way from Sterling Heights, Michigan, to Finerville, Arizona, and he'd begun to doubt the directions given by his rental car's GPS. On a dusty road, he stopped to look around, seeing acres and acres of land that was hot, dry, and starkly rural. Squinting against the burning sun, he scanned the horizon, which seemed bleached of color and empty of life. Only moments after leaving the A/C, his skin felt parched and stretched. Shading his hand, he turned until he saw a low roof some distance to his right. Getting back into the car, he drove toward it.

The place stood a half mile off the road, its walls so long unpainted that its original color was unknowable. A few dilapidated outbuildings flanked it, animal shelters with no current purpose. On the hard-packed driveway sat a pickup that something heavy had dropped on, caving the sides of the bed inward and twisting the tailgate so it had to be tied closed.

A woman answered his knock, stocky, dark-haired, wearing what appeared to be a permanently irritated expression. Melissa Tillotson had been suggested by the school's elementary principal as the only remaining person who'd known Caleb well. "He and Melissa rode the bus together every day," she'd told Drew. "Neither had any friends, but they were…I guess the word would be *allies*."

The woman who'd been Caleb Green's ally waited in distrustful silence for her unexpected visitor to explain himself. In her dull, dark eyes, Drew saw neither intelligence nor interest. "I'm looking for people who knew Florence and Caleb Smithers," he said, "The school gave me your name."

"Yeah?"

He made a quick assessment. "I'm willing to pay for your time."

"How much?"

"A hundred dollars, if what you have to say helps me out." When she frowned, he added, "They're both dead, so you don't have to worry about blowback."

"Caleb's dead?"

"Over a year now."

As Melissa pulled the door open, it ground against the warped wooden floor. "Come in." She didn't wait to see if he followed but went down a narrow hallway. "The place is messy, but I like it this way."

The house was beyond messy. A narrow path wound through waist-high piles of stuff, none of which seemed to be in use. It was simply there. She led him from one room to the next, all equally full, and they finally came to a dinette table set against a sliding glass door that probably hadn't been opened in years. Boxes stacked against it almost obscured the view. There were two chairs at the table, one piled with clothing. Tillotson moved the stack to the floor and tilted her head to indicate he should sit. "My momma was big on garage sales," she said, taking the other chair. "I got the bug from her."

"Sounds interesting," Drew lied.

If she noticed his false tone, she didn't comment on it. "I like owning things somebody else used to have."

"I'm Andrew McMahon." He passed a business card across the table to her. "You grew up in this house, right?"

"It's mine now. Momma and Daddy both died." She glanced at a photo that hung on the wall, a younger version of herself with two tired-looking adults. "Daddy had Parkinson's, so that took a long time." Picking up a rooster-shaped toothpick dispenser, she selected one. "As soon as he was gone, Momma got sick with the cancer. They say that happens a lot, from the stress." She removed something from a back tooth with the pick and then set it at one side of her mouth. "By the time she died, I was kind of past the idea of leaving."

"I'm sorry about your parents." Drew gave it a beat. "Caleb was your friend?"

"We hung out." Her eyes turned dreamy. "When I was little, I thought we were s'pose to be with each other, like Forrest Gump and Jenny."

The comparison to Jenny suggested a disturbing image of her childhood. "Where did Caleb and his grandmother live?"

"If you go by the road, it's a mile from here, but over that ridge, it's not that far." She pointed, and Drew leaned forward to see out the narrow slice of unobstructed glass. "We used to meet in that little woody spot along the top."

"You were about ten?"

"When he left, yeah, but we started back in kindergarten. We had the longest bus ride of any kids. Caleb sat with me every day, and we pretended we didn't hear the others making fun of us."

"Why did they do that?"

She waved away her childhood misery. "I had holey pants and that. Caleb's grandma made him wear button-up white dress shirts and a tie."

"And the other kids made fun."

"Yeah. When Aunt Florence died, Caleb had to go live with his mom. After that I was mostly by myself at school."

"Tell me about Caleb."

Her gaze dropped to the table. "He could do stuff."

"Such as?"

"Catch tree lizards. Pile rocks into pretty stacks…what do they call them?"

"Cairns."

"Yeah. We had a bunch of those." She paused to choose a memory. "In school, Caleb beat everybody when they had races." In her voice Drew heard the leftover hero-worship of a lonely little girl. Her tone hardened as she added, "He used to say when he got big enough, he'd kill Daddy, so he couldn't come in my bedroom at night anymore."

Having no idea what to do with that information, Drew asked, "What was Caleb's home life like?"

"Fine." Her tone was breezy, but he saw darkness gather behind her eyes.

"The hundred is conditional, Ms. Tillotson. You have to be honest."

"Oh." Possibly to give herself time to consider that, the woman asked, "Do you want a glass of water or…water?"

"No but thank you." She had started to rise from the chair, but she sat back down. Drew waited expectantly, holding her gaze.

Licking her lips, she finally said, "People think people are one way, you know, but lots of times that ain't true."

That quizzical statement lay between them for a while. McMahon waited. Swallowing, Melissa finally said, "Aunt Florence, everybody called her. She was big in the church. She took casseroles to houses where somebody died. She wrote letters to the paper about the meaning of Christmas and Easter and how we shouldn't celebrate them as days off or times to get gifts and candy. We should remember what a holiday represents."

"A pillar of the community. I heard that in town."

Melissa's face twisted. "What you didn't hear is when no one else was around, Aunt Florence was different."

McMahon rubbed his neck. "Everyone I spoke to said good things about her."

"But you never talked to Caleb, did you?"

"Well, no. He was dead before I ever heard of him."

She gave him a long, speculative look. "So why do you care now? Why are you offering money to hear about him?" Her eyes narrowed. "I ain't seen your money neither. You better not be lying about paying for my help, or I'll call the sheriff and tell him you made improper advances toward me."

Though McMahon guessed the sheriff was wise enough to know better, he took out two fifty-dollar bills Sliding one across the table, he kept his hand on the other. "Can you prove Florence abused her grandson?"

Her brow furrowed. "I know what Caleb told me." She sat up in her chair, as if hearing a voice in her head. "She didn't beat him or nothing, but Florence said her job was to teach Caleb to do right. She said if his faith was strong enough, he'd be a good man, like his dad never was."

"His dad."

"Virgil was a bad kid, I guess. Ran away, changed his name, never even called his mom until he got his girlfriend pregnant."

"Give me an example of this faith Caleb was supposed to develop."

"It was everything. Every single thing." Her eyes turned up as she recalled. "Once he got the flu. He felt awful, but his grandma believed sickness is all in a person's mind. 'If your faith is strong,' she told Caleb, 'you won't get sick.' He tried to be strong, but he couldn't help it. He threw up." Tillotson's gaze met Drew's. "Florence made him eat his own vomit. Said he had to show his body that he was stronger than any germs."

Drew's stomach roiled at the image. "Anything else?"

"She made him memorize Bible verses every day. If he couldn't recite them perfect, he got no supper. Once she saw his shoelace was untied, and she locked him in the corn crib, even though it was awful cold that night. She said only bad boys go around looking sloppy."

"No one stopped her?"

Melissa gave him a look. "Who would do that?"

"Social services? The school counsellor?"

"Aunt Florence told Caleb nobody wanted him. His dad was dead. His mother gave him up. She told awful stories about foster care, how they'd rape him every night, because they're all child molesters."

"Didn't anyone ever tell him the truth?"

"Who'd you believe when you were little, your family or some adult with coffee breath and dandruff?" Tillotson tucked two strands of hair behind her ears. "That's why I never told on Daddy. I knew they'd take me away and I'd never see Momma again."

Drew was again at a loss for words, but she went on. "We both hated school, but Caleb told me just do enough to keep the teachers off our back." Her eyes hardened. "He was right. If you do their stupid homework, nobody cares if you're okay or not." She turned toward the window and the ridge beyond it, perhaps remembering the two misfit kids who'd met there. "Everyone said we were shy, but when it was just him and me, we talked a lot."

"Did Caleb ever stand up to his grandmother?"

She shook her head, and her expression indicated she didn't think that would have been possible.

McMahon had long suspected Caleb was mentally disturbed, which explained, even if it didn't justify, his mother shooting him in his bed. If his grandmother's mistreatment had made him hate women, he might well have transferred that hatred to Nettie. "Did Caleb ever hurt you, Ms. Tillotson?"

She eyed the other fifty. "He did stuff that scared me, but no, he never hurt me."

"Tell me what he did that scared you."

She shook her head, unwilling, but Drew shifted the fifty a little toward her. When she spoke again, her voice was low and flat. "One time he brought this kitten he found along the road." A smile changed her face from sulky to sweet. "He let me hold it for a while, and it was real soft. I said maybe Daddy would let me keep it, but Caleb said we had to kill it…and then he did."

Drew noted the omission of details. "How did he kill the kitten?"

"You don't want to know." She pressed her fists against her eyes. "Sometimes at night it's like a movie playing in my head, and I can't make it stop." Setting both hands on the table, she extended them toward him. "Caleb was my only friend, but after that I was scared of him. It wasn't much later that Aunt Florence died. Caleb didn't want to be with his mom, but he said maybe she had money. Maybe he'd be moving to a place with air conditioning and a swimming pool."

"Did you ever hear from him again?"

"No." Her head sank almost to her chest. "I missed having somebody to talk to, but honestly, I was kinda relieved when Caleb moved away."

Chapter Twenty-Six

Ruth-February 7

"Nathan Tanner is dead." Kim burst into the office in the East Wing where Ruth sat at her desk, a lamp on either side to light her work.

Looking up with a frown, she said, "Tanner? Really?"

Kim handed Ruth her phone, and she skimmed the article. "He fell overboard?"

"In the night," Kim said. "His body washed ashore a day later."

Ruth made a *tsk* sound. "Such a shame when a person's talent is wasted by addiction."

"You think he fell because he was drunk?"

Ruth handed the phone back. "That seems to me a reasonable assumption."

"When he was…here, Tanner told me that he intended to stop drinking."

Ruth clicked on "Print," and a whirr sounded from a spot below her desktop. "Addicts always say that. I suppose a few actually do it." Taking up a few sheets of paper, she passed them to Kim. "Will you look this over and correct any errors you find?"

"Sure." Kim scanned the first paragraph and then looked up, eyes wide. "The President is ending programs for single mothers?"

"To cut fraud." Ruth explained. "Women can't keep having babies so they can live on welfare."

"Hasn't that 'welfare mothers cheat the system' story been discredited?"

Ruth rolled her eyes, but just a little. "Can you honestly say you haven't stood behind a woman at checkout who bought steaks and Pepsi with her Bridge card?"

"What does that prove?" Kim's tone turned argumentative. "Statistics—"

"It happens every day, Kimmie, all over the nation." Clicking the cam of her ball point pen, Ruth added instructions at the top of a document. "Voters are sick of welfare moms with brand-new cell phones and mani-pedis every week."

Kim scanned the sheet again. "How does this line up with your contention that kids do better if their mothers stay home with them?"

Ruth paused, unsure if Kim was ready to hear her argument. "It's best if women with children don't work outside the home."

"How can a woman take care of her kids if she has no job and no government support?"

"With a husband who has a job." Kim's mouth opened, but Ruth raised a hand. "For years we've been telling women they can 'have it all,' but that's not true. Women who want children should have them, but if they do, they should commit to raising them. Mom should be there when the kids come home each day. She should be in contact with teachers, so school and home function together for the children's benefit. Mom should monitor her kids' behavior, keep them out of gangs and on the right path." Ruth spread her hands. "Can you honestly say there's anything wrong with that?"

"What about women who want to use their talents for more than child-rearing?"

Ruth set the pen aside and met Kim's gaze. "Well, a woman who loves learning might home-school her kids. Those with a mind for business might open home-based stores. The internet is perfect for that." As Kim's expression turned darker, Ruth finished, "Our children are important, Kimmie. Everything else has to take second place."

Kim waved the papers she held. "Yet you'd cut support for those children."

Ruth sighed. This was going to be harder than she'd thought. "It's biology at its most basic. Women are meant to have babies and nurture them. Men are meant to provide for their families."

"What if a woman wants to be a doctor or rocket scientist?"

"Then she should be one. But we give up some things to get other things."

"You're saying a woman can't have kids if she wants a career." Kim's cheeks reddened, and her voice quivered.

"The finer points will be worked out by each couple, but yes. We believe women should make a choice: work or family."

"But—"

Ruth didn't wait for Kim's next objection. "I'm sure there would be men willing to stay home with the children. If a woman is more economically viable, then that makes sense. As long as there's a parent on duty in the home." Standing, she went to the window and looked at the snow-topped bushes, the monochrome lawn, and the sidewalks lined with piled snow. "For too long in this country, we've let exceptions make the rules. It's time to set our standards by what the majority wants, not what misfits and outcasts demand."

Kim's expression revealed that she was still upset, but instead of arguing, she made a muttered excuse about things to do and left, her back stiff with tension. Disheartened that someone so close to her was unable to see what she saw clearly, Ruth bit her lip. A few seconds later she went back to work. Her sister would understand in time, when the plan was in place and results became known.

Ruth felt the Mandell administration had found the pulse of the nation and begun responding to its needs. While she was less sure of the right way with international politics, she'd found a solution that worked well on two fronts. She'd handed most foreign policy duties over to the Vice President, Cary Stockwell. He'd served on the Foreign Affairs Committee for years, so he knew how things should go, and as a bonus, his duties there kept Stockwell out of the President's business.

Ruth glanced at the clock. Almost nine. Hurrying upstairs, she arrived to find Butch on the sofa and Dr. Chalmers taking his leave. A smile lit Butch's face. "Doc says I'm doing good, Ruthie."

"Doing *well*, Sweetheart," she corrected. "I'm thrilled to hear it. Mary made the muffins you like. Why don't you get a few for the doctor to take with him?"

As Butch headed for the kitchen, Ruth asked, "How is he really, doctor?"

His expression revealed reluctance. "I wish I had better news, ma'am." He hesitated before delivering his diagnosis. "It isn't the stroke that's holding Butch back. He has early-onset Alzheimer's."

Ruth had suspected it for some time, but it was still a shock to hear her fears confirmed. Butch repeated himself and often couldn't come up with a word or name that should have been familiar to him. Behind his eyes was a look of confusion. Though he smiled and pretended to know what was going on, Ruth knew he was frequently lost. "What can be done?"

"There are medications that slow progression, and we'll get him started on them right away." He met her gaze. "But that won't be enough. President Mandell can't meet the demands of his office."

"If you're willing to treat his illness and keep quiet about it, Eric, we can still make this work."

He licked his lips. "I'm not sure you understand. He—"

"Great things are under way," Ruth interrupted. "We can't let the failure of one brain get in the way."

"Even if that man is the President?"

Ruth bit back an impatient reply. "Do you trust me, Doctor?"

"Of course."

"And you know my husband trusts me, yes?"

"He does."

"The things Butch promised the nation can be done, despite this…problem. Butch has a gift for speaking persuasively. He can read from a teleprompter. He'll be watched over, guided, and protected. We—you and I and the multitudes who support Butch—can't let his dream die."

The doctor began putting his medical equipment into a leather bag, perhaps to give himself time to think. Closing the clasps with twin clicks, he said, "There will come a time when his condition can't be hidden anymore."

"I understand, but until then, we move forward." Meaningfully she added, "Your reward will of course be commensurate with your role."

Butch returned from the kitchen, carrying a box and wearing a sheepish grin. "Mary gave me a dozen, Doc. If there are only eleven in there now, I expect you to treat the case of the disappearing muffin as a state secret."

Chapter Twenty-Seven

Kim-February 8

When Drew McMahon called, Kim almost let it go to voicemail. She had a zillion things to do, and she'd been feeling guilty about sending him to dig into Caleb Green's past. Ruth wouldn't approve. For sure Nettie wouldn't approve. Though Dr. Foeller would be professionally interested in what he found out, even she might balk at what could only be termed snooping.

But she wanted to know. "Hello, Drew."

"Hi, Kim. How's the weather in D.C.?"

"Gray as gunmetal and rainy. It's been ticking at my window since five a.m. How about you?"

"I'd welcome some of your rain. This place is like those desert scenes in old movies, bone dry with wavy stuff in the distance. I'm at a motel you wouldn't send your worst enemy to. I'm pretty sure the cockroaches have fleas."

She chuckled. "If you're trying to save on expenses, it's not necessary."

"Nope. I'm in the middle of Abso-Nowhere, U.S.A. Only motel for miles."

"You found the grandmother's place."

"Finerville, Arizona. I have to tell you, there's nothing finer about it."

"And what have you learned?"

"Caleb was a mediocre student. Only one teacher remembered him, and she didn't have much to say except that he dressed funny. Because of his clothes, the other kids called him names like Pee Wee Herman and Professor Frink. The pastor at their church remembered the grandmother, Aunt Florence, as a good woman, though he admits that her views were a little to the right of Joseph McCarthy's. Caleb attended church and Sunday school regularly. Pastor was happy that Florence had such an upright grandson, since her boy Virgil was a disappointment to everyone."

"I guess a woman beater does qualify as a disappointment."

"Right." Drew paused as a semi passed, making it difficult to hear. "The sheriff wasn't around back then, but I asked him to look back in the records. Lots on Virgil, from drunken brawling to selling cocaine. Nothing on Caleb, but I guess that's to be expected when he left so young."

"I can tell from your voice there's more."

"Hey, you don't even know me that well yet."

"Still."

"Yes. Caleb's closest friend tells a different story about Aunt Florence. She says the old woman made Caleb's life hell."

"Oh, no. Why didn't the authorities take him away from her?"

"No one knew. When she was diagnosed with diabetes, she wouldn't take insulin or change her habits. She told the doctor she trusted God more than she trusted him. One day while Caleb was at school, she went into a coma and died."

"You said she made Caleb's life hell."

"With disastrous results. The friend saw him kill a kitten, and it was...bad."

"Oh, God." Kim ran a hand through her hair, forgetting she was supposed to appear with the First Lady in a few minutes. "This could help Nettie, right? If he was disturbed and she had reasons for what she did…"

"I wanted to bring Caleb's background in, his drinking and inability to keep a job, as part of her defense. She wouldn't let me."

"She blames herself for him being…whatever he was."

"Probably." After a brief silence, Drew asked, "What should I do now?"

"Go home." Kim spoke firmly, though her voice held traces of regret. "Send me your notes and a bill for your time and travel. Once I've had a chance to think it through, I'll decide what to do with what you learned."

After a second silence, Drew said, "We could discuss it in person some time."

She almost dismissed the suggestion, and later she wondered why she hadn't. Life was crazy busy, and she wasn't looking for entanglements of any kind. She told herself it was for Nettie, that Drew was someone she could talk to about her sister. He wouldn't tell anyone. And for some reason, she remembered his blue eyes and the scent he used, like fresh air and birch trees. "Let me get caught up a little, and I'll call you."

"Great."

As she put down the phone, Kim felt a flutter of happiness. Maybe a friend was what she needed right now, even if he seemed interested in being more than that.

Chapter Twenty-Eight

Ruth-February 10

"Mrs. Mandell." Ruth turned to see Morris Blake, Butch's Attorney General, hurrying to catch up with her in the hallway. "Can I talk with you a sec?"

"I'm honored, Mr. A.G." She made a mock bow, grinning, since she'd known Morris long before he became Attorney General. He'd been married to her former roommate Molly briefly, but they'd both moved on. Molly was now on Husband #3. Leading the way into her office, Ruth indicated two chairs in a corner that were less formal than the desk area. As Blake sat, she turned on a torchiere lamp between the chairs before seating herself. "How are things with you, Morris?"

"Fine, fine." His expression belied the words, and his hands fumbled at his tie. "I'm sorry to be blunt, but do you think the President is…all right?"

Ruth took a second to prepare herself for a conversation she'd been dreading. "Of course he is, Morris. He had an exhausting campaign, and now he faces the work of doing what we promised the American people. It's not surprising that he's a little forgetful."

"Ruth, he's made some serious errors lately."

She smoothed her hair. "I don't know what you mean."

"Yesterday he called me Martin. He told some of us he intends to take a week off at the end of the month to go duck hunting." Blake hesitated, but then finished doggedly, "It's like he doesn't know he's President."

Ruth leaned forward and put a hand on Blake's arm. "Morris, you sound positively paranoid."

"You don't think Butch is…distracted?"

"Overwhelmed, maybe, but he has the constitution of an ox. He's adjusting to the demands of a very difficult job."

"All right, then." Blake stood. "I should go. I've got lots to see to myself." He paused. "There are some pretty serious legal challenges to some of the changes we're making."

"People often react badly when the old ways are tossed out, Morris. Things will settle down."

"I hope so."

As soon as he was gone, Ruth hurried to Gavin Croft's office. He was alone, his body bent toward his computer monitor and his face screwed tight with concentration. Seeing her in the doorway, he rose and gave her his full attention. "Morris Blake just came in to ask if Butch is okay."

"How did you answer?"

"I said he's fine, but I could tell he didn't believe me." She folded her hands, pressing her thumbs together. "Morris has been Butch's friend forever. He knows there's something wrong."

"Which is why I wouldn't have given him the A.G. job." Croft's objection had been overruled by others, including Ruth, who felt that since Blake was so strongly associated with Butch, it would have been suspicious if he were overlooked. Croft adjusted his necktie. "I'm afraid he'll have to go." He watched Ruth as he spoke, probably fearing she'd object.

Instead she asked, "You can arrange that?"

"I can if you support me with the President."

Doubtful, she asked, "How would it be done?"

"Blake has…carnal weaknesses, as you've no doubt heard. We'll put him in a position where he can either resign his post or be exposed as a sexual predator. When he makes his decision, it will help if the President accepts it."

"What if Blake goes public with his claim that Butch is incompetent?"

"The indiscretions I mentioned will ensure that he keeps quiet." Croft tapped on the desktop with a finger. "You might prepare the President to okay the person I propose as Blake's replacement."

"Who will that be?"

"I have Kenneth Betzer in mind."

"I've never heard of him."

"He's fairly obscure, but Judge Betzer is ambitious. He's never received the recognition he believes he deserves."

"Will he support the Unity Project's goals?"

Croft's smile was wolfish. "He will if we make him Attorney General of the United States." Turning, Croft pulled open a drawer and began sorting through files. "Betzer is exceptionally talented at formulating legal arguments that achieve a specific result."

"I see."

Croft must have sensed doubt, because he said, "Sometimes those around us can't take the long view, but once we move our agenda ahead, they'll see the good that results."

It seemed at times that Croft could read her mind. "We only want what's best for everyone."

Sorting through the papers on his desk, Croft found the sheet he'd sought and gave it to Ruth. "Here's information on Betzer you can use to familiarize the President with his qualifications."

If he remembers, Ruth thought. "I'll see to it."

She turned to go, but Croft said, "Perhaps we might address the concern Blake mentioned."

Ruth's spine spasmed, but she hid it by reaching out and adjusting her paperweight. Was Croft having second thoughts about supporting a disabled President whose wife made decisions for him? Meeting his gaze, she said, "Of course, Mr. Croft."

He clasped his hands at his waist. "The President's recovery has been slower than we hoped."

Butch complained frequently of being too tired to meet with committees or listen to briefings. More than once, he'd become lost in the White House. Ruth noticed that Croft invented excuses to walk with him, tacitly guiding Butch to his destinations. He'd also begun greeting people by name, which she suspected was his way of refreshing the President's memory.

Whenever possible, Ruth tried to be where Butch was. She accompanied him to policy meetings, despite raised eyebrows and discreet sniffs of disapproval. When foreign dignitaries visited the Oval Office, she sent Kim to have tea with the wives while she stayed for conversations about trade and defense. For the most part, Ruth remained silent, evincing polite interest in the proceedings but no intent to participate. Later she explained the important concepts to Butch, though more and more, his interest wandered. He'd never really wanted the Presidency, Ruth knew, and now that his brain didn't function properly, he rebelled at the work it required.

The bright spot was Butch's love of attention. He was always willing to stand before the cameras and act the part of the nation's leader. If they kept his speeches short and let others explain the fine points, they muddled through.

Still, the time had come for her and Croft to admit their mutual problem openly and plot—no, she corrected—*plan* what could be done about it. "He has Alzheimer's," she said, and Croft's soft gasp revealed that she'd confirmed his fears. "Only you, I, and his doctor know. We need to protect him so his work can be completed."

"Others have noticed his confusion," Croft said. "One woman on staff suggested, rather timidly, that we look into Article Twenty-five. I told her that was both disloyal and ridiculous." He paused, meeting her eye. "With your help, the President can continue to eradicate the problems we've failed to address for decades."

For a moment Ruth remained silent. She wasn't naive enough to believe Croft's allegiance was without personal motivation. On his own, with his watery voice and rat-like face, Croft would never sway the hearts of voters. But he liked being the power behind the throne. While she doubted he truly believed in their cause, Ruth guessed he would support whatever—whoever—helped him keep his position of power.

Was it right to use a flawed but capable man to achieve her ends, or should she let the plans she and Butch had made fail? If Croft helped her make excellent ideas into workable reality, she decided, where was the harm? Her motives were pure, even if his weren't.

"Who has concerns about the President other than Morris Blake, Mr. Croft?"

"The staffer I mentioned now works for the ambassador to Liechtenstein." He waited for her to smile at his cleverness. When Ruth obliged him, he went on in a more serious tone. "More worrisome is our head of Homeland Security, Daniel Stone, who's more and more outspoken on the President's lapses. Yesterday, I met with him privately and asked that he keep such thoughts to himself. I believe I convinced him things will improve, but it might be wise to consider replacing him as well."

"Two top men leaving the administration within months of Butch's swearing in? That won't look good."

"True." Croft considered. "What if we—I mean the President, of course—put a trusted man in as Stone's second-in-command? At best, he might convince Stone that the President is fine. At the least, he could keep us informed as to Stone's intentions."

"Who could do that?"

"Secret Service experience has given Josh Bennigan sufficient background for the post, and we know that he's loyal to President Mandell—to both of you." He paused. "Some of us recognize that your contributions are as important as your husband's." Though the remark was ingratiating, Ruth couldn't help but smile. It was nice to have her efforts applauded, even by a sycophant like Croft.

This was their moment to attack the nation's problems and fix them, and Ruth would not let it slip away due to her husband's weakness.

"All right then, Gavin. Let's talk frankly about how we can protect the President from embarrassment."

Chapter Twenty-Nine

Nettie-February 17

"How is the greenhouse project going?" Dr. Foeller asked at the beginning of a session.

Nettie glanced out the window, where threatening gray skies contrasted starkly with Foeller's peaceful office. The greenhouse was around the corner, at the side of the building, and she wished she were there now, shifting pots and pinching off dead leaves. Still, approval of her request for a chance to grow things had come with a tacit expectation that she'd be more forthcoming about her past. "It's good. Been a while since I stuck my hands in dirt."

"I understand you and your son had a truck garden."

"I moved us to the farm where I grew up when…when the chance came along." As she spoke, Nettie thought of her parents and the ruin she'd made of their lives and their property. It was like a physical blow, but she forced herself to go on. "I thought it would be good for Caleb to learn how to grow things."

"And did he take to it?"

She chuckled grimly. "The only part he liked was the selling."

"He preferred interacting with people to tending plants."

"He enjoyed cheating our customers." Nettie ran a hand along the back of her neck. "I had to watch him like a hawk."

"How does one cheat while selling produce?"

"He'd take a quart of squashed berries and scatter fresh ones on top. He'd use the old thumb-on-the-scale trick. Or I'd hear him tell customers that our fruit was grown from heritage seeds, which it wasn't."

"Why did he do that, do you think?"

"Caleb liked putting things over on others." Nettie picked at some dirt under her fingernail. "When I would try to explain why that was wrong, he'd say, 'Come on, Mom. It's fun.'" Distressed at the stab of disloyalty the revelation caused her, she added, "Kids don't see things the way adults do. Anyway, I'm glad to have the chance to grow things again."

Though Nettie thought of the greenhouse as hers, she shared it with two other inmates, Olin Dobbs, and Pearl Rivers. Olin was a man of few words, while Pearl seldom shut up. Olin watched Nettie carefully and copied what she did, while Pearl seemed interested in nothing except escaping the watchful eyes of the guards.

Though Martha's Place was a prison, the feeling of being incarcerated was diminished where possible. Staff all wore the same uniform, with only an arm patch to differentiate guards from cooks, nurses, and cleaners. Guards carried Tasers in discreet holsters that might have held cell phones instead of weapons. The enclosure wall was lined with gracefully decorative (though short) shrubs, and the watchtowers hinted more of Tintagel than Sing-Sing. Inmates wore either sweatpants or shorts paired with t-shirts or hoodies. The fact that "PRISONER" was stenciled in large print on each piece was only fair, Nettie admitted.

The new greenhouse, a silvery polycarbonate and aluminum structure, sat east of the main house, about thirty yards from the kitchen door. Two modules joined made an area 8x24, and a ragtag assortment of tables gleaned from secondhand shops sat along either side. "You can grow food for us," Foeller had commented. "That way we all benefit."

And they did. The kitchen staff was pleased when quick-growing vegetables like bok choy, mustard greens, and radishes were ready in only a few weeks. Soon Kim got vegetables to take home when she visited: baby potatoes, a bag of fingerling carrots, and even a pint of strawberries, which Nettie put in a tissue box lined with toilet paper to protect them from bruising.

For the first time in over a year, Nettie had work she was enthusiastic about. She drew diagrams, so plants sat in places best suited to their needs. She plotted how to rotate her stock over the seasons so there would always be fresh food available. Once, with her hands buried in potting soil, she caught herself humming a tuneless melody, as her dad had done as he worked around the farm.

Pearl was a trial. While she insisted she'd learned "everything" about growing things, from her parents' full-time gardener, she had neither knowledge nor experience with plants, and she did her work so haphazardly that Nettie often redid it after she left.

Olin was different. He was there each morning when Nettie arrived, waiting for her to tell him what to do. At first, he said little except, "How much fertilizer on these, Miz Nettie?" Over time, he began talking a little when Pearl wasn't around. At first Nettie struggled to decipher his speech due to a combination of factors: his Virginia tidewater accent, his unfamiliar terminology (like calling bags *pokes)*, and his unfortunate tendency to mumble. Olin called her "Miz Nettie," which she hoped wasn't because she was white. She preferred to think of it as respect for her age, which was twice his.

Though she mostly remained separate from other prisoners, Nettie grew to like Olin, which led to curiosity as to his reason for being in prison. She'd never heard anyone ask a newcomer, "What are you in for?" like they did in movies, so she kept their communication focused on work. Still, Olin didn't seem violent or prone to bursts of anger. She couldn't imagine him hurting anyone. He was certainly no white-collar criminal, not an embezzler or hedge-fund cheat. Since his crime had interested Dr. Foeller enough to bring him here, there were probably surprising elements. As they spoke of bean plants and onion sets, Nettie found herself hoping he wasn't guilty of something she'd hate, like child molestation or mail-bombing strangers.

Pearl's crime was not a secret. While she dumped potting soil everywhere and set trays in the wrong section of the greenhouse, she bragged about enlisting her boyfriend's help with burgling her neighbors' house when they went on vacation. She and Charley had giggled the whole time they were inside, she reported, but the fun ended the next day, when they learned there was video of them leaving the premises with bags of stolen goods. "He blabbed everything to the cops and got a reduced sentence," Pearl told Nettie and Olin. "Why did I ever believe that creep loved me?"

To convince the trustees at Martha's Place to let their daughter serve her sentence there instead of a state facility, Pearl's wealthy parents had made a large donation. "Dr. Foeller isn't thrilled about having me here," Pearl said. "She rambles on and on about how I need to recognize the property rights of others." Since Nettie noticed that Pearl helped herself to her cigarettes whenever she felt like it, it was clear the counselling sessions hadn't yet borne fruit.

Chapter Thirty

Kim-March 17

Kim was setting name cards at places around a table in the Old Family Dining Room, where the First Lady would soon lunch with a delegation of female attorneys. Lit by sconces and chandeliers, the room glowed with tradition and class. While the event was mostly social, Ruth had commented that she'd probably get an earful about Butch's adjustments to the court system.

To dispose of the backlog of cases that plagued the nation's courts, President Mandell had begun appointing "tertiary jurists," functionaries charged with ferreting out frivolous lawsuits and streamlining cases where the defendants were recidivists. A tertiary jurist had to okay a lawsuit before it could move into the court system. Those arrested for a crime they'd been convicted of previously went before a tertiary jurist, who made a ruling on the spot. The rulings were subject to appeal in a traditional court setting, but a defendant who lost his appeal got the maximum sentence. In addition, the attorney who filed the appeal was deemed ineligible to serve as a tertiary jurist in the future.

Many traditional judges expressed outrage at what they saw as a perversion of the system, and late-night comics and newspaper editorials scoffed at "Jurist Judy" courts. But Attorney General Blake, Solicitor General Keogh, and others held that the system was justifiable under the law. No one was influencing judges' decisions; they were simply reducing the number of cases they had to deal with. Accused criminals were heard by trained legalists, and if they disagreed with the verdict, the traditional process remained open to them.

Many lawyers supported the plan, likely because tertiary jurists would be chosen from their ranks. The legal field was overcrowded, and a steady paycheck from the government was a nice incentive, resulting in less need for ambulance-chasing.

Citizens approved of the new system as well. "For years, we've wasted the time and resources of our courts," a popular blogger argued. "This plan keeps the system moving, without crybabies and recidivists clogging things up."

The administration had also begun major changes to the nation's prison system. All minimum-security prisons were turning their focus to vocational education. Convicted criminals were tested on arrival, and from that came individual goals for rehabilitation, not a blanket sentence of *X* number of years. When inmates reached their goals, they were immediately eligible for parole. They weren't just dropped into society again, either. Deals were made with businesses, who monitored workers' behavior in exchange for their labor as well as preferred status with government contracts. Though it was too early in the program's existence to tell, the early results looked good. Kim saw possible red flags with employers serving as parole officers, but—

"Sorry." A deep voice interrupted her thought. "I didn't mean to bother you."

Kim turned to see a thin, dark-skinned young man in the doorway. He looked like he belonged in middle school, with a thin frame and black-rimmed glasses that hid most of his face. His suit was so new it almost crinkled, and a plain black necktie hinted he wanted desperately to appear more mature than he looked.

"You're fine," Kim told him. "I'm doing the seating for today's luncheon."

"I have the programs."

"Great. Set one on each plate, please, and leave the extras on the side table."

He nodded, obviously nervous. Stepping forward, he dropped some of the programs then hit a chair as he bent to retrieve them, almost upsetting a water glass. "I don't think we've met," Kim said. "I'm Kim Dailey."

Clearing his throat, he said, "Harley Stark."

"Are you new to the White House?"

"My third day."

"Well, it's nice to meet you, Harley." She asked the question commonly put to White House staffers. "Where's home?"

"Gatlinburg, Tennessee."

"I've heard it's beautiful there."

"We think so." Now that she'd heard a few words, she noticed the slight flattening of the young man's vowels. *Think* sounded more like *thank.*

"And what's your job here?"

"Mostly I do whatever Mr. Croft tells me to."

Kim refrained from expressing condolences. "I'm sure that's interesting."

Perhaps picking up on her hesitation, Stark grinned. "He's really smart."

"Yes." Unable to think of anything kind to say about Croft, Kim returned to her work. "And you're seeing the way the White House operates. That's exciting."

"It is, but I guess I've got a lot to learn." Drawing himself to a stiff posture, he mimicked Croft's pedantic tone. "'You should listen more and speak less, Mr. Stark.'"

His performance was spot on, and Kim studied the cards in her hand, hiding a smile. If Stark was learning to be discreet, it wasn't immediately obvious. "Listening is an excellent skill to develop when working in government."

"Yes," he agreed, "but when I *do* listen, I get in trouble for *that.*"

"How?" She was counting chairs and spoke more from politeness than real interest.

"My first day here, I was working in a corner, and I heard Mr. Croft and this Assistant Secretary of Something talking about a guy named Tanner. He seemed pretty important to them, so later, I asked Mr. Croft who that was. He got this down-his-nose look and accused me of eavesdropping." Raising his shoulders, Harley finished, "So am I supposed to listen when Croft talks or not?"

It took a second for the name to register. Why had they been discussing Nathan Tanner?

Unaware of her confusion, Stark continued moving around the table, setting a program atop each plate. "Do you like living in the White House, Ms. Dailey?"

Kim chuckled. "Sure. Where else would I meet a sultan on Tuesday and the quarterback for the Vikings on Wednesday?"

A thin voice made them both jump. "Aren't you supposed to be setting up for the President's meeting this afternoon, Mr. Stark?" Gavin Croft stood in the doorway, his face pinched with irritation.

"It's not until two," Stark replied. "I told Ms. Alba I'd run these down for her."

"Do you work for her or for President Mandell?"

Stark took a breath. "The President."

Feeling sorry for the kid, Kim said, "Mr. Stark would have been gone by now if I hadn't got him chatting about his hometown." To Stark she said, "It was so nice to meet you, Harley. Thanks for your help."

Croft frowned but said no more. He'd grown prickly with Kim lately, probably because she sometimes questioned his methods. He made no secret—at least when Ruth was absent—of his opinion that she was both naïve and nosy. Exchanges between them had become icily polite, and Kim noted with chagrin that when decisions were made, Ruth sided with Croft more often than with her.

In fact, Ruth had shifted from disliking Croft to defending him. "Butch is too friendly for his own good," she told Kim. "Gavin is very protective of the President." Kim knew that important people often used "attack dogs," to perform unpleasant tasks such as disciplining staff and putting enemies in their place. Still, Croft's delight in those tasks turned her stomach. What Ruth interpreted as protecting Butch, Kim saw as crushing anyone who disagreed with him.

"The room looks beautiful, Kimmie." They turned to see Ruth in the doorway. "Well, hello, Harley."

"Good morning, Mrs. Mandell."

"Did you find that place I told you about?"

His left hand moved to his opposite forearm, where Kim saw a dark spot mostly covered by his shirtsleeve. "Um, yes, ma'am. They said they can remove it."

"Good. I'm sure you'll be pleased once it's gone." Coming to his side, she put a hand on his shoulder. "We all make decisions we regret later, and tattoos are always in that category."

Stark's response lacked enthusiasm, but Ruth didn't seem to notice. Turning to Croft she said, "Can we look into giving the FCC more power over advertising, Gavin? There are misleading ads everywhere and they make me sick."

Kim detected the slightest hint of irritation in Croft's eyes, but what he said was, "What a good idea, Mrs. Mandell. I'll look into it and see what might be done."

"Thank you, Gavin. I was sure you'd help."

He inclined his head in what seemed like a bow. "I'm always amazed at the scope of your dedication to the American people."

Kim looked to Ruth, wondering if the man's toadying tone registered, but Ruth only smiled. Clearing his throat, Croft said, "If you ladies will excuse us, Mr. Stark and I have work to do." Giving Stark a meaningful look, he moved past Ruth and then stopped to wait for the young man to precede him down the hall.

When they were gone, Kim said, "Stark seems like a nice kid."

"I'm told he's very bright. His father represents Tennessee in Congress, and he was difficult about a certain vote until Gavin had the brilliant idea of offering his son a job at the White House."

"Tit for tat." Hearing her own tone, Kim knew she didn't sound approving.

Ruth patted her arm. "It's the way things work in this town, Kimmie."

"I suppose. I hope he does well."

"He'll learn." Ruth touched her own forearm absently. "That boy had "UT" inked onto his arm in big, bright orange letters." She shook her head. "Ah, youth, those years of cluelessness and poor decision-making."

Chapter Thirty-One

Ruth-March 24

Entering the President's Study, Ruth found the drapes tucked aside and the window cracked open to let in the stiff breeze. Butch complained these days that he felt dizzy when the room was too warm. He was seated on the couch, deep in conversation with Morris Blake, who appeared pale and tense. Seeing Ruth in the doorway, his gaze went to Butch, clearly pleading. "We'll talk about this again later, Morris."

"My mind is made up, sir."

Butch's gaze followed Blake as he excused himself and left. "Morris wants to resign his post, effective at the end of the month."

"Really."

A sigh indicated the depth of her husband's unhappiness. "I tried to talk him out of it, but he said something about a storm he can't weather." Butch made an impatient gesture, knocking over a photo of the two of them that sat on his desktop. "I told him we'll stand by him," he said as he righted it. "That should get him through whatever trouble he's in."

"What if he doesn't want to stay, Sweetie? What if he'd rather walk away from the White House than have whatever he's facing become public knowledge?"

A now-familiar look of confusion settled on Butch's face. "But he's been my friend for…I don't know, years."

"Morris might be quitting *because* he's your friend, Butch. To protect you."

Butch rubbed at his face as if trying to erase the frown that had formed. "This town grinds people down. Everyone's ready to throw a guy under the bus."

"Then be grateful Morris isn't the type to drag you under with him." Ruth massaged her husband's shoulders, and he made a moan of pleasure. "I've heard good things about a judge out west. We might look at him to replace Morris."

"Umm." A moment later he said, "Ben called."

"Really? What's he up to?"

Butch sniffed. "That boy only calls when he needs something, either money or help getting out of trouble."

She paused in her kneading. “What is it this time?”

The President put his hand over hers. “I forget. Croft said he’d see to it.”

Chapter Thirty-Two

Nettie-March 29

Nettie was watching two women play ping-pong in the recreation room when Kim arrived. Though she never said it aloud, Kim's visits and her work in the greenhouse were all that made Nettie's existence worthwhile these days. She tried not to be envious of the time Kim spent with Ruth. No doubt it was more exciting than visiting a worn-out criminal like herself.

"Hey, sis." Rising, she led the way to an alcove where two chairs flanked a small table. "They're deep cleaning my room, so I can't go back there for a while." Grinning, she added, "No doubt they search for contraband while they're in there, but I've got no worries."

"This is fine." Kim shivered. "The wind out there is nasty."

Nettie gave her a sly smile. "I wouldn't know. I don't get out much."

Kim's grin revealed relief that Nettie could joke about her imprisonment.

"Tell me all about life in the White House."

"It's different than I expected. I thought it would be weird, having all the security and working in such a historic setting. But after a few days, it's just the place where you live."

Nettie glanced around them. "I know what you mean."

"It's kind of hard, you know?" Kim fiddled with the zipper on her jacket, avoiding Nettie's gaze.

"Kim, if you're unhappy as Ruth's little helper, you don't have to stay."

"It's not a question of happiness. I didn't realize how…I don't know, how momentous the job would be." Unzipping the jacket and removing it, she draped it across the chair back, taking great care to set it straight. "You know things you don't want to know, and they feel wrong, but you kind of owe allegiance, so you go along." She gave the jacket a final pat. "Like I said, it's hard."

Nettie waited until Kim looked at her again. "You can tell me anything, Kim. I won't criticize or judge you, and I won't pass it on to anyone else."

Her response sounded like a laugh, but also like distress. "I don't know where to start."

"Tell me the first thing that bothered you."

"I'm betraying a confidence." Kim put out a hand as if to touch her then drew it back. "I need to know what you think."

Nettie almost said that what she thought didn't matter, but equivocation wasn't what Kim needed. A secret hung like a weight around her neck, and she thought telling it would bring relief. Nettie didn't believe sharing was particularly cathartic, but if Kim did, she was willing to listen.

Haltingly at first, Kim told her about the stroke Butch Mandell had suffered on inauguration day, the cover-up, and the substitution of an actor until Butch was well enough to return. She ended with a question that was partly a plea. "Do you think we did the wrong thing, Nettie?"

Sugarcoating wasn't Nettie's style. "Legally, yes, but that's not the question you're struggling with. You want to know if it was morally wrong, which, I'm sorry to say, is your question to answer. Since things are back to normal now and the right man is in the Oval Office, how much does it matter?"

"I feel like we cheated the American public."

"There's precedent for hiding a President's weakness. FDR's polio, Lincoln's bouts of depression, and Reagan's dementia, to name a few. The President is a figurehead for the nation. As such, people like to think of him as healthy in body and mind."

Kim still seemed doubtful. "I hope Butch is really back to full health."

"If he isn't, he's got Ruth," Nettie said. "She's tough enough for both of them."

Kim's feet shifted impatiently, scraping across the tile floor. "But Ruth wasn't elected President."

Nettie regarded her for a few seconds. "Does that change things for you?"

"Well, no. Ruth will always do what she thinks is best for the country."

"I'm sure she has a plan for everything."

"What do you mean?"

"Ruth has never been one to question herself." She picked at a crack on the tabletop with a fingernail. "I suppose that's good. I question every move I make, and look how I ended up."

Kim seemed to take her admission as a sign. "Nettie, I've learned some things about Caleb's grandmother. He had it rough with her, didn't he?"

Nettie covered her anger—at least she hoped she did—and said calmly, "Where did you get that information?"

Kim looked down at her hands again. "We wanted to find something, some information that would help you in the future."

"We?"

"Drew McMahon did the leg work."

"Drew." She chuckled softly. "My un-shady lawyer."

"Caleb's experiences in his early years explain—"

"Nothing. And they don't change the fact that I killed him."

"But if he threatened your safety, they'd take that into account when you come up for parole."

Nettie turned her gaze to the impervious window. "I don't need you to get me out of here, Kim. I'm exactly where I should be, so you and Drew McMahon need to leave it alone."

Chapter Thirty-Three

Kim-April 5

"Ms. Dailey, there's a man trying to get hold of you. He's called several times, but you were always busy. I left messages, but..." The aide glanced at Kim's desk, which was completely covered with printouts of a speech Ruth was slated to give to the nation's largest teachers' association. She'd left a note asking Kim to make it into a cogent whole, so she'd printed out Ruth's notes and spread the sheets out, trying different arrangements. "Your desk looks like an explosion at a paper factory."

Kim grinned. "I know. I can't even open a window and let the breeze in for fear of ruining my work." She lifted pages, careful not to disrupt the order she was for the most part pleased with, until she found a bit of lavender paper: *Call Edmund* and a number.

"He's in D.C., and he wants to see you," the aide said. "He called again this morning to ask if I'd passed on his messages." Her tone was tinged with insult at the suggestion she hadn't done her job.

Thanking the aide, Kim went back to work on the speech. Once she had the order down, she booted her computer and cut and pasted until the file was arranged correctly. Next she inserted segues, so the text flowed naturally. As she worked, Kim asked herself if she wanted to talk to her ex after all this time. If she did contact Ed, would it be to demand an explanation, or simply to tell him off? She even considered notifying Mr. Calver that the person who'd really stolen his money was back from wherever he'd gone with his ill-gotten gains.

In the end she texted the number Edmund had left: *Meet me Ariella's Diner 19th Street noon.*

At a light knock on her office door frame, Kim looked up to see Morris Blake, his expression grim. "Can I talk to you for a minute, Ms. Dailey?"

That was a departure for Blake, who'd called her Kim from the first day they met. Though he was witty and entertaining, she'd been warned by other females on staff to refuse Blake's offers of "working together" on a task and the even more blatant, "Let's celebrate with a drink." The man was a womanizer, and rumors circulated of women bought off after they complained he'd groped them. At least one claimed he'd gotten her drunk and then raped her. Kim sometimes wondered if Butch knew, but Blake was a valuable asset, a master of the sound bite. Whispers said his behavior was tolerated because he could put an argument into a few, concise words and deliver the message with an assurance that convinced people that it was true.

Today Blake seemed a different man. "Come in." Kim's office, no more than a cubbyhole, was currently hers alone. Blake closed the door, which made her uncomfortable, but because his demeanor was so grave, she ignored the threat to her reputation. Indicating a chair, she asked, "What's up?"

"I'm leaving my post as Attorney General."

"What? Morris, are you ill?" She stopped, aware that guessing was counterproductive.

"I need to focus on my family." The words sounded practiced. "Work here has been immensely rewarding, but I feel I've neglected my wife. And my children will be grown and gone before I know it."

It was a common explanation from government officials who'd been forced to resign, but one didn't say that aloud. "The President will be sorry to lose you."

As Kim wondered why Blake was telling her personally about his upcoming departure, he provided the answer. "Your sister Ruth, she listens to you, right?"

She chuckled. "I'm not so sure that's true."

"But you and she spend time together. You talk." When she nodded, Blake leaned toward her, setting his hands on his knees. "Gavin Croft has too much influence over Ruth."

Surprised by the straightforward statement, Kim struggled for an objective response. "Mr. Croft is…" *Evil* was the word that came to mind. "…resourceful."

"Please, warn your sister to be careful," Blake said. "Croft's agenda has nothing to do with unity or consensus."

"If you're concerned, why don't you warn her?"

Blake crossed his hands at his waist, and Kim got a disturbing image of him being led from the White House in handcuffs. "I waited too long." His chin dropped almost to his chest as he said, "I kept thinking Butch would slap Croft down." For once the eloquent Attorney General seemed to struggle to put the right words together. "Butch is no rocket scientist, but he has—had—clear goals for correcting some of the ways this country has gone wrong." Kim nodded understanding, and after massaging his temples briefly, he went on. "Since the election, he's lost focus, which has allowed Croft to…" He ran his hands down the sides of his face and pressed them against his mouth, as if physically stopping himself from saying too much. He ended by rephrasing his earlier plea. "Try to get Ruth to see that Croft needs to be controlled."

Kim drew some quick conclusions. First, Blake was being forced out of his position. Second, Blake knew Butch wasn't fully capable of carrying out his job as President. He'd seen that Ruth was the real power, and Croft was manipulating her. And third, he wanted Kim to do something about it.

"I'll speak to her, but Morris, you know I'm only Ruth's—What do they call it? Her body woman."

"Family matters," Blake said. "If she'll listen to anyone, it's you."

When he was gone, Kim considered who might go with her to make Ruth examine Croft's motives and her own actions. Her first thought was Ben. Ruth hung on her son's every word, and surely he'd noticed his father's forgetfulness.

That wouldn't work. Ben's arrogance had grown of late, and he treated everyone but his parents with thinly veiled contempt. She might enlist one of the girls, but Ruth's imperious attitude toward them suggested she'd ignore their advice right along with Kim's. While Kim respected Vice President Stockwell, Ruth did not. And the First Lady's body woman couldn't very well call a Supreme Court Justice or a powerful senator and say, "We need to chat about the First Lady's behavior."

There was more to consider. If Kim told what she knew, it would come out that Ruth had concealed Butch's stroke. That would land Ruth in a lot of trouble, and Kim would be an accessory. She chuckled grimly. If she talked, the result might be some sort of record. All three Kovaleskys in prison: one for murder, two for treason.

Kim's phone alarm beeped, indicating it was time to leave for her lunch date with Edmund. Setting Blake's visit at the back of her mind, Kim went out to deal with yet another criminal.

Kim arrived at Ariella's, an old-style diner updated for the Capitol crowd, right on time. She was halfway through a Pepsi when Edmund stepped into the doorway and stopped, temporarily blinded by the change from bright sunlight to mood lighting. Seeing her, he waved tentatively, and Kim felt an unwelcome stab of affection for the boyish man she'd married. Though his light-hearted view of life had charmed her for a long time, theirs had not been a great love. They'd worked well as a team, tolerated each other's foibles, and had an active sex life. She had never asked herself if there might be more.

It wasn't like the love Butch and Ruth have for each other. She'd seen their devotion up close, the glances that communicated without words, the intuitive knowing what the other would do or say. It was almost magical. Kim sometimes wondered if Butch's indifference to all things intellectual bothered Ruth, but it didn't seem to. She didn't laugh when he assumed *Crime and Punishment* was a new cop show on TV. Butch had provided Ruth with wealth and social status. *And lately*, Kim's mind whispered, *power too.*

Edmund approached her table, his expression wary. Should she hug him? Give him a cold stare? Slap his face? In the end she merely waited while he slid into the seat opposite and set both elbows on the table. "Sorry I'm late, but I got lost. It's good to see you, Kim."

His casual tone sent her in the direction of anger. "Yeah, Ed? Is it really?"

He regarded her quizzically, trying to read her mood. "Is something wrong?"

She avoided the question. "How was the Arctic adventure?"

A grin lit his face. "You can't imagine what it's like down there." Taking out his phone, he began pressing buttons. When he found what he wanted, Ed turned the phone toward her. "You don't have to go through them all, but it's so cool."

Kim looked down at the first photo: Edmund arriving at McMurdo Station, which brought to mind the old mining towns in movies. Scrolling through, she saw him on a forklift, his body rounded by multiple layers of clothing as he moved crates into a warehouse. She knew it was Ed by the scarf he wore, one she'd bought him for Christmas a few years back. Another photo showed him at a table with others, all in flannel shirts and knit caps, all mugging for the camera. The next showed him reading in his bunk, unaware he was being photographed.

Ed put in bits of explanation as she scrolled. "When the C-130s come in, we unload them and separate the gear. Some of it is general supplies, and some is research equipment. My job is storing it where the scientists can find it."

Intrigued despite herself Kim asked, "How did you get this post, Ed?"

Unwrapping his flatware, he toyed with the spoon. "I always wanted to see Antarctica, and you and I were growing farther apart by the day. At this...party we went to, I got talking to someone, and I said I wished I could chuck everything and go there." He extended a hand across the tabletop in a plea for understanding. "This friend said if I really wanted to go, the NSF is always looking for station support workers. I asked what the qualifications were, and she laughed and asked if I could drive a forklift."

"You work for the National Science Foundation?"

He shrugged. "It's not a permanent job. You spend a summer there—theirs, not ours—and come home in February. If you want, you apply to go back the next October." He grinned. "I probably will. It's different, but it's...I don't know..." Taking up the phone, he flipped through the pictures and then showed her one. "Those are the Southern Lights, *aurora australis*. Are they amazing or what?"

She had to admit they were spectacular. After a moment she said, "Why did you steal from Calver PR, Ed? If you needed money to pay for your trip, you could have told me, and we'd have figured it out together."

His gaze, which had been focused on the photo, rose, his eyes full of innocent surprise. "What in the heck are you talking about?"

Chapter Thirty-Four

Ruth-April 8

The briefing began in an orderly fashion. Butch's press secretary, Glenda Delacroix, stepped into the glaring lights and made a few announcements of general interest. Next, she answered questions about the Family Initiative and the administration's ongoing work to provide national health care.

A half hour in, Delacroix shifted tone. "Ladies and gentlemen, the President has an announcement he'd like to make in person. If you'll give us a minute, we'll get him out here so he can address you directly."

An anticipatory rustle passed through the room. Reporters readied themselves, checking their cameras, finding a fresh sheet of note paper, or messaging their stations to be ready for breaking news.

In less than two minutes, Butch Mandell entered, his relaxed smile in place, and took the podium. "Good afternoon, folks. We're making some changes in how we deal with the press going forward. Glenda will get into all the details with you, but before she does, I want to put things into perspective."

"Over the last few decades, the press, like our two political parties, has become more and more partisan. The twenty-four-hour news cycle took that partisanship from mildly annoying to a critical weakness. Due to their endless need for content, stations present hours of analysis, or what passes for analysis. Anyone with eyes can see that it often boils down to opinions and speculation. Now when I got elected, I asked experts from different groups how we might make the information our citizens receive more objective."

Feet shifted, and an undercurrent of disapproval murmured through the room. Here and there, hands rose as reporters readied themselves to ask questions or lodge protests.

The President seemed not to notice. "I can give you an example from right here in this room. Ms. Lorna D'Agostino." His gaze found an attractive newswoman well known on the east coast. "I've heard you tell a story about the day there was an explosion in Manchester. Do you remember it?"

She seemed reluctant but answered, "Yes, sir."

"You were in your dressing room, getting ready for your newscast, when an assistant came to tell you there was something going on downtown. He told you to come to the set right away. Is that correct?"

Even more reluctantly, "Yes."

"At your news manager's direction, you went on camera to report the incident. With footage of screaming people running from the city center in the background, you spoke for several minutes, speculating on a possible attack on America and never admitting you knew *absolutely nothing* about the situation." Mandell's smile remained in place as he went on, but his voice took on a serious tone. "It turned out that the 'crisis' was an explosion caused by a cracked gas main. No bomb. No terrorists. No one hurt." He spoke to the reporter directly. "Now, you tell that story to demonstrate how tough your job is. But I believe the American people would prefer reporters know the facts before they start talking."

The woman spoke in a defensive tone. "But everyone—"

"Exactly." He pointed a finger at her. "All news outlets do the same thing. Reporters tell viewers there was one gunman when there were two. They report an arrest when there was none. In the competition to be first, accuracy gets left behind." Butch's gaze swept across the room, including everyone there in his criticism. "You want big stories, and accuracy suffers because of it."

More hands went up, but Mandell ignored them. "Anyone know what the statistics are on our citizens' trust of the press?" The hands went down. "Less than 50%. As low as 40%. Should our citizens tolerate misinformed reporting? Partisan slants? 'Experts' with an agenda? Accusations of lying on both sides of every issue?"

He paused, but now no one seemed to want to speak. In fact, a few heads lowered as if ashamed of the truth he'd presented.

"Before elections, the modern press is like a circus ringmaster, shouting, "Look! This candidate made an outrageous statement! Now look over here! This candidate is accused of this and this and this." Leaning over the podium, Butch stared down those still able to meet his gaze. "It doesn't matter if the accusations are true or false. It doesn't matter if a candidate makes a complete fool of himself. Your bosses want customers, and you want your name on an article or your face on a screen." He paused dramatically. "It has to stop."

After a few seconds of silence, a reporter asked, "What are you proposing, sir?"

"Glenda will lay it all out for you." The President picked up his notes. "I wanted you to hear the reasons directly from me."

When Butch was gone, Delacroix took the podium again, causing nervous titters as she fiddled to get the microphone back down to her level.

"President Mandell is proposing a Fairness Doctrine much like the one this nation abandoned in 1987. The goal is to discourage reporting and analysis that presents only one side of an issue." Delacroix waited for some muttering to subside before going on. "We will require every news organization, no matter how large or small, to designate an oversight manager, one person responsible for maintaining truth and balance in the reports they release. The doctrine will extend to internet entities as well as television and print. Oversight managers will be vetted by the White House, and once they're in place, will have the power to sanction individuals who pass on unproven material. If a station continues to offer unbalanced reports, the oversight manager will be legally liable."

"What if these managers and the Mandell administration don't agree on what's balanced, or even what's true?"

"Violations of the Fairness Doctrine will be heard by a special tribunal," Delacroix replied. "If their case is lost, the news source will be permanently banned and its management fined or even jailed." She followed the gasp of surprise with a firm statement. "The citizens of this nation are tired of half-truths and exaggeration. Get your act together, people."

In the stunned silence that followed, Delacroix closed the folder before her. "I'll be here again tomorrow to take your questions." With that, she left the podium.

The President's new idea was understandably unpopular with all branches of the news media. Editorials bemoaned the perils of information controlled by the government. But ordinary citizens were more accepting. "Butch wants news people to be honest, that's all," a popular blogger commented. "He wants us to get the straight story."

Ruth's reaction to Butch's speech was relief. He got through it without a single mistake, and his charm lessened the sting of his words. She was pleased to have helped with writing the new policy. Though the media would never approve of every decision Butch made, they'd be much more careful now about how they said so.

Morris Blake's departure as the nation's Attorney General brought surprisingly little interest. In his announcement, he thanked Butch for appointing him but claimed to be overwhelmed with the work involved. Ruth's code of conduct kept the staff from blabbing about his character, and the new press standards meant most outlets were afraid to even whisper unfounded accusations. Interest moved on to the Supreme Court, where changes to immigration policy were being tested. The new A.G. proved himself from the first, offering the creative argument that the Court had no standing to rule, since only non-citizens were concerned. In the end, the justices agreed, leaving policymaking to the executive branch. Croft crowed—though only to Ruth—that choosing Kenneth Betzer as Attorney General had been perfect.

"He's everything we hoped for. Without judicial interference, we'll solve the problem of undocumented immigrants within a few months."

His obvious glee made Ruth uncomfortable. "You make it sound like we set out to derail the justice system."

"Of course not," he assured her, "but we have to be proactive. For too long, factions and legal saboteurs have stood in the way of solving this country's problems."

"True," Ruth said thoughtfully. "If we want good outcomes for everyone, we have to use all the means at our disposal."

Chapter Thirty-Five

Nettie-April 10

Nettie came into the greenhouse one morning to find Olin bent over the toolbox, cleaning dirt off a trowel with a rag. "Always at it early, aren't you?" His startled jump made her laugh. "Relax. I didn't mean to scare you to death."

He chuckled, but his eyes didn't light up the way they usually did when he was amused. "Getting things ready for the day."

Pearl showed up, a half-eaten doughnut in hand. "Hey," she greeted them. Focusing her gaze on Olin she asked, "Did I see you walk past my door in the middle of the night?"

He rolled his eyes. "How would I be out there after lockdown?"

"I don't know," Pearl said airily. "But *I'm* not somebody's *favorite*." To Nettie she said, "Have you seen him kiss ass with the guards? You'd think he was trying out for some new reality show." Tracing an imaginary marquee in the air, she said in an announcer's tone, "*Jailhouse Shenanigans*. What will Olin get away with next?"

Nettie took Olin's side. "It doesn't hurt to be friendly."

"None of them like me, especially the women," Pearl said with a sniff. "Jealous bitches."

The next day, Nettie discovered the tunnel. Busy with a visitor, Pearl hadn't come to the greenhouse. About an hour into their work time, Olin went to the kitchen to get the scraps the cooks saved for them: eggshells to fertilize, coffee grounds to keep slugs away, and fruit rinds to repel aphids.

While he was gone, Nettie decided to move a table to a flatter spot, so it didn't teeter every time it was touched. She set the trays atop it on the ground, careful not to break fragile seedling stems. Getting down on her knees, she dragged several bags of potting soil off the stretcher shelf underneath. Once that was done, the table moved easily, and she set it on a more level spot. Turning back, Nettie saw a tarp on the ground where the table had been. Raising one corner, she gasped in surprise. The tarp covered a hole about two feet in diameter. Stuffed in the opening was a bundle of cloth, and she dragged it out and unrolled it. A denim coverall, its elbows and knees caked with dirt. Wrapped inside it was a spade that had gone missing weeks ago. She recalled Olin saying he'd broken it and tossed it in the trash.

Nettie stood for a few seconds, holding the bundle and putting it all together. Olin was digging his way out of Martha's Place.

Where did the tunnel go? Outside the prison, of course, but Olin couldn't simply pop out of the ground on the opposite side of the wall and saunter away. There were cameras. There were guards. Even if he evaded them and made it to the street, an escapee with "PRISONER" written on the back of his shirt and the leg of his pants was bound to raise an alarm. At the very least, a passer-by would whip out a cell phone and record the escape to post on Instagram. How did he hope to succeed?

Should Nettie tell Dr. Foeller what Olin was up to? The doctor had been good to her, but Olin was…a friend, or as close to one as she had in this place. He took pains to do the heaviest work. On the days when the walls closed in and made her want to scream, he told corny jokes until she laughed. And he had never once asked what the First Lady was really like or why Nettie had murdered her only child.

If Olin was some kind of maniac, he might repeat his crime if free. And even if he wasn't a danger to others, it was likely he'd be caught, returned to his original prison, and punished for the attempt. He might even be hurt in the process. Telling on Olin could protect him, even save his life.

But even as those thoughts raced through her mind, Nettie was putting things back the way they'd been. The decision was too big to make on the spur of the moment. She needed time to think.

When Olin returned, he began crushing the eggshells they'd been given into fine pieces with a hammer while Nettie sliced banana peels into thin strips. As they worked, she asked, "Why are you in prison, Olin?"

His response was so long in coming she thought there wouldn't be one. Finally, he said, "I was convicted of aggravated rape."

"Want to tell me about it?"

He gave a mirthless chuckle. "Do you want to tell me about shooting your son in the chest?"

"I'm trying to decide if I should report the tunnel under this greenhouse."

His eyes blazed hot, and she suppressed a shiver. Olin could easily kill her if he chose, using one of the tools within reach or even his bare hands. Nettie turned and looked him in the eye. "I need to hear your story."

The angry expression faded, replaced by a look of pleading sincerity. "I need to prove I didn't rape anyone." No doubt aware of how many prisoners claimed they were innocent, he added, "I got an alibi, but she doesn't know she's my alibi."

"How can that be?"

Olin didn't seem eager to tell his story, but in the end, he did. "Me and two friends went to Lauderdale for spring break. At a bar on the beach, I met a girl who was into games. She said we shouldn't use real names. We'd have what she called a 'happy hookup' and then forget about it." He pounded the eggshells with a little more force than necessary. "She said I could call her Belle, like the girl in *Beauty and the Beast*. I said fine, then I was Denzel Washington's illegitimate son Malik. We left the bar together and had sex on the beach. Around two, she got up, said she was flying home later that morning, so she had to go. It was warm, and the sound of the waves was nice, so I stayed where I was. When the sun came up, I opened my eyes to find this cop standing over me. He asked what I was doing, and I said I'd had a few drinks and needed to sleep them off. The guy checked my ID and then told me to move along." His lips twitched. "That should have been the end of the story."

"Did Belle claim you raped her?"

"No. On the same beach that night, a girl named Noreen Gray went walking by herself. She was attacked, beaten pretty badly, and raped."

Nettie had begun to see where this was going. "She thought it was you."

"If she'd reported the rape then, it would have been different, but she cleaned herself up and invented a story about a dune buggy accident to explain her bruises. Then she went back to Minnesota and tried to forget what happened."

"But she couldn't."

"No. She started having nightmares. After a while she couldn't make herself leave the house. Finally, the story came out, and her parents called the Fort Lauderdale police. Noreen described her attacker as a black man about six feet tall with big hands." Olin held out his hands, which Nettie had already noticed were larger than most. "As soon as the cop who'd rousted me on the beach heard that, he decided he knew who the rapist was. He had my name from these things called field interview records the cops make whenever they speak to someone."

"They had to have more evidence than that to convict you."

Olin chuckled, but the sound wasn't happy. "Have you seen what color I am?"

"I'd say you're a shade of human," Nettie replied, "but I know it isn't always that way in our justice system."

"You got that right. Noreen was sure she recognized me. My lawyer suggested she might have seen me earlier in the evening. He said it was dark on the beach, so she couldn't be certain. She said she was, and she cried so hard the judge had to take a recess. Other people testified I'd been romancing white girls all week, like that was a crime." He grimaced. "I told them I was with someone at the time, but I couldn't prove it. The prosecutor brought in stuff I'd been charged with before, a few scams and whatever. He made me seem like the biggest liar on the planet." He shook his head. "The only person who could have straightened things out was Belle, and she was gone. I didn't know her name, where she'd been staying, or where she came from."

"Your lawyer should have paid someone to track her down."

"I didn't have money for that, and besides, I don't think he believed me. Public defenders get this mind-set, you know?"

Nettie thought of Drew McMahon, who'd done his best for her despite her record, her lack of cooperation, and her attitude. She wished she'd been kinder to him. "How'd you get to come here, to Martha's Place?"

"Dr. Foeller heard about my case and decided I fit her study criteria." He sniffed. "She wants me to tell her what made me snap, attack an innocent woman, and beat her bloody." Rolling his eyes, Olin finished, "If I don't give it up pretty soon, I'm afraid she's gonna toss me back into real prison."

"If you were free, what could you do to help yourself?"

His jaw flexed. "Find Belle."

"You'll break out of prison and look for a girl you have no idea how to locate."

"I came up with a starting point." Olin gestured at his own head. "For months, I went over every second of that night, trying to recall any clue. Finally, this memory popped into my head. Belle had a graduation cap sticker on her phone that said *Purlingham High School Class of '20.* I must have noticed it and then forgot it, but your brain stores everything, right? One night when I was almost asleep, that little sticker came into my mind like I was seeing it in real life. I looked up Purlingham online first chance I got. It's this little dot on the map in Vermont."

"You could find Belle by looking at photos in their high school yearbooks."

"Right."

"But even if she vouched for you, you'd still be in trouble for escaping prison."

He spread his hands. "I'm gonna hope they consider that I wasn't supposed to be here in the first place, you know?"

Nettie turned to practical matters. "Where's this tunnel you're digging headed?"

Olin looked around to assure they were alone. "A hundred and fifty years ago, at the time this place was built, people had started to understand the causes of disease. Homeowners who had the money for it had these brick tunnels built to drain standing water away from their homes."

"How do you know that?"

"Every once in a while, they collapse. The traffic breaks them down, and bam! You got a hole eight feet deep, sometimes in the middle of a street. It's always big on the local news."

"Martha's Place has a tunnel like that?"

"It's marked on the original property records." He raised a finger as a caution. "Now, it's not for sure, but there was never much reason to fill those tunnels in. Property owners usually blocked both ends and forgot about them. Our tunnel should connect with the city's sewer system, making an underground path all the way to Shockoe Bottom and the James River."

Nettie smiled. "You found a way to get out of here, but you couldn't go digging up the yard to look for it."

"Until you asked for a greenhouse. When the guys came to set it up, I sort of steered them to this spot."

"Are you sure it's down there?"

He frowned. "I had to guess at the location, since I can't go out and measure." He nodded toward the spot where she'd found the tunnel. "I went down four feet. Now I'm branching out, looking for bricks instead of dirt."

Nettie heard disappointment in his tone. "It's harder than you imagined."

Olin scratched his ear. "So far, my pilot holes just keep going."

"What does that mean?"

His response was preceded by a long sigh. "It means I have to keep digging."

"What if the old tunnel caved in years ago?"

"There'd be a depression in the ground."

Which would have been filled in to smooth the lawn, she almost said, but Olin didn't want to hear that. "What happens when you find the shaft?"

"I pry some bricks out, climb in, make my way to the river, and leave Richmond for Vermont."

"With no money, no ID, one clue to the girl you're looking for, and no idea what she'll say if you find her."

His jaw jutted. "Nobody but me is gonna do it."

Sensing she couldn't dissuade him, Nettie asked, "How did you manage to dig this hole?"

"I work at night. There's a boarded-up coal chute in the basement, and I fixed it so I can slide it open and crawl out."

"Video surveillance?"

"Cameras record where they're pointed. Whenever I got the chance, I started nudging them a little to one side." Reaching up, he pantomimed slapping something overhead. "After a while they were far enough off center that I can scuttle along the wall and avoid being seen."

"Nobody noticed? Nobody fixed it?"

"My guess is that every shift hopes the next one will fix it, but nobody wants to get out a ladder, climb up there, and re-center all the cameras."

Nettie admitted it was human nature to put off small, laborious tasks. “Okay. But we’re locked in our cells from nine at night till seven in the morning.”

Olin blushed. “Pearl was right about me being somebody’s favorite. One of the night girls leaves my door unlocked when she does the bed check at ten. I sneak out, dig until around two, and then when her partner has his meal break, her and me spend some quality time in the staff lounge. Just before he comes back on duty at three, she locks me in my cell again.”

“I can’t believe she’d jeopardize her job like that.”

“She doesn’t know I can get outside. And even if I did, there’s the wall.” Olin tilted his head at Nettie. “Breaking the rules is no big thing if you convince yourself it won’t matter.”

Nettie’s head nodded in unconscious agreement. She’d lived for years believing nothing mattered, and as a result, she’d broken plenty of rules. Instead of arguing further, she regarded Olin with a wry smile. “You dig half the night, work with me all morning, and keep your guard girlfriend happy in the wee hours. You’ve got to be exhausted.”

He shrugged, youth dismissing the concerns of age. “I nap in the afternoons.”

Nettie had one more question. “Where’s the dirt?”

“I scatter it, like the guy in that Shawshank movie. Across the lawn. In the flowerbeds.” He smiled. “In y’all’s plant trays.”

“You spread the dirt from your tunnel on my turnips.” He raised his shoulders in a silent question: *Why not?* “You are a clever devil, Olin Dobbs.”

He looked at her, his face serious. “What you going to do about it, Miz Nettie?”

She sighed. “I’m going to advise you that it’s a terrible idea, and then I’m going to pretend I never moved that table.”

Chapter Thirty-Six

Kim-April 12

Kim was surprised when Drew McMahon called to say he was on his way to D.C. "Can you get away for dinner?"

"How—?" Ignoring the rush of joy she felt, she said, "Never mind. When and where?"

"I made reservations for six at the fanciest of the four restaurants at my hotel."

"You seem pretty sure of yourself." Kim didn't mind. In fact, she was excited by the prospect of seeing him.

"You say you have no social life. I'm trying to help a girl out."

For their meeting Kim chose a dress Ruth had complimented, saying it slimmed her silhouette. Ruth's hair stylist had provided some kind of magic potion that relaxed the kinky waves Kim had fought all her life, so she no longer had to tame her thick hair with barrettes or a scrunchie. Checking her mirror image, Kim saw anxiety in her eyes and stuck her tongue out, making fun of herself. "Stop acting like it's a blind date," she said aloud. "He's seen you at your worst, all red-eyed and blotchy from crying."

Rodgers, the man usually assigned to be Kim's driver, pulled up at the restaurant entrance at five minutes to six. When he opened the car door, she hesitated. "I'm not sure when you should come back for me."

"It doesn't matter. When you call, I'll come."

Kim suspected Rodgers reported what she did outside the White House to Ruth, since the First Lady seemed to want to know everything about those around her. Kim still had no idea how Ruth had learned of her contact with Drew, but she'd allowed her to believe it continued because Kim found him attractive. Ruth didn't need to know about their inquiries into Nettie's past. She was sure to comment that in trying to understand their sister's crime, Kim was wasting Drew's time and her money.

"Tell you what," she said to Rodgers. "I'll take a taxi back."

Drew McMahon waited at a booth along the side wall, and he waved discreetly to get her attention. He looked the same as he had when they'd met two years earlier, when she recalled thinking almost from the first that Nettie could trust him. Drew's approach to the law probably explained why he was still in solo practice, why he would never have a stable of wealthy clients, and why he had cared so much about things Nettie had not.

A waiter followed Kim to the table, and she ordered a glass of Sauvignon Blanc. Though she found it sour, Ruth's voice sounded in her head. "It has fewer calories than most wines."

Kim and Drew engaged in small talk, perusing the menu, until the waiter returned with her wine, took their orders, and withdrew. Over drinks, she told him the full story of why she'd left Michigan, ending with her recent meeting with her ex. "I believe Edmund is telling the truth," she said. "He was completely surprised to hear there was money missing at Calver PR."

"Then your boss made up the story so he could fire you?"

"Or someone made it look like Edmund and I were cheating."

"Who'd do that?"

"Honestly, I can't think of anyone."

"Maybe another employee took the money and framed you two for it."

She shook her head helplessly. "That's the only explanation I can think of, but I can't figure out how they managed it."

"You should contact your former boss and let him know there's a criminal on his staff." When Kim hesitated, Drew asked, "Would you like me to do it?"

"Would you? I doubt Mr. Calver will admit he's wrong on my say-so."

"I'll go down there first thing Monday morning and see him in person."

With that out of the way, they turned to discussing Drew's trip to Arizona. He went over everything again, filling in details he'd skipped on the phone.

"Could Caleb's old friend—Melissa—be exaggerating?" Kim asked.

"No." He didn't elaborate, but Kim surmised that the woman's manner had convinced him as much as her words.

She sipped at her wine, tempted to ask Drew what he thought she should do next. That wasn't his decision to make, nor was it fair to expect him to be her sounding board. "I appreciate your help," she said. "What do I owe you?"

He produced a bill that was far too low, and they haggled briefly. Drew insisted it was exactly right. "I missed a whole week of winter in Detroit, and I felt the sun on my neck," he argued. "That's worth a discount."

The food arrived, and by tacit consent, they moved to other topics. "I bet it's interesting to be so close to the people who make this country go," Drew said.

Kim shrugged. "Interesting, yes, but you know what? They're all people. They have bad breath, flat feet, and zits they hide with concealer."

"But you see what's behind the events, like when the Attorney General suddenly decides he needs to spend more time with his family." He gave her a sidelong glance. "I sense there's more to that than what was said in public."

Out of respect for Butch—and probably pressure from Gavin Croft—Blake had kept his doubts about the President's competence to himself. Kim suspected that others in the administration took Blake's departure as a warning. Loyalty was required. Questioning the status quo was cause for dismissal.

That wasn't a burden she could share with McMahon—or anyone, for that matter. In fact, Kim even regretted telling Nettie as much as she had. Still, Nettie was unlikely to pass on what she knew, while an attorney might feel compelled to act if he suspected a White House cover-up.

"I let others decide the big things," she said lightly. "Now tell me, how's life in Detroit?"

Taking the cue, Drew turned to a summary of things she might have missed: the Lions' choice of yet another new assistant coach, a new live theater venue, and the rumor that a former mayor was mounting a comeback. Kim made suitable comments, becoming more relaxed than she'd been in...how long?

When they finally pushed their plates aside, Drew gave Kim a direct, possibly flirty, look. "When Mrs. Mandell comes on TV, I always look to see if you're with her, but you're pretty good at staying out of the limelight."

"I'm a worker bee. No reason for anyone to focus on me."

He raised a hand like a kid in a classroom. "I have a reason. I like your face."

"You're one citizen. The rest focus on our lovely First Lady."

"We each have our favorite," Drew said, "and you're lovely too."

She felt her face warm, but her brain cautioned, *You've got way too much on your plate to let a man into your life right now.* A mischievous voice in another part countered, *It isn't a lifelong commitment, though. It's just dinner.*

As the waiter cleared away their meal, Kim and Drew moved to a raised table in the bar and ordered drinks. Conversation wandered over a dozen topics, and they found shared interests such as police procedural mysteries and Renaissance art. "Next time, I'll take you to the National Gallery," Kim said. "It's amazing."

"Is next weekend too soon?"

She laughed. "Drew, you can't be running out here every few days."

"Who says I can't?" His expression turned serious. "Mrs. Cinelli's slip and fall at Target can wait. Right now, all I can think about is the next time I see you."

In Drew McMahon's presence, Kim felt like a part of her that had been frozen solid was beginning to thaw. With other men, she smiled and even laughed, but she didn't experience the glow of warmth in her chest that rose when his gaze met hers. She found herself telling Drew about her upcoming high school reunion and her ambivalence about attending. "I want to see everyone, but I'm not sure I can face it, you know?"

"If you don't want to go alone, I could be your plus one."

She let out a small whoop of objection. "You'd be bored to death in twenty minutes."

"I'm not easily bored," he replied. "And bringing a date would protect you from getting stuck with that twice-divorced former classmate who collects vintage lunchboxes and brings homemade venison jerky for everyone to try." He took on a playfully bashful air. "I clean up pretty good, and I promise to behave."

Kim considered it. "My friends have been hounding me about coming."

"Let's do it." He took out his phone. "Give me a date and time, and I'll make sure I have clean underwear."

Laughing, Kim looked up the information in her own phone so Drew could enter it in his. She watched as he did, thinking that he looked cute when he was concentrating. Suddenly a question came to mind. Had she dismissed her driver to be considerate, or had she been subconsciously expecting to spend the night with McMahon? The idea was appealing.

Her phone buzzed in her hand, causing her to jump. "Excuse me," she said to Drew. "Hey, Ruth."

"Are you in for the evening?"

"Um, no, not yet."

"Oh." Disappointment was obvious in her voice.

"What do you need?"

"Nothing. I was going to run a few things by you…No. It can wait until tomorrow. I have no right to interrupt your evening."

"That's all right." She checked her watch. "I can come by in half an hour, if that works for you."

"No, really, Kimmie. Enjoy whatever it is you're doing."

"Ruth, I'll be there in half an hour." As she spoke, Kim saw Drew's smile falter a little. The evening wasn't going to end the way he'd imagined either.

The Mandells' family-dinner-together custom was tested under the strains of the Presidency, but Ruth cajoled and accommodated to get everyone to attend. Kim was invited, of course, and she enjoyed the company of the younger girls, with their crushes and their rapid, half-word teen-speak. She saw a little of herself in Grace, a young wife learning the ways of marriage. She found Ben irritating, though he was carefully polite when he spoke to her. Rumors of his bad behavior abounded among the staff, so while Ruth cited Ben's many achievements at college, Harley Stark confided that he was often in trouble. Once he'd grumbled, "Mr. Croft should leave me alone for a while and work on the President's kid."

Shortly after they finished dinner, Butch was called out due to a tense situation in Southeast Asia. Ruth went along, leaving Kim with the Mandell children. Ben immediately made his excuses and left, hinting that he had more interesting places to be. Kim didn't mind, because she liked listening to the girls when they let their guard down. "Mom's all husty about Leah's boyfriend," Maddy told Kim and Grace. "His dad's a barber and his mom clerks at a Dollar Store."

"Where did you even meet this boy?" Grace asked Leah. "You had to know The Mom would disapprove."

"She wouldn't know if Maddy hadn't told," Leah complained.

Grace's expression showed empathy for her little sister. "I had a normal boyfriend once. His dad worked for our dad, but after someone saw me kissing him, his family got transferred to Texas." She crossed her arms as if chilled. "I figure Mom made it happen. Couldn't have me falling for a nobody."

"But now you're married to Jason," Maddy said, "so it's all good."

"Right," Grace murmured, but Kim saw a trace of regret in her niece's eyes.

"Me and Zack aren't a big deal," Leah said. "He's cute, so we text back and forth a lot." As an afterward she muttered, "That's all we can do, since Ms. Nine-letters monitors my every move outside the White House."

"Ms. Nine-letters?" Grace repeated.

"FLOTUSRPM," Maddy informed her. "That's what the staff calls her, so I made up my own nickname from the nine letters."

"First Lady of the United States Ruth Patricia Mandell," Grace translated. "Our mom isn't 'The Mom' anymore."

"She's everybody's The Mom now," Leah said. "She can tell the whole country what to do, and they have to do it."

Chapter Thirty-Seven

Ruth-April 14

"We hear reports of a wave of refugees from Central America heading to our southern border, Mr. President. Are you prepared to keep them from entering the country illegally?"

President Mandell glanced toward his wife, who raised a brow, acknowledging her correct prediction of the day's first question. Setting his hands on the edges of the podium, Butch faced the array of camera lights and spoke earnestly. "Let's look at a few facts first. For starters, the danger we've been warned about for years, that criminal aliens swarm across our borders with the intent to create mayhem, is largely fiction. Movies love to portray non-citizens as drug dealers and human traffickers, but the vast majority are hard-working, honest people. The media"–He smiled and rephrased—"the *old* media, blew crimes committed by non-citizens out of all proportion, because fear sells, and too many want to believe that the bad guys aren't 'us.' They're nasty strangers with an evil agenda." He paused, highlighting what came next. "Evidence collected and analyzed annually reveals that aliens, even those here illegally, are not a significant crime problem."

"We also know that most undocumented individuals don't enter the country via our southern border. They come from all over the world, usually on visas, and fail to return home. Now that's a problem we need to address, but it can't be solved with higher walls and more patrols."

A reporter raised a hand, but Butch signaled for her to wait until he finished. "There's a third point to consider. This country needs laborers to do the jobs our own workforce can't or won't do. We allow guest workers for that purpose, and it works." Again he paused, removing his glasses and leaning toward his audience. "Now, because America is the land of opportunity, those workers want to stay. And as soon as they can, those who are able leave the low-paying jobs in the fields and find better ones. That means we are constantly in need of new workers." Butch raised his hands, palms out. "Like it or not, without a periodic influx of non-citizens, your food won't be harvested, your lawns won't be mowed, and your children won't be tended. We are wise to welcome those who want to come here to work."

"Even if they wade the Rio Grande at midnight?" a reporter shouted.

Croft wrote on his iPad with a stylus, and Ruth saw Butch look down at his synced device on the lectern to read the man's name. "We can make crossings like that unnecessary, Dennis. We can give guest workers honest employment in a manner that's fair to them, to our own workers, *and* to employers." Butch looked at the teleprompter, reading the words Ruth had written. "We'll begin by sorting all guest workers onto employment tracks, according to what they can do. We're in the process of hiring investigators to do that, and we'll boost their productivity with the best technology available, including facial recognition to weed out any with criminal backgrounds." Butch dropped a bombshell, though his expression remained pleasant. "As a condition of entry, all foreign workers must agree to an implanted tracking device."

The room buzzed, and an outraged man opined, "That sounds like something from a science fiction novel."

"According to exhaustive polling," Butch replied evenly, "that's what our citizens want. The vast majority of Americans don't object to outsiders coming here to work. They just don't want them wandering the country unsupervised."

Butch paused, his eyes challenging anyone in the room to argue the point. When no one did, he went on. "We're currently recruiting businesspeople to sponsor guest workers once they've been vetted. These employers will take responsibility for their workers' well-being and their behavior. After two years, if a worker has demonstrated readiness, he or she can begin the process of becoming a citizen."

"What about their families?"

"Up to four non-employable dependents may accompany each worker: a spouse, kids, even Grandma." Butch grinned. "Now, she might never make it to full citizenship, but the rest have a fair shot if they behave themselves." He raised a finger. "The worker is responsible for his dependents' conduct. If any one of them commits a serious crime, they'll all be sent back to their country of origin."

"Wouldn't that put their lives in danger?" someone asked.

Arching a brow, Butch responded as Ruth had coached him to. "Wouldn't that give them incentive to behave?"

Though editorials speculated on possible misuse of the President's new policy, most admitted it was better than previous systems. One editor summed it up: *Work, a place to live, and the chance for citizenship is what our ancestors came here for. If we can offer those things to others without endangering ourselves, why wouldn't we?*

ICE was expanded, and its agents were charged with tracking down undocumented persons already in the country. "The search isn't punitive," Press Secretary Delacroix explained, "but the law is the law. Those with jobs and no serious offenses will be slotted into the process the President mentioned, but their cases will be heard after those who made legitimate applications for entry. Any undocumented person with a felony on record will be returned to his or her home country."

As in other cases, the pragmatism of Mandell's position won most citizens over. Americans were tired of arguing rights and wrongs, and there were provisions in the new policies to satisfy both sides of the argument. The President often paraphrased the Rolling Stones: "We can't all get what we want, but together we can figure out what we need."

All of the nation's big arguments were approached in similar ways. Pollution, drug abuse, campaign finance reform, and a dozen other issues that had in the past been powder kegs became, if not completely fixable, less sectarian. Mandell created what became known as "Gangs of Twelve," six Senators and six Congressmen recognized as experts in a particular area. Chosen from both parties and the ranks of independents, the "gangs" sat down to hammer out legislation that codified policies initiated through executive orders. To those who complained the President was usurping Congressional authority, Delacroix explained, "Executive orders create a trial period for a policy, so we can see what works and what does not. Congress will turn workable practices into law and readdress those it feels are flawed."

In general, Congress was willing to work with President Mandell. "They're terrified of losing power," Ruth told Kim as they fine-tuned the wording of a pending announcement. "They never dreamed a third-party candidate could win, and now they're falling all over themselves to prove to their constituents that the mess of the last decade wasn't due to partisanship on their part." Her voice took on a low, rumbly tone. "'Everyone else was pig-headed and dishonest, my fellow Americans, but not me.'"

"The cooperation is amazing," Kim said. "I hope it continues."

"Oh, it won't." Ruth's snicker was un-like her dignified First Lady persona. "But right now, voters view Congress as a bunch of spoiled brats. Butch is the parent who's taken them in hand. If they oppose him, their constituents will rebel."

"I've heard he's facing some challenges in the courts."

"True." Ruth's tone hinted they were frivolous. "Luckily, most of our current judges favor a literal interpretation of the law. If the Constitution doesn't explicitly say the President *can't* do this or that, he should have his way."

"Are you saying Butch has no restrictions?"

Ruth tilted her head. "He's possibly the most powerful President we've had outside wartime. Voters love him, the courts support his right to act, and Congress is afraid to deny him what he wants."

Kim's expression hinted at disapproval, and Ruth felt a stab of regret. She wished her sister could see that Butch's growing power meant they could accomplish great things, especially if they acted decisively in his first term in office.

Chapter Thirty-Eight

Kim-April 14

On Monday morning, Drew called Kim a few minutes after ten. Clouds hung over D.C. like overstuffed sacks, and she warned that a storm might interfere with the call.

"I'll talk fast, but you need to hear this. Your employer—"

"Former employer."

"Right. Calver was apologetic. It seems the whole Kim and Edmund stealing from the company thing was a mistake."

"He put me through all that because of a *mistake*?"

"As I said, he was apologetic. This auditor, supposedly part of a well-known Detroit firm, called and offered a free audit as a way to prove they could do a better job than the guys Calver had been using. Is he kind of known for being cheap?"

Kim giggled. "*Free* is Mr. Calver's favorite word."

"That's the vibe I got. Anyway, this new auditor digs up convincing evidence of your supposed crime."

"Which got me fired."

"Yes, but a month later, Calver tried to contact the man, and the phone number he'd been given no longer worked. He called the firm and learned they'd never heard of the guy."

"Weird."

"Calver immediately had a new audit done, which showed no evidence of fraud." Like movie music highlighting important dialogue, Drew's words were underscored with thunder.

"I can't believe it."

"Calver says he made amends as best he could. He had no number for you, but he contacted your sister and arranged to return the money. He asked her to have you call so he could apologize, but you never did. I think he was terrified that you'd sue." He waited until a crash of thunder faded. "Ruth didn't tell you any of this?"

"No. The money was hers anyway, and I would guess that in her Ruth-like way, she decided it was best if I wasn't given the confusing choice of going back to my old life or staying here." Inside, Kim shook with anger, but she was determined not to let it color her voice. "Who did it, Drew? Why did a fake auditor make up evidence to get Ed and me in trouble?"

"Since your ex had left the firm by then, I think it was done to get you fired."

"I need to talk to Edmund again. I'll call you back tonight."

Kim put the phone down, tears stinging her eyes. Ruth could have relieved her mind so easily, but she'd let her go on feeling misunderstood, rejected, and indebted. Why?

The storm broke then. Watching the lightning bursts across the sky, Kim tried to puzzle out her sister's need to have her around. While she understood the political benefit to having a "normal" sister balance the negative image people had of Nettie, that wasn't all of it. In some unacknowledged part of herself, did Ruth need Kim's approval?

When the storm faded to low rumbles, Kim called her ex-husband. Edmund answered immediately. "Hey, Kim."

"The embezzlement thing was a mistake, Ed. Calver knows we didn't steal from him."

"That's good. I mean, I don't plan to go back to PR, but if I ever had to, I'm glad that mess isn't hanging over my head."

"When you told me about going to Antarctica, you mentioned a person who helped you make the contacts needed to get signed on. Who was that?"

He didn't answer for a few seconds. When he did, he sounded apologetic. "It was at Grace and Jason's wedding. I'd had a bit to drink, and I told her how you and I had drifted apart. I said I'd been thinking about leaving. She asked where I'd go if I could choose any place I wanted. She made it a joke, said I was too old to become an astronaut or dance with the New York Ballet." He chuckled at the memory. "Anyway, when I said my dream was spending time in Antarctica, she laughed and said that was easy."

"She?" Kim prompted impatiently.

"Ruth. Don't be mad at her, Kim, but she hooked me up with a guy at the National Science Foundation. That's how I got invited to McMurdo."

It took a while for Kim to get Ruth alone, but that was probably good. Some of her anger had burned away by the time the last staffer packed up and left for the day. "Ruth, why didn't you tell me that my supposed embezzlement turned out to be fake?"

Ruth had been sorting papers into a desktop file, but she stopped, looking embarrassed. "Oh. I guess I forgot all about it."

"You forgot to tell me I wasn't suspected of criminal activity anymore?"

"I'm sorry, Kimmie. You might have noticed that I'm a little busy these days. Someone named Calver called and said there'd been a terrible mistake. He wanted to speak to you, but you were out that day, visiting Nettie." Ruth's brow tightened. "I gave him some grief about it, told him the whole thing was his fault. He was quite apologetic, and we made arrangements for return of the hundred thousand I'd loaned you." She tapped her lips with a finger. "I meant to tell you as soon as we got a few minutes alone, but when does that happen these days? At some point, I simply forgot about it." Coyly she added, "It might have been Freudian. I certainly don't want you moving back to Michigan and leaving me bereft."

The explanation poked a large hole in the bubble of Kim's indignation, but she had one more question to ask. "Why didn't you tell me it was you who helped Ed get work in Antarctica?"

Ruth seemed confused. "I did?" She leaned her face on her fist for a moment, thinking. "We talked at Grace's wedding. He was very unhappy, and I saw that he was making you unhappy too." Reaching out, Ruth touched Kim's arm. "I never thought Ed was a good match for you. Now, I think you know it too."

She was right. While Kim had been hurt by Ed's desertion, she was better off without him. And he seemed more content as well. Ruth had really done nothing wrong.

Kim didn't have much time for social media, but on weekends she'd check to see how things were back in Berlin. Friends there posted pictures of their kids playing sports, their husbands ice fishing on Lake Huron, and themselves at girls' lunches, holding up wine glasses and mugging for the camera. Kim always clicked to "like" the photos, though Michigan seemed very, very far away.

That night, with her window open to let in the rain-washed air, she perused her Facebook notifications and noticed a tiny "1" at the top of her home page. Someone who wasn't a Facebook friend had sent a private message. It was up to her to decide whether to open it or ignore it.

After a brief argument with herself, Kim read the note. *Ms. Dailey, please give your sister a message for me. I don't know how else to reach her. Tell her Nathan Tanner was murdered.*

Well.

She navigated to the sender's profile. Her name was Bonnie Amour, and she listed her profession as actress. Her cover photo showed a curvaceous brunette with a come-hither look that was overdone. Other photos on her page were the same: lots of makeup, lots of cleavage. Her latest messages concerned recent heartbreak and a struggle to accept great loss.

Apparently, she'd been Nathan Tanner's friend. *Murdered?*

Kim didn't respond to the message. In fact, she forgot about it over the next few days, which were hectic. It was Thursday evening before she returned to Facebook to send a birthday note to her friend Kelly. Being there reminded her of the message, and on an impulse, she replied with her cell phone number and a time: *Friday p.m., 3-5:00.*

Friday turned out to be a mess. She completely forgot the message she'd sent and wouldn't have answered the unknown caller if she hadn't been arranging the trip to her reunion. "Kim Dailey."

"It's Bonnie. Bonnie Armentrout."

"Who?"

"On Facebook I use my stage name, but Armentrout is my real name, in case you want to check me out."

"All right, Bonnie. I'm not sure why you contacted me."

"I need you to tell Mrs. Mandell there's a killer on the President's staff."

That stopped Kim for a second. Finally, she said, "Ms.—um, Bonnie—"

"Please listen, because I'm not trying to scam you. Me and Nathan were in love. We met on the cruise ship, and it was like we'd been looking for each other all our lives. You know how that is?"

Not really. "Um-hum."

"They called and asked him to come to the White House without really telling him why. When he got back, Nathan told me everything, about…you know, the thing with President Mandell. He wasn't supposed to talk about it, but him and me didn't have any secrets." Pride colored her voice as she added, "Nathan did a really good job, don't you think? I mean, after he told me, I watched the clips again, and I still had trouble believing it was Nathan."

Kim didn't respond. No way was she going to admit to any of this.

"So Nathan came back to the ship, and I gotta tell you, Ms. Dailey, that week did him a world of good. I mean, I loved the guy, but I won't deny he had a problem with booze. After D.C., he was a different person. Said he'd given up drinking for good, and we were gonna get married. He'd get a regular job, but we'd live where I could pursue my career, either L.A. or New York."

"He sounds like a good man."

"He was. But here's the thing." Her voice grew tearful. "One night Nathan said to me, 'Bonnie, there's a Secret Service agent on board who was in on things when I pretended to be President Mandell.'" Her voice tightened. "I said it was probably one of those doppel-whatevers, you know?"

"Doppelgangers."

"Yeah, that. But Nathan said he looked exactly like this Bennigan, except he had a mustache. Nathan was in a passageway and this door opened and there he was. Nathan said, 'Agent Bennigan?' and the guy said, 'You got me confused with someone else.' But he went back inside the room like he'd changed his mind about going out."

"That was the name he said? Bennigan?"

"Yeah. Do you know him?"

Again, Kim didn't confirm anything. "I was making sure I heard you correctly."

But she was picturing Bennigan's expressionless face. Since Butch had come to the White House, Bennigan and Croft had grown closer. Josh now served as Assistant Head of Homeland Security, but Kim noticed he took his cues from Croft more than from his superior.

Had Croft decided that letting Tanner live was too great a risk? Had Josh Bennigan followed the entertainer to Alaska and pushed him off the cruise ship?

No. That wasn't possible. She was letting the fact that she disliked Croft lead her into conspiracy theories.

"Ms. Armentrout, I really appreciate your call. I will look into this."

"Good. I can help with—"

"We won't be speaking again. While I appreciate the information, this needs to be handled through official channels."

"As long as Nathan gets justice," Bonnie said. "He helped the President. He didn't deserve to die for it."

Chapter Thirty-Nine

Nettie-April 15

Spring had expanded Nettie's growing venture to include a vegetable patch outside the greenhouse. A pleasant young man from a nearby nursery tilled up a section of the yard, and she made diagram after diagram, plotting how to maximize both indoor and outdoor planting space. She was unfamiliar with Virginia's growing season and viable crops, but Olin, a native of Norfolk (which sounded like Nawfuk when he said it), warned of long, hot days when the sun beat down on the tender plants like flames. She adjusted her plans accordingly.

One morning Pearl dumped a whole flat of seedlings on the planks that served as a walkway through the greenhouse. While she fussed and excused herself from blame, Nettie bent to try to save what she could. "Olin, will you ask inside for a broom and dustpan?"

He went off, and Nettie worked silently, replacing the tiny plants in their cups and firming the dirt around them while Pearl dithered. She didn't apologize, Pearl never did, but she apparently decided to make up for her carelessness with information. "Do you know there are people checking up on you?"

Nettie looked up, surprised. "Who?"

Pearl shrugged. "Foeller reports to somebody. I heard her on the phone." Nettie imagined Pearl lurking outside the doctor's office. Sneakiness seemed to be part of her nature.

"Are you sure she was talking about me?"

"You're the only Nettie I can think of." Pearl seemed pleased to have piqued her curiosity. "Doc said good things, like how you're quiet and cooperative."

What made the monotonous life of Janet Waller of interest outside the prison?

"Pearl, will you get the hose, please? We need to resettle the dirt around the roots to keep the air out." Nettie always explained what she was doing, though Pearl seldom showed any interest.

When she returned, Nettie gently watered the plants. "Did you hear Dr. Foeller say a name?" she asked casually.

Pearl's eyes rolled upward, and her nose scrunched. "She called him Mr. Craft, or Crawford, maybe."

Nettie filed the name away in her mind. When next she saw her, she'd ask Kim about someone named Craft, Crawford, or something similar.

Chapter Forty

Drew-May 3

As Drew McMahon prepared court cases, drafted wills, and advised clients on the eccentricities of the legal system, his thoughts often strayed to Caleb Green. What had the man done to make his mother, who by all accounts had done her best to raise him well, kill him as he slept? Neglecting the case of a woman who wanted to sue her neighbor for having three Schnauzers when the city's ordinance limited dog ownership to two, he pulled up the files on Nettie Waller's case and read everything again, looking for a thread to pull.

Nettie had at first been almost blank, answering questions with only a yes or a no. Once she realized Drew truly wanted to help, she'd warmed to him a little, but that hadn't made her any more forthcoming. "Let's not waste the court's time, Mr. McMahon. Do what you have to and move on."

Nettie's reticence indicated that she blamed herself for Caleb's faults. Now that he knew Green had been abused as a child, Drew wondered how messed up he'd been. After staring into space and tapping on his desktop with a pen for several minutes, he called the dog-hater and told her he couldn't help with her lawsuit. Putting a sign on his office door that said, *Closed until Monday,* he escaped into the thin spring sunshine. He'd go to Berlin and talk to people who'd known Caleb Green as an adult. He should have done that in the first place, no matter what Nettie ordered. At home, Drew packed a bag, and at the last minute, tossed his fishing gear in the trunk. May was a good time for bluegill, and there was good fishing in the rivers of Michigan's Thumb.

The bunkhouse was now home to a young man with an old man's scowl, his sharp-faced wife, and three noisy children under school age. Nettie's greenhouse stood empty and neglected, its plastic walls pierced in several places with tatters flapping in the breeze. When Drew asked if they'd known Caleb and Nettie, the husband shook his head, a frown creasing his brow. The woman leaned forward, her eyes wide. "Want to see where it happened?"

Drew politely declined. "I'm interested in finding Caleb's friends." They couldn't supply any names, but the woman said, "I heard he used to hang out at the Ace a lot. It's right in the middle of town." Leaning in again, she added, "He was there the night he died. Came home, went to bed, and then *bang!* His mom goes in and shoots him." She pointed. "It's right down there if you want to—"

"Thanks for your time."

The Ace was almost exactly in the middle of Berlin, with a coin laundry on one side and an abandoned clothing store on the other. It wasn't quite noon, but two men sat at the bar, sipping beers and ignoring each other, while the bartender busied herself near the back. Since both customers were drinking Budweiser, McMahon asked for the same.

"I'm interested in talking to someone who knew Caleb Green," he announced as the woman slapped a coaster on the bar and set a frosty-cold beer atop it. The patrons narrowed their eyes, apparently trying to remember who that was. The bartender stopped dead for a few seconds, as if zapped by a magic spell. When she recovered, she returned to her task at the back without comment.

"Caleb Green left here one night a while back and went home, where his mother shot him dead."

At the reminder, the men nodded like twin marionettes. "Oh, yeah," the older one said. "Used to come in a lot, didn't he, Holly?" He frowned. "I don't think him and me ever spoke."

"He never bothered nobody," the other said. "Guess his ma went nuts. Shame."

That seemed to be all they had to offer. The bartender remained where she was. Drew sensed that she was hiding.

"Miss, I have some calls to make," he said. Pointing at a sign over the till, he asked, "Can you bring me an order of those jalapeno poppers?"

She turned to look at him, her deep-brown eyes blank. "Sure."

Drew took his beer, went to the table farthest from the bar, and played games on his phone until Holly brought his order. "They're really hot," she warned, setting the cardboard boat before him. "I brought extra napkins."

"Did you know Caleb Green?"

He thought she'd deny it, but all she said was, "I don't want to be involved in whatever you're doing."

"I'm trying to find out why the guy's mother felt she had to kill him."

Her eyes narrowed. "Never met her. Don't know why she did what she did."

"But you know something about Green. Something that makes you uneasy."

Sighing, she tossed him a bone. "Caleb used to come in here with a line of sh—stuff about how he was going to do this or go there. He'd leave Berlin for a while, but he always ended up back at his mom's."

"She supported him?"

She shrugged. "He'd get a job someplace or another, but it was never 'right' for him, you know?" Holly made air quotes around the word. "The boss hated him. The work didn't fit his skill set. It wasn't getting him where he needed to be."

"Did you and Caleb ever date?"

She shook her head. "I have a kid. Don't need creeps hanging around."

"Caleb was creepy?"

Glancing at her regulars, Holly kept her voice low. "I wouldn't have let Caleb Green within a mile of my daughter."

"Tell me why." Her bottom lip rose, pressing the top one into a downward arc, and he said, "I'm not just nosy. I'm Nettie Waller's lawyer, and I'm hoping to get her paroled. If she was afraid of him, I need to prove it."

When Holly looked over her shoulder again, Drew understood her reluctance. If they're smart, small-town businesspeople don't blab to strangers about the locals. But her customers were watching the TV above the bar, and Holly wanted to tell him about Caleb. He waited, biting into a greasy, tasty popper and washing it down with beer.

"One night after I closed up, my car wouldn't start. I was about to call my brother to pick me up when Caleb came along, driving that beater pickup his mother had. He said he didn't know how to fix my car, but he'd give me a ride home." She bit her bottom lip. "I knew him from the bar. It wasn't like I was getting in with a stranger."

"You accepted."

"Yeah." Her lower lip quivered slightly as she took in a breath and went on. "Halfway to my house, he turned down this two-track road the loggers use. I said, 'Where are you going?' but he didn't answer me. He went maybe two hundred yards, just out of sight from the road, and stopped. I couldn't see his face in the dark, but it creeped me out big time when he said, 'I've been thinking about you a lot, Holly.'"

"What did you do?"

"At first I played it cool, said I had a boyfriend and wasn't looking for a relationship." She stopped, fiddling with the collar of her shirt as if it suddenly felt too tight.

"And—?"

"He said, 'I'm not looking for a relationship either, Holly.' He grabbed my purse and tossed it behind the seat, so I couldn't reach my phone. Then he says, 'I've got a friend who's been teaching me about women. He knows how bitches should be handled.' Then he laughed, and I almost wet my pants." Holly's lips quivered again. "I told myself Caleb was just a jerk who got off on playing games, but that wasn't how it felt."

"What happened then?"

For the first time, she smiled. "Would you believe coyote hunters?" She used the local pronunciation, *KAI yoot*. "I'm sitting there wondering if I should fight him, jump out of the truck and run, or try to talk him out of whatever he had in mind. All of a sudden, these headlights come out of the woods, right at us. Caleb's truck blocked the road, and before he could stop me, I got out and ran to the other truck. It was two guys I knew a little because they come into the bar most weekends."

"What did you say?"

"Caleb was right behind me, and he started in about how good it was that they came along, because we'd stopped to talk and now his truck wouldn't start. He said our cells weren't getting a signal."

"You didn't contradict him?"

She shook her head. "I just wanted to get away, and I was afraid they wouldn't believe how bad he'd scared me." Her lashes, joined by mascara into tarry strips, lowered briefly. "I'm not exactly Snow White, if you know what I mean."

"Caleb's word against yours."

A huff of air said it was worse than that. "Some in this town would say a girl that went with some guy at two in the morning got what she deserved."

Rape is rape under the law, no matter who the victim is, but McMahon knew that in the world Holly inhabited, she might not be seen as a victim. "At least you got away."

"I asked the hunters for a ride home, said I'd send a tow truck for Caleb, and they said sure. He couldn't object to that, so I got my purse and left with them."

"And you were okay then?"

"They thought it was hilarious that Creepy Caleb got stuck out in the woods." She rolled her eyes. "I didn't send a tow truck, either, 'cuz there wasn't a thing wrong with that pickup." As final evidence she added, "The guy at the garage said somebody disconnected my car's battery cables."

"How did Caleb react to all this when you saw him again?"

Holly's expression turned outraged. "Like it never happened. In fact, I kind of wondered if I dreamed it."

"But you didn't."

"If those guys hadn't come along, Caleb would have raped me. If I told on him, he'd have said I asked for it." She glanced around before speaking again. "For a long time, I was scared to close the bar by myself. I kept imagining Caleb and his buddy Marlon waiting for me outside."

Drew had been wiping the grease from his hands with a napkin, but he stopped and looked up at her. "The friend Caleb mentioned was Marlon?"

"Yeah." She shivered. "I bet he's a real sweetheart."

"Right. Birds of a feather."

Outside, McMahon cleaned the remaining fry grease from his hands with sanitizer and a garage towel before touching the steering wheel of the Audi Cabriolet he counted as both transportation and investment. A spring storm had blown in, destroying his plan for a few hours of fishing. He drove southward, ruminating on the name Caleb Green had mentioned to Holly. *Marlon* wasn't a common name, but a particular Marlon came to mind. Gerald M. Tilman, now imprisoned for life, had raped and murdered at least three women. The press had dubbed him the "Garbage Man," since he'd sometimes left his victims' bodies in trash bins. At trial he'd been referred to by his given name, Gerald, but Drew recalled reading that Tilman had usually gone by his middle name, Marlon.

Lightning flashed overhead, and intermittent spates of heavy rain forced him to slow down and hope no driver ahead stopped entirely, blocking the road. Even with the strain of driving under those conditions, he felt a niggling in his gut. What if Caleb Green had known Gerald Marlon Tilman, a man suspected of at least eight murders?

He tried to remember what he knew of the case. Prosecutors had charged Tilman with only the cases where they had enough evidence to convict: one in Lapeer where he'd been caught dumping the body of a woman he'd raped and strangled, another in Port Huron, and a third in the town of Port Sanilac.

As an attorney, McMahon had been interested mostly in how the case was presented and defended. Tilman had refused to speak to anyone except his lawyer, an ambitious woman who insisted someone else was the Garbage Man. She pointed out that the crimes differed in detail, and she claimed that Tilman could not possibly have committed some of them. At the time of one murder, he'd been hospitalized with appendicitis.

"Only TV killers do exactly the same thing every time," the prosecutor had countered. "And even murderers sometimes need emergency surgery."

The prosecution's best evidence was that Tilman had been caught dumping a body. A kid walking home from his girlfriend's house at night saw a man behind a restaurant, pulling a large, tarp-wrapped object from the trunk of his car. The kid's father happened to be a local sheriff's deputy, and officers arrived at the scene in time to catch Tilman before he drove away.

Tilman was linked to two other cases through the testimony of witnesses, an ID on a security video, and his palm print on a victim's car door. Found guilty, he was sentenced to three life terms, to be served consecutively. He would never step foot outside a prison again. Drew guessed there'd been frustration among the authorities at being unable to close the other five cases, but they no doubt consoled themselves with the certainty that the Garbage Man was done killing.

I've got a friend who's been teaching me about women.

How much of this did Kim Dailey need to hear? Though Drew hated the idea of upsetting her, Kim was no shrinking violet. Soft, yes, and perhaps a little naive, but she adjusted quickly to reality. She wouldn't enjoy what he had to tell, but she'd really hate it if he kept secrets from her.

Braking for a large puddle in the road, Drew realized he was letting his imagination take things too far. The idea that Caleb Green knew the Garbage Man was pure speculation on his part. He needed to do a lot more thinking and maybe even some research before he shared his disturbing theory with Kim.

Chapter Forty-One

Ruth-May 5

KLX News blog-Darla Banks

With cherry blossoms blooming outside the window, this reporter sat down with First Lady Ruth Mandell for a wide-ranging talk about how the first sixteen months of the Mandell administration has gone. It's no secret in D.C. that the President's wife is a strong influence on him, though Mrs. Mandell downplayed that when I joined her in her tastefully decorated space a few doors down from the Oval Office. "We're partners," she said. "In effective partnerships, each party listens to the other. Butch is the President, the person voters put in office. I have opinions, but he has the final say."

My interview with Mrs. Mandell will be aired in its entirety on Sunday morning, but here are two excerpts that demonstrate her unique perspective on American life.

DB: We've heard complaints that government spending is on the rise, Mrs. Mandell. Can you explain why that isn't a bad thing?

RPM: Our new procedures are sometimes expensive to implement, but they'll save money in the long run. Butch's referee program discourages legislators from proposing pork-barrel projects. Tertiary jurists save our courts time and money and punish repeat offenders. Our new military arbitrators work with the Pentagon on its budget, and costs are already down twenty percent. Consensus groups save time by teaming Congressional representatives with experts on all sides of an issue. We no longer wait for committees in one house of Congress to spend months probing a topic, introducing legislation, sending it back to committee, and then finally voting on it, only to send it to the other house, where the process starts over. All committees are now joint, and their job is to sit down together and solve problems. The administration takes the lead, helping Congress organize itself, which, though I shouldn't say it, they've never been able to do efficiently.

In each of the cases I've mentioned, we've spent a little at the outset to save a lot in years to come. A more efficient government will lessen the burden on American taxpayers.

DB: You've long held that family roles need to be strengthened, and you've faced criticism for advocating that women leave the workforce. Would you comment on that?

RPM: It's never made sense to me that women pay half their salaries for someone else to raise their kids. We want our children to share our values, yet we leave them with caregivers whose social class, economic level, religion, education, or culture is vastly different. No matter how well-intentioned the caregivers are, kids aren't raised the way they'd be with Mom there.

On a personal note, I left today's interview with a lot to think about. While I'm on the job, my two children are at a day care center. They're safe and supervised, but as their mother, shouldn't I be their biggest influence? Ruth Mandell makes a woman think about what it is to be a woman.

Be sure to tune in to KLX for Sunday Selections at 9:00 a.m. and hear more of our First Lady's fascinating comments.

Sunlight warmed the morning as Ruth and Kim left the White House and visited a public school that had adopted creative approaches to learning. After listening to presentations from teachers and students, Ruth gave a short speech. While she promised support for public education, she mentioned the need for private schools focused on specific goals. "Religious instruction has always been one reason for private education," she said, "but we need private schools dedicated to the arts, vocational training, and special education. Our public schools do a good job for most children, but we all know students who would benefit from a different approach. Some have special talents; some have special needs. Some have no desire to go to college, and some can't adjust to the traditional school-day model. If we encourage private schools that appeal to those students, we relieve the burden on public schools and let them concentrate on what they do well."

"Good speech," Kim commented afterward. "Should play well on both sides."

"That's the whole idea of consensus." Ruth was staring over the driver's shoulder. "You know what's always bothered me?"

"What?"

"Car dashboards are all different. Why is that?"

"I suppose it depends on the company."

"Yes, but you get used to the turn signal being on the right side of the steering column. Then you get a new car and it's on the left. It could cause an accident."

Kim chuckled. "How long has it been since you even drove a car?"

Ruth smiled, acknowledging it had been a while. "Still, lots of things in this country would be easier to use if they were uniform. Why don't credit card readers all work the same way? Why are gas pumps different at different stations? Why can't phones all operate the same?"

"It's…I don't know."

"Think about confused senior citizens, inexperienced teenagers, or busy housewives. Why should they have to adjust to these useless variances every day?" Ruth thumped her fist on the armrest. "We should see what can be done."

"You haven't got enough to do without reorganizing the world's businesses?"

Her right brow rose. "That's what's great about having a little power, Kimmie. Other people gladly do the work, both because my suggestions make sense and because they like to make me happy."

Ruth sat in the semi-dark family room, relishing the quiet. Her feet were killing her. Dinner had been long, and it was after midnight when their guests had been escorted to their rooms. She'd worn higher heels than usual, since the ambassador's wife was a tall, willowy type who made her feel like Thumbelina. She'd pay for it, but at least she'd met the woman's gaze—almost.

She hadn't forgotten her complaint earlier in the day. Before joining Butch in bed (He was already snoring), Ruth composed an email to the FTC director, using Butch's account.

> Would like regulations that encourage standardization in business, so users and consumers can easily use items they need daily. As an example, a size ten should always be the same, no matter the brand. Clocks should work the same way, so the average adult can set the time without asking some geeky teenager to help. Every website should have a similar landing page, so users easily find what they're looking for.
>
> Please submit ideas for new regs within a month, as we are eager to get started on this.

Ruth turned away from the computer. In the morning when she was fresh, she'd check the email for errors and then send it. She went to bed pleased that she'd again found a way to make life better for everyone.

But when she came downstairs in the morning, Croft was waiting at her office door. Once they were inside, he said, "We've got riots in some of the ACs." Though they were officially known as "guest worker settlements," White House staffers called the areas where foreign workers were housed "alien camps" or "ACs."

"What's the problem?"

"The usual complaints. Conditions are primitive. Employers use them as slaves."

"Have our guests forgotten the horrible places they came from?" Ruth paced for a few seconds. "What do you recommend?"

"The President stated our policy publicly. We need to respond with decision."

"You mean with force?"

"I know it seems harsh, but these people are neither as fair-minded nor as altruistic as you are. The only way to prevent more trouble is to remove the agitators and show the rest that we mean business. If we let these people come into our country to work, they must recognize our right to set the rules."

Ruth had stopped to look at Croft as he spoke, but when he finished, she did some more pacing. "All right," she finally said. "Send in a Special Ops team, arrest the leaders of the protest, and deport them immediately. Tell the rest they'll receive the same treatment if they don't go back to work. Once that's done, organize the workers into teams of twenty. Each team should meet to discuss, and then submit three ideas on how to improve conditions in the camps. Tell them we'll look into their complaints, but at the same time, require them to report those who try to stir up trouble. Remind them they can all be deported if we decide it isn't worth it to deal with them." Nodding, Croft turned to leave, but Ruth had another idea. "Give each team leader some sort of badge—No, let's do jackets with patches that say, 'TEAM LEADER' or something similar. Authority is a big motivator."

"Excellent idea, Mrs. Mandell. I'll see to it."

When Croft was gone, Ruth sent the email she'd composed the night before, and then sat staring at the computer screen. Once, and it seemed a long time ago, she'd been prepared to be a traditional First Lady. She'd adopt a cause, attend events, and smile for the cameras. But as Butch's inability to lead became obvious, she'd happily stepped into his shoes. *I like it,* Ruth thought. *I like solving problems and having the power to see that my suggestions are turned into actions.*

Other First Ladies had, to differing extents and under differing circumstances, become the power behind the President. Ruth Mandell had the opportunity to improve the nation she loved, and she intended to make the most of it.

Leaving a brunch with business leaders that afternoon, Ruth and Kim moved through a light rain, surrounded by a circle of watchful Secret Service agents and protected by umbrellas held over their heads. As the limousine exited the venue, two homeless men wove through the traffic ahead, knocking on car windows and asking for money. Ruth shook her head. "Such a shame."

"I know." Kim turned to watch the pair recede as the car went on.

They rode on in silence, but as they entered the White House grounds, Ruth said, "We could do something with them."

Kim had already forgotten. "Do something with who?"

"Whom." Ruth caught herself frowning and relaxed her forehead, determined not to get deep furrows between her eyes like Nettie had. "The homeless. We could send them somewhere to be rehabilitated, so they don't make nuisances of themselves on our streets. They need to go somewhere and learn to be self-sufficient, like the old communes."

Her voice teasing, Kim asked, "Are we going back to the sixties?"

"They'd get whatever they need to get better. If they're addicts, we help them get clean. If they have PTSD, we provide counselling and support. If they need to re-establish self-esteem, we find them meaningful work to do."

"Aren't those things available now in some form or another?"

Kim's lack of imagination was often like a pin stuck in Ruth's balloon of confidence. "Current programs are voluntary. Do you think it's smart to let someone with a diseased mind decide what he will or won't do?" She put a hand on Kim's arm. "Think how differently things might have turned out if someone had intervened with Nettie early on, someone who didn't let her make all those bad decisions."

Kim frowned. "If fixing people were that simple, someone would have done it already."

"Maybe no one's tried hard enough." Ruth spoke lightly, but in her mind, she was well on the way to creating a plan.

Chapter Forty-Two

Kim-May 5

Harley Stark flicked the office lights on and off twice to get Kim's attention. "We're having cake in the VP's office. It's his birthday."

"Oh, right. I have a card somewhere in this mess. I'll find it and be right there."

Glancing at the envelopes piled on her desk, Harley asked, "Can I help? The Cardinal is gone for the day, so he isn't looming over my shoulder."

After Nettie told Kim about Gavin Croft's calls to Martha's Place to check up on her, they'd nicknamed him "The Cardinal," a reference to the diabolical character in Dumas' musketeer stories. In an unguarded moment, Kim had mentioned the nickname to Harley, who, to her surprise, knew all about Cardinal Richelieu's behind-the-throne machinations. He'd begun referring to the Chief of Staff by that name when he and Kim were alone.

"Could you drop this stack off at Lucy's office on your way? She's going to check for duplicates before we mail them."

"Sure. What about the others?"

"Ruth wants to sign those personally before I send them out."

"All of them?" Harley set the finished mail into a tray for transport. "Mrs. Mandell certainly is a hard worker."

"I think the word is *indefatigable*."

"Was she always like that? All organized and do-it-this-way?" His tone held a hint of resentment, and Kim recalled Ruth insisting, albeit gently, that Harley have his college tattoo removed.

"She used to clean my room and then say, 'This is how it should always look.'" Kim massaged her fingers, which ached from addressing fifty invitations to a White House supper by hand, as Ruth had instructed. "It drove her crazy that I didn't care how messy my room was, but I was maybe eight years old."

"Does she ever run out of energy?"

"Not when she's on a mission to make something better." Out of loyalty she didn't add—*to her way of thinking*.

"No disrespect to her," Harley said, "but I'd just as soon work with you." With the heedlessness Kim had come to expect from him, he added, "And I could go for a long time without dealing with Master Ben and his 'situations' again."

"What situations?"

"Croft had me help Ben deal with a problem." Belatedly aware he'd said too much, Harley backtracked. "I figured you knew, since it was family stuff."

"I guess I missed it in the fuss of getting ready for the English delegation." Though Kim wondered what action of Ben's had required intervention from the U.S. government, she didn't question Harley, since it was, as he'd said, "family stuff."

"Here's Cary's card. Let's go see what kind of cake we get."

Ben's "situation" and Croft's intervention made Kim curious, so she decided to ask Ruth directly. In an infrequent moment when the two of them weren't surrounded by others, she asked, "What's Ben up to that concerns Mr. Croft?"

"Where did you hear that?" Ruth sounded snappish, but a second later, she regained control. "Gavin served as intermediary in a dispute to help Ben out."

"Who was involved?"

Though a sigh hinted she didn't want to answer, Ruth did. "Ben and a young woman had a…misunderstanding. They'd both been drinking, and you know how those things go. She accused him of inappropriate behavior, exactly the sort of thing one expects when an unscrupulous woman spends time alone with the President's son." Ruth licked her lips. "Since Gavin is an attorney, he offered to make the girl aware of the dangers of attempted extortion."

Kim was tempted to ask if they'd even considered that the girl might be telling the truth, but she bit her tongue. No sense telling a mother her son was arrogant and entitled. Certainly not a mother like Ruth.

Interested to learn what others thought of the President and his advisors, Kim began infiltrating the various White House cliques. She invented names for them in her head: the Up-and-Comings, who ate lunch at their desks in order to be available to some Cabinet member; the Here-for-the-Glory types, who avoided work but managed to stand behind their bosses when the cameras started rolling; and the My-Parents-Are-So-Proud set, who did exactly as ordered, because being sent home to Duluth or El Paso or Panama City Beach was the worst disgrace they could imagine. While Kim didn't fit in any of the groups, they were all welcoming, so she began fraternizing, both at and after work.

Croft was often the target of the griping, though Kim noticed a lowering of volume when someone recounted the latest outrage. He was rumored to have ears everywhere, and his revenge was swift. Anyone Croft believed disloyal, from Cabinet heads to the guy who opened doors for the President, might find himself out of the White House and unemployable as well.

Among the whines about long hours, coworkers' snubs, and prickly bosses, Kim heard opinions on the rapidly dissipating search for consensus. Most commissions, committees, and citizen panels formed in Butch's first months in office had been proclaimed successful (whether that was true or not) and disbanded. Generally, the staff approved. "All they did was argue," one aide complained. "Then they'd get all mad because the President wasn't paying enough attention to their precious topic, like that was the only thing he had to deal with."

Feeling disloyal and a little foolish, Kim started keeping track of things that didn't seem right to her. Unsure how secure her computer was, she went low-tech, buying a fancifully decorated notebook and using her own form of shorthand to set down dates, times, and incidents where she believed pressure was applied or bribes offered. When the White House announced that the business task force was in complete agreement on new tax legislation, she wrote down the names of those she knew had disagreed and kept track of what happened to their careers. If she found out what had been used to pressure them into compliance, she wrote that down too.

Though it felt like paranoia, Kim didn't keep the notebook in her living space or work area. Instead, she set it at the bottom of a stack of manuals in a room where documents were printed, laminated, and bound. From the layer of dust on top, she concluded that no one consulted paper manuals anymore. It was easier to ask the internet, *What do I do when the printer jams?*

Chapter Forty-Three

Kim-May 10

"What I'm finding out isn't pretty," Drew's hesitant tone indicated he'd considered not telling her what he'd discovered.

"I have to hear it all," she replied, "but not on this phone."

"They listen in on your calls?"

She sighed. "I'd rather not take the chance."

Though she suspected he wanted to, Drew didn't ask for specifics. "Okay. Call me from a different phone."

Kim glanced out at the blustery day, unsure how she'd do that. "Give me an hour."

Putting on a light coat, she left the White House and walked to the Mall. A girl of about fifteen sat on a bench, apparently waiting for someone. She shivered in the too-thin jacket she wore, and Kim smiled to herself, recalling those days of youth when fashion dictates one's level of comfort. The girl held a phone before her like a talisman, and Kim said, "Hi. I'm sorry to bother you, but I left my phone in my office, and I need to make a quick call." When raised brows hinted the girl was about to refuse, Kim added, "It's worth fifty bucks to me not to have to go all the way back inside. It'll be a really short call."

The girl waited while Kim pulled the fifty-dollar bill she kept folded small in a side pocket of her purse for emergencies, and the exchange was made. She'd memorized Drew's number, and when he answered she said only, "It's me." Aware that the phone's owner was listening, Kim spoke quietly in response to Drew's instructions.

"Buy one of those prepaid phones at a box store. I'll get one too. Send a text message to this phone and give me your new phone's number…Let's see." He paused to think. "Send the number using questions that I'll know the answer to but no one else will. For example, if you ask, 'What color did I wear the day we first met?' The answer is *blue,* so that would give me the number four. Or you could ask what time your first appointment was. I know your area code is 202, so you can skip that and just give me clues to the last eight digits."

"You remember what color I wore a year ago?"

"I remember everything about that meeting."

Embarrassed, Kim said, "Got it," and ended the call. Returning the phone to its owner, she headed for the bus stop.

As she rode, Kim chastised herself for the cloak-and-dagger behavior she and Drew were engaging in. She had no proof she was under scrutiny, only hints from things Harley said in his offhand way or looks that she saw pass between Ruth and Gavin Croft.

The day before, Kim had brought Ruth an article from the internet that claimed the camps for undocumented immigrants were little better than prisons. The writer described employers sending semi-trucks each morning to take workers to their fields or factories. They returned them to the camps at night, where food was scarce, sanitation was lacking, and protests were met with force.

Ruth had responded with an angry wave. "You can't give credence to journalists who don't even sign their names, Kimmie."

"He doesn't give his name because he could be prosecuted for disseminating what you call fake news."

"Well, it is fake. Some despicable nobody is trying to bring us down with lies."

"Ms. Dailey," Croft had said in an oily tone, "these outliers always have an agenda. That's exactly why we instituted changes to the rules of reporting."

"George Orwell would disagree." Kim quoted: "*Freedom of the press, if it means anything at all, means the freedom to criticize and oppose.*"

Ruth sniffed disdainfully. "Isn't Orwell the one who wrote the book about pigs?" She and Croft exchanged a glance that said tales of talking animals had no place in the real world.

At that point Kim had invented an errand and left, feeling it was best to walk away.

An hour after she'd left it, Kim returned to the park bench, which was now empty. The wind had picked up, and her hair blew around her face as she sent the list of questions she'd worked out on the bus ride back. While her acquaintance with Andrew McMahon was neither long nor deep, they'd grabbed lunch one day when he was first assigned Nettie's case. She'd racked her brain to recall things they'd talked about once the subject of Nettie's fate had been discussed, and she hoped he recalled the same things she did.

Her number was 883-5016

For 8, she wrote: *MI favorite I can't stand* (The answer was kielbasa, which he'd ordered.)

8: *Same as above*

3: *# of times I visited yr office*

5: *childhood dog's name* (Candy. While Ruth might remember that, she'd never been a dog person)

0: *# of times I've had sushi*

1: *Fob on my keychain* (a ***1*** in U of M's colors, which he'd teased her about, being a Michigan State grad)

6: *sport I won't watch on TV* (tennis)

After checking to be sure no one could hear, she answered her new phone when it rang for the first time. "Did we do it?"

Drew chuckled. "We're into spy craft now: untraceable phones and coded messages."

"I know it sounds weird, but people know that you and I talk."

"Why would anyone care?"

"Because you connect to Nettie. I'm pretty sure they don't want me opening that can of worms a second time."

"Isn't this administration supposed to be different? Open, honest, all that?"

"That's what Butch wanted—wants, but not everyone shares his view. They say the words and hold their faces right, but too many are busily increasing their wealth and power."

"And they spy on people like you, hoping to find weaknesses they can exploit."

"Yes." Her spine tingled as she imagined a van nearby with a parabolic listening device aimed in her direction.

"No offense, but why does your opinion matter so much?"

Kim bit her lip. "Everyone around Ruth, from her staff to her kids, tells her how great she is, how wise and good. I can't say things I don't believe, so I guess that makes me a challenge for her."

Drew paused, taking that in. "Still, the two of us talking isn't exactly a national issue. And helping Nettie out doesn't threaten the administration."

"Appearances matter a lot to Ruth. She's embarrassed that she comes from a dinky town, and she remembers our youth in negative terms, like when we had to be careful not to show up at school with cow manure on the soles of our shoes. Now she hates that there's a killer in her immediate family. To balance that, she likes me beside her, smiling as she saves the country from itself. I think she wants Nettie to stay out of sight and hopefully out of the public mind."

"She doesn't care that Nettie might have had cause for what she did?"

"If Nettie was afraid of Caleb, people might ask why her wealthy sister didn't do more to defend her from a murder charge. For Ruth, it's better if all the previous nastiness isn't dragged into the limelight again." Kim sighed. "I don't want to hurt Butch or Ruth or their goals, but I'm positive Nettie is not a monster who killed her son for no reason."

"I never believed she was, and what I'm learning bears that out." Drew told Kim Holly's story, ending with, "She admits Caleb never laid a hand on her, so I suppose he might have been the type who gets a thrill out of scaring women. But she was convinced he meant to rape her."

"My God." Kim realized, though she didn't say it aloud, that sexual threat was part of the weirdness she'd felt when Caleb visited her home. The way he'd looked at her. His tone of voice. Had he considered raping his own aunt?

"Abuse as a child can be a big factor for rapists," Drew was saying. "Because they had no power as kids, they take it by forcing themselves on women."

Someone called Drew's name, and he said, "I have to go. Call me on this phone anytime. I'll keep it handy."

Kim put the extra phone in a side pocket of her purse, her mind boiling with a dozen emotions. If Nettie had discovered that her son was a rapist, what would that have done to her?

Chapter Forty-Four

Drew-May 14

Drew McMahon began collecting everything the legal system had to offer on Caleb Green. He re-read the reports he'd obtained at the time of Nettie's trial. He called or visited police stations and sheriff's offices in the Thumb area, asking what, if anything, they'd known about Green. He hoped that putting bits and pieces together would either prove or disprove what he thought—what he feared—might be true.

Green's juvenile record began with an arrest for shoplifting at age eleven. A store owner who saw the boy pocket a bottle of Tylenol and leave followed Caleb out, dragged him back inside, and called the police. Reading the report, Drew sensed that the cop had felt compassion for a fatherless kid from a low-income household. *Boy says took pills for mom—headaches.* Nettie had paid for the stolen item and ordered her son to apologize to the owner, which he'd done without hesitation.

The second arrest came three years later, and this time it was more serious. On the school bus one afternoon, Caleb punched a girl several years older than he, breaking her front tooth. He claimed that she'd harassed him for weeks, calling him "raggedy boy" and "loser." Both had received counseling. The psychiatrist noted in her letter to the judge, *Caleb spoke freely and smiled often, but I got the feeling I saw only the boy he thinks he's supposed to be.*

There were other scrapes with the law, one serious enough that Caleb had worn a tether for several months. A restraining order was issued after a girl claimed he stalked her. Caleb's attorney argued that in a small town, it was inevitable that two teens would show up in the same places.

The most interesting item involved Caleb being questioned about a murder in a town where he worked. The detective on the case thought he had his man until Tilman was arrested. Once it was established that Tilman was responsible for the deaths of several women in southeastern Michigan, other unsolved crimes were assumed to be the work of the Garbage Man.

Drew drove north to Lapeer to interview Detective Patrick Lazarowitz, who'd questioned Caleb about the rape/murder. "I had this feeling Green was my guy," Lazarowitz confided. "The victim shopped at the store where he worked. A customer had reported him for saying 'creepy things' when he carried out her groceries. There was this look to him, this glint in his eyes that said, '*I did it, but you'll never prove it.*'" He combed through his spiky hair with his fingers. "I wanted it to be him, you know?"

"Then they arrested Tilman."

"Yeah." The detective frowned. "There were some differences that bothered me, but my captain said, 'Pat, how many serial killers you think we got operating in southeast Michigan?'" He massaged his neck. "It made sense, you know?"

"You said there were differences?"

"Some of the bodies weren't left in trash bins. And in two cases I know about, the women's keys were taken, probably as souvenirs. Tilman didn't do that."

"Did you tell your captain about Caleb?"

"What's to tell? A kid that got in trouble. A guy that couldn't hold a job and gave me bad vibes. Not exactly a damning profile."

"Did you ever meet his mother?"

"Yeah, I went to talk to her." He leaned over to peer at his notes. "Janet."

"What was your impression?"

The detective chuckled. "She asked me more questions than I asked her. Wanted to know everything I could tell her about Tilman and the murders. Guess she was afraid, being out there all by herself most of the time. Of course, I couldn't tell her everything, but I tried to set her mind at ease."

"Did you succeed?"

"I don't know." He shook his head. "Later on, she calls me out of the blue to ask how we knew Tilman was our guy. By then I'd read enough to be pretty sure, and that's what I told her. She said, 'Then you don't believe my son has done anything wrong?'" He rubbed at his jaw. "Now, to be honest, I still figured Green was guilty of something, but Tilman was our guy. I put her mind at ease, said her son was okay." Glancing at the clock, Lazarowitz rose from his chair. "I'm due in court in fifteen minutes, so…"

Drew put away his notebook. "Thanks for your time. The fact that you suspected Caleb Green of murder tells me a lot."

"But I was wrong. And even if I wasn't, the guy's dead now." Lazarowitz opened the door and let McMahon precede him. "When I read about it, I felt bad for the mother. I bet that punk did stuff that scared her into killing him."

"She insists he never hurt her. And he was in bed, sound asleep."

"Doesn't mean she wasn't afraid of what he *might* do." They stopped at the head of the stairway. "I've had parents tell me they know their kid will commit a horrible crime someday. They don't know who they'll hurt or when, but there's this ache in their guts, like a warning."

Drew headed for his car, turning what he knew over and over in his mind. According to Kim, Caleb blamed Nettie for leaving him with his demented grandmother. That first crime, the stolen bottle of Tylenol. Had Caleb considered murdering his mother that first year?

If so, he'd changed his mind. Caleb might have figured out that Nettie's guilt made her susceptible to his demands. He must have seen that she'd never deny him a bed, a meal, and anything else she could provide. What, then, had he done or said that pushed her to murder? What had Nettie known about Caleb Green that no one else did?

When he got back to his office, Drew wrote to the prison in Ionia, Michigan, asking for permission to interview Gerald Marlon Tilman.

Chapter Forty-Five

Kim-June 10

As summer turned the city to a sea of flowers a second time, the Mandell administration scoured the corners of the republic for dirt and dust, streamlining old methods and pushing Congress to enact new laws. Objections that arose were drowned out in the celebratory mood that swept the nation. Party One wasn't blocking Party Two's agenda. Decisions were made, and things got done.

Early on, Butch had issued an executive order creating a new breed of public servants called *referees*. Appointed by the President, their task was, as he put it, "to stick their noses into everybody's business." Referees investigated complaints from everywhere, from legal watchdogs to private citizens. They recommended changes to practices that were deemed redundant or counterproductive. They presented their findings first to the Congressional representatives involved. For example, if construction of a bridge in Delaware was delayed and the referee suspected corruption, he notified both the senator and the representative from the district. As Press Secretary Delacroix explained it, "Referees don't take a 'side.' They simply observe and report, encouraging elected officials to fix the problem. But if they act within a reasonable time, the referee will move up the chain of command."

That meant the President's Council of Citizen Justice, a group that heard testimony from all sides. Anyone who refused to appear before the council in a timely manner was hunted down and brought before them in handcuffs. The Council could fine or even jail those judged guilty of misbehavior. Challenges to the Council were few, and when they occurred, the courts almost always sided with its ruling.

"Citizens are sick of waiting years for problems to be solved," Butch said in a speech that outlined the referees' more notable successes. "Shady contractors and building inspectors who look the other way will be found out, and everybody who isn't doing his job will be sorry if the CCJ has to intervene."

Kim learned (and wrote in her book) that any judge who ruled against referees' recommendations was reported to Kenneth Betzer, who quietly shifted him to the corners of jurisprudence. "If they don't see the value in what we do," she overheard Betzer telling Ruth, "they can adjudicate traffic cases and disputes over copyright infringement."

Lobbyists were bound by strict new rules. "Incentives" for elected officials were banned. No trips to the Caribbean. No secret contributions to a re-election campaign. Not even an invitation to lunch or golf. If business wasn't done on the record, a referee was likely to show up and ask embarrassing questions.

With publicity that bordered on propaganda in Kim's mind, Butch was elevated to a god-like standard. He was on TV almost daily, signing executive orders with an expression appropriate to the material they contained. Those "Busy President" shots were teamed with "Down-to-Earth President" moments. On sunny days, Butch might appear on the White House lawn in shorts and a t-shirt to play fetch with his dog or stroll peacefully with a childhood friend from Pennsylvania.

Kim and other insiders knew that Butch had little real interest in the work his office demanded. That was all right, Ruth insisted, because voters had the strong leader they wanted, a man who looked directly into the cameras and said things that calmed their fears.

It was hard to disagree with their success. The nation's First Couple behaved with dignity. They established consistent policies that were easy to understand and enforce. They seemed to have the nation's good in mind in whatever they did.

But Kim knew what was happening behind the scenes. Gavin Croft had files on everyone's private lives, and he used them to force members of Congress to put their heads down and go along. When some members resigned, citing ill health or family concerns, fresh faces appeared, often independents who admired the President and were eager to follow his lead. Through it all, Ruth's hand guided things. She coached Butch, she cajoled malcontents, and she convinced the public that things were getting better every day.

"How do you do it?" Kim asked her. "Every day it's something new. Foreign visitors, domestic issues, one problem after another, all day long."

"I love it," Ruth replied. "We're making a difference."

"What if something you do backfires and makes a situation worse?"

Ruth's expression revealed genuine surprise. "A person can't succeed if she doubts herself, Kimmie."

Madison *Reporter* June 10, 2026

> *Gun control is an issue most legislators take pains to avoid, but President Mandell claims a solution is in the making. Shortly after taking office, Mandell created a commission made up of gun manufacturers, anti-gun groups, psychologists, the NRA, and a half-dozen other entities vocal on the issue. He asked them to "wade through the hype and address the core problem." There was muttering in Congress, since the 1997 Dickey Amendment bans spending government money to study gun problems, but Mandell ignored the objections. "It's time to get past old thinking. No more thoughts, prayers, and promises. We're going to take action."*
>
> *It is the President's position that both sides of the issue have not been honest and open with the public. "Gun defenders don't want ownership restricted," Mandell's press secretary told reporters. "They scream, 'Second Amendment! Second Amendment!' instead of seeking workable solutions. Those against gun ownership refuse to acknowledge that common sense practices like requiring trigger locks and firearm safety classes can greatly reduce gun deaths. They'd rather eliminate whole classes of firearms in the vain hope that no one will kill anyone if a certain type of gun isn't available."*
>
> *When the inevitable question of mass shootings arose, Delacroix responded, "The murders of school children or mall shoppers are horrible and tragic, but here are the facts. Of the 15,000 murders committed with guns any given year in this country, a miniscule number are the result of mass shootings. In 2021, for example, it was 373. While that number represents too many lives lost, guns are one thing and mental illness is another. Terrorism is different from either of those. Mandell's*

Firearms Commission is tasked with reducing gun deaths while recognizing the right to bear arms."

Today's briefing also introduced a new use of the referendum, a direct vote by all citizens, as a tool for lawmakers. "With today's technology," Secretary Delacroix explained, "it's possible to let citizens weigh in on important questions by actually having them vote on legislation before Congress does. While a referendum won't be binding, it will send Congress a clear indication of what their constituents want."

Constitutional scholars immediately weighed in. Some believe a referendum would damage representative government. Others acknowledge that Congress long ago stopped representing individual voters. "The referendum would bypass business interests, corporate money, and lobbyists' pressure," one analyst concluded. "With it, voters could indicate what they want done. Members of Congress will have to decide if they want to stand with their constituents or stand in their way."

"I don't recall Butch ever mentioning referendums." Kim said as they watched the talking heads discuss the idea. "It sounds more like a Gavin Croft plan to manipulate Congress."

Ruth's gaze was cool. "Today's technology allows it, so why not hear what voters have to say on a given issue?"

Kim broached a dangerous topic. "Butch doesn't show much interest in his job these days, Ruth. Is he okay?"

"He's fine," she responded crisply. "He was there when we came up with this idea, and Butch wholeheartedly approves of the referendum as a way of finding consensus."

"That's good." Though Kim's tone remained mild, her words belied it. "After all, Butch was elected President, no one else."

Chapter Forty-Six

Drew-June 12

Marlon Tilman was housed in the I-Max, a maximum-security prison in Ionia, Michigan. To see him, Drew McMahon had submitted a written request. Once he was checked out, Tilman was asked if he wanted to meet with a man he'd never heard of. Hoping to intrigue the prisoner enough to agree to see him, Drew put *Need information only you can provide* as his reason for visiting.

"Tilman hasn't been a good boy, so he's been in Level V for a while," the man who called Drew reported. "But he's out now, and the visit's been okayed by the powers that be."

"Great. Thanks."

Drew drove two hours west to the city of Ionia on one of those summer days where it seems like the trees are breathing in sunlight as they fatten and turn deep green. The scenery almost—but not quite—dispelled his dread of entering Michigan's most secure prison. He'd been inside jails, of course, but this was a giant step deeper into the world of crime and punishment. Drew was both intrigued and anxious as he stopped at the gate for instructions on how to proceed. The facility felt like a medieval castle on steroids, with a stun fence surrounding it and cameras everywhere. He'd read that it was aging and overcrowded these days since, on Michigan's long list of things that needed fixing, prisons ranked after roads, schools, bridges, toxic water lines, and a host of other concerns.

The chill at his backbone intensified as Drew entered the facility, went through the pat-down and other procedures the visit required, and was led into the bowels of the prison. Though he knew better, his imagination conjured a scenario where a stone-faced guard said, "Nobody told me you could leave." That came from TV shows where the hero went in undercover and then couldn't get anyone to believe he didn't belong there. Heroic friends always got the TV character out, but McMahon hadn't told anyone, even Kim, where he was going to be.

His mood was lifted by a guide who was either naturally chatty or pleased to converse with someone unlikely to shiv him if he turned his back. "Your guy was in solitary until yesterday, which is why your request was delayed. That's good for you, because he's probably ready to talk to just about anybody."

"Does Tilman have friends here?"

That got him a look. "Nobody here has friends the way you think of it."

"What did he do to get solitary?"

The guard hesitated. They probably weren't supposed to gossip about the inner workings of the place, but in the end, the story was too good to resist. "There was a prisoner giving Tilman grief, and he ended up with eyedrops in his coffee."

"I heard that can be bad."

"Yeah. His breathing got all funny. Someone saw Tilman swipe a bottle that one of the guards carries with him, so they figured out pretty quick what was wrong and who did it."

They'd come to their destination, an open room where bored-looking guards stood at each entrance and visitors, mostly women, waited at what could only be called stalls, each peering through a glass partition for the man she'd come to visit. Every few seconds a prisoner entered on the opposite side, located a familiar face, and came forward. They each picked up phones that hung beside them so they could communicate. One woman put her hand on the glass, and the man did the same, touching without touching.

When Tilman stepped through the door and stopped to survey the visitors, Drew recognized him from newspaper photos. Marlon Tilman had a nest of wavy blond hair, high cheekbones under large blue eyes, and a mouth that might be called *sensuous*, with lips that were a little slack, a little wet. There was nothing of cruelty in his expression, no hint of what he was capable of.

Tilman's hands rested at his waist in loose fists, hinting at shackles recently removed. The guard pointed toward Drew and spoke, and the prisoner waved as if they'd met on the street. Coming forward, he sat and picked up the phone. "Mr. McMahon."

"Thanks for meeting with me."

Tilman's smooth brow creased briefly. "For a while, there were reporters every day, asking about my parents, my brothers, did I wet the bed in middle school. Any tidbit no one had printed yet."

"But your kind of notoriety fades with time."

Tilman's blue eyes turned icy. "You're here, so something has changed."

"I'm interested in your acquaintance with a guy named Caleb Green."

He blinked once. "Never heard of him."

"That's funny. He told a witness you were 'teaching him about women.'"

The man's free hand flashed a dismissive gesture. "Men lie to impress the ladies."

"You once lived two blocks from the grocery store where Green worked. One of your victims was probably abducted from the store's parking lot."

Drew had read everything he could find on Tilman. According to several sources, he was cunning but not particularly intelligent. And like many criminals, he had a colossal ego. With a hint of derision in his voice Drew said, "I suppose no one wants to admit his protege is more successful than he."

"My *protege*? You've got to be kidding." Remembering his earlier denial, Tilman backtracked. "I worked alone."

"Caleb said you were teaching him." Judging it was time for flattery, he added, "He said you were the master, and he wanted to learn everything he could from you."

After Tilman thought about that for a while, he raised his index finger. "I let him *watch*. Once."

Tilman's confirmation of an association with Caleb Green struck Drew silent for a few seconds. Caleb had learned from the Garbage Man. What had he done with the lesson?

Lost in a memory, Tilman stroked the side of his face. "He got all quiet when it was done. We talked once afterward, and then I never heard from him again." His chin rose, and Drew guessed Caleb's rejection had hurt. "No problem. I went my own way." He leaned toward the glass until his forehead almost touched it. "I figure young Caleb had the desire but not the guts."

"To kill."

His smile made Drew's flesh crawl. "It isn't as easy as you might think."

"How does the topic of murder come up between casual acquaintances?"

Tilman touched his temple with a forefinger. "When there's anger under the skin, it slips out through a man's eyes."

Lazarowitz had commented on Caleb's disquieting gaze. "How did you meet Green?"

"I was in the store getting groceries one day, and here was this kid, setting out canned goods." Tilman rested an elbow on the shelf before him. "We got talking, and I mentioned I was into watching a martial arts form called Belizekal. He said there was an exhibition in Port Huron that weekend. The guy who was supposed to ride over there with him had canceled because of some bullshit arrest. I offered to buy the second ticket."

"You and Green hit it off."

"Yes." A moment of introspection hit, and he said, "I never had a lot of friends, but he and I started hanging out, visiting the local bars."

"When did you share your, um, secret activities with him?"

"You mean, how do you tell a new acquaintance that you kill people?" He made a wry face. "Probably the same way a gay man comes out to his best friend." Tilman cradled his chin in his free hand. "You toss out a hint. If your listener doesn't make a strong objection, you move to a bigger hint. Et cetera, et cetera, et cetera."

"Did Green tell you his secrets too?"

"No." Tilman's eyes glowed. "He listened, like a star-struck teenager. I was doing things he'd fantasized about, and he wanted to know everything."

"Because he hated women?"

Tilman nodded. "Caleb said his grandmother was the devil and his mother was a waste of skin."

"Do you think he could have acted on his own, using what you…showed him?"

"If he did, I have no knowledge of it." Tilman sounded almost prim as he added, "I will say that some of the cases they tried to pin on me are not mine."

"Did you tell the police that?"

"Sure." He rolled his eyes to indicate how far that had gone. They said, 'Gee, Marlon, we'll check that out.' Hah."

"Are you saying that some of the deaths blamed on you might have been Caleb's doing?"

"Cops are always happy to close murder cases. Now, I have a number I know are mine. The others?" He flipped a hand. "Anyone might have done them."

"You never mentioned Caleb's name to the police?"

Tilman's chin rose. "Why would I do that?"

"Weren't you jealous that you got caught and he didn't?"

"Can you prove he killed anyone?"

"No."

"Then why would I be jealous? I don't think the kid has the nerve to do what I did." Tilman jabbed his chest with a thumb. "What I got away with for years." As an afterthought he added, "But if he *is* on the hunt today, it's because he learned from a master."

Suddenly Drew felt like he couldn't breathe. He stood, sending the chair skidding backward, and spoke in a tone of repressed fury. "Just so you know, *Master,* Caleb Green can't benefit from your expertise these days. His mother, that 'waste of skin' he spoke of, put him down with three shots to the chest."

Chapter Forty-Seven

Nettie-June 21

When Kim visited Nettie on a mild day in June, they walked through the greenhouse together. The heat gave the place an earthy smell, and Kim asked a lot of questions as they went. Nettie was pleased that she recognized how important the greenhouse was to her.

When Nettie questioned her about life at the White House, Kim's response was a question. "Do you think Ruth could ever, um, go over the edge?"

"What do you mean?"

"She's changing everything, from kids' toys to how we store nuclear missiles. Butch pays no attention, and Ruth gets…I don't know…stubborn if other people don't see things the way she does."

Nettie removed a dead leaf from a tomato plant. "That's our Ruth."

"At home, Ruth was like my second mom, pushing me in the direction she thought I should go. You were more a buddy type sister, and I liked that you didn't tell me what to do."

A familiar sense of guilt swept over Nettie. She'd traded her beautiful little sister's admiration for a life of crap. Reaching out, she straightened a pot that sat crooked in its tray before answering Kim's original question. "Ruth might smile and say she could be wrong, but she doesn't believe it."

Kim's gaze remained on the pot as she recounted a memory. "I intended to go to Delta College, where I could have played softball. Ruth said softball isn't life, and she had this long list of arguments for U of M. The professors were better. The student body wasn't made up of 'yokels.' They had better extracurricular activities." Kim giggled. "Like I would ever have joined drama or debate."

"She never could see past her own opinions," Nettie said.

"According to Ruth, I was too young to know what I'd want to do once I 'escaped' Berlin."

"You went along."

"And ended up with a debt it took me years to pay off." She waved a hand. "It's my fault. I should have stuck to my guns."

They left the greenhouse, and Nettie took out her cigarettes and lit one. "Confidence was always Ruth's gift," she said after a long drag. “It used to make me jealous. I felt like everything I did was wrong. I smiled too much. I laughed too loud. I talked when I should listen and made dumb comments.”

“Really? You never seemed unsure of yourself to me. I mean, you were the big drama star in the family.”

“Life’s easier with a fake persona and someone else’s words in your mouth.”

“Still,” Kim said, “believing that you’re right isn’t the same as *being* right. There’s no consensus at the White House now. It’s all about what Ruth wants.”

“People go along with that?”

“Cardinal Croft is an expert at manipulation.” Kim’s lips twisted. “From how we respond to natural disasters to where the coffee wagon sets up, Ruth decides what should happen and he arranges it.”

“What about Butch?”

“I’m not sure what’s wrong with him.” She sniffed. “He’s around, but he seems tuned out, like he doesn’t care.”

A shiver of dread passed along Nettie’s spine. “You’re saying that seasoned politicians and Harvard lawyers let the President’s wife tell them what to do?”

“Most of them are sycophants who do whatever they’re told. Others like the rewards they get for obedience. Those who argue with policy find themselves out of D.C., usually to someplace remote and unglamorous, or they face rumors of corruption or mental illness.” Kim spread her hands. “The people who are left get Ruth what she wants.”

“I knew Ruth was pushy, but—”

“She’s doing good things,” Kim said. “It’s just that it isn’t right for one individual to have so much power.”

“Would you be happier if you got out?”

Kim bit her lip. “I think—I hope—I’m helping by sticking around. I let Ruth know when I believe she’s wrong. Not in public, of course, but when we’re alone.”

“Does it change anything?”

“Not as often as I’d like.”

Nettie shifted her cigarette to the other hand, since the breeze sent the smoke directly at Kim. "What if it becomes too hard to stay?"

She sighed. "I'll think of a reason, and I'll go."

With a sly smile, Nettie said, "Tell her you're running off with my former lawyer."

"She'd have plenty to say about that." They walked on a few steps, and Kim said, "The other night I dreamed you and I bought a lodge in the Porcupine Mountains, way north in Michigan's Upper Peninsula. The place had a chalet roof and cantilevered porch where we sat and drank wine and looked out at the view." She scraped at the sidewalk with a foot. "I remember feeling at peace."

"Can we get a dog in your next dream? I miss having pets." Nettie didn't say out loud that she hadn't been comfortable bringing animals into the house with Caleb around.

"Sure," Kim said. "A collie, like our old Candy." Her phone beeped, and she sighed. "Time to go, I guess. It's really nice here." She blushed, realizing prison wasn't 'nice' for Nettie.

"It isn't bad," Nettie said. "This place keeps me in, but it also keeps stuff out."

Though Nettie couldn't help Kim make the decision she feared was imminent, she began paying closer attention to news reporting. In general, the media seemed to favor the Mandell administration and its changes, but when she observed closely, Nettie detected falseness in the carefully chosen adjectives, repeated buzzwords, and frequent nods of approbation. Like Congressmen and judges who feared retribution from the executive branch, reporters chose not to rock the boat and risk getting their press credentials removed. One large news organization had already been banned from the airwaves for pursuing an "un-American agenda" and "standing in the way of progress toward a consensus government."

Ruth's latest crusade was against "trash" on the internet. "We tolerate too much that isn't uplifting," she'd said in an interview. "President Mandell called together some inventive minds, who've created a new internet site. *Callout* will focus on giving our citizens truthful information in a timely manner. There's a section for each Cabinet department and government agency, and I get a site all to myself. It's called *FLOTUSRPM*, and I hope to do my part to stop misinformation and meanness online. We're starting to monitor social media sites for accuracy, and we will require each site to adopt rigorous standards of truth or be banned from operating."

"Damn straight," said an inmate sitting nearby. "It's about time they stopped all the lies that get passed around."

But whose truths will replace what's banned? Nettie asked herself. A second later, she decided it wasn't worth fretting over. Ruth was Ruth, and Kim would have to decide when she'd had enough. As would the American public, she suspected.

Chapter Forty-Eight

Ruth-July 14

Ruth sat at her desk, a single lamp lighting her work. Outside, the sky was bright, but she'd drawn the blinds so as not to become distracted from the many things she wanted to get done before noon. Hearing a throat-clearing sound, she looked up to find Croft standing deferentially in the doorway. When she gestured for him to enter, he said, "I'm sorry to bother you, ma'am, but we're getting pushback from the Health Care Consensus Committee."

Ruth's head came up. "Who?"

"Mostly Senator Diller, but he's got support from Dr. Crandall and a few others."

"What's the problem?"

"They claim it's impossible to predict future costs, so it's a mistake to cap fees for specific treatments."

Ruth paused to absorb that. "Suggestions?"

"If we let them continue to set prices, the citizen reps will be furious." She waited, and he nodded as if he'd received a telepathic message. "I could adjust the wording, slip in something about executive oversight. That should placate them but still achieve the results we want."

"How will you get your 'adjustments' past the lawyers?"

He waved a hand. "Bury them in boilerplate."

After a second pause, Ruth nodded. "See to it."

The door opened, and Butch put his head in. "What are you two plotting?"

"Scheduling stuff." At a nod from Ruth, Croft excused himself and left the First Couple alone. As if she hadn't been discussing it moments before, she asked, "How's the strategy session on health care going?"

"Rocky, they tell me. One of the docs told Yaklin the medical people are about ready to give up."

"Did he explain that you're counting on their cooperation?"

"I think—I don't remember what he said." His brows met. "Ruthie, I'm having trouble. My mind won't do what I want it to."

She took a breath before answering. "Dr. Chalmers said that's to be expected, Butch. You need time to get back to normal."

Butch looked confused. "Back from what?"

"You had some…weakness, remember?"

"Oh." From his expression, it was clear he didn't, and tears stung Ruth's eyes. She loved this man so much, and it hurt to see him diminished, to recognize that what they'd planned together was now in large part her responsibility alone.

As she adjusted the knot of his tie, Butch took her hand. "Maybe we should put the new health care plan on hold for a while."

"No." She spoke more abruptly than she'd meant to, but she couldn't let defeatism interfere with what needed to be done. These days, Gavin Croft understood her aspirations better than the man she loved did. Better than the staff. Better than her own sister.

"The health care people say they've compromised all they can," Butch said, and Ruth felt a flicker of joy that he recalled the issue at hand. "They won't give up their right to set prices."

"Let's sit in on the afternoon session," Ruth told him. "Your presence will do a lot to assure everyone on the panel they'll get the best deal possible."

"You know how much I hate meetings," he muttered. "These days I can't even remember who's who."

Smiling up at him, Ruth promised, "I'll be right beside you. If it's too boring, we'll write naughty notes to each other."

The session resumed after lunch, and a rustle of anticipation went through the room when the President and First Lady entered. "Does anyone mind if we sit in?" Butch asked.

There was a scramble to provide two more chairs at the table. Butch seated his wife and took the place beside her. "We're here to observe," he told the group. "We hear great things are coming out of these meetings, so we got excited about getting an early peek at your results."

Butch paused, and Ruth saw that he wasn't sure how to continue. "Ms. Calkins, please go ahead," she said. "We're eager to see how you're getting this done."

Betsy Calkins was visibly nervous at having them present, but she tapped her notes into a neat pile and said, "Before lunch we were addressing some issues that are…difficult."

A man interrupted, speaking bluntly. "Frankly, Mr. President, the plan you're touting will destroy the health care industry."

"Not destroy," a man next to Calkins corrected, "reform. Jobs lost in insurance will simply migrate to the new system."

Ruth recognized the speaker as Croft's man, Connor Yaklin, who'd helped draft the Universal Health Coverage Plan. "We'll need record-keepers to assure efficient service and prompt payment. Investigators will monitor patients to see that they follow medical advice they're given."

"About that," one of the doctors glanced at Butch, clicked his pen nervously, and then stated his concern. "My patients won't be thrilled to learn that someone's going to demand they follow my orders."

"That's the trade-off," Yaklin said. "If people want free healthcare, they need to listen to the experts."

"But it feels like we'd be spying on them," a woman said.

"Because we would be." Ruth recognized Senator Diller, who had been vocal about his objections to the plan.

Yaklin raised his hands like a conductor readying an orchestra to begin. "Every year, you insurance people send your members health questionnaires, right? You follow up with suggestions on how patients can improve their health." Turning his hands down, he touched the stack of papers before him. "This plan takes the next logical step. We make healthcare better by *requiring* that patients take their doctors' advice." He pointed at a frowning man across from him. "If Dr. Walker there prescribes a CPAP machine for sleep apnea, his patient should wear the darned thing, not toss it in a drawer."

"But treatments vary," Walker replied. "Even doctors don't agree what's best."

"We'll use the best scientific information available, which is all anyone can do." Yaklin tapped his pen on the tabletop. "We all know, for example, that smoking is devastating to a person's health. Why should we spend millions treating COPD or lung cancer for patients who lack the will power to save their own lives?"

Betsy Calkins spoke, more confident now that she had support. "That's another instance where the present system folds into the new one. Former insurance agents can support patients' efforts to change their unhealthy lifestyles by becoming consultants, coaches, and trainers."

Yaklin nodded. "Upper management will still hire, monitor staff, and track health trends. People at all levels of the health care industry can expect similar work with similar compensation."

That wasn't completely true. Croft proposed that once they'd broken the stranglehold insurance companies had on health care, they'd be able to cut jobs and save money. That aim was hidden in phrases like, "In the event of" and "Under unusual circumstances."

A man who'd been quiet thus far spoke. "The devil will be in the details."

"Agreed," Yaklin said. "We need to see the plan in action, so we can find the problem areas." He made a sweeping gesture that included the whole table. "Next year and every year after, this committee will reconvene. We'll make adjustments until we get a system that works for everyone."

Seeing doubt on more than a few faces, Ruth elbowed Butch lightly. When he cleared his throat, the room fell silent. "Mrs. Mandell and I want you to know how grateful we are to you all for working so hard on this," he said formally. "You've done more than anyone could have expected in a short time, and what I've heard here today makes me hope we can send this bill to Congress soon." He turned his head slowly, making eye contact with each person in turn, and spoke as if the matter were settled. "The American people need what this committee has hammered out for them, and they—and I—will always be grateful to you."

Around the table frowns eased, and Ruth heard, or imagined, a hiss of released tension. Butch Mandell approved of their work. The healthcare bill would go to Congress where, after Croft tweaked the wording, it would become law.

"I predict there'll be screaming on both sides about this," Harley Stark said the next day. He'd been assigned to type the final wording into the computer for dissemination to lawmakers.

The young man is useful in a dozen ways, Ruth thought, *too bad he can't seem to master the art of keeping quiet.*

Blithely unaware, Harley finished, "The way I read this, we get healthcare but give up a big chunk of independence in exchange."

Ruth checked an item off her long to-do list. "Well, *I* predict that Americans will take the President's word when he says the outcome will be good for everyone."

Chapter Forty-Nine

Nettie-July-31

The sun was a dim, watery ball behind thin clouds as Nettie walked to the greenhouse one morning late in July. Rain had dripped from the sky for days, a slow leak that seemed unlikely to ever end. Olin seemed restless, and Nettie thought he had something to tell her, but Pearl was there. He spent an hour making fertilizer and glowering as Pearl went on at length about two inmates who were supposedly "getting busy" behind the dryers in the laundry room. When she couldn't stand Olin's antsy behavior any longer, Nettie asked Pearl to take a basket of green beans inside to the cooks.

As soon as she was gone Nettie turned to Olin. "What is it?"

"I found the tunnel." She'd hoped he'd given up, since his night-time probes had until now resulted in failure. "It's deeper than I expected, but once I chop out a few bricks, I'll be gone."

"How long before you go?"

"Tomorrow night."

"There's probably a grate at the other end," Nettie warned. "You don't have a welder in your back pocket, do you?"

"I've got my eye on a crowbar in the maintenance guy's toolbox. He won't miss it until it's too late."

Nettie had the unusual and uncomfortable urge to hug Olin. She would miss the young man who had come to feel more like a son to her than her own son ever had. Since that would make them both uncomfortable, she said, "Good luck. Find Belle and set the record straight."

"I will," he said firmly. As an afterthought, he added, "Did you ever think about getting out of here?"

"No," she replied. "I'm exactly where I belong."

When disaster struck the next afternoon, Nettie wondered if Fate had sent Olin a message. If so, it was in the guise of Pearl, who set a basket of tomatoes in the center of an aisle and went off to do something else. Since his vision was blocked by a stack of trays he was carrying, Olin tripped on the basket and went sprawling. Pearl immediately began squawking excuses, and Olin spoke to Nettie between clenched teeth. "My ankle's broke. I felt it snap."

He was whisked off to the nearest emergency room, and Nettie cleaned up the mess of spilled pots and squashed tomatoes. Maybe, she thought as she worked, Olin would use his recovery time to reconsider the escape. She couldn't imagine crawling underground like a badger and coming out who knew where. A person would have to be desperate to attempt something like that.

Chapter Fifty

Kim-September 5

Kim flew to Detroit on Labor Day weekend, and Drew picked her up at the airport. She'd been nervous about their date, because Drew had seemed to cool toward her lately. He didn't ask when he could come to D.C. to visit, and he called less often, citing a heavy caseload. She didn't have a lot of time to worry about his pulling away, but when she had a few moments to herself after a busy day, Kim felt an empty space in her life she hadn't noticed before Drew came into it.

Today, Drew seemed to be his old self as he led her from the terminal and set her suitcase in the back seat of his Cabriolet. She praised the car's condition, as she guessed she was supposed to do. It wouldn't do to tell the proud owner she couldn't tell one vehicle from another and only cared that it would get her from Point A to Point B. Getting in, she lowered the visor to shield her eyes from the blinding sunlight and waited impatiently for the A/C to kick in.

At her hotel, Kim gave herself a break from government affairs by avoiding both the television and her phone. Instead, she napped and looked out the window at the traffic until time to dress for the reunion. In the quiet, she tried to remember the time before she was part of the Mandell administration, before she felt faintly guilty for ignoring the delusions she helped it create and foster day by day.

Drew returned at four, and they headed north to Berlin. "I hope you aren't disappointed," Kim said as they drove. "Berlin has a lot of really nice people, but we've also got our share of rednecks."

"Are you telling me I'm overdressed?"

"You look great." Kim had trouble deciding if people she liked were physically attractive or not, but she thought Drew was. "Are you ready to deal with embarrassing questions like, 'When will we hear wedding bells for you two?'"

"You forget," he said loftily, "I am fully trained in the art of rhetoric."

The evening turned out to be fun, despite the heat and the questions. Drew listened with interest to stories of high school hijinks and laughed on cue. "Your date's cute," Margo said at the snack table. "Is it serious?"

Kim piled chips on a plate and added a spoonful of salsa. "We haven't been dating that long."

Mary Van Andel followed her into the restroom, supposedly to check her makeup. "Your new guy seems fun," she crooned. "I bet he's great in the bedroom."

Choosing her words carefully, Kim responded, "Drew's been great everywhere we've been."

They sat with Kelly, her husband, and three other couples. Conversation was relaxed, and though Drew let the others talk most of the time, he told a couple of anecdotes about practicing law in Detroit that brought giggles and guffaws.

"I warn you," Kelly's husband Logan told Drew after his fourth beer. "This girl was the toughest one on her soccer team." In the overly wise manner of the drunk, he finished, "Give her grief, and she will come *after* you."

Catching Kim's eye, Drew said, "She'll get no grief from me."

When the band began, they danced. Drew's moves were easy to follow, and Kim felt comfortable, content, and...*protected* was an odd word, but his arms seemed like a safe place to be.

On the drive back to Detroit, she asked if he'd had a good time. "I did, though apart from me and a couple of outsider husbands, everyone there knew everyone else. That's hard for me to imagine, coming out of Dearborn High."

"Most of them haven't changed much."

"You mean gossips are still gossiping and complainers are still complaining?"

"Yup. Knowing a kid in third grade pretty much predicts how he'll be as an adult."

"I think circumstances play a role," he said. "Like your sister Ruth. You say she's always been assertive, but she channeled that in positive ways, and now she's helping to lead the whole country."

Kim chuckled. "And if he were here, Dad would say it's because she loves telling people what to do."

As they drove on, Drew began showing signs of nervousness. He tapped the heel of his hand on the steering wheel. He cleared his throat as if about to speak, but then he didn't. "What are you thinking about so hard?" Kim asked.

"It's—stuff I've been working on."

"Does that 'stuff' have to do with me and my family?"

A long pause. "Maybe."

"And does it have to do with why you've been kind of distant lately?"

Drew let out a puff of air. "Yes." He ran a hand through his hair, and she caught a whiff of the outdoorsy scent she liked. "I hate to ruin a beautiful evening, but I have three pieces of information you need to hear, and since your flight tomorrow is pretty early, I guess we should deal with it tonight."

"Tell me," she demanded.

For a while Drew rambled. "I-I didn't know if I should tell you, and then I decided I had to, but I didn't want to do it by phone. It felt like we should be together when you hear it, which is really dumb, I know. I'm nothing to you, but you shouldn't have to deal with this all by yourself and there's nobody—"

"It's okay, Drew," she interrupted. "Just tell me."

He started with the name the barmaid had mentioned, the man Caleb said was "teaching" him about women. Then, he told her about his interview with Tilman. Kim shivered as he recreated the atmosphere at the prison and the man's arrogance. "He said that?" Kim asked when he finished. "He said he let Caleb watch?"

"Yes."

"Dear God."

"There's more." He told her about a detective he'd visited who for a time suspected Caleb of murdering a local woman. When he mentioned that in some cases the victim's keys had been taken, Kim thought for a few seconds that she was going to vomit. Clutching her stomach until she regained control, she turned to Drew. "When I cleared out Caleb's room, I found a box of keychains."

"How many?"

"I'm not sure." Her tongue felt thick and slow. "Four, maybe five."

Drew was silent for a few seconds, but then he said, "Well, I guess that's good. It's evidence we can use to prove what he did. The police can match—"

"I threw them away."

"Oh."

The realization of what they now knew sat between them like a boulder. What could she about what Drew had revealed? What could he say that would help her deal with it?

The answer, as far as Kim could tell, was nothing.

To forestall further conversation, she turned on the radio and pressed button after button. Nothing that came through the speakers registered, due to a wild roaring inside her head. She felt numb and at the same time wracked with pain. She felt like crying but also like screaming. Vainly she tried to pull her thoughts into some kind of order, but they buzzed behind her eyes like angry hornets. The terrors that Caleb had endured as a child. The horrors he had inflicted on innocent women. And the fact that Nettie had learned somehow what her son was doing and had seen no recourse but to remove him from the earth.

Drew apparently sensed that she needed time, so they rode without speaking for miles. Finally, he reached over and put a hand on her arm. The touch, as light as it was, felt like a lifeline, pulling her back from an abyss of despair. When she could trust her voice again, Kim said, "You said you had three pieces of information."

"You've had enough to deal with for one night."

"It's all right. I want to know everything you know."

He glanced sidelong at her as if judging her state of mind. "Okay. I couldn't stop wondering who got you fired, so yesterday I called Calver PR and asked for a description of the fake auditor. Your old boss said the guy was about forty, with black hair combed straight back and a fake tan that got streaky at the back of his neck."

"Gavin Croft," Kim whispered.

He turned to look at her. "Doesn't he work for the President?"

"No. I mean, yes, he does, but please, forget what I just said."

When they got to Kim's hotel, Drew seemed unwilling to leave her alone, and Kim wasn't sure she wanted to be. They went to the bar for a nightcap, and by tacit consent abandoned the topic of Caleb Green and what he'd done. Instead, they talked about their dreams, which for Drew was time to fish. When Kim claimed she wanted nothing but peace and quiet, he said teasingly that she'd chosen a terrible place to search for that.

It began with light touches and long looks. Soon they were sharing slow kisses in the dark corner of the booth. When the bar closed, it felt completely natural for Kim to invite Drew to her room.

Kim's flight to D.C. passed quickly. She'd awoken with a firm resolve to present everything she knew to Ruth and force her to deal with it. She'd force her sister to face Croft's underhandedness, and she'd make her help Nettie get justice. As First Lady, she could ask for a reexamination of the case. Evidence would be found linking Caleb to at least one unsolved murder, and that would prove that Nettie had cause for what she'd done.

Though she'd learned horrible things, the weekend had provided wonderful moments too. Her night with Drew was …*unprecedented* wasn't a common word for a sexual encounter, but it fit. While Kim's experience with lovemaking was limited, being with Drew helped her understand for the first time what all the fuss was about.

Chapter Fifty-One

Ruth-September 6

"The...relationship I mentioned to you has moved on to a new phase," Croft said when Ruth came downstairs. She'd taken to getting a few hours of work in on Sunday mornings, before she and Butch attended services. She often wondered if Croft slept at all, since no matter what time she arrived or left her office, light showed under his door. Today he waited for her in a dark alcove, his presence revealed only by the light from his phone.

Unlocking her door, Ruth led the way inside, took her place at the desk, and lit the lamp. "What new phase?"

"After her reunion, your sister and Mr. McMahon spent the night together."

"I see. What have you learned about him?"

"In February he went to Arizona, where he interviewed people from Caleb Green's childhood."

"Oh, good grief. Are we never going to be done with this?"

"Since then," Croft went on, "McMahon interviewed people in your hometown to find out what sort of person Green was. And he visited the state prison recently, where he interviewed a serial killer named Gerald Tilman."

"Is he representing the man in some capacity?"

"Not that I can determine. A few years back, Tilman lived near a grocery store where your nephew worked. The two men were seen together in local bars a few times."

Ruth pressed two fingers to her lips. "Gavin, I want to know everything Mr. McMahon knows about Caleb Green."

Croft nodded. "I'll put Josh Bennigan on it."

Butch was more confused and unhappy than usual all morning, so she ordered their afternoon schedule cleared and had lunch served to just the two of them. As they ate an excellent chicken salad served on croissants, Butch said suddenly, "Ruthie, what would you say if I told you I'm thinking of resigning?"

Shock traveled through her like a jolt of electricity. After a few seconds she managed, "Why do you say that, Sweetheart?"

Butch set his fork aside. "We both know I can't cut the mustard anymore, and that puts a burden on you. I miss home, and I'm tired of being asked about this and that and whatever. If I step aside, Cary's perfectly capable of finishing out the term."

"But we have so much yet to do, Butch. We haven't acted on climate change, and we still need to put the banking industry in order."

"Someone else will have to do it." Before Ruth could marshal her arguments, he went on. "I'll announce that my health is poor, and I don't feel I can fulfill my duties."

"I can." It was out before she could stop it, and Butch's head jerked at her decisive tone. Forcing a calm she didn't feel, Ruth said more softly, "Honey, have I done something wrong?"

"No, of course not. It's—"

"You had a vision for our nation, and I've done my best to make it a reality. Now, if you think I can't achieve the goals we set together, then say so." She dropped her gaze. "I've been doing what I thought you wanted."

"No, Ruth, you've done a great job. It's me. I'm not doing my part."

"Sweetheart, as long as you keep the public on our side, you're doing your part." Reaching over, she put her hand on his. "The team you chose is great, so I've got all the help I need."

Butch picked up his fork again. "If you're sure it isn't too much."

"It's not," she told him softly. "I love what I'm doing for you and for the nation."

That wasn't the last trying conversation for the day. When Butch went to take a nap and she returned to her office, Ruth found Kim waiting, her posture tense and her expression disquieted. "What can I do for you, Kimmie?"

"I have new information about Nettie's case."

Because the day had already been trying, Ruth responded with uncharacteristic irritation. "Don't you have enough to do without wasting time on a matter that's already settled?"

"But she might have had a good reason for what she did."

Ruth turned away, pressed her hands together for a moment, and then turned back. "Nettie shot a defenseless man, one she admits had never hurt her or even threatened to." She took a step toward Kim. "You told me she wants you to leave it alone. So do I, so why won't you do it?"

"Then you won't help?"

"I'm sorry for Nettie, Kim, but she chose her path."

"All right then." Kim's expression turned stony. "Since you have so little sympathy for criminals, maybe you'll deal with one close to home. Croft framed Edmund and me for the embezzlement at Calver PR."

"How do you know this?"

"I can't say, but it's true."

After a long pause, Ruth said, "If it is, I'll deal with him."

"Deal with him how?"

"Until I have more than your word for it, I'm not sure."

Kim shook her head angrily. "At the very least, he should be fired. And as far as I'm concerned, he should be prosecuted."

"Do you realize how much that would damage all that we're trying to accomplish?" Kim's mouth opened, but Ruth went on. "If Gavin did as you claim, he did it for me. I was under a tremendous amount of strain. I'd said more than once that having you to help me out would be a big relief." She rubbed at her forehead. "Now that I think of it, he suggested once that I ask you to leave your job. I said I had, but you'd turned me down. He must have thought—" She took a step toward Kim, one hand outstretched. "He was trying to help."

Kim backed away until she came to the window and could go no farther. "Help? Ruth, he turned my life to crap."

"But it worked out, didn't it? You're a part of something important now. While the method might have been misguided, the result is good for both of us."

Kim was silent, but her eyes blazed with anger. Ruth took several deep breaths to quiet her racing heartbeat. Kim's inability to understand the importance of Gavin Croft to her plans had long been bothersome, but thus far, she had deferred to Ruth's judgment. The personal aspect of this revelation was making it harder for her, but Ruth hoped she'd come around once she'd had time to think things through.

That hope was dashed when Kim took a sheet of paper from her jacket pocket. "Is this the 'something important' we're part of? This New Day for America?"

"Where did you get that?"

"Someone left it in the copier."

That was a lie. Ruth was scrupulously careful about keeping track of how many copies were made of their more daring plans. She'd find out where Kim got one in time, but at the moment she had to decide how to respond. Opening the draperies, she looked outside and said brightly, "Funny how we had such lovely sunshine this morning and now we have clouds and rain."

Ignoring her attempt at deflection, Kim said, "This…Ruth, it's crazy."

She went to her desk and sat, which restored her confidence, like a ship's commander stepping onto the bridge. "New Day isn't solid yet, but we're considering—"

"Denying women jobs? Refusing credit to females?" Kim's voice was shrill. "This would make it almost impossible for women to live independently."

Ruth gave it a beat, so Kim could calm down. "Do you know how many women in this country are mired in debt?"

Raising the sheet of paper, she waved it angrily. "And your solution is to make them dependent on men?"

"If women return to their biological role as family caregivers, men will step up and take care of them."

"What if they don't want to be taken care of?"

"You're thinking of lesbians, but we have special provisions for them. While children can't be allowed in single-sex homes, consenting adults will be able to establish legal partnerships." Ruth smiled. "There will be no discrimination against Rainbow People."

"You plan to make my husband responsible for my behavior. How does he see that I do as he demands?"

"I would expect that the two of you would sit down and discuss that before the wedding."

"But if he controls everything, what are my options?"

Ruth smiled. "Clever wives have always found ways to get what they want."

"So we go back to manipulating men with sexual favors?" Kim was as angry as Ruth had ever seen her. "Will we cinch ourselves to achieve wasp waists and flirt from behind our fans? How progressive your Unity Project is."

Gesturing at the document that Kim held as if it were a dirty rag, Ruth said, "But it's the solution to multiple problems, starting with unemployment. If women leave the work force, there will be a job for every man. Mothers will be available to monitor their kids' behavior, preventing much of the delinquency and substance abuse we see today." As if Kim had objected, she said, "But it won't be Mom's job alone. If a boy takes a gun and shoots up his school, both parents will be charged as accessories. If an unmarried girl gets pregnant, both her family and the boy's will be required to support the child financially." Unable to look at Kim's angry face, Ruth took up a pen and pretended to check a sheet of figures on her desk. "We need to revive group morals and family responsibility. We need to take care of each other." After a moment she added, "Even if it feels somewhat artificial at first."

Kim consulted the sheet again. "What about the last paragraph? What's 'concentration of funds'?"

"Again, those are only ideas we've been discussing—Butch and the team." Ruth cleared her throat before continuing. "A person with too many choices often makes bad ones, and society pays for it, over and over. Since so many in the general population lack financial skills, we thought that employers might help workers be more responsible." Her throat felt dry, and she considered getting a water from the minifridge. No. It would make her look nervous, and she wasn't, not really. "Instead of being handed a weekly paycheck, employees could have savings accounts at work. When they withdraw funds, they'd be required to justify the expenditure." Ruth's tone brightened at the imagined result. "No more incidents where Dad drinks up two weeks' pay in one night at the bar. No more moms getting expensive mani/pedis while the children have no school clothes." She interlaced her fingers. "What we're doing, Kimmie, is forming bonds. Mothers take care of children. Husbands take care of wives. Employers take care of workers. Everyone is connected; everyone benefits."

Kim's tone was contemptuous. "Sounds like the feudal system to me."

"You really should read more nonfiction." Ruth made her tone teasing, though sweat prickled in her armpits. "Gavin tells me that New Day is based on classic ideals for societal order. Laborers do necessary work; soldiers defend from invasion and insurrection; and leaders make the rules. In our version, women control everything, since they raise the laborers, soldiers, and leaders of tomorrow."

"The hand that rocks the cradle rules the world." Kim tossed the paper onto the desk, where it slid off the other side and onto the floor. "People don't fit into neatly preassigned boxes, Ruth."

"They might if they understood the benefits." She made her smile bigger, though her lips felt tight. "There's strength in a system where each level of society is responsible *for* those below it and responsible *to* those above. I'd like to see that strength in place in our nation, and I'm not the only one."

Chapter Fifty-Two

Nettie-October 2

Prison was in many ways perfect for Nettie. She had useful work to do, was left to herself for the most part, and was required to be no more than superficially polite to other people. The problem with life is that worry follows us wherever we are, and few of us can set it aside completely.

Nettie's worries varied from day to day, but they boiled down to three concerns. One was Olin. While she told herself there was nothing she could do to stop him from attempting an escape as soon as his ankle healed, and while she reminded herself he was both inventive and capable, she still feared for his safety. He might become lost underground and wander aimlessly until he either died or was forced to emerge, at which point he'd be apprehended. If he did escape Richmond, he faced a journey without resources and a mission likely to result in failure. The girl he sought might have moved. She might not want to become involved in his defense. She might be married and unwilling to tell her husband about her one-night stand on a beach in Florida. It made Nettie angry, this worry, because she didn't want to care what happened to Olin. Who was he that she should lie awake and fret about his future?

Nettie's second worry was for the nation. Things Kim had said drew her attention to news reports, and these days Ruth was always there, smiling as she explained that the President was elbow-deep in reforms and had asked her to say a few words for him. Though proud of Ruth's success, Nettie knew that any question her sister faced was answered according to her own views and standards. Ruth saw life in simple terms, but in her current role, the questions were complex. Her solutions would not always be welcomed or even grudgingly accepted. Nettie feared that would make Ruth dangerous.

Her final and biggest worry was for Kim. She didn't share everything she knew, but Nettie noted her growing uncertainty as to her role in the Mandell administration. At her September visit, she'd said her reunion was fun, Drew was fine, and things at the White House were crazy, as always. But she didn't sound like she'd had fun, and while Nettie guessed Kim cared for Drew, she seemed reluctant to talk about him. Had he done something to upset her?

And what about her relationship with Ruth? The more attention Nettie paid to the nation's direction, the more she believed that Kim would at some point have to take a stand against the President, and, more importantly for Kim, against Ruth. What would happen if she announced that she was leaving the White House? It depended on how much Ruth wanted—needed—her younger sister to go along. That led to another disturbing thought. What would her own role be if Kim and Ruth came to a schism? For the first time, she realized there might have been more to moving her to Martha's Place than keeping her out of the public eye. Would the sister who never doubted herself use the sister who always did to keep Kim on her side?

Chapter Fifty-Three

Kim-October 18

Kim felt bad about lying, but she knew Ruth would disapprove of her weekend plans. She was flying to Tampa to meet Bonnie Armentrout, girlfriend to the deceased Nathan Tanner. Kim told a half-truth. She was meeting Drew McMahon for a mini vacation. "Dozens of up-and-coming young men here in Washington would love to take you on a romantic weekend," Ruth commented, "and you choose Mr. Aw-Shucks, Esquire?"

"The heart wants what it wants," Kim sang. Though Ruth made a sound like an unhappy hen, she didn't say more. They'd established a kind of truce, where Ruth didn't share her ideas for saving the nation with Kim, and Kim didn't offer opinions. It worked, sort of.

Stepping off the plane into Florida's heat, Kim found Drew waiting, a gym bag slung over one shoulder. "Got in an hour ago. I thought we'd ride together."

They took a cab to a hotel near where Bonnie was performing in a revue. Dropping off their bags, they went to the restaurant where they'd agreed to meet her. While they waited, Kim told Drew everything she hadn't shared up to that point: Butch's stroke, Croft's machinations, and the increasingly dictatorial behavior of the nation's First Lady. She had decided if wasn't fair of her to drag him further into her activities without fully informing him.

As she talked, Drew used the same word, over and over. "Wow." When she finished, he said, "I have questions, but I think I'd better let all that sit in my brain for a while."

"Okay," Kim said. "Bonnie should be here soon."

She wasn't. Eventually, they ordered and ate, expecting she'd arrive before they finished. When she didn't, Kim called her. No answer.

"Let's find the club where she's working. Maybe she's there."

"Rehearsal started ten minutes ago," a woman told them after they banged on the entry door for a long time. When Kim explained that Bonnie had missed an appointment, she said, "Barry might let you watch until the dancers take a break. Then you could talk to her."

There was another wait before someone came to the closed double doors of the performance area. Music from inside drowned out Drew's rapping, but finally he was heard and a harassed looking man jerked one door open a few inches. "What?"

"Sorry to interrupt," Kim said, "but we were supposed to meet Bonnie Amour over an hour ago. Is she here?"

"She didn't show." The man gestured at the stage behind him. "I'm trying to work out how to cover if she isn't here tonight." With that he closed the door in her face.

Kim turned to Drew. "Any ideas?"

"Someone in the show must know Bonnie," he replied. "Let's wait until they finish and see what we can find out."

About twenty minutes later, ten sweaty women came through the doors, chattering like blue jays and gulping water from plastic or metal cooler cups. Kim stopped one, who pointed out a young woman named Mitzi, Bonnie's current roommate. "She went out for a run this morning," Mitzi told them. "Haven't seen her since."

"Do you know what she planned to do today?"

"She was meeting a woman for lunch—I guess that was you, right? Other than that, she should be here." Mitzi looked concerned. "I hope she's okay."

But she wasn't. By nightfall, the police had contacted Mitzi, who called Kim, as promised. "They found her—her body in an alley," Mitzi said. "Her purse is missing, and so is her engagement ring." Her voice turned tearful. "Some creep killed her for a few bucks and a half-carat diamond."

When Kim relayed the news, Drew frowned in concern. "This doesn't feel like a random thing to me."

"Do you think I got Bonnie killed, Drew? She contacted me. Now she's dead."

"That wouldn't be your fault. That would be whoever is trying to make sure the story of the President's stroke never comes out."

"Gavin Croft." She bit her lip. "What can we do?"

"Right now, I think we need to keep our heads down."

That sentiment was reinforced when Kim returned to the White House on Sunday evening. A Secret Service agent whose name she didn't know stopped her on the stairs, gripping her forearm. "Ms. Dailey, you need to watch what you do."

At first, she thought he was joking, but his expression said he wasn't. "Why?"

"You're going to get somebody hurt, maybe yourself, maybe someone you care about." A woman above them started down the stairs, heels clicking on the marble treads. Glancing up at her, the man released Kim's arm and continued on his way.

As she went on, Kim's mind repeated the message. *Watch what you do.* Was it a caution or a warning?

Chapter Fifty-Four

Ruth-same day

Kim didn't often visit the President's apartment in the White House, so when she showed up at the door Sunday evening, Ruth steeled herself for yet another difficult encounter. Butch was watching TV and hardly noticed when Kim was escorted in, but Ruth set aside a folder emblazoned with the Presidential seal and stood to greet her sister.

"Ruth, we need to talk. You have to hear this or…I don't know what I'll do."

Leading the way to a small study, Ruth indicated Kim should sit. "Okay, I'm listening." For reasons she couldn't have explained, Ruth closed the blinds as Kim recounted Andrew McMahon's investigation and the conclusions they'd formed as to why Nettie murdered her son. Then she relayed a conversation with a woman who insisted Nathan Tanner was murdered. The woman herself was now dead.

Fighting to show no emotion, Ruth sat down opposite Kim. "Who else knows about this?"

"No one. Only Drew and me."

"I can't believe you brought McMahon into this. Can you imagine what some basement blogger would do with these lurid stories you've concocted from a few speculative comments and a couple of conspiracy theorists?"

Kim shook her head. "He won't tell anyone. He wouldn't."

Ruth's gaze focused. "He cares for you."

Kim's hands flailed at the air like startled birds. "We haven't really had time to consider that, but he wants to help Nettie."

Leaning forward, Ruth touched Kim's knee. "He can't help her, Kimmie, and neither can you. It's too late."

"It's not. We'll reopen the case and reexamine the evidence. If Caleb was—"

"Kim!" Ruth's voice sounded harsh in her own ears, and she paused to calm herself before going on. "It's bad enough that I have a murderer for a sibling. Now you want to tell the world that our family produced a monster far worse than Nettie? What good would that do anyone?"

"It could get her out of prison."

"Has she indicated a desire to get out? Has she given any sign she's unhappy where she is?"

"Well, no. Nettie thinks she deserves to be locked up, but that's because—"

"—because Nettie is weak," Ruth interrupted. "She never took hold of her life and made it into something worthwhile. My God, how many chances does she get? It's—"

Seeing Kim's expression, Ruth stopped herself. "I'm sorry. That wasn't fair." Smoothing her hair, she took a deep breath. "This comes at a really bad time. We've arranged a face-to-face meeting next week with the Chinese leadership, and we desperately need to avoid distractions. So far, we've experienced none of the personal scandals that plagued other administrations. But if you insist on pursuing your questions, who knows where it will lead?"

"I don't want to make trouble..." Reluctance was evident in Kim's tone, but behind it was resolve. She didn't want to, but she would.

"Tell you what. Keep what you know about Caleb to yourself for a week. Nettie's fine where she is for that long, and once this China thing is over, I'll have time to figure out how to minimize the damage it will cause when the story comes out. And I'll see that the death of this Bonnie is investigated fully. I'll have Gavin—"

"Ruth, Croft is right in the middle of this."

She laughed, though it took effort. "I know you dislike him, but Gavin Croft is indispensable to me—and to Butch." Ruth went back to her original question. "I'm asking you to give us a week to look into your revelations. Can you do that much for me?"

"I guess so."

"Great. Now, come and help me choose what to wear to that Colonial Descendants Luncheon tomorrow. They're a bunch of snobs, so I don't want to show up looking like a Polish kid from the Michigan sticks."

Chapter Fifty-Five

Nettie-October 19

"Tonight's the night," Olin told Nettie. Rain pelted against the walls, making it hard to hear his words. "My ankle is good to go."

Nettie looked out at the gray morning, the soggy darkness of trees and buildings soaked with moisture. Whether he succeeded or failed, Olin would not return to Martha's Place. "I hope you aren't giving up a gilded cage for something a lot less hospitable."

"I gotta try it. You should keep the hole a secret. In case—"

"I told you," she interrupted, "I have no desire to escape."

"But if they find it, they'll know where to look for me, and besides, they'll suspect you knew. You don't have to do much, just hide the hole in the morning, like I been doing."

Nettie nodded, but she realized she'd have to do better than Olin had. Because he'd spent so much time there, the greenhouse would be thoroughly searched. If the table was moved, his route would be obvious.

The next morning when she came down for breakfast, Olin's usual place was empty. Grabbing a breakfast pastry and a cup of coffee, Nettie told the guard she was heading to the greenhouse early. "My tomato plants looked pale yesterday. I want to set them in the sun for an hour before it gets too hot."

Agreeably, the man escorted her to the greenhouse, gave it a cursory glance from the doorway, and then left her to her work. The table sat off to one side, revealing the tunnel opening. Getting a trowel, Nettie dug up a square six inches deep around the edges of the hole. Taking two shelves from a unit in the corner, she laid them over the opening and set four growing trays filled with spinach seedlings on top. Last, she dumped potting soil between and around the plastic trays, smoothing the edges so it appeared to be a patch of plants growing directly from the ground.

When it was discovered that Olin was missing, the greenhouse was searched, as she'd expected. Nettie stood near the doorway, her heart beating faster than normal, as the guards moved tables and stuck their noses into everything.

"What's this?" one of them demanded when he came to the square of seedlings.

"Spinach does better planted directly in the ground, but it doesn't need a lot of light." As she spoke, Nettie said a little prayer that the man wasn't a backyard gardener. "Now the tomatoes over there don't mind being in pots as long as they get lots of sun, so we put them outside for a while every day." She blathered on, making things up as she went, until the man's eyes glazed with disinterest.

The search turned up no clues as to how Olin had left Martha's Place or where he'd gone. "We believe that Mr. Dobbs saw an opportunity and took it," the police chief told reporters. "Perhaps a delivery truck was left unattended. Trucks are searched at the gate, of course, but he might have found a spot no one thought to look at, like the roof of the vehicle."

There was some confusion about the time of the escape. According to the records, Olin was in his room for the ten o'clock bed check. Nettie knew differently, but the guard who was Olin's "friend" couldn't admit to her part without losing her job.

Nettie hoped Olin's success would continue, but she wasn't optimistic. He was without resources, and his photo was shown on TV screens all over the city. How far could he get? All day, as she tolerated Pearl's inane chatter, she missed Olin's...was *friendship* the right word? It had been so long since she had a friend that Nettie wasn't sure how that felt.

As rumors concerning Olin's escape continued to buzz through Martha's Place, Nettie wondered which of the guards had been his unwitting assistant. There were only two females on night duty, and she'd had no dealings with either. They came on at ten p.m. and left at six, during which time she was in bed, either asleep or reading. She'd seen their faces at the spyhole as they made bed checks. One was about twenty-five, with deep-red hair and large, round eyes. The other, perhaps a decade older, wore an expression that hinted at general misanthropy.

Nettie asked the younger woman to get her some ibuprofen, claiming she'd strained her back at the greenhouse. She brought her two pills and passed them through the slot in the door, her manner pleasant without being friendly. Nettie asked, "Is it true they haven't caught Olin Dobbs yet?"

The guard's expression turned serious. "Yeah. It's been a nightmare for the third shift. Police asking questions, Dr. Foeller all sad and embarrassed, and reporters everywhere." Her tone turned angry. "I had three of them waiting at my house when I woke up."

"They think he had help from one of you?"

"I guess." Her brows turned squiggly. "I told them it wasn't me and they should get out of my face."

"I saw him in the greenhouse every day, but I never dreamed what he was up to." After a momentary hesitation Nettie added, "He was definitely hot."

"Yeah," she agreed. "You wouldn't think he'd have to rape anyone."

Steeling herself for the lie, Nettie said, "He didn't have to as far as I was concerned."

The guard's eyes widened, but Nettie saw no hint of either anger or envy. It was more like disbelief. "Um, I hope your back feels better."

"Thanks."

The next night, the other female guard had duty on the second floor, and again Nettie asked for ibuprofen. This time the assent was more grudging, as if she didn't want to be bothered. When the pills arrived, Nettie asked, "Have they found Olin Dobbs yet?"

"No."

"I'm really going to miss that guy. We used to…you know…in the greenhouse."

There it was. A flash of jealousy she couldn't hide. "Take your pills," she said. "Then go to sleep."

Nettie sank onto her narrow bed, pleased. Kim had once said that in D.C., bits of gossip were stored away for future use against both friends and enemies. While a guard was neither of those things, it couldn't hurt to have ammunition in case of a future firestorm.

Chapter Fifty-Six

Kim-October21

Kim paused outside the President's office, carrying a stack of documents that required more than the autopen signatures used for most of his correspondence: a personalized birthday card for an important senator, a thank-you to a particularly generous supporter, and other special messages.

Inside, Gavin Croft was speaking. She'd hoped he wouldn't be there, but that was a vain hope these days. Peeping in, she saw, before windows open to the October sun, that Croft sat at the President's desk. Outrage flooded through her like a wave. How dare he?

"You concluded the business then?" Croft was saying.

"I did." Though she couldn't see Croft's guest, the voice was Josh Bennigan's. "I was back in time for the Secretary's barbeque."

"Good," Croft said. "Another loose end tied up."

Kim knocked then and went in. Butch sat on a sofa at one side of the room, watching an old movie. Croft remained in the President's chair, meeting Kim's gaze with a touch of challenge. Bennigan turned to watch her approach, his expression blank, as usual. Deliberately, she turned and went to Butch, who looked up from the TV and smiled. "Hey, Little Sister."

"Mr. President, I brought some letters for you to sign."

"No sweat, Bernadette." He turned to look at Kim. "Did you see my speech on infrastructure?"

"I did. It was very convincing."

With a gesture in Croft's direction Butch said, "I have good help."

Croft bowed, evincing humility Kim knew he didn't feel. "It's an honor to help you save our nation from itself, Mr. President."

Butch chuckled. "Now, Gavin, it wasn't as bad as all that."

"It was going that way, sir, but you've turned things around nicely."

"Whatever a man can do, he should do." As Butch spoke, Kim was again reminded of a talking bird. Who'd taught him that pretty phrase? Having said it, the President of the United States returned to watching Sly Stallone kill bad guys.

Kim turned to Croft, intrigued by the first sign of real conviction she'd ever heard from him. "Do you really believe we were headed for destruction?"

"Republics end in one of two ways, Ms. Dailey: civil war and fracturing, or the assumption of power by a strong leader."

"A dictator."

He grimaced at the term. "Can you look me in the eye and tell me the average citizen is capable of choosing who should lead?" He glanced at Bennigan as if seeking a more receptive audience than Kim. "Show the masses a rich man, and they say, 'He must be smart, or he wouldn't have so much money.' Offer a gifted speaker, and they believe his every golden word. Present them with a war hero, the son of a former President, even a retired actor, and some will find reasons to believe that he perfectly grasps the complexities of government and has their best interests at heart." He made an impatient huff. "Perhaps one in twenty voters is both willing and able to sort through the rhetoric and arrive at an informed decision."

"What about Butch? Are you saying the voters didn't choose wisely there?"

"The American people stumbled onto a golden opportunity, and by some miracle, they took it." Croft pointed a finger at her. "If they're wise, they'll keep this administration in power for as long as possible."

There was so much to unpack in his statement that Kim didn't have a response. Abruptly, Croft changed the topic. "I'll see that he signs the items you brought and have someone return them to you."

Kim wanted to stay, to order Croft out of the President's chair—out of the room, the building, and the city, for that matter. Taking a moment to calm herself, she did none of those things. What good would it do, when Ruth let him do as he pleased?

She started back to her office, dissecting what she'd heard before they knew she was there. Bennigan had made a quick trip somewhere on Saturday, to tie up a "loose end." When the suspicion of what his errand had been came to her, Kim made a detour.

"I found a pair of sunglasses in the Rose Garden," she told the aide at the Homeland Security front desk. "They look like the ones I've seen Josh Bennigan wearing."

"He isn't in right now," the serious-looking young man informed her. "If you're going past Mr. Croft's office, you might find him there."

"Thanks. I'll do that." She turned as if to leave but asked, "He wasn't in Florida this weekend, was he? I could have sworn I saw him at the Tampa airport Saturday morning."

"He did go to Florida," the guy said, "but he flew down Friday late and came back Saturday afternoon."

"Is it possible that I could speak with Nettie, Dr. Foeller?"

"You're coming down?"

"No. I'd like to speak to her on the phone."

"Oh. Clients can receive calls on Thursday evenings."

"I…I'd like to speak with her today. I need advice."

"I see." Kim heard a drawer slide open. "Give me a number where she can reach you, and I'll have her call as soon as possible."

"Thanks. It isn't an emergency. I just need to talk to her."

"I understand," Foeller said. "Despite her faults, Nettie is a person you feel you can turn to when things are a mess."

An hour later, Kim's second phone rang, and she answered, "Nettie?"

"It's me. What's up?"

"I don't know what to do. I think Josh Bennigan might have killed the woman I told you about. Nathan Tanner's girlfriend."

The pause that followed was long. "Kim, are you sure your imagination isn't working overtime?"

Setting her forehead into her palm, Kim tried to press away the tension there. "I went to Florida to meet with her. She never showed up, and later they found her dead from an apparent robbery. I just found out that Bennigan went to Tampa last weekend, and I heard him and Croft talking about a loose end they'd tied up."

"Okay." Another long pause. "Let's look at what you know for sure. She claimed Bennigan was on the ship the night Tanner died, but you only have her word for that."

"And now she's dead. That's a pretty big coincidence." Kim rubbed at her forehead again. "I've tried to get Ruth to look into what Croft and Bennigan are doing, but she refuses to listen. Do you think I should try again?"

After yet another pause, Nettie said, "Is there someone else who can help?"

"I can't think of anyone. People here are either convinced Ruth and Butch are gods, or they're scared to say anything. The other day, one of the Secret Service agents kind of threatened me. He said I need to be more careful."

"Careful of what?"

"I'm not sure, but it felt like he was telling me to keep my big mouth shut." She shivered. "Since then it seems like the guy is everywhere I go, watching me."

"This is a Secret Service agent?"

"Yes. His name is Everett Mero, and I heard he's one of Ruth's favorites."

Nettie's voice lowered. "Kim, you do need to be careful. You don't want to get in the way of people with that kind of power."

Kim assured her sister that she'd do that, but when she hung up the phone, she muttered, "I'm already in the way. The question is, do I jump on the bandwagon or get run over by it?"

Chapter Fifty-Seven

Ruth-October 21

The update Croft provided was irritating enough, but his nasal twang intensified Ruth's irritation. "I understand," she said, cutting off his recitation of Kim's interference, "but I assure you, my sister will not create public problems for us."

His thin lips tightened. "Ms. Dailey doesn't grasp the scope of your vision, ma'am. She could endanger the work we're doing."

"We now know my nephew was a violent man." She couldn't bring herself to use the term *serial killer*. "Kim has agreed to remain quiet about that until we decide how to deal with it."

"I hope she meant it. Your husband's enemies would love to get their hands on such sensational information."

"Caleb's…oddness…can't hurt Butch," Ruth said. "He's the most popular President in decades."

"But any scandal is injurious at this critical point." He went to the window and parted the blinds, looking out at the bright October day. "We're already dealing with pushback from Congress on some of our reforms."

Attorney General Betzer, who'd come to Ruth's office with Croft, sided with Ruth. "The mud-slingers can't hurt us, Gavin. We've got dirt to throw back at anyone who tries to come at us."

Ruth saw Croft shoot Betzer a look of warning. She'd long suspected Croft used Morris Blake's replacement as a source for gathering information to be used against their detractors. That was an internal matter; Ruth chose to focus on the long view. While individuals who spoke out might suffer temporary embarrassment and even loss of their position in the government, the overall goal of unity was to benefit everyone. Croft protected Ruth from the harsh realities of leadership because he respected her ethics. His discretion was a sign of loyalty.

Clearing his throat, Croft said, "If you're sure Ms. Dailey will do as you ask, we'll go ahead with what's necessary for events to proceed on schedule."

Picking up a stack of papers, Ruth tapped them into a tidy pile and set them back down. "Even if Kim were to speak up, no one would listen."

"Perhaps not on her own, but with support..." Croft left it a question.

"Yes, there is that. What can be done about the lawyer?"

"I can see to him." Croft sniffed. "Ms. Dailey also spends a great deal of time with the Vice President."

She waved dismissively. "He's perfectly happy dressing up and cutting ribbons."

"Stockwell was a formidable senator in his day."

"And now he's old." Ruth crossed her arms in a dismissive gesture. "The Vice Presidency is an empty honor, but it's still an honor. Cary would never jeopardize his position by making waves."

Though he made no argument, Croft's stiff posture indicated he wasn't satisfied. "All right," she said after a moment. "If you're so worried about Kim, we'll give her what she wants." Sitting down at her computer, she said, "I'll draft a letter to the parole board."

Chapter Fifty-Eight

Nettie-October 22

Pearl ran through the gray rain with her head down, giggling as she reached the greenhouse. Tossing her hood back, she asked, "Did you know you're getting out of here tomorrow, Nettie?"

Shock left her unable to do anything but repeat the important words. "Out? Tomorrow?"

"Foeller told one of the guards he's going to escort you to the train station in the morning. Some guy named Bennigan will meet you there and take you to D.C." Pearl's eyes were wide. "You're really related to Mrs. Mandell? I thought somebody made that up. I mean, you're…different from her."

"You got that right. Did you hear a time mentioned?"

"The early train, Dr. Foeller said."

What was Ruth up to now? Kim believed Bennigan was responsible for the deaths of Nathan Tanner and his girlfriend. Did Ruth hope to control Kim through her concern for Nettie, or had Croft and his minion decided the First Lady would be better off if her criminal sister disappeared completely? Either way, Nettie decided, she wouldn't be around when they came for her.

Since Olin left, she'd been tantalized by the knowledge that escape was possible. While she deserved to be in prison, there was nowhere on earth she'd erase the memory of herself loading a gun, walking to the back of the house, and ending the life she'd created. With that to face every day, life itself was a prison.

What would it be like to live on her own again, to decide what she ate and when she went to bed? How would it be to walk beside a river and know she could go as far as she wanted, with no wall ahead to stop her?

Though she derided herself for it, Nettie sometimes imagined what it would be like to be free. She'd have a garden, of course. She'd get herself a dog and experience again that unquestioning, loyal companionship she remembered from childhood. Candy at her feet while she read. Candy helping her bring the cows in for milking. Candy sliding his big head under her hand to prompt petting. No questions. No judgment. Only a presence beside her.

Forcing herself back to reality, Nettie gave her ditzy helper the first and last compliment she ever would. “You’re a good kid, Pearl. Thanks for telling me.”

Chapter Fifty-Nine

Kim-Same Day

When her second phone rang, Kim knew it had to be Drew, but she almost didn't recognize the voice that spoke. "Kim, I'm in trouble."

"Hang on." There was no one else in the room, but she moved to the window and looked out at the blustery day, so that anyone coming in wouldn't hear. "What's wrong?"

"I'm being charged with witness tampering and extortion."

"What? Drew—"

"A juror in my current trial went to the judge and said I'd offered him money to vote to acquit."

"You would never do that."

"There's video of me stopping him in the courthouse hallway. Kim, I swear I've never spoken to the man."

"How could there be video?"

"It has to be AI-generated imagery. They can make it look like a guy was someplace he wasn't."

"Can't it be identified as fake?"

"It's pretty difficult." Drew paused. "We know who's behind this."

"Gavin Croft."

"Do you think Ruth knows?"

"No." She hoped she spoke the truth. "What will you do?"

After a moment of hesitation he said, "It's probably best if you don't know."

She opened her mouth to argue, but he was right. "Please get word to me when you're safe."

"I will, if I can."

As Kim put the phone into her pocket, a wave of loneliness threatened to overwhelm her. With it came the realization that she'd ruined Drew's life. If she'd never told him what she knew, never asked him to help her, he'd still be the respected attorney he'd always been. Now he had two choices: be punished for things he hadn't done or run to where Croft couldn't find him.

Croft had to be stopped, but she couldn't do it by herself. There was only one person who could control him. Shaking with dread, Kim went in search of her sister.

Ruth was in the Treaty Room, examining diagrams of what looked like a weapon. "Can I speak to you alone, please, Ruth?"

At the note in Kim's voice, she looked up, and Kim saw her lips thin slightly. "Of course, Kimmie." Turning to her staff she said, "Will you excuse us for a few minutes?"

The others left the room. Ruth stepped away from the table, drawing Kim to a cushioned seat big enough for them to sit together. She left her hand on Kim's shoulder as she asked, "What's upset you now?"

Briefly she told her about Drew's trouble, ending with, "He's done nothing wrong, and I want—I hope you can help."

Ruth put a spread hand on her chest. "What could I do?"

She made an angry gesture. "It's all lies, Ruth. If you asked them to investigate more carefully, they'd find that out."

"But you said there are witnesses. And video."

"All faked."

Ruth set her hands in her lap before speaking. "How would it look if the First Lady started sticking her nose into legal affairs in Michigan?"

Kim clutched her stomach, trying to still the shaking inside. "It would look," she said distinctly, "like you care about justice."

"But if I interfere because your friend is in trouble, doesn't that smack of corruption?" Her gaze met Kim's. "If Drew McMahon is innocent, he'll be exonerated. If he is guilty, he'll have to accept his punishment. The laws in this country apply to everyone."

"He's been set up." She almost added names but stopped herself in time. "Your influence can make things right." She added in a whisper, "Please."

Ruth's expression turned stoic: a saint in a museum painting, sad but noble, burdened but brave. "I can't help a criminal escape punishment simply because you're in love with him, Kimmie."

"Drew didn't do what he's being accused of."

"Then let the system work," Ruth said. "We've used it for two centuries. It will turn out well in the end."

The next day, Kim found an article in the *Detroit Free Press* with the headline: *Local Attorney Sought.* It explained that Andrew McMahon had gone missing after police questioned him on possible interference with the justice system. *Mr. McMahon's attorney admits he can no longer reach his client by phone, and McMahon's apartment is deserted, with items missing that indicate possible flight.*

At the end there was the usual appeal for information from the public. Kim shivered, imagining Drew slinking through crowded spaces to…where? The airport? Not likely. A bus terminal? Maybe. He'd leave the country, maybe head to…

She stopped. What did she know about flight to escape arrest? Drew might know more. At the very least he'd probably had a few former clients whose methods of eluding the police failed, so he'd know what didn't work.

Chapter Sixty

Nettie-Same Day

When Dr. Foeller arrived at the greenhouse, damp spots on her shoulders from the rain, Nettie gave no hint she knew what the visit was about. Glancing around to see that they were alone, Foeller said, "You're being released in the morning." She handed Nettie a sheet of paper that said Janet Waller had been granted parole at the request of Hiram and Ruth Mandell, who would take responsibility for her care and behavior.

"Why?"

"No idea." After a pause Foeller said, "It's probably wrong of me to ask questions at this juncture. Our association is over, or it will be soon, so I have nothing to offer in exchange for the truth." Her thin face seemed to grow thinner. "I want to know, not for the book or for my case files. Were you afraid your son was going to kill you?"

"No." Her jaw felt stiff, like half-set concrete.

"Then I believe you were sure he'd hurt someone else."

In a voice that wouldn't stay firm, she said, "He already had."

"He admitted that?"

"Not voluntarily." Her voice dropped to a murmur. "I told him I knew what he'd done, and he didn't deny it."

"When did you realize how disturbed Caleb was?"

She shook her head. "Once in Tucson, a neighbor mentioned that her puppy had gone missing. Another time, a woman stopped to ask if we'd seen her cat. Both times I caught a look on Caleb's face that made my stomach flip. When my parents died, I thought if we lived on the farm, I could help him…change."

"That didn't happen."

"I'd try to convince myself he was better." Nettie rubbed her arms as if she were freezing. "But I knew in my gut he wasn't. I contacted a half-dozen agencies, always anonymously, and asked what could be done for a child with latent homicidal tendencies. Every one of them said there had to be more than a mother's suspicion." She huffed derisively and took on the tone of a professional person trying to sooth an unreasonable parent. "Only with evidence of seriously deviant behavior, Ms. Waller, can a judge order incarceration and treatment."

"The Catch-22 of dealing with dangerous psychopaths," Foeller said. "We can't stop them from hurting someone until they hurt someone."

"He wouldn't have been a psychopath if I hadn't left him with that monster." Her hands moved up her neck and covered her ears, as if to shut out a voice only she could hear. "When Caleb left home at seventeen, I didn't know whether to be worried or relieved. He came back a year later with no explanation, and that became the pattern. He'd leave for a while, but he always showed up again. When he was sober, he hardly spoke to me. But when he got drunk, he'd tell me what Florence used to do to him."

"What that woman did wasn't your fault."

Nettie's hands slid to her chest. "I was his mother. I should have protected him."

"You didn't even know where he was."

"And instead of finding out, I got drunk or high, day after day, while my son was tied to his bed in that God-forsaken farmhouse." Nettie picked some dirt from under her thumbnail. "She used to sit in a chair beside him, holding a butcher knife and telling him what she might do—what God was telling her she might *have* to do—because he was such a bad boy." Her last words were a groan. "She told him he had no soul."

"Did you send Caleb for counselling?"

"Twice, but he was good with strangers, and to be honest, you don't get the best psychologists in Berlin, Michigan. Caleb would look sad and admit that yes, he got angry at times, but now that he was with his real mother, he was getting better. He said he was sorry he'd been troublesome, and he'd learned a lot from talking about it with a caring professional." She added an observation. "Both counsellors felt sure they'd made progress with the boy's issues."

Foeller nodded, accepting the possibility of self-delusional therapists. "How did you learn how bad it really was?"

"I'd been suspicious of his coming and going for a long time. He'd be okay at home for a while, but then he'd get antsy, rubbing his hands and pacing. Over time I figured out that meant he'd be moving out again soon." Nettie swiped at her hair with a hand, pushing it off her forehead. "I wasn't supposed to go into Caleb's room, but one day he'd taken my phone charger and I needed it, so I did. On his dresser was a box I'd never seen before. I opened it, and inside were three key chains, none of them the type of thing Caleb would carry. It meant nothing to me, so I put the top back on the box, found my charger, and left."

Nettie ran a hand down the back of her neck. "Soon after that, Caleb left home for a few months. When he came back, a fourth key chain showed up in the box."

Foeller shook her head as if rejecting the conclusion Nettie had drawn. "They could have been gifts."

"When I looked into the box that second time, a conversation I'd overheard a few years earlier came to mind. Caleb was about twenty-two then, and he was on the phone, saying how amazing 'it' had been. How he'd never felt like that before. How 'she' was the perfect choice. It made my skin crawl."

"Are you implying that he and someone else—?"

"At the time I dismissed it. I told myself he and a friend were reliving a threesome with some willing party girl. But I think I knew differently, even then. The tone of Caleb's voice, the—" Nettie stopped, fingering the cigarette pack in her pocket.

"From that conversation and the key chains, you suspected Caleb was committing…crimes."

"I started combing the news for attacks against women, and I found out that in Indiana, during the most recent time Caleb was gone from home, a woman had been abducted from a store parking lot, raped, and strangled. Her car was found in a lake a few miles from her home."

"What did you do?"

"That night when he came home from the bar, I told him I knew he was…hurting women. I said he had to get help, or I'd go to the police."

"What was his response?"

"He said, 'I'm pretty sure the cops don't operate on Mom vibes.'" Nettie's voice went even softer. "Then he said, 'I visited your sister Kim the other day.' When I asked why, he said, 'I wanted her to get me a job at her firm, but she was no help at all.' Then, in this really casual tone, he added, 'She's nice-looking though. I left her place thinking, *There's a gal who'd look good on a coroner's slab.*'"

Foeller made an odd sound, and Nettie met her gaze. "Do you see, Susan? Do you understand why I couldn't let my son wake up even one more morning?"

For a few seconds Foeller struggled for something to say. Finally, she said, "I'm so sorry, Nettie. I can't say if what you did was right or wrong, but it's good that the President and his wife want to help you put it behind you."

"Yeah," Nettie replied. "I'll be sure to thank them when I see them."

Fourteen hours later, Nettie was a mess, mentally and physically. She wasn't sure which was worse, dragging herself through the absolute blackness like a mole, or turning on her stolen flashlight and seeing how narrow the passage ahead was. Her breath came in half-panicked gasps, and she felt like she was in a nightmare that she couldn't awake and end. Forcing herself forward with elbows and knees, she whispered aloud every few feet, "Go on. You can't go back." A horrible thought formed in her traumatized mind. What if Olin had suffocated down here? What if she came upon his corpse, blocking her way and foretelling her own brief future?

After what seemed hours, her left elbow encountered a different hardness. Praying it wasn't a rock, Nettie felt with her hand and found man-made rectangles, the brick of the tunnel. Turning on her light, she surveyed the opening Olin had made, feeling its edges to assure herself it was real. Could she wriggle through? If Olin had, she could. Still, Nettie hesitated. What lay below? Mud and filth, for sure. How deep? There might be rats or snakes, probably rats *and* snakes. And the image of Olin's corpse somewhere before her seemed glued to the back of her mind. The authorities had found no leads, no sightings. The chance that he'd died in the tunnels was as likely as the chance he was on his way to Vermont.

"Go on," Nettie whispered aloud. "You can't go back."

By threatening to reveal her part in Olin's escape, she'd forced the guard to leave her cell unlocked. Once the bed check was done, Nettie left her cell and, avoiding security cameras as Olin had instructed, made her way to the kitchen. It took precious minutes to figure out his trick for opening the old coal chute. As she worked, it seemed that rough hands hovered at her back, ready to grab her by the collar and drag her back to where she belonged.

Once she mastered the secret exit, she'd dodged her way to the greenhouse, moved the table, and dug out the plant trays that hid the hole. Guards would see the mess as soon as they entered in the morning, so her escape route would be obvious. At best, Nettie had six hours to make her way through the tunnel to the sewers and on to an exit. After that, she had no idea what she'd do.

Turning onto her back, she grasped the edge of the hole, pulled her body forward, and let her feet down, feeling a brief panic when they touched nothing. Arms shaking, she lowered herself a little farther and was rewarded with a brush of something semisolid. With a sinking feeling that was both physical and emotional, she let go and squished into the muck at the base of the tunnel.

The shaft was low, smelly, and dank. It was so dark that her light revealed little of what was ahead, no better, she thought, than carrying a lit cigarette. There, with her heart still racing from the crawl through Olin's burrow and her nose assailed with noxious odors, Nettie felt the desire for a smoke like a thousand tiny demons stomping through her brain and body. Forgetting the slime on her hands and the root tendrils that caught at her hair, she imagined herself taking out the pack, shaking out a cigarette, and leaning against the bricks while she drew smoke deep into her lungs. A second later, she laughed aloud. She was in twenty kinds of danger and possibly steeped in methane gas. Rats might even now be sniffing at her ankles, and all she could think of was satisfying her dirty habit.

"No more," she said aloud. "If I live through this, I quit."

With that decided, she began wading through the ancient tunnel. She felt like a seeker from mythology, blind, bent, and fearful of what lay ahead. To keep her courage up, she told herself that not finding Olin's body meant he'd made it, though she had no proof of that. He might even now be on his way to a state prison with the prospect of years added to his sentence for the attempt.

The downward slope was gentle, but she felt it in her thighs as she waded through muck that pulled at her feet with ugly sucking sounds. Once the Martha's Place tunnel joined Richmond's municipal drainage system, navigating the various lines would become a problem, but Olin had said that by following the direction of flow, she'd eventually reach the James River.

At the end of the old brick tunnel, she found proof that Olin had made it that far. An iron grate that separated the shafts was missing two bars, making a hole big enough to crawl through. She wondered how long it had taken him to saw through them with his stolen hack saw. She was lucky he'd gone first, opening the way so all she had to do was duck through the hole.

The main drainage tunnel had slightly better amenities, smooth walls and a solid bottom with only a few inches of smelly water covering it. Still, with each step a new fear arose. Would she be overcome by gas and pass out? Would she get lost in the darkness? Would she miss an exit? If she found one, where would she emerge? And what if it rained again? Would a surge of water push her off her feet, sweeping her along in the filth until she succumbed to the flow and drowned?

Stopping periodically, Nettie pointed her pitiful light upward, looking for an exit hatch. It seemed she'd been down there forever, and she couldn't tell whether it was fact or fear that made her feel like she was going deeper into the earth.

Focused on what was above, she failed to see an impediment before her. As her foot caught, she fell forward, breaking her fall with her hands, but unable to keep her face out of the effluviant water. Quickly pushing herself up, Nettie used her shirt to wipe away what she could, spitting to clear her lips and nostrils.

When she realized she'd dropped the flashlight when she fell, panic threatened to overcome her. How would she know which way was forward? How would she see dangers ahead? She had to find the light. Without it, she'd go mad.

Swallowing her disgust, Nettie knelt on the tunnel floor and crawled forward, searching with outstretched hands in widening circles. Up close, the smell almost gagged her, and the rough surfaces scraped her fingertips raw. After what felt like hours but was probably only a few minutes, she heard something bump against the tunnel wall. After a few seconds of groping, she found the plastic cylinder, pulled it to her, and pressed the switch. No beam of light rewarded her effort. She sobbed aloud, defeated by the unforgiving blackness.

Could she go back and find the hole that led to Martha's Place? Light was plentiful there. She'd find dry clothes and warm blankets. It was prison, but anything was better than dying down here, alone and blind. In a gesture of frustration, she shook the flashlight, tapping it against her palm. After a few tries, the light came on. "All *right*!" she shouted, and her voice echoed around her like a thousand happy Netties.

Turning the light off to save the batteries, she sat for a few seconds, willing herself to ignore the cold, the damp, and the unknown. "Go on," she whispered. "You can't go back."

"Unnnh." The sound came from behind her, and Nettie froze. Something was in the sewer with her. Rats, most likely, but possibly worse, perhaps a boa constrictor dumped by a jaded pet owner. A moment later, the sound repeated, and she realized she hadn't tripped over some*thing*. She'd tripped over some*one*.

She crawled back a few feet, reaching out in the blackness. "Olin?"

"Unnnh."

"Olin, is that you? It's Nettie."

"Netteh." She turned on the flashlight and saw Olin, filthy and half-aware, with his back against the curved wall, legs outstretched, and one arm wrapped around his stomach as if he had a bellyache. The right side of his forehead was scraped raw, and his eyes only opened halfway.

"What happened, Olin? Why are you still down here?"

"Hurt. Arm." He pointed upward. "Manhole."

Shining the light upward, she saw a metal ladder and above it, small, dim circles of light that had to be drain holes. "That's our way out, right?"

"I tried—" Olin struggled to focus. "Got the cover up, but a car came and—hit it. Knocked me—ladder."

He'd been both lucky and unlucky. His attempt to lift the heavy cover had failed, but he might easily have been killed in the resulting fall.

Turning the flashlight off again, she asked, "What are your injuries?"

"Shoulder's broke, or maybe dislocated. Hurts like hell." His voice was weak. "No way I could get back up there and try again."

"You've been stuck down here all this time?"

"Ran out of food a while ago. Water too."

"Here." She took out the bottle of water she'd stuffed down her bra and wiped the top off on the inside of her sleeve. "Drink."

The bottle left her hand, and she heard him swallow. After a few seconds he said, "Good."

"Can you walk?"

"Maybe." She heard him shift his legs. "How long?"

"Three days, Olin. You left Martha's Place three days ago."

"You followed me?"

"I'll explain later." Olin's injury complicated her escape, but he knew the tunnel system and she didn't. Taking a granola bar from her pocket, she said, "Eat this. Then have more water."

When he finished, Olin's voice sounded stronger, though he groaned each time he moved. Despite his obvious pain, she heard humor in his voice as he said, "Good you came along. Didn't want to spend the rest of my life down here."

"Me neither," she replied. "If I help you up the ladder, do you think the two of us can move that cover out of the way?"

Olin's chuckle ended in a cough. "Do we got a choice?"

"No. They'll see the tunnel in the morning and come after us. Come on." Clumsily, they climbed the ladder together, rung by rung. Olin grunted with each step but didn't stop. At the top, Nettie turned on her light to see what they were dealing with. The cover sat in a metal rim. Through the drain holes, she could see light and not much else. If they got the cover out of the way, they'd emerge in the middle of a street. There was no other choice, so they'd simply have to be careful.

"Okay." Nettie stuffed the flashlight into her pocket. "Tell me what to do."

"I'll put my good shoulder against it and lift. Once it's out of the frame, you need to roll it off to the side."

"Got it."

Nettie had to position her arms on either side of Olin, which made it difficult to guide a chunk of metal that weighed as much as she did out of its resting place. What if her hands slipped? The impact might knock them both off the ladder. Hearing his labored breathing, she doubted Olin could survive another fall.

Again, no choice. They had to do this, and it had to work the first time. She felt Olin ready himself, bracing his feet on either side of hers. His hot breath hit her cheek as he took the weight of the cover onto his back. When he grunted, “Go!” Nettie pushed upward with both arms but harder with her right. At first the weight resisted their efforts, but Olin gave a mighty groan and pushed harder. The result was a slice of light only she could see. “That’s it,” she panted. “On three.” Her joints burned with effort as she counted through clenched teeth. “One. Two. Three!” With a burst of combined energy, they pushed the cover onto the pavement, where its metallic clunk sounded to Nettie’s ears like the bells of St. Mary’s. Peeping out at the street, she saw that for the moment, it was deserted.

Crawling out, she turned to help Olin. “Let’s go.”

“We gotta put it back.”

Nettie sighed, acknowledging the wisdom of concealing their exit point. The street was still deserted, so Olin sat on the pavement, holding his injured arm with his good one, and pushed with his feet while she guided the cover into place. When it finally seated with a grind and a clunk, she set her hands on her hips, stretched her aching back, and looked around.

A half-block away was a cemetery where tall, wide headstones offered concealment. She pointed; Olin grunted approval. She helped him to his feet, and together they hurried through its gates and into darkness.

Chapter Sixty-One

Kim-October 23

Harley Stark poked his nose into Kim's office, where she was creating a work schedule for Ruth's growing staff. "Could I speak with you, Ms. Dailey?"

"Of course. I think that's it for now," she told the two aides who'd been helping her. As they went off in a cloud of moderately expensive perfume, one of them gave Harley a glance of interest, but he didn't notice. "What's wrong?" Kim asked when they were alone.

Taking a deep breath, he took a bunch of folded papers from his jacket and laid them on her desk. "They plan to make the Presidency a lifetime position."

Harley had become increasingly critical of the Mandell administration, often asking if she approved of this action or if she knew about that protest. Kim had avoided committing herself, but she couldn't help listening when Harley passed on rumors about suppression of so-called "malcontents." Though unsure what she'd do with it, Kim always entered the information in her notebook, adding what she knew of each situation. Sometimes she berated herself for it. Her careful notes and stealthy eavesdropping would never add up to anything. She was no freedom fighter, and rebellion was highly unlikely. Most citizens were perfectly happy with the current leadership. At least, what they knew of it.

Harley pointed at the papers. "Look at them before you say anything." Picking up the sheets, Kim scanned one after another: emails, phone texts, and handwritten notes he'd copied, no doubt at great risk to his position in the White House. "Some of us know this is wrong, Ms. Dailey. We're hoping you can help."

"Me? Why?"

A swallow revealed the extent of his nervousness. "I don't know what happened, but Mandell quit trying. Now, the First Lady pretty much does as she wants, and she's gotten pretty tyrannical."

"Oh, come on, Harley."

He raised a hand, palm out, as if begging her to listen. "Some really good people in history turned bad when they got power over others. Bloody Mary tried to save England by killing Protestants.

Queen Isabella thought the Inquisition would save souls." With each name, he tapped a finger on her desktop. "Peter the Great. Oliver Cromwell. Napoleon. The list goes on."

"Ruth isn't burning anyone at the stake." But she got the gist of Harley's argument. "She means well—I mean, she did at first. Now Ruth can't stop herself from trying to make everyone do what she says."

Harley's expression revealed relief, and Kim realized that it had been hard for him to come to her. She could have him fired, discredited, maybe even imprisoned.

"Croft is the villain in all this," she said.

"With help from Bennigan and Betzer," Harley agreed. "Those of us who oppose them have to be careful, because they've got everybody spying on everybody else. Even the Secret Service guys report to Croft."

Kim clicked at her teeth with a fingernail. "You really think they plan to seize power?"

"It won't seem that way." He gestured at the papers he'd given her. "In there you'll see how they plan to convince the voters that a long-term Presidency for Mandell will fix all our problems. They'll hold a referendum on it, and the result will be a landslide victory—even if it isn't." Harley's smile was grim. "Congress will be stuck between opposing the so-called will of the people or making that result into law."

"What will they do with those who refuse to go along?"

Taking the sheets from her, Harley leafed through until he found a passage. Kim scanned it quickly and then read it again, more slowly. "Patriot Instruction Camps?"

"All over the country they've been building these camps, they said for guest workers, ex-cons, and the homeless." Harley adjusted his glasses. "What they didn't tell you is that people who speak out against this administration also end up in those places." He sniffed. "I'm probably a candidate, since I haven't exactly been subtle about my disapproval."

"Surely the press will object."

"But they've been clamping down on the media. They've expanded post-9-11 laws, they monitor news agencies, private phones, even the internet. I can still get information via the Dark

Web, but even that is dangerous. My sources change their web addresses daily to keep from being caught and 'camped.'"

"This is a civilized country," Kim objected. "They can't get away with this."

Harley's expression turned sad. "Do you know what most people want, Kim? They want to believe that everything is okay. For years now, nobody agreed what was right and what was wrong. Do black lives matter, or is it blue lives? Does life begin at conception, or should a woman control her body? Will strangers be allowed to come here and settle, or do we keep our country the way it was in the Good Old Days? Is the government responsible for making everyone's life better, or should every person achieve his own success? Everybody had a side, but nobody could satisfy the other side's objections.

"Then Butch Mandell came along, as handsome as JFK and as personable as Reagan. He explains that the measures they're taking are for the good of everyone. Now people might grumble about little parts they disagree with, but they're happy the nation finally has the unified leadership it's needed for a long time."

"But people will object if things go too far."

Harley made a sound of disagreement. "I don't think they'll know what 'too far' is until it's too late."

Kneading the muscles at the back of her neck, Kim said, "Are you saying an educated electorate will lose rights they've always enjoyed and accept a repressive government because they trust and admire one man? I can't imagine it."

"Germans were well educated, yet Hitler convinced them only he could solve their problems. In the 1970s, Iranian women went from miniskirts to hijab in a matter of months."

"Neither of those countries is the U.S.A."

"But the situations were similar." Harley made his points, raising fingers as he spoke. "Growing economic disparity between rich and poor. Government forcing citizens to accept concepts they aren't comfortable with, like non-English-speaking communities and transgender equality. People feel that their values are threatened by the demands of minorities and outsiders."

As he spoke, Kim wrapped her arms around herself, feeling as if the temperature in the room were dropping.

"It isn't about being smart or loving democracy," he finished. "It's about believing those who claim they can make things better."

"Americans will give up their freedom to get standardized gas pumps and street corners with no homeless people."

"By the time they realize what they've done, it will be too late to go back." Harley went silent, letting Kim think it through.

After a moment, she asked, "Why have you brought me all this?"

"We hope you still have influence with the First Lady." When Kim raised a hand, ready to deny it, he said, "Someone has to talk to her."

She squirmed in her chair. "How much time do you think we have?"

"From what I hear, they plan to act after the midterm elections next month. Independents will win big, but most of them lack experience and, to be honest, quite a few of them are whackos. Under President Mandell's guidance, New Day for America will launch. Members of Congress will be promised all kinds of things, and most will go along, thinking they're part of a big national awakening. When the dust settles, they'll be a rubber-stamp body, allowed to make speeches and posture for the folks back home, but essentially powerless."

Kim dug her nails into her upper arms. "I'm not sure we can stop this, Harley."

"I'm not sure either," he replied, "but we hope you might be able to talk to Mrs. Mandell, make her see this is wrong."

"I'll do what I can, but you have to understand that I have no authority to tell anybody anything."

"Shred those sheets once you've read them," Harley warned. "Somebody is always looking over your shoulder."

Kim nodded, but she had a better idea. Harley's evidence would go into her notebook, so when the time came, she could prove to her sister that her plans for the nation rested on misguided "solutions" and rotten underlings.

Later that day, Kim exited a doorway and almost bumped into Josh Bennigan. He didn't excuse himself, so she didn't either. To her surprise, he spoke. "What have you got there, Ms. Dailey?"

It was the notebook, which suddenly felt like dry ice, burning the skin of her hands. "I take notes on the food preferences of White House visitors," she said, though she felt her face warm at the lie. "I also note allergies, religious restrictions on food, things like that."

"I find that interesting. Could I have a look?"

Suddenly Kim's teeth felt too big for her mouth. "Well, the First Lady needs me to make some calls before end of day. I'd be happy to show you another time."

"Of course." His eyes never left hers as he stepped aside, an acknowledgment that he knew she was lying. Kim hurried off down the corridor, thinking that now she'd have to get an exact duplicate of this notebook and make her lie into truth, in case Bennigan asked a second time to see her notes on food.

Chapter Sixty-Two

Ruth-Same Day

"What do you mean, she isn't there?" Ruth had been leaving the White House when her phone rang, and the sky, which was a blend of gray tones, seemed to turn a shade darker as she listened.

Bennigan was apologetic. "They had an inmate escape a few days ago, ma'am. It looks like she followed the same route."

"One assumes your people can locate her quickly."

"We will, ma'am. No question."

"I prefer it be done quietly. No APBs, no cops on the street hauling my sister into some station house."

"I'll see to it."

"All right. Get back here as soon as you can so the three of us can talk."

Ruth immediately cancelled her appointment and called Gavin Croft. "When can you come to my office? It's important."

Apparently detecting tension in her voice, he didn't ask questions. "Give me an hour, ma'am."

Chapter Sixty-Three

Nettie-Same Day

They slumped behind an oversized tombstone until the sun's first rays peeped over the horizon. The temperature dropped as the night waned, so they huddled together, sharing body heat. Nettie dozed intermittently but woke as Olin struggled clumsily to his feet. "Time to move."

Through the gray dawn, she peered at the street below. "Where are we going?"

"First, we gotta get this crap off us."

Nettie was in favor of that until she saw where he pointed. Across the street was a park with a fountain. "There?" she asked incredulously.

His pain-wracked expression changed briefly to a grin. "You got a better idea?"

"But it's cold. We'll be even colder wet."

"Think of it as one of them Polar Bear Plunges y'all have up north."

She admitted, though reluctantly, that a bath was necessary. They smelled horrible, and a simple change of clothes wouldn't be enough. Trudging behind Olin, she approached the fountain. It was small, with two tiers of flowing water. After checking to see that no one was nearby, they crawled in, Nettie supporting Olin as he stepped over the basin edge. They crouched under the fall of water, letting it flow over their heads and through their clothing. Though Nettie's teeth chattered by the time they were done, it felt good to be clean again. When they'd climbed back onto the grass, she suggested turning their prison clothing inside out to hide the word stenciled on each piece. She helped Olin with his pants, but the shirt was too difficult to remove and replace over his damaged shoulder. Nettie wrung each piece as dry as she could, but the cold, clammy fabric stuck to their legs and chilled their bones.

"We're not noticeable," she said sardonically. "Wet as hounds, clothes inside out, and you look like you got sideswiped by a freight train."

"We'll be getting out of sight again pretty soon." Olin shivered violently, and his face was the color of clay.

"Are you going to be all right?" she asked. A second later she chided herself, *Shut up, dummy. You aren't helping one bit.*

Ignoring her query, he pointed. "Capitol Square is that way. Under it is a tunnel system people used to use to get around. It's mostly closed now and off limits to the public. If we can find the entrance I read about online, we can hide down there until we figure out what to do next."

Nettie adjusted her damp sweatpants. "I'm not sure I ever want to go underground again."

Olin's grin revealed the ghost of his old self. "I hear that."

The walk to Capitol Square was nerve-wracking, but they met only one other person, a man walking his dog. As he neared, she put an arm around Olin, hiding the word on the back of his sweatshirt. The man, preoccupied with getting the dog to do his business, hardly spared them a glance.

The tunnel entrance, Olin said, was in the lobby of an office building. When they located the address, the entry doors were locked. "Too early," he muttered. They found a place to wait behind some hydrangea bushes, where they shivered and tried to make themselves invisible until a security guard came to open the doors. Though she didn't have a watch, Nettie guessed it was 7:00 a.m. When the guard was gone, they entered the lobby and began searching for the tunnel entrance. "It will look like the door to a janitor's closet," Olin said as he led the way. "And it should be right...here."

The door was padlocked, and Nettie gave a groan of disappointment. "I brought along one of Doc Foeller's paring knives," Olin said. "If you hold that lock steady, I can get it open."

They managed it, though it wasn't a smooth operation. Nettie had trouble focusing. There had to be surveillance cameras, which meant someone was watching them. When she mentioned it, Olin didn't seem worried. "They don't watch those things in real life like they do in the movies. I mean, how boring would that be?" Rolling his head, he called her attention to a camera near them. "Besides, they're mostly aimed at entry doors and places where hallways connect." He went back to work, and Nettie focused on holding the padlock steady and trying to adopt her companion's casual attitude.

When a soft click signaled Olin's success, they hurried through the door. Reaching back, Nettie closed the padlock on its staple, hoping a casual observer wouldn't notice the hasp wasn't in place. Then she followed Olin, who limped down two flights of stairs, leaning heavily on the railing.

At the bottom, they stopped to survey their new hiding place. The passage was dry and lit by low-wattage sconces placed every thirty feet. Many of them were burnt out, hinting that maintenance was spotty. Nettie sincerely hoped replacements weren't scheduled for today.

Machinery narrowed what had once been an open path, and the hum of fans and engines made a constant, low music. No longer used for foot traffic, the old tunnel now housed ugly metal hulks required for the comfort and convenience of those in the buildings above.

"People might come through sometimes," Olin said, peering ahead, "but we'll hear them in time to hide."

Down a side passage, they found a diagram posted as a guide. "This thing goes on forever," Olin said, and the tenor of his voice told Nettie he was almost out of energy.

"Sit," she ordered. "I'll find us some water and maybe food."

Water turned out to be easy. Down the next side passage was a janitor's alcove with a tap and a shallow floor basin for cleaning mops. Finding an empty soda can, she rinsed it, filled it from the tap, and drank enough to slake her own thirst before refilling it for Olin.

While he gulped the water she left him again, determined to locate food. Along the tunnel, staircases led to back doors of various businesses and organizations, but they were all securely locked. She continued through several passages, careful to pay attention to the route so she could get back to Olin. At the fourth or fifth turn, she stopped, feeling desperate. Half-starved, hurt, and exhausted, Olin needed fuel, but the tunnel offered nothing. Did she dare go back outside?

A little farther down, a staircase led to a door with "Delton Museum" stenciled on it. When she climbed the steps and grasped the knob, she found it locked, as the others before it had been, but above the door was a vent that Nettie guessed was a no-frills exhaust for the A/C. It covered a space about two feet high by three feet wide. She'd brought the paring knife along. If the screws were flatheads, life would be good.

Going back down the stairs, Nettie retraced her steps until she found a mesh trash basket she'd passed earlier. Hauling it up the steps to the doorway, she inverted it and climbed on top. Balance was precarious, since the basket wasn't meant to be used as a booster, but she started work on the screws, which cooperated by turning easily. When she set the vent down, carefully so it made no sound, she could see into a cluttered room that contained stacks of boxes and a desk with an ancient-looking computer tower, monitor and keyboard. Though the place was lit only by the blue light of the computer's power supply, she saw logos like "Hanes" and "Giftees" on the boxes. Storage for the museum's gift store, she decided. That was good, because those boxes might contain things they needed.

On the minus side, her trash basket booster wasn't high enough to let her do more than look. Like a mirage in the desert, the room was tempting but unreachable.

No. It couldn't be unreachable. She needed that room to be *reachable*.

Returning to the tunnel, Nettie searched until she came upon a galvanized bucket full of sand, no doubt left to serve as an ashtray for workers who slipped into the tunnels to smoke. Dumping the sand on the floor, she took the bucket and went back up the stairs.

Climbing onto the inverted wastebasket again, Nettie spread her feet to its outer edges, set the bucket upside down between them, and stepped onto it. A foot higher than before, she was able to grasp the edge, brace her feet on the door, and pull herself up until she could set one knee on the opening. In seconds she was sitting with one foot inside and one out. She pulled her sweatshirt hood up and tied it tightly, leaving only her eyes showing. If there was a surveillance camera inside, they'd soon figure out who she was, but, she thought, *One does what one can.*

Bringing her other foot through the opening, she turned to face the wall and lowered one foot and then the other to the desktop below, setting her weight on it only when she was sure it wouldn't collapse under her. Easing herself down, she surveyed the room, still peeping from the neck hole of her shirt.

Opening the nearest box, she helped herself to useful items, a table runner to make a sling for Olin; a long, colorful peasant blouse to replace her prison shirt and cover the worst of the stains on her pants; and a couple of raincoats with the U of V logo for warmth. Thinking of Olin's injured arm, she sorted through a box until she found a "Virginia Is for Lovers" sweatshirt that zipped in front. Another box contained stadium blankets, which she took to use for bedding. When her pile of goods became unwieldy, she added a tote bag with a clever meme about science being science, whether you believe in it or not.

No food. Going to the door at the opposite side of the room, Nettie peered out at the gift shop itself. A clock over the entry said it was almost eight, which meant that people would soon be arriving for work. She had to hurry. Before opening the door, she unplugged everything she could find, hoping to disable alarms and surveillance cameras. No loud noises sounded as she moved quickly through the aisles, keeping her flashlight beam aimed low. At the front, she found a tray of candy bars next to the cash register. "Breakfast," she whispered as she stuffed her pockets, waistband, and bra, choosing bars that contained nuts, oats, peanut butter, or coconut. Next to the counter was a small refrigerator, and she took four bottles of Gatorade. On her way back to the storeroom, she stopped at a table of assorted caps and chose two with the broadest bills she could find.

Working quickly, Nettie tidied the place, closing the boxes so the missing items weren't immediately evident. She packed what she'd taken into the tote bag, added a pair of scissors from the desk, fastened the bag's handles together with mailing tape, and stuffed it through the opening. Back in the tunnel, she replaced the vent, the bucket, and the trash bin, gathered up what had spilled from the tote when it rolled down the stairs, and started back to Olin, bent like an old-time peddler.

Almost back to where she'd left him, she heard footsteps and stopped dead. They came from some distance, but whoever it was seemed to be headed her way. Hurrying the last few steps to where Olin sat, she whispered, "Gotta go. Company coming."

She helped him stand and heard him suppress a moan of pain. With the tote straps over her other shoulder, she led the way to the nearest staircase and helped him up the steps. At the top was a sign: "No Exit: Alarm Will Sound." It was too late to go back down, but a small recess at one side was out of view from below. If they were still, whoever was there might pass by unknowing.

Olin sensed the need for quiet, and she saw him press his lips together to hold his pain inside. They stood, bodies touching and backs pressed against the wall. Nettie's mind buzzed with worry. What if this was the exit the person meant to take? What if guards were required to investigate each staircase as they made rounds? What if the passer-by heard Olin's labored breathing?

The interloper whistled softly as he walked. Suddenly the sound ended with a grunt of surprise. Peeping out, Nettie saw a disheveled, bearded man in dark jeans and a dirty hoodie. On the steps lay one of the caps she'd taken from the shop. It had fallen out of her bag as she helped Olin up the stairs.

"You!" The man's voice was harsh and commanding. "Come out of there."

Olin put a hand on Nettie's arm and shook his head, but she had already assessed their options. The newcomer was obviously a vagrant, but his assertive demand hinted he wasn't the passive kind. If she remained in the alcove, she and Olin were cornered and vulnerable. In the open, she had a better chance to either fight or run, leading him away from Olin. If she was lucky, she might be able to talk him into leaving her alone. Squeezing Olin's good arm, Nettie set down the tote bag and stepped into view. "I'm not here to make trouble."

"This my space," the man said belligerently. "Don't nobody come through without me getting something for it."

It was a lie, of course, but he saw her position as weak and his as strong. Nettie saw sadism in his eyes, pleasure at coming upon a lone female he could frighten and bully. He shifted his body, and she saw that he carried a length of pipe about an inch in diameter. A cheap but effective weapon, easily wiped clean and tossed away if necessary. He circled it in a threatening manner.

"I'm just passing through," she said calmly. "No threat to you."

"Come down here."

Olin made a negative sound, but Nettie put a hand behind her back to signal him to stay quiet. Putting every bit of acting talent she had into her movements, she obeyed, appearing both reluctant to approach her tormentor and afraid not to. She kept her eyes downcast, as if unable to look away from the weapon. The man reacted as she'd hoped, moving his feet from an offensive position to a more relaxed stance.

The downfall of arrogant men is their own arrogance.

As she reached the bottom step, Nettie took a single long stride, quickly closing the gap between herself and the man. With her right hand, she grabbed the end of the pipe and twisted it toward the weakest point in his grip, the gap where thumb and fingers met. The surprise of her move made the pipe hers. At the same time, she punched out with her fist, catching him full on the nose. When he staggered backward a step, she hit him on the outside of the knee with the pipe.

The expletives that followed were garbled, but their message came through.

"Get out," Nettie ordered. "Now, or I'll put you down for good."

Her would-be attacker didn't need further urging. Limping, rasping, and cursing, he skittered down the tunnel.

When a door slammed somewhere in the distance, Olin came down the stairs, stooping to pick up the cap she'd dropped. Setting it on her head, he said, "Man, Nettie, you got skills!"

"I've dealt with violent men before," she said calmly, though her breathing was ragged. "They don't expect you to take the initiative, but sometimes it's all you can do."

"Will he come back?"

"Not today. Let me show you what I found."

They moved into the light spill of a working sconce, and Nettie took out the food she'd stored in her clothes and then began unloading the tote bag. Olin opened a candy bar at once, took a large bite, and chewed while she took the sweatshirt and raincoat out and removed the tags. Using the scissors she'd lifted from the office desk, she cut Olin's sweatshirt off and gently helped him put the new one on. Next, she fashioned a sling from the table runner. Once the arm was immobilized, some of the tension left Olin's face. She helped him slide the windbreaker on, leaving the right sleeve empty. The jackets hung to mid-thigh, so while the knees and hems of their pants were still grimy, they looked respectable enough from the waist up.

While Olin ate a second candy bar, Nettie took off her Martha's Place sweatshirt and replaced it with the colorful blouse she'd stolen for herself. As she zipped the jacket over it, Olin joked, "You're a real fashionista."

"Yeah, right." Rolling up their discarded clothes, she stuffed them into the tote. When she tried to set the second cap on Olin's head, it teetered precariously due to his oversized cloud of hair. Chuckling, he had her cut a strip from his prison sweatshirt to use as a do-rag. When he set the cap over it, Nettie said, "You look like a member of Wu-Tang Clan."

Olin gave the cap a tug, so the bill covered his brows. "Works for me."

"We need to disguise our faces, but this is all I could find for right now. Later we can add glasses or whatever."

"Sure," he said sardonically. "We'll buy 'em with the cash we brought along."

Nettie looked back toward the storeroom door. "I should have looked for money in the desk."

"Probably all locked away." He took a third candy bar and unwrapped it. "You should have a couple of these."

She took one. "Let's go." As they walked, she said, "You need to get that shoulder looked at."

"I'm fine."

"We need money and a place to hide until they stop looking for us."

"How's that gonna happen? You're the First Lady's sister."

He was right. Her disappearance was going to be big news.

Unless the First Lady didn't want it to be.

Chapter Sixty-Four

Kim-Same Day

"Kim, come in." Vice President Cary Stockwell rose and gestured her forward. He and two aides were seated around a table, their heads together as they examined a schematic of some kind.

"Am I interrupting?"

"Kevin and Don brought in some proposals for my security in New York City next week. Hard to balance interacting with the crowd and protecting me from some crazy who's convinced I'm a demon from Neptune." Turning to his aides, he said, "Give us a few minutes, will you, guys?"

They rose, power drinks in hand, and left. "You appear to be a woman on a mission," Cary observed. "In ten minutes, those two will stick their noses in and wave the daily schedule at me, so talk fast."

"Okay." Suddenly, Kim had no idea where to start. After making herself half-crazy trying to come up with a way to convince Ruth she had to seriously reconsider her path, she'd thought of Cary. The VP had the knowledge, the background, and the Constitutional authority to act. He could present Ruth with the choice between being reasonable or facing Butch's removal from office. But it was a momentous step. She was betraying her sister in ways Ruth would never understand. To make matters worse, Kim didn't have a clue where to begin or how much to tell. Her eyes prickled with tears, making her want to run from the room. How could she explain the situation to Cary if she started sobbing like a depressed teenager?

"Let's have a drink." He turned to a small refrigerator next to his chair. "Coke or Sprite?"

"Coke, please." Kim drank pop—soda, Cary called it— only with the Vice President. He loved it, and since he was amazingly healthy at seventy, she figured sugar worked for him.

He passed her a can, took one for himself, and led the way to four upholstered chairs set in a circle at one side of the room. A switch on the wall changed the lighting from overhead lighting to a glow that lit the corner they occupied. Indicating she should sit, he followed suit and popped the top on his drink. By the time all that was accomplished, Kim was better able to control her emotions. "I have things I need to tell you."

"I'm listening."

She hesitated, wondering for the hundredth time if this was wise. It was possible Stockwell knew exactly what Ruth and Butch were up to. If he agreed with their plan, he'd probably call for Kim's arrest. Like Drew, she'd be discredited, her behavior explained by rumors of mental illness or naked ambition.

But Ruth spoke of Cary Stockwell in dismissive terms, and Kim doubted she trusted him enough to include him in plans for a government takeover. That too was a problem. If Stockwell was as weak as Ruth believed, what could he do to help?

She eased into it, beginning with her family's running joke that Ruth was a dictator in velvet gloves. Stockwell's nod indicated he knew the First Lady well enough to conclude that it was still true. More confidently, Kim explained her suspicion that Gavin Croft and his associates indulged in dirty tricks. "I'm sure Ruth doesn't know how far things go," she said, "but it gets worse all the time."

Again, Stockwell nodded, his grave expression hinting that he shared her fear.

"Now I have to tell you about my other sister. I'm sorry to make this a family saga, but I recently learned why Nettie killed her son. I told Ruth she had cause for what she did, but she claims Nettie wants to be in prison."

"And does she?"

"Well, yes, but I think she's punishing herself too harshly."

He took a sip. "We tend to do that. At least some of us do."

Next, she told Cary how Drew McMahon had done the leg work for her on Nettie's case. "In return, he's being accused of things that aren't true," she said. "I think Gavin Croft is trying to keep him quiet about my nephew's crimes."

"To spare the First Lady embarrassment."

"Yes. Ruth says we can't let family skeletons ruin the success they've had."

"Success."

Kim heard something in his tone. "You don't agree with what they've done?"

A sigh. A large swig of Coke. Finally, Stockwell said, "Judged on the surface, this administration has done amazing things in a very short time. But if you look closely, it's not pretty."

"What do you mean?"

"Women are being forced from the labor market. Our 'guest workers' aren't treated fairly, nor are the homeless and the mentally handicapped. Businesses use them for cheap labor and ignore their rights without penalty. He chuckled grimly. "They like that part, but in the next breath, they're complaining about Ruth's meddling, like her demand for identical dashboards and universal thermostats." He turned the soda can in his hands absently. "Mrs. Mandell likes her cell phone, so they all should be exactly like it. She prefers that credit cards be swiped, not tapped or chipped." Cary's smile was bitter. "When your sister turns her eye to a practice or a product, engineers shudder. Behind her back, they've begun to call it 'getting Ruthed.'"

Kim wondered if Harley knew the term. No doubt he'd spared her feelings when possible, not disparaging her sister any more than necessary to get his message across. "Why do they put up with it?"

"Butch is a popular figure, as is his wife, and Croft is an expert at applying pressure. Betzer can word a document so that it means whatever he wants it to, and Bennigan uses the power of Homeland Security to deal with even the smallest rebellions." Cary's brows met like warring clouds. "You'd be surprised at how fearful my former colleagues in the Senate have become."

"I've noticed that D.C. isn't exactly overflowing with moral courage."

Leaning back in his chair, Cary set one leg over the other. "Some of us do what we can, in the shadows. Your friend Harley, for example. He's good about keeping me and the other malcontents informed as to what Croft is up to."

Kim sighed. "If you know this administration has gone wrong, why have you gone along with it?"

He took a drink. "I made my thoughts known privately to the President, but he's...*diminished* is the only word I can think of."

"Diminished. Yes."

"When I first met Butch, I found him a little shallow, a little hokey, but honest, and therefore not without possibilities. These days, it's like he's standing a long way off and can hardly hear me speaking."

"He had a stroke." She hadn't meant to say it, but there it was. "The night of his inauguration. Ruth covered it up."

Cary rubbed his chin. "The slip in the shower. I wondered about that."

"She says he's recovered but I think the way he is gives her freedom to…"

"Run the country her way?"

Her lips quivered, so she took a sip of Coke. Swallowing, she said, "Yes."

"I'm afraid there isn't much we can do about it, Kim. The current Cabinet is made up of yes-men. They aren't going to invoke the 25th Amendment and put themselves out of a job."

"If we told them about the stroke, would it change things?"

"That depends. Can you prove what you've told me?"

Kim shook her head. "The people who know will never speak up, and the actor who took Butch's place is dead."

Stockwell pointed a finger at her. "You need to be careful, Kim. If Croft knew you'd told me all this, he'd come after you."

Kim felt a stab of regret. "I hope I haven't put you in danger, Cary."

"We need an excuse." He considered briefly. "What's Butch's birthday?"

"April something."

"How about Ruth?"

"December 2nd."

"All right. If anyone asks, the two of us met to begin planning a surprise birthday celebration for her." Kim nodded understanding, and they both rose. "I'll continue exploring the options, but again, we must be careful. These are powerful people, and they'll swat us like flies if they learn we're coming after them." His smile was rueful. "I'll be made to look senile and delusional. Lord knows what they'd do to discredit you."

Kim was still scared, but she felt a little less alone. "Thanks for believing me."

"No, thank you for trusting me. I've dithered for too long over what to do, but you helped me face the truth. It's time to stop acting like a politician and time to become a statesman."

When Kim left the VP's office, Everett Mero, the Secret Service agent who'd given her the warning, waited in the corridor. He watched her approach, his forehead slightly creased, but didn't speak. Kim felt the urge to mention Ruth's birthday, but it would have been odd to explain her visit to one of the silent guardians who protected the President. Instead, she looked down at the floor, as if she didn't notice Mero standing there.

Chapter Sixty-Five

Ruth-Same Day

As Croft and Bennigan sat stiffly in straight-backed chairs, Ruth paced her office. "We'll find her," Bennigan said for at least the fourth time. He received no response.

Croft's comment mirrored Ruth's thought. "Ms. Dailey knows where she is. If she doesn't, she soon will."

Ruth had stopped at the window, and she closed the blinds against the bright sunlight. "I suppose the two of them have put their heads together and reached the conclusion that I'm the evil sister." Turning to Bennigan, she asked, "You're watching Kim, yes?"

"We monitor her calls. Her driver reports where she goes when she leaves the grounds. I'm not sure what else we can do."

Ruth's arms were crossed, and her fingers beat a rhythm on her upper arm for a moment. "Don't just track Kim. Follow everyone she speaks to, anyone she's friendly with on the staff." She rubbed her hands together as if they were cold. "Nettie will contact her. She'll have to. And when she does, Kim will do what she can to help."

As the men went off to do her bidding, Ruth continued pacing, her usually peaceful demeanor gone. Why couldn't people see what she was trying to accomplish? And why did her beloved younger sister refuse to even try?

For a horrible moment, Ruth doubted everything. Despite her hard work, not everyone approved of her policies. She'd noticed looks exchanged between Croft and Bennigan, acknowledging things she was never told. Then there were the fleeting expressions she glimpsed on the faces of those around her, flashes of irritation that seemed to say, "Here she goes again." Those looks hinted that her ideas were…What? Unwelcome? Unachievable? Petty?

Kim claimed she was sticking her nose into every aspect of American life, but how could she allow so much to go on that was wasteful and counterproductive? Surely it was wrong to see things that need fixing and not do something about them.

But reports trickled in from all over the country. Groups were organizing to oppose what they termed the President's "overreach." Women objected to the steady shifting to an all-male workforce.

Visiting workers claimed their bosses treated them badly and no one cared. Hospitals claimed that the new health care plan was creating chaos. And the roar against standardization was deafening. While Ruth tried to make life easier, people screamed in outrage because they no longer had a choice between squeeze-and-turn and push-and-turn pill bottles.

Ruth worked sixteen hours a day, six days a week (and often Sunday evenings, though she didn't admit that), only to face petty objections to her common-sense rules. Croft had every right to act against the malcontents who screamed about their rights. Once they shut up, Americans would see how smoothly the country could run.

We're a nation with too many critics, she thought. *There aren't not enough good citizens who are willing to let a leader of principal show them the way.*

Chapter Sixty-Six

Nettie-October 24

Nettie and Olin spent the day in the tunnels, listening for footsteps and resting to rebuild their strength. Choosing a spot where a sconce was burned out, they lay covered in their blankets, alternately dozing and discussing. Olin's plan had been to hitch a ride north with a passing trucker, but he couldn't function on his own with his shoulder injury. Still, travel would be more difficult with two people of different ages, a male and a female, one white and one black. Their photos had probably been on the news all day, and police everywhere were looking for them. "I have to contact my sister in D.C.," Nettie said. "She'll give us money, which will give us options."

"She won't rat you out?"

"No." Nettie smiled. "She won't like it, but she'll keep quiet."

"Then I guess we're heading to our nation's capital."

That presented its own set of challenges, but Nettie used a trick she'd learned long ago, when she needed to travel secretly and for free. Huddled outside an all-night gas station, they watched for pickup trucks. Each time one stopped, Nettie approached and asked the driver if he was going to D.C. When the sixth one gave an affirmative answer, she asked if she might ride along. He refused, which she'd expected, given her disheveled appearance.

When he went inside to use the rest room, she and Olin climbed into the back of the truck. Huddling in the shadows at the front of the bed, they covered themselves with a dark-hued stadium blanket. Nettie bit her lip as the man returned to his truck, but he climbed into the cab without noticing he had passengers. Soon they heard the heavy beat of the driver's music and the slap of his hands on the steering wheel as he did impromptu duets with the drummer.

The ride was cold, and she worried about how the bumps must aggravate Olin's damaged shoulder. As they lay quietly, side by side, Nettie pondered the question that had caused her to run: Why had Ruth arranged her freedom? Only one reason fit what she knew of the situation: Ruth planned to use Nettie to control Kim. That meant Ruth and her coterie feared Kim was a threat to their power.

Originally, she'd meant to disappear and let Kim know later that she was okay, but now Nettie felt responsible for Olin. If she could get his shoulder seen to and give him bus ticket money, she'd have done what she could for him. That meant asking for help, and Kim was the only person she could trust.

Lights overhead became more frequent, and traffic picked up. She felt Olin scoot toward her so they could speak softly. "You awake?"

"Too cold to sleep."

"I've been paying attention to the signs. I think we should get out now, because we're in an area I'm a little familiar with."

"Okay. You're the one who's been here before."

"Next red light, stay low and roll over the right-hand side. I'll follow."

It was dangerous. They might be hit by oncoming traffic. A passer-by might alert the driver to their presence. And she knew what it would cost Olin to slide over the pickup wall and land on the pavement. "Got it."

Their unknowing chauffeur never saw them go. He'd joined the vocalist, castigating a woman named Diana for her cold heart and hot body. Olin made a muted groan when he jumped, but Nettie steadied him with an arm around his waist. The driver of the car behind them looked surprised and then suspicious, but Nettie waved and gave him a big smile, as if the whole thing was a joke. Shaking his head, the man sped off, and she and Olin rested for a while on a bus stop bench.

"We're here," he said, adjusting his makeshift sling. "Now what?"

"If you think you can manage it, I want you to meet with my sister."

"Why don't you go?"

"If I go, Kim won't want me to leave. You can tell her what we need and then walk away."

He managed a laugh. "We hope."

"Yes. She might be watched, so we'll have to be careful."

Chapter Sixty-Seven

Kim-Same Day

"Why can't I visit?" Kim had come to see Nettie, to talk with her about the steps she was taking to stop Ruth. She didn't recognize the man who met her at the outer gate of Martha's Place. He wore sunglasses, though the day was cloudy, and his blank expression said he wasn't there to be helpful.

"The prisoners are not available to visitors at this time."

Over his shoulder she saw police cars and vans parked outside the building. People moved around the yard with purpose, obviously searching, and fear struck Kim like a hammer blow. "I need to speak with Dr. Foeller."

"She isn't available."

"I can wait. When might she be able to see me?"

"Dr. Foeller is gone from the property indefinitely." His tone said she'd get no more information. Trying to appear confused but not suspicious, Kim got into the waiting Uber car. "Drive a few blocks and then find a place to park, will you?" she asked. The driver obeyed while she located the business card Foeller had given her and entered the number handwritten on the back. The phone rang six times before she heard a voice that was female and young. "Hello?"

"Hi. I'm Kim, a friend of Susan's. Can I speak to her?"

"She's…gone."

"What do you mean?"

"Men came in the middle of the night and arrested her." The last few words came in a rising tone. She was close to tears.

The daughter was—what had the doctor said? Eleven. She had to be terrified. "I'm so sorry…Dylan, right?"

"Yeah."

"Are you alone, Dylan?"

"No. Uncle Frank's here."

Reluctantly, Kim took advantage of the girl's youth. "Dylan, I can help your mother, but I need to know exactly what happened. Do you know why she was arrested?"

"They said she cheated Medicare—or maybe Medicaid. I forget."

Kim had been framed and dismissed from her job. Drew had been framed for corruption. Now they'd made it appear that Foeller too was a criminal.

"Who's on the phone, Dylan?" The voice was male.

"A friend of Mom's."

Next, Kim heard a man's voice. "Who is this?"

Quickly, she ended the call. She'd used the burner phone, but with the power of the government against her, how safe was it? If they'd arrested Drew, they had his, and there were only calls to this number in its memory. Leaning toward the driver she asked, "Is there a Walmart nearby?"

In fifteen minutes, Kim had a new phone. She tossed the old one into a trash can as she left the store. It meant Drew couldn't call, but she doubted he could anyway. He was on the run, and that was her fault.

Feeling she had nowhere else to go, Kim returned to the White House and buried herself in work. Ruth came and went but seemed preoccupied. Kim didn't mention her wasted trip to Richmond, and Ruth didn't ask about it. What would she say when she learned Nettie was gone?

Or had Ruth arranged Nettie's disappearance? What better way to keep Kim quiet than to hold Nettie's future hostage?

No. Ruth had done things that were wrong, but her heart was in the right place. If she and Nettie could sit down with Ruth, they'd help her see her mistakes and correct them. She'd get rid of Croft and his cronies. She'd close the camps, stop suppressing dissent, and let the government operate as it was meant to.

At that moment Kim's cell phone—the one associated with her name—burbled. She didn't recognize the number on caller ID, so she didn't answer. It was an hour before she noticed she had a voice mail. "Ms. Dailey," said a male voice, "this is the Owl Bookshop. The Laura Lippman novel you ordered came in. You can pick it up at your convenience." He gave their closing time and wished her a pleasant day.

She hadn't ordered a book, and she'd never heard of the Owl Bookshop. But she had told Nettie she was eager to read Lippman's upcoming release. "I'm going out for a while," she told Ruth. "I have an order to pick up."

"There are staffers who'd do that for you, Kimmie."

"I don't mind. The sun is out, and I'll have time to browse a little before they close for the day."

Kim's driver stopped in traffic near the bookshop. "I'll park up there," he said, indicating a lot farther down.

"Great. I'll walk up when I'm done, so you don't have to make a left in this mess." She added a warning. "It might be a while. Inside a bookstore, I tend to lose all track of time."

Rodgers slid his phone out of his pocket. "I've got my entertainment right here." Kim got out, tapped the trunk to let him know she was clear, and watched him drive off. The first thing he'd do, she guessed, was call the White House and report her location to Gavin Croft. He'd probably been told it was part of the job. *How easily we accept what we're told by those in authority when it doesn't seem like a big deal.*

The bookstore was sprinkled with patrons: some tourists, a mom with two small children, an elderly man perusing the War & Military section. Behind the counter, a clerk tapped away at a computer keyboard. Kim didn't approach, aware the woman had no order with her name on it. The call had been to get her here, to see Nettie. At least, that's what she hoped.

Unsure what her next move should be, Kim went to the new releases section. As she made a show of perusing the shelves, a young black man in a bright orange windbreaker passed behind her. One sleeve hung empty, and a piece of cloth around his neck held his arm at his chest. He moved carefully, fearful of jostling or being jostled. In her ear she heard, "Give me a few seconds then come to the cookbook section."

Kim did as he said, but when she got there, the area was empty. Picking up a book on Greek cooking, she paged through it for a few seconds, looking around without appearing to. She was at the back of the store, in an alcove with bookshelves on three sides. On her left was a doorway marked "Employees Only." Patrons moved behind her, but at the moment, no one seemed interested in food preparation. There was a convex mirror in a corner overhead, and she stepped back a little so that she could see what was behind her. At first she saw no one of interest, but a flash of movement caught her attention. Rodgers. He peered at her suspiciously for a moment then moved off, phone at his ear.

"Ms. Dailey?" The voice came from her left, and she turned to see the man standing in the doorway of the stockroom. He held the hinged door open a few inches so that she could see him, but it was unlikely anyone else would. "Nettie sent me. We need your help."

"Of course." Realizing she'd agreed too easily, she amended, "If you can prove what you say."

He smiled. "I'm supposed to show you this." Reaching into his jacket pocket, he took out a bracelet made of braided thread.

"Oh my God," Realizing she'd almost shouted, Kim clapped a hand over her mouth. Leaning back, she checked the convex mirror again. No sign of Rodgers. "I made that for her when I was still in elementary school."

"I think it means a lot to her," the man said. "She threatened to thrash me if I lose it."

"Okay, you're with Nettie." Kim spoke softly, and she put back the book she'd been holding and took up a different one. "I'd like to know why, but we don't have time. Is she okay?"

"She's okay. Her and me escaped from Martha's Place, but we got nothing."

"How can I help?"

"We need money."

"I figured that." She'd brought along five hundred dollars in cash, which she took from her pocket and put into the book, making sure he saw the cover before she put it back and took up another. "I can arrange more, but it can't come directly from me." Taking out her phone, Kim looked up a number and read it to him. "Can you remember that?"

"Give it to me one more time."

She did, and he nodded. "Got it."

"In about an hour, call that number and tell the woman who answers that your name is Benny Franklin. She'll get you the money. You just need to work out where to meet her. She'll be flying in, so the airport is probably best."

"Okay." The man lowered his head as if the next part was embarrassing. "She made me promise to ask about seeing a doctor. I messed up my shoulder, and she says I'm no use to her if I don't get it fixed."

That was a problem Kim hadn't anticipated, but she quickly saw a possibility. The man was taller than Harley, but they shared general features, white teeth, a thin frame, and small, low-set ears. "I'm going to ask a friend of mine to pick you up right outside this place at…let's say 6:00, after he gets out of work. You and he aren't twins by any means, but you're similar enough that I think you could use his insurance info at one of those urgent care places." Realizing Harley had every right to refuse her request, she added, "If he doesn't show up by 6:30, call me again and we'll go a different way." He nodded, and she went on, "What do I call you?"

A grin lit his face. "I kind of like Benny Franklin."

"All right, Benny. When you get the money, you're going to take my sister away from here, right?"

He nodded. "I need to go north. Nettie can travel with me. Once we take care of business I got up there, I'll see about getting her a new identity."

"You can do that?"

A shrug. "I know people."

"Great. I'll ask my friend to help you get treatment. Once that's done, you and Nettie get on a bus and get out of D.C."

Kim wasn't looking directly at the man, but she heard a change in his tone. "She told me to say that you need to get away too."

"Don't worry about me." She chose her purchase, a book of 20-minute recipes. "Tell her we'll figure out a way to see each other once it's safe."

"Okay. You should leave now. I'll pick up the money and then go out the back."

When Kim returned to the White House, Ruth met her in the hallway. "How was the excursion?"

Kim felt like a terrible person. Ruth had been so good to her, and she was going behind her back to help Nettie and working against what Ruth held most dear. She took a large breath and let it out before answering, hoping to make her voice sound normal. "Material for long evenings in my room." She showed Ruth the book, which she'd had the presence of mind to buy before leaving the store.

"Knowing you, it'll be finished in a day and a half." In a casual tone, she asked, "How was your visit with Nettie today?"

"They wouldn't let me see her or Doctor Foeller. There must be a virus, or maybe an emergency."

Ruth shivered delicately. "I hope she's all right."

"Last night I dreamed Nettie and I bought a farm and lived there quietly, just the two of us. Is it weird that I'm dreaming about being away from people?"

"I don't think it's *weird,* exactly," Ruth replied. "But to be honest, I don't understand why you'd want to."

Chapter Sixty-Eight

Nettie-Same Day

The Med-View Urgent Care Center receptionist looked up to see two African American men enter and approach her desk. One wore a dapper suit; the other a UVA windbreaker with one sleeve empty. Grasping the desk as if he might faint, he said, "I need to see a doctor about my shoulder."

"What's the trouble?"

"I was working on my car and the jack slipped. I took a pretty good hit."

"May I see your identification and your insurance information please?"

"Sure." Using the opposite hand, the man took out a wallet. His companion helped him find the cards she'd asked for. The woman entered information into her computer, asked for fifty dollars, and then said, "Take a seat over there. We'll call when we're ready."

The two men retreated to the chairs along the opposite wall. A few minutes later a woman came out and said, "Mr. Stark? Would you come with me, please?"

Both men rose and followed her to a room, where she opened the door and stood aside. "Take a seat on the exam table. Doctor will be with you shortly."

Once she was gone, Harley helped Olin get onto the table and gently removed the windbreaker. "I think we did it."

Olin chuckled, though his face was tight with pain. "I hope your insurance covers pain pills, dude, because this hurts like a bitch."

Nettie was a bundle of nerves after a man in an apple-red Buick pulled up at the corner outside the bookstore, identified himself as Kim's friend, and whisked Olin away for medical treatment. Nettie's job was to take a cab to the airport, meet a plane from Detroit, and receive the money Kim had arranged with her lawyer, Abigail Pelletier. If the woman was puzzled by the odd request that she bring ten thousand dollars to D.C. and hand it over to a woman in a UVA windbreaker, she apparently trusted Kim enough to do as she asked.

The cab ride was expensive, and the clouds that had moved in to hide the sinking sun didn't help Nettie's mood. What if the woman couldn't get a flight on short notice? What if a storm between Detroit and D.C. delayed her arrival? Should Nettie wait at the airport? If she did, would Olin assume she'd been caught? Why hadn't she used Kim's money to buy phones so they could—

Shaking herself mentally, Nettie cut off her litany of worries. Being out of prison was its own sort of prison. Options required choices. Companionship brought responsibility. Being a person, not an inmate, was hard.

At the airport, Nettie gave the cabbie a decent but not generous tip, hoping he'd recall only an elderly woman who listened to his stories and smiled at his jokes. They'd bought Olin reading glasses that made him look, he claimed, like Malcolm X. She'd bought glasses too, and a gray, tightly curled wig that, when she settled it over her own hair, recalled her grandmother and the sharp smell of the permanent wave lotion she'd used. Buying makeup for the first time in decades, she'd painted on an unrecognizable face: black brows, green eyeshadow, and enough rouge and lipstick for a Vegas revue.

Inside the terminal, she found the gate where Abigail would be arriving and waited as passengers came down the jet bridge. She recognized the woman from the description she'd provided, noting the large purse slung over her shoulder. When she chose a spot in a corner and sat down, Nettie approached. "Ms. Pelletier? I'm Kim's friend, and I'm here for Benny Franklin's package."

Recognition showed in the lawyer's eyes, but she only nodded. Taking a small purse out of the large one, she put its strap over her shoulder and pushed the larger bag toward Nettie. "Why couldn't I have wired this?"

"It's best if you don't know."

"Okay then. I need to hit the restroom before I get on a plane headed west." With a grimace, she added, "Can't deal with airplane lavatories."

"Thank you."

The response was a cheerful wave. Taking the purse, Nettie left the terminal for the taxi stand and directed the driver to the motel where they'd rented a room for the night.

Olin was there, his shoulder wrapped in elastic bandage and his arm supported by a proper sling. "Your man was pretty cool," he said, his words slightly slurred. "We got the job done." Pointing to a bottle of pills on the nightstand, he added, "He even took me to the pharmacy afterward."

"What's the verdict on your shoulder?"

"Dislocated. Hurt like hell when the doc put it back in, but it feels okay now."

"I'm glad it was fixable with one visit."

"Yeah. If I needed surgery—no way that would happen for a while." He gestured at the bag she carried. "Is that our stake?"

"It is."

"Your sister's buddy gave me his old university ID card. I think it will work, 'cause bus stations don't usually check those things too close. Tomorrow morning, we get on a bus for Vermont."

"You do, Olin. I'm staying in D.C. until I'm sure Kim is okay."

Chapter Sixty-Nine

Ruth-October 25

"You were smart to suggest watching your sister's friends," Josh Bennigan told Ruth the next morning. It was five a.m., and only the desk lamp was lit, so Ruth's face was shadowed. "Yesterday after work, the kid from Tennessee had an errand you'll be interested in." He described how Harley Stark had picked up a stranger and taken him to a local walk-in clinic. "The woman at reception said Stark came in with a dislocated shoulder. We think the two men switched identities and the other guy was treated, not Stark."

"Kim arranged this," Ruth said. "The man's connected to Nettie somehow."

"He matches the description of Olin Dobbs, a rapist who escaped Martha's Place a few days before your sister did. It's likely he dug the tunnel she used to get away."

"Where is he now?"

"We followed him to a motel out in Mount Pleasant. Clerk says he checked in alone. Paid cash for the room."

"I assume you have men watching the motel."

"Yes."

"Find out if anyone has joined this man with the damaged shoulder."

After a brief call, Bennigan reported, "My guy says a woman went into the room last night around eight. They assumed it was a…professional lady, since Dobbs has spent the last two years in prison. They did say she wasn't exactly what you'd expect a twenty-something guy to choose for a paid companion."

"Send a team to pick them up—quietly—and take them to…" She turned. "Gavin? A private place I can reach quickly?"

"I'll arrange it, Mrs. Mandell."

"Good. I have meetings most of the day, but I'll clear my evening schedule."

Chapter Seventy

Nettie-Same Day

Nettie had begun to think she was doomed to a life underground. She'd escaped prison through a tunnel, hidden from capture in a tunnel, and now she was in the custody of Secret Service agents, who'd stowed her away in yet another tunnel.

The only good part was that Olin was already on his way north when agents showed up at the motel and ordered her to come with them. He'd tried to argue against leaving her, but the pain pills he'd been given left him slightly goofy, unable to form coherent sentences. Nettie had convinced him to go, promising she'd follow in a day or two.

Knowing the police would be looking for a young black man with lots of hair who was traveling with an older white woman, she'd changed what she could. Using the scissors she'd stolen from the museum, Nettie cut Olin's hair close to his scalp. Then she'd started calling Lyft drivers, chatting with several until she found one who seemed helpful but not too inquisitive. She explained that her stepson had wrecked his car and his shoulder on the Beltway and therefore needed help getting home to Vermont. Her nephew was unfamiliar with the city, and he'd been given Percocet for his pain, so she feared he might not be able to manage buying a ticket and getting on the right bus without help. Since she had to work in the morning, she couldn't see to it, but she could offer a large tip if the driver would help "Harley Stark" get on his way home.

Around midnight, she'd sneaked Olin out a side door of the motel, led him to a gap in the fence that surrounded it, and pointed him at the gas station a few blocks down where his driver waited. Looking out windows on all sides of the motel, she'd decided that unless they had a half-dozen people watching, Olin's departure by that route would go undetected. As he walked away, his gait slightly uneven, she tried to figure his odds for success. With his cropped hair, fake nose ring, and new, slightly upscale clothes, he looked completely different. He had Stark's ID. And anyone watching the bus station would see two men approach the ticket counter and then head for the bus together, apparently sharing a destination.

"Purlingham." Olin had said when they parted. "Come find me in Purlingham, Vermont." Nettie nodded, though she made no promises.

Now she could concentrate on getting Kim to leave the White House.

But that plan had changed when a heavy knock on her motel room door signaled trouble. With terse commands, three agents had escorted Nettie to a car, which took them to the Treasury building. They'd led her inside and down a set of steps. After a series of passageways, they'd come to a door much like the one she and Olin had used to enter the tunnels in Richmond. Blank and innocuous, it was accessed by passing a badge over a reader. After more passageways and a downward elevator ride, the men had left her in a closet-sized room one of them called "the bunker." Nettie guessed she was somewhere under the White House, in one of the safe places a President could be taken in an emergency. Despite the upholstered furniture and well-stocked kitchenette, the artificial light, piped-in air, and hatch doors gave the place a depressing, prison-like air.

Nettie didn't know how long she was there. She helped herself to food from a fridge and used the teensy bathroom a few times. Finally, the door opened and a man stepped inside, checked the room, and nodded an okay. Ruth appeared, looking as fresh and lovely as always. "You can wait outside, Don. I'll be fine."

Nodding again, the man left, and Ruth stepped toward her. "Nettie."

"Ruth. Nice waiting area you've got here."

"We're under the White House, as you've probably guessed. This tunnel was built in 1987, to protect President Reagan in the event of a terrorist attack. It's accessed by secret staircases, one outside the Oval Office and another in a closet in the Residence."

When Nettie said nothing, Ruth turned brisk. "You're quite a problem for me."

"I never intended to be."

She chuckled dryly. "You were never very good at predicting consequences." Nettie was silent, tacitly admitting it was true, and Ruth went on. "Kimmie is convinced there was a miscarriage of justice in your prison sentence."

"I told her I deserved what I got."

Ruth's smile thinned. "Too bad she didn't take your word for it."

"I tried to make her stay away." That wasn't altogether true. At first she had, but later, not so much.

"Now you've escaped from the prison you admit you deserve, and Kim has helped you remain at large. More embarrassment for me and for Butch."

"She didn't—"

"Don't lie to me. I know exactly what she's done."

"All right, but she didn't intend to mess things up for you. Kim assumed I'd leave the city and disappear."

"Which you should have done." Ruth tilted her head. "Where's the black man?"

"Gone."

"We'll find him." Ruth fiddled with her jade and gold bracelet. "I understand he has an aunt in Chicago. He'll likely go there."

It was a relief to hear they'd be looking for Olin in the wrong part of the country. "I assume he's a dead man if you find him."

Ruth looked shocked. "Why do you say that?"

"People who get in your way tend to die."

"That's not true."

"What happened to that actor, Tanner? And his girlfriend the dancer?"

"Tanner died in a drunken accident. I understand the woman was mugged and killed in an unsafe area of the city."

"Do you believe that, or is it what you tell yourself so you can keep going?"

Ruth chose an oblique response. "Our goal has never been to hurt anyone."

Nettie grew angry, and her hands flexed in her lap. "You had a prisoner at Huron Valley shove me down the stairs, so I'd accept a spot at Martha's Place."

"I didn't—" Whatever she'd intended to say, Ruth changed her approach. "If you weren't so stubborn, you'd have gone to Virginia when first asked."

"So you had me attacked. How do you justify that?"

"The good of the many sometimes requires the temporary discomfort of a few."

"I think the few would disagree."

“People—the majority—approve of my actions. Our actions,” she corrected.

“Ruth, you’ve fallen into the mode of dictators everywhere: *My way is best because I say it is.”*

She waved dismissively. “You speak as if we’re beheading dissidents on the National Mall. We’re instituting logical reforms. Most people understand their value.”

“And if they don’t?”

“It’s the responsibility of government to keep order.”

“Order? I’d call it tyranny.”

Ruth sniffed, ending attempts at justification. “We’re getting nowhere, so here’s my offer. You have the power to save Olin Dobbs — trouble. Dr. Foeller too.”

Nettie’s heart sank. “What have you done to Susan?”

“She’s facing fraud charges.” Her gaze met Nettie’s. “But they could be dropped.”

“If I do what?”

“Talk to Kim. Convince her that you want to disappear.”

“Disappear?”

“Your release has already gone through. We’ll bury the news of your escape and announce that you’ve chosen to retreat to a secret place and live a private life.”

Nettie could have wished for nothing more. She had no desire to field questions from nosy reporters and curious neighbors. But she suspected she’d be a hostage, used to pressure Kim into going along with Ruth’s so-called reforms. Her safety would require Kim’s silence.

“I’ll agree, if Kim is given the same offer.”

“Kim doesn’t want to go live in the middle of nowhere,” Ruth snapped.

Nettie leaned back in her chair and folded her arms. “Let’s ask her.”

Ruth paced the length of the table, turned, and came back, her serene expression restored. “Agent Mero will bring you up to the residence later tonight, and you, Kim, and I will sort this out.” She sniffed as if something smelled bad. “While I’m sure Kim will choose to keep her position at the White House, I know you. You’ll need to hear it directly from her, or you won’t believe it.”

Chapter Seventy-One

Kim-Same Day

It was after ten p.m. when Harley knocked on Kim's apartment door to say that Ruth wanted to see her in the Treaty Room. The White House offices were different late at night, with its usual busy-ness gone and the lighting dimmed. When they reached the door, Agent Mero was waiting. He turned the handle and stepped back, allowing Kim to enter. Without being asked, Harley followed Kim into the room.

Ruth and Nettie sat in a corner, Ruth on a settee and Nettie in a straight-back chair. "Wait outside," Ruth ordered when she saw Harley. "This is a family meeting."

Harley's eyes met Kim's, seeking guidance. He didn't know everything that was going on, but he knew enough to be concerned. When Kim nodded slightly, he said, "I'll be right outside the door. Call if you need anything."

Her sisters were in shadow, their backs to the lamp on Ruth's desk, but Kim read tension in Nettie's posture. Ruth rose. "Look who showed up, Kimmie."

For reasons she couldn't have explained, she said, "Kim. Not Kimmie."

"Oh." There was a world of understanding in the word. "Have a seat, *Kim.* We need to talk."

Kim stepped toward them. "Nettie, are you all right?"

"I'm fine." She looked odd, with a shirt she'd never have chosen for herself, heavy makeup, and matted hair. Her face drooped with exhaustion, making her look as old as she had at Caleb's trial.

Drawing a chair to a spot equally distant from her sisters, Kim asked, "What's Nettie doing here, Ruth?"

"She escaped from Martha's Place, as you well know, but she wasn't wise enough to simply disappear. Now it's up to me to decide what to do about my sister the prison escapee." She turned to Nettie. "I had things all worked out, but you screwed everything up, as usual."

Nettie spoke to Kim. "I had to talk to you before I left."

"You *had* to." Ruth's voice vibrated with anger. "It's always about you, Nettie. What *you* want. What *you* decide." Kim tried to speak, but a dam had broken, and Ruth's emotions spilled like an overturned bucket. "I did rings around you in school, but you were the drama star. I worked hard at home, but Mom and Dad went on and on about how well Nettie sang in church last Sunday. I got a full ride to U of M, but they were too upset about you running away with your small-town Romeo to even notice." She jabbed a thumb at her own chest. "*I* married a man who supported me. *I* had children who didn't turn out to be serial killers, because *I* took care of them. What did I get for it? Nothing. Until the day they died, Mom and Dad were still trying to fix things for Poor Nettie." She turned on Kim. "Now you're doing the same thing. You care more about *her* situation than you do about the good I'm doing for this country."

"What is it you want from us, Ruth?" Nettie's voice was low and flat, as if the answer didn't matter.

Ruth spoke first to Kim. "I'd like a little loyalty from the sister I've made part of my staff." Turning to Nettie she continued, "And I'd be ecstatic if your depraved son's horrible crimes never become the topic of discussion on every TV show and coffee klatch in the country."

"Because it dims your chances of becoming Queen Ruth?"

She made a disdainful gesture. "I don't want a title, and you know it. But yes, there are calls for Butch to become President for life." Kim took breath to argue, but Ruth raised a hand. "I know, he's not himself right now, but he'll improve in time. And I've started bringing Ben into things. Before long, he'll be prepared to take over." She extended her hands, pleading for understanding. "So much in this country needs fixing. It can't be done in four years, or even eight."

Kim leaned forward and took Ruth's outstretched hand in hers. "You've lost sight of the goals Butch had as President, Sis. Unity. Fairness. Consensus."

"It's all about you," Nettie added. "What you think. What you want."

Ruth looked from Kim to Nettie and back again. Snatching her hand away, she knitted her fingers so tightly that her knuckles turned white. "Neither of you understands what we're trying to do."

"You're right," Nettie said. "We don't see how steamrolling civil rights and suppressing dissent is the new American way."

Kim said more gently, "You govern through subterfuge and lies. Do you really expect us to go along with that?"

"You don't have to 'go along,'" Ruth said angrily, "but I can't let you openly oppose us. Family should present a united front."

"You mean stand beside you and support a government takeover?" Nettie asked.

Ruth's face reddened. "It isn't a takeover if the people demand it. The average citizen doesn't want to decide what's wrong and what's right. They'd rather have someone they trust make good things happen. *I* am making things happen. *We* are," she amended. "Butch and I."

Voices sounded in the hallway, then a peremptory knock. The door opened, and Gavin Croft entered, with Josh Bennigan close behind. "Ma'am, is everything all right in here?"

"Yes," Ruth answered. "Mr. Croft, Mr. Bennigan, this is my sister Nettie. I've offered to see that she's taken care of for life if she agrees to live quietly in the place I asked you to arrange."

Kim was looking at Ruth, but her peripheral vision caught a look that passed between Croft and Bennigan. "Ma'am, we believe we have the ideal spot." He turned to Nettie, indicating with a raised brow that it was time for her to respond.

Instead, Nettie spoke to Kim. "I told Ruth I'm willing to do as she asks, as long as you're allowed the same choice."

It seemed the universe paused and focused on Kim, waiting for her answer. Croft's left eye squinted, like a villain from Charles Dickens. Bennigan watched with what appeared to be casual interest. Ruth leaned toward her, as if her spirit might reach out and lead Kim to the correct decision. Only Nettie looked away, hiding her eyes. Kim rose and went to the window, turning her back on Ruth in order to utter the words she needed to say. "I don't approve of what's going on."

In a second Ruth was at her side, sliding an arm around her waist. Though it was meant to be comforting, it felt as if she'd been put in chains. "I've tried to help you, Kimmi—Kim. I gave you a job better than any you'd have found on your own, a place to live that's the envy of everyone, and a chance to be part of historic events. If you stay on, I'll include you in the decision-making process. When you're better informed, you'll see that I know what I'm doing."

"And if I go with Nettie?"

Ruth almost pushed her away. "If you go with Nettie? *If?*" She took a breath before continuing, and her voice sounded like tightly drawn piano wire. "You'll pledge to keep what you know to yourself. You'll leave us to our work."

After a long pause, Kim said, "All right. We'll go. Tonight."

Through stiff lips Ruth said, "Josh, please arrange it."

Bennigan shifted his feet and said nothing. It was Croft who spoke. "If I might make a suggestion, ma'am. Ms. Dailey's abrupt departure will seem unusual if we don't lay some groundwork." Turning to Kim, he asked in a formal tone, "Might we persuade you to let your sister go ahead while you stay on for a day or two?"

Kim hesitated, but Ruth took hold of her arm. "I get that you want to go, and I won't stand in your way. But if you're present when the announcement is made, the public will understand that things are all right between us."

It was horrible, feeling that she'd chosen one sister over the other. In a small voice, Kim said, "I suppose that's okay." She glanced at Nettie, who studied her own hands as if she'd never seen them before.

"All right, then it's settled." Ruth sounded almost cheerful. "Nettie, Josh will see that you're taken to…" She turned to Croft. "Where will we send her?"

"It's a farmhouse in Tennessee. I believe it will be perfect for them, ma'am."

A certain blandness in his tone made Kim's shoulders shift, but Ruth seemed pleased. "A nice location? A comfortable house?"

"I'm told the place has been recently renovated. There's some acreage, so Ms. Waller can have a vegetable patch." With an air of friendliness uncommon to him, Croft finished, "They say the view from the back porch is stunning."

Ruth turned off the desk lamp, a signal that they were finished. "Thank you, Gavin, for your help and concern."

"It's my job, ma'am, but I should add that it's also my pleasure to assist the most dedicated public servant I've ever known."

"Well, then." Ruth went to a bookshelf on the east wall. "Let's get this done before we're interrupted." She pressed a concealed button, opening a panel Kim had heard about but never seen. Behind the doorway was a platform about six feet square. A blank wall, adorned with nothing but a fire extinguisher, faced them. On the right Kim saw a railing and a narrow spiral staircase.

Bennigan stepped onto the platform and pressed a button on the wall to the left. Leaning back in her chair, Kim saw two metal doors slide open, revealing an elevator car. Turning, he made a mock-gallant gesture toward Nettie, signaling she should enter.

Ignoring Bennigan, Nettie approached Kim and took her in her arms. The embrace was longer and tighter than she'd expected, and Kim whispered in her ear, "I won't be far behind you."

"Watch the Cardinal, Kim. Do not trust him for a minute." Releasing her, Nettie crossed the platform and entered the elevator.

"Nettie," Ruth said, "I hope you know that I wish you well."

Nettie didn't answer. She looked once more at Kim, and in her eyes was regret and something else, maybe fear. Suddenly it was as if a cloth had passed over a foggy window, and Kim saw everything clearly. "Stop!" she ordered, but Bennigan had already pressed a button. "Ruth, they're going to kill her."

"Oh, for—" Ruth clucked, but Kim was already on the move. Diving past Croft, she ran onto the platform and lunged at the closing elevator doors. Nettie took a step forward, but Bennigan reached out with a meaty fist, grabbed her collar, and jerked her backward. In the quickly narrowing strip of vision, Kim saw him punch Nettie with his other fist. The doors came together, blocking Kim's view, but her last image of her sister, dazed and struggling to remain on her feet, seemed burned into her brain.

Croft and Ruth had followed Kim through the doorway and onto the platform. His face tight with irritation, Croft turned and closed the secret doorway, making it unlikely anyone would hear if Kim called for help.

Had Ruth seen what Bennigan did? "Ruth, you can't let him take Nettie. He's going to kill her."

"Do you hear how ridiculous you sound, Kim?"

"Bennigan isn't taking Nettie to Tennessee," Kim insisted. "They lied to us." She pointed at Croft. "He's lying to you."

The platform was lit with blue bulbs. In their glow, Ruth, with her flawless skin and perfect hair, appeared otherworldly, like a goddess of some ancient cult. When she spoke, it was to Croft. "Tell me the truth. Where is he taking my sister?"

He sighed. "Mrs. Mandell, I never meant to deceive you, but here's the situation. If we let your sisters go wherever they choose, they'll make trouble." A familiar oiliness crept into his tone, and Kim's lips curled as he gave her a false look of concern. "I'm afraid Janet is jealous of your success, and she's infected Ms. Dailey here with lies and distortion. Neither of your sisters has your vision, ma'am. They don't understand what it takes to pull a nation from the brink of chaos."

"What do you intend to do with them?"

Croft's forehead creased as he composed his answer. *His lie*, Kim amended. "The farm in Tennessee is, um, secure. We would keep them sequestered there for a time, so they don't pass on what they *think* they know."

"You intend to lock them up."

Kim took a step toward her. "Ruth, think about what happened to Nathan Tanner. Croft told Bennigan to kill Nettie."

Croft chuckled, though it sounded fake. "You've both heard every word I said since arriving, so I'm not sure when I would have done that." To Ruth he said, "After the interim elections, if things go as they should, a disgruntled secretary and a convicted criminal won't affect our plans, no matter what nonsense they try to peddle."

"So they'll be confined until November." Ruth raised a hand. "That's only a few weeks, Kim."

"Yes." When Ruth hesitated, Croft went on. "While I know how important family is to you, ma'am, this is vital to our success."

"Family is everything," Ruth said slowly, "at least, it is in theory. But as a practical matter, it can be disruptive." She turned to Kim. "I'm afraid I agree with Gavin. We can't trust you two not to stick your noses into our business.

"Ruth, you can't—"

She put up a hand. "I gave you everything, and you've thrown it back in my face. I'm finished with you."

How much did she understand? How much did she choose not to? "Ruth, these men *kill* people."

Ruth drew herself up indignantly. "These men do as I tell them. They understand who's in charge, don't you, Gavin?"

"As you know, ma'am, I'm fully committed to your—"

Kim made her move then, pushing past Croft and heading for the stairs. She almost made it, but he reached over the railing, caught her by the shirt collar, and pulled her backward. She landed on the concrete floor, jolting the back of her head painfully, but she rolled to one side, twisting until his fingers lost their hold. She pushed herself to her feet, though her vision swirled and her eyes didn't focus. Croft stood between her and the stairs, arms raised slightly as if daring her to try again. Though she doubted she could defeat him one on one, Kim had to get past him somehow.

On her left, Ruth launched a tirade that was part lecture, part babble. "Kimmie, I want you to calm down and listen to me. We'll work this out. We'll announce that the pressure you've been under led to nervous collapse. We'll say you've retreated somewhere to rest. No one needs to know we've disagreed."

As Ruth ranted and repeated herself, her tone pedantic and her promises unlikely, Croft guarded the entry to the stairs. Eyeing Kim like a cobra watches its prey, he mirrored her movements, stepping whichever way she did.

"We can—" "We will—" "Kimmie, listen—" Ruth kept talking, but her pleas faded to unintelligible squawking in Kim's ears.

Ignoring her throbbing head, Kim struggled to formulate a plan. There was nothing available for use as a weapon. Screaming for help was probably useless, even dangerous if the wrong people showed up. In the end it came down to a desperate feint to the right followed by a dodge to the left. Without much trouble, Croft figured it out, and his fingers closed on her right arm, pinching so tightly she gasped in pain. Pulling her backward, Croft caught hold of her other arm with his free hand. For a few seconds they stood face to face, each wide-eyed and panting. When Kim let her arms go limp, Croft's mouth turned up in the slightest of smiles, convinced she'd given up. Quickly, Kim brought both hands up and pushed her elbows out sharply, breaking his grip. She hoped it hurt, and it seemed to, because she heard him mutter, "Bitch!" under his breath. In answer, Kim punched Croft hard, aiming at his throat. Since she'd never actually struck a fellow human being on purpose before, the blow landed low, allowing Croft's collarbone to absorb some of the impact. He didn't go down, but he did turn away, holding his throat and making choking sounds. Despite everything, Kim felt a tiny glow of gratification.

She started for the stairway again, but another pair of hands pulled at her arm. "Kim, stop." Though tiny, Ruth was strengthened by agitation, and her nails dug painfully into Kim's skin as she ordered, "Stop this foolishness and *listen to me*."

Kim glanced at Croft, who was slowly straightening from the crouch that pain and lack of oxygen had caused. Any second he would turn on her again, as strong as before and twice as angry. "Let go!" she ordered, trying to jerk her arm free.

Ruth paid no attention, and her expression revealed manic determination. "Kimmie, listen. Kimmie, please, *listen*!"

"No!" Kim shouted, and she shoved her sister hard. Ruth let go, but at the same moment, Croft attacked again, grabbing Kim by the hair and pulling her backward. Her head tilted toward the ceiling, and her feet stumbled as she tried to remain upright. Croft slid an arm around her neck and squeezed, and she struggled to pull in air. Desperate, she reached over her shoulders with both hands and clawed at his face. Unable to see, she flailed at him, and was rewarded when her nails connected with soft flesh. Croft roared with pain, and his arm slid from her throat. He didn't let go of her hair, however. Twisting cruelly, he used it to swing Kim around and smash her into the concrete wall. Her shoulder struck first, then her head followed from the whiplash effect. As pain radiated through Kim's whole body, Croft released his hold, and she slid down the grainy surface, landing painfully on her knees. Again her vision blurred, and she saw two versions of Croft standing over her. One hand covered his right eye, and blood poured from between the fingers. The remaining eye focused on her, and Kim knew he would kill her if he could. With a roar like a wounded animal, Croft drew back a foot, ready to kick her into submission. Summoning the last of her strength and calculating around her double vision, she grabbed the foot and pushed it sharply upward, sending Croft to the floor. When she could focus again, he lay flat on his back, dazed and gasping to regain his breath.

"Ms. Dailey, are you here?" a muffled voice called from the Treaty Room.

"Harley. We're on the escape platform."

A pause. "Okay. I don't know how to open the door, but I'll get someone."

Croft continued to make ugly, wheezing noises. Kim looked around for her sister, but Ruth wasn't on the platform. Had she gone back into the White House? No, the door was closed. The elevator was still and silent. There was only one other place she could be.

Rising, Kim went to the spiral stairs, looked down, and let out an anguished cry. Ruth lay completely still on the landing below, her limbs splayed like a doll tossed on the sidewalk. Rising, Croft hobbled to where Kim stood. When he saw, he made a soft groan, and his energy seemed to drain away, like water spilled on the ground.

A grind sounded behind them, and Harley appeared, his face tight with apprehension. With him was Everett Mero, his hand on his service weapon. "Kim, are you all right?"

"Josh Bennigan took Nettie." Her voice was faint from fear, exertion, and shock. "He's going to kill her." She waited for Croft to call her a liar, but he seemed not to hear.

Taking out his phone, Harley made a call. "Bennigan left the premises with an older woman," he reported a minute later. "He said he'd be back in an hour."

"Not Tennessee, then."

"What?"

"Never mind. Please, you've got to find him."

"Agent Mero," Harley said, "will you get your people on it?" Mero stood back, his gaze hopping from Kim to Croft and back again. When Croft made no eye contact, he took out his phone and stepped into the Treaty Room.

Harley turned back to Kim. "Where's—?" His eyes widened. "Hey!"

Leaning forward, Harley pushed Kim hard, sending her reeling to one side. She cried out in surprise but caught the railing and managed to stay on her feet. Behind her, Harley grunted in pain, and turning, Kim saw him drop to the floor. Gavin Croft stood over him, the fire extinguisher he'd ripped from the wall raised in both hands, ready to strike a second blow.

Pushing off from the rail, Kim rammed her shoulder into Croft's back. As he stumbled forward, Harley delivered a sharp kick to the outside of his knee with the heel of his shoe. Howling in pain,

Croft dropped his improvised weapon, which clattered to the floor and rolled into a corner. Leaning heavily on the handrail, he clutched the damaged joint, moaning softly.

"What's going on?" Mero stood in the doorway, his phone still in hand.

"Shoot this woman," Croft ordered between gasps. "She murdered the First Lady." When he pointed down the stairs, Agent Mero stepped forward to look. His eyes widened when he saw Ruth.

"Shoot!" Croft repeated. "I order you to kill her."

Time slowed. Kim saw Mero's gaze flick to her and then back to Croft. Harley lay on the concrete platform, his head bleeding from the blow he'd taken to save Kim. Mero drew his weapon, his face taut. Kim couldn't take her eyes off the gun, its metal handle in Mero's hand, its muzzle coming up, up, and pointing...

At Gavin Croft. Mero fired a single shot that reverberated in the small space. Croft immediately fell to the floor, his body slack. After stepping forward to assure that he was dead, Mero went to the doorway and spoke to someone in the Treaty Room. "Secure this door. Don't let anyone in without my say so."

"We need medical help," Kim said. "Harley's hurt, and Ruth…she fell."

Mero went down the steps, felt Ruth's carotid with two fingers, and said what they already knew. "She's gone."

Don't think about that right now, Kim thought. *Think about how to save Nettie.* But it was too late for that too. She'd lost both sisters, and she blamed herself. No matter what else they'd done, their love for her had contributed to their destruction.

"Are you all right?"

Kim rubbed at her bruised shoulder. "Nothing serious."

"Okay, then see if you can stop Stark's bleeding." He handed her a handkerchief, which she pressed against the gash. Harley gave her a weak grin but seemed unable to speak. *Another person hurt on my account*, she thought. Mero called for EMS, but the medical team he summoned was apparently neither ordinary nor random.

"Tell me what happened," he said as he put away his phone. "The short version."

"Ruth was going to let Croft and Bennigan kill my sister. I tried to stop her, we struggled, and she fell."

Mero chewed at his lip. "Okay. It's best if neither you nor Stark is around when this gets out."

"But it's my fault she's dead," Kim objected. "I'll have to give some sort of statement."

Mero shook his head. "I've already spoken to the Vice President." A slight arch of his brow told Kim that Mero and Cary were allies. "He wants you and Stark gone. We'll come up with suitable explanations for your absence, starting several hours ago."

"You're going to lie about what happened tonight?"

"Most definitely." Noting Kim's confusion, Mero explained, "People close to the First Lady, like Bennigan and Betzer, are going to do their best to hold onto power. They'll prop up that poor, clueless bastard we call President and claim you planned to kill him too, so that Stockwell could run the country." Mero smiled grimly. "They'll probably give me the Medal of Freedom for stopping you."

"I'll tell the truth," Kim said firmly. "It was an accident."

"Do you think no one knows how much you disapprove of this administration? Or that you and Stockwell share doughnuts and soda several times a week? Or that Stark has been snooping into all kinds of places he shouldn't?" Kim was struck silent, recognizing for the first time how Cary and Harley might both be hurt by what had happened.

"If you stay, they'll come after you," Mero went on, "and I'll be honest. You're in no way equipped to deal with liars as talented as those people are."

"Can they be stopped?"

"The VP will work on that, but not if he's implicated because of his friendship with you."

"But I killed her," Kim said, her voice wavering.

"You did what you had to do. Now it's my job to get you and Stark out of town before the firestorm starts."

A soft knock sounded, and Mero opened the door for two businesslike EMTs. After a few words with him they separated, one going to where Ruth lay and one to Croft. Moments later, both shook their heads. Easing Kim out of the way, the woman removed the handkerchief to examine the long, deep gash on the back of Harley's head. Looking up at Kim's anxious face, she said, "It's ugly, but it doesn't look like his skull fractured."

"Patch him up quickly," Mero ordered. "He won't be going to a hospital." Nodding, the woman opened her kit. In minutes she'd wrapped the wound tightly and given Harley shots of what Kim guessed were antibiotics and painkillers. By the time that was done, Mero had made several more phone calls. Someone brought a zip-up jacket that hid the bloodstains on Harley's shirt. He managed to stand, albeit shakily, and Mero said, "This way." He helped him into the elevator, where Kim replaced him as Harley's support while the agent pressed the correct buttons. "Get off at Stop 3," he ordered, exiting the car. "Go through the kitchen, and you'll be directed from there."

Kim objected one last time. "I can't leave. I'm responsible—"

"Ms. Dailey," Mero interrupted, "Stark needs your help."

His gaze met hers, and Kim realized he was asking her to trust him. Mero, and by extension, Cary Stockwell, wanted her to leave Washington tonight. *I can be free from this place forever*, she thought. That was followed by, *But never free from what I've done.*

She put her free hand on Harley's arm. "I'll take good care of him."

"Leave through the kitchen. You'll find a car in the lot behind the Eisenhower Building. Keys are in it."

When the elevator stopped, Kim steered Harley toward the kitchen. A woman stood by the exit door, and Kim feared for a moment they'd be arrested. Instead, the agent handed Kim a phone and the purse she'd left in her bedroom. "GPS is already programmed for a motel near the Canadian border. Stay there until someone brings you new ID papers, so you can cross into Quebec."

Kim hesitated. These people had sworn an oath to protect the First Family. If she and Harley were killed leaving the White House grounds, the whole mess might be explained as an unfortunate family dispute.

"Everything okay?" Harley mumbled, and Kim assured him it was. She had to trust that Mero had their interests at heart.

Chapter Seventy-Two

Kim-October 26

Kim drove north in the starless night, listening to news stories that told everything and nothing. The First Lady of the United States was dead, as was the President's Chief of Staff, Gavin Croft. No details were available. The President had retreated to his apartments and would see no one.

That turned the nation's eyes to the Vice President, who promised solemnly that the inquiry into the night's events would be thorough. "We know this much," Carroll Stockwell told the nation, "There's no nefarious purpose here, no foreign plot, no domestic terrorism. It's likely a tragic mistake was made that led to the deaths of two of this country's brightest stars. Whatever the explanation is, we will find it." His calm demeanor and firm assurance quieted the fears of the American people, and while speculation continued, there was no panic.

Kim stopped in a mid-sized town and bought supplies, a few pieces of clothing, some packaged food and the medical items Harley needed. He slept most of the way, though she made him eat some chicken nuggets from a drive-thru so the pain pills she'd been given would be better tolerated. She questioned him periodically, fearing a concussion, but he seemed lucid enough, just sleepy from the medication he'd been given. In the motel, she unbandaged his wound, replacing the whole head wrapping with a large patch that could be covered by a knit cap she'd found on a rack. When she apologized for her ineptitude as a nurse, Harley said, "It's okay, Ms. Dailey. Tennessee boys are tough." With that, he settled himself on the bed and promptly went back to sleep.

Late the next afternoon, Kim answered a knock to find a sealed manila envelope resting against the door. She opened the documents and studied her new self: Camilla Brooks, born in Ontario, currently a resident of Saskatchewan. There was an address and a note: *House is in your name. Will make arrangements for your friend when he's able to decide what he wants to do. C.* It took her a second to realize that Cary, the acting President of the United States, had written it.

They crossed the border at midnight at a tiny post in Maine where the single guard on duty was so lonesome for company that she treated Kim like a long-time friend. After glancing at their documents, she asked, "Can you turn on the interior lights for me, hon?" She obeyed, and the woman craned her neck to look at Harley. "Have a hard day, did he?"

Forcing a cheerful tone, she replied, "Traffic has been a nightmare. I told him I'd take a turn driving now that we're out of that mess."

"And where are you and this young man headed, Ms. Brooks?"

"Prince Edward Island. Henry's fiancée, my niece, is from there, and she wanted their wedding to be in the church where she grew up. I volunteered to be his chauffeur and his guide to all things Canadian."

The border guard nodded, acknowledging the right of brides to be demanding. "When is the wedding?"

"Sunday afternoon." She forced a smile. "If I push it, I'll get there in time to rest up before the ceremony."

The guard handed their passports back. "I hope everything goes well."

"Thanks. Me too."

Two miles down the road—not the road that would have taken them to PEI—two cars sat parked on the shoulder…the *verge*, she supposed she should call it now that she was Canadian, sort of. One car, a Ford Escape, was empty, and a man she'd never seen before leaned against the driver's side of the other, a Honda CRV, talking to the person inside. He put up a hand to signal she should stop, and Kim fought a wave of panic. It had all been too easy, and now she'd been caught. She and Harley would go to prison for the rest of their lives, and that was the best-case scenario.

Then the occupant of the Honda exited, his face revealed in her headlights. "Drew!" she said.

Harley stirred in the back seat. "What?"

"It's okay, Harley. I think we made it."

Six months later, Kim sat on the cantilevered porch at the back of the lodge in Saskatchewan where she and Drew lived as Camilla and Tom Brooks. She was pleased with the background invented for them: naturalists who'd come to the area to study moose habitat.

"It's boring enough to keep the neighbors disinterested," Drew commented, to which she'd replied, "What neighbors?"

It was true they had few contacts, at least with human beings. Harley had opted to return to the U.S., where he served as aide to a senator on the committee investigating corruption in the Mandell administration. He was invaluable in that cause, not only because of his own experiences, but also because Kim had told him where to find her notebook full of dates, names, and specifics. Bennigan and Betzer had both been removed from their respective offices, and they both faced serious criminal charges.

As she sipped her morning coffee, Kim watched two deer nip daintily at the tulips she'd planted along the edge of the clearing. It had been a waste of effort—unless one considered it worthwhile to offer shy woodland creatures new and exotic foods to try. Humans were the interlopers here, but she and Drew had been advised to stay isolated for at least a year. Then, Everett Mero suggested, Tom and Camilla would be safe to travel if they liked, even spend their winters in a warmer place.

Gavin Croft, the President's trusted advisor, had killed the First Lady and been himself killed by Secret Service agents. The medical examiner announced he'd found a large brain tumor, which had caused a drastic personality change in Croft. Staff members came forward to say they'd noted erratic behavior from the Chief of Staff in the weeks before his death, but no one recognized the seriousness of the situation until it was too late. Reading that, Kim recalled Croft suggesting they might blame Nettie's crime on an undiagnosed brain tumor. At least the idea hadn't gone to waste.

Two days after his wife's death, President Mandell resigned. While the official reason was inconsolable grief, there were rumors that Mandell had had a stroke upon hearing the news and was fully incapacitated. Still, he sent the American people a final message, asking them to respect his privacy and follow the new President, Cary Stockwell, as they would have followed him and his beloved Ruth.

President Stockwell said little in public about Butch Mandell or his wife. He encouraged the nation to let Congress do its job and focus on the future. As Croft's methods were scrapped and his cadre of accomplices removed, leaders in the Senate and House cautiously reasserted themselves. From what Kim could tell at a distance,

Stockwell's Senate experience provided him with a pool of decent lawmakers to draw from, and with their help, he was quietly undoing the evils of the last two years.

She didn't envy him the job, since brawling had broken out between factions who wanted to keep the "Mandell reforms" and those who claimed that many of them were illegal. That was natural, Kim decided. Democracy is a messy business. If Ruth and Butch had accomplished anything, they'd made the point that swinging from liberal to conservative every few years was counterproductive. The Unity Project's legacy would be the acknowledgment that problem-solving involves listening, discussion, and compromise. Ruth had made a lasting contribution, and Kim felt she'd have been glad to know that.

On the phone she'd been given the night she left D.C., Kim received occasional text messages from Everett Mero, keeping her informed. *No 1 lkng 4 U* came a week after they'd moved into the house. On TV, she often saw Mero standing behind President Stockwell, which led her to wonder if his warning to be careful had come from Cary. It had been her own fear that made it into a threat. Both the Vice President and the Secret Service agent must have been frustrated to know that so much was wrong when they had so little power to change it.

One day in December, she'd noticed a message on the phone: *Call this number at ten p.m. any Wednesday night.* After conferring with Drew, she called, and Cary Stockwell said, "Hey, Kim. I just wanted to hear you say that you're all right."

"Cary, it's so good to hear your voice. I can't thank you enough for…everything."

"As long as you're okay, what I did was little enough."

Her gaze met Drew's. "I'm good."

"Excellent. I have things to tell you, and of course they're private things. Except for your young man, no one can know."

"Of course."

"First, as to your older sister, Nettie. We fear she drowned in the Potomac."

Kim knew Nettie was dead, but it hurt to hear it put into words. "When I heard that Bennigan told the guards he'd be back in an hour, I guessed it would be something like that."

The President sighed. “A wicked man, for sure. I doubt it will help you to hear this, but she managed to take him with her. We found his body the next day.”

“But not hers?”

“No. A witness saw a man and a woman struggling on a bridge. He hurried to help, but before he got there, they both went over. By the time he called the police, the current had carried them downstream. Bennigan’s body caught on a piece of half-submerged metal, which is how they found it.”

“Both my sisters gone. It’s hard to accept.”

“I’m truly sorry, Kim. I know Ruth meant well, but given the power to change lives, some of us find it hard to ignore our own conceits.” He sighed. “If it helps, I use her mistakes as a lesson, to make sure I never let my ego take over.”

“If only leaders everywhere were so wise. Thanks for calling, Mr. President.”

“Nice to talk to you again, Kim. And I’ll always be Cary to you. Get used to it.”

No one in D.C. had paid much attention to where Kim Dailey was. When asked, the new White House press secretary said she’d left the area, preferring to be alone with er grief. Mrs. Stockwell, the new First Lady, would of course choose her own staff.

The cost of Kim’s crime was isolation from almost everything she’d ever known, and she accepted it gladly. After weeks of long walks and late-night conversations with Drew, she came to terms with Ruth’s death. Yes, she’d killed her sister, but she couldn’t say what she might have done differently. She had to live with it.

Even as information emerged about wrongs done in the name of unity, Ruth and Butch Mandell remained symbols of great leadership. Gavin Croft was generally believed to be guilty of everything from lying to the President to murdering those who got in his way. No one seemed willing to admit how deeply Ruth was involved in the repressive government the Mandell Unity Project had instituted.

Kim discovered a bright spot one day while reading Yahoo news: Olin Dobbs’ rape conviction had been re-examined when a Vermont woman came forward to swear he’d been with her on the night in question. "Belle" had snapped pictures over the course of the evening, proving what Dobbs had always claimed.

Once the story circulated, another woman came forward to say she'd been raped that same month in much the same manner. She'd kept it quiet, and when a tall black man was arrested and found guilty, considered justice done. Unlike Olin's accuser, this woman had held onto her clothing. Once Olin was cleared, the DNA evidence on her underwear led police to the real rapist. Olin was declared innocent, and the justice system decided to ignore his escape from Martha's Place.

From the same article, Kim learned that Dr. Foeller was back where she belonged. No mention was made of her arrest, but Kim assumed it had been declared a mistake. Foeller would never know the true story of Nettie's death, but at least she was free from further harassment.

Drew came outside, carrying a mug of coffee in one hand. With the other he rubbed his head until his hair stood up at his crown. "Morning."

She pointed at the doe and fawn grazing not twenty yards away. He moved slowly to a chair so as not to spook them, and they sat together in silence, watching. A noise made the deer start, and in a heartbeat, they were gone. A car had come up the drive.

Visitors made Kim uncomfortable, but Drew said, "I'll go." Patting her shoulder, he went inside and through the house to the front door.

She heard his exclamation of surprise. Pleased, not alarmed. Rising, she went inside. The door stood open, and Kim saw a car backing out of their drive. A black man who seemed vaguely familiar waved once before heading down the road. Kim turned to where Drew stood on the porch, his face split with a wide grin. Stepping across the threshold, she found someone she'd never expected to see again.

"Nettie!" Her voice was choked. "We thought—"

Her sister's smile was uncharacteristically smug. "To quote Mark Twain: 'The report of my death was an exaggeration.'"

About the Author

Peg Herring is the author of acclaimed series like the Simon and Elizabeth Historical Mysteries and several standalones such as *Deceiving Elvera*. She lives in northern Lower Michigan with her husband of many years.

Visit http://www.pegherring.com for Strong Women, Great Stories

Books by Peg Herring

Available at major booksellers in print and e-book formats. Many are also available as audio books. (Series listed in order.)

***

The Kidnap Capers (Suspense with cozy tendencies)

KIDNAP.org

Pharma Con

The Trouble with Dad

***

The Simon & Elizabeth Mysteries (Tudor Era Historical)

Her Highness' First Murder

Poison, Your Grace

The Lady Flirts with Death

Her Majesty's Mischief

***

The Loser Mysteries (Contemporary Mystery/Suspense)

Killing Silence

Killing Memories

Killing Despair

Clan Macbeth (Historical Romance, Medieval Scotland)

Macbeth's Niece

Double Toil & Trouble

***

<u>Mercedes Maxwell Suspense Series</u> (with Historical Implications)

Shakespeare's Blood

Charlie Dickens' Documents

***

<u>Standalone Mysteries/Suspense</u>

Somebody Doesn't Like Sarah Leigh (contemporary cozy mystery)

Her Ex-GI P.I. ('60s-era mystery)

Not Dead Yet... ('60s-era paranormal mystery)

Deceiving Elvera

Writing as Maggie Pill: Cozy Mysteries- http://maggiepill.maggiepillmysteries

<u>The Sleuth Sisters Mystery Series</u>

The Sleuth Sisters

3 Sleuths, 2 Dogs, 1 Murder

Murder in the Boonies

Sleuthing at Sweet Springs

Eat, Drink, and Be Wary

Peril, Plots, and Puppies

Captured, Escape, Repeat

***

<u>Trailer Park Tales</u>

Once Upon a Trailer Park

Twice the Crime This Time

***

<u>The Max & Lucy Mysteries</u>

Cutest Little Killer

CPSIA information can be obtained
at www.ICGtesting.com
Printed in the USA
LVHW032335091221
705823LV00001B/31

9 781944 50234